MANDATORY RELOAD

THE SEQUEL TO *B-ZONE*

Life is training.

Al Voth

BY
AL VOTH

TRIGGER PRESS INTERNATIONAL
SPRUCE GROVE, ALBERTA, CANADA

Copyright © by Alan J. Voth
First Printed in 2001
Printed in Canada

THE PUBLISHER

Trigger Press International
Box 3713
Spruce Grove, Alberta, Canada
T7X 3A9
www.triggerpress.com

Canadian Cataloguing in Publication Data
Voth, Al,   1953 –
   Mandatory Reload

   "The sequel to B-Zone"--t.p.
   ISBN 0-9685050-1-5

   I. Title.
PS8593.O84M36 2001   C813'.54   C2001-911452-4
PR9199.3.V67M36 2001

Cover Photo: Jordan Photographic
Cover Design: Penny Snell
Cover Gun built by: Scott Finnebraatten
Printing: Quality Color Press

AUTHOR'S NOTE

Have you ever noticed how often our heroes possess a high level of proficiency with the weapons of their time? David's skill with a sling and stone was used to defeat Goliath; Robin Hood owned the longbow; William Tell a master of the crossbow; Zorro the greatest swordsman of his time, and the Lone Ranger was better with his brace of Colt 45's than any gunslinger who walked a dusty street in the Old West. In each case the weapon evolves with the times, but the hero stays the same—fighting evil, rescuing the innocent and righting wrongs.

Ultimately, all these heroes owe their existence to writers; historical heroes to those who chronicle their stories and fictional heroes to the artists who create them for stage, screen or the printed page. The origin of actual historical heroes, whose lives writers record, is self-evident. Fictional heroes are commonly viewed as the product of nothing but imagination. I'm not so sure that's true. I suspect their seeds actually exist somewhere in reality.

Our generation probably has more fictional heroes than any other, but are they great heroes? I don't think they can be until they've established their durability over time. Once we become history ourselves and that nostalgic perspective mellows how our age is perceived, who will our great heroes be? A sports star? I doubt it. An international spy? A super-hero? A police officer is a fair bet. But maybe, just maybe it'll be a person like Nathan Burdett, whose skill level with firearms is exceeded only by his iron will to do the right thing.

To those readers unfamiliar with firearms and the people who use them, I can assure you that the equipment and technology described in this novel all exist in common usage. That's easy enough for most people to believe. However, likely shocking to the uninitiated, will be that the skill levels described herein are also accurate. It's important to note that this stratospheric skill level exists largely outside the world of the firearms professional—as embodied by the police and military—and resides almost exclusively in the world of the sportsman. People unfamiliar with the world of firearms may find that as hard to believe as the skill levels I portray in this story, but it is undeniably true. The point is proven continuously in open competition where the winner is invariably a sportsman. There are of course, military or police professionals who do emerge victorious in shoulder to shoulder competition. When they do, it is because they are sportsmen as well and have refined and honed their basic skills in that sporting world. Either way it is the sporting challenge that drives people to compete with others and pushes their skill level to the limits of human ability.

Some people are uncomfortable that those with the greatest firearm skills in our society do not necessarily wear a uniform. For those people, let me assure you that the dedication, giftedness, and discipline involved to attain this skill level ensures it will remain the exclusive preserve of good and honest men and women.

Allow me a reminder that, as noted on the front cover, this is a sequel. That, of course, means if you want to get the most out of this story you should read *B-Zone* first. If you're one of the many thousands who have already done so, allow me to thank you for the investment of time you made to enjoy one of my stories.

Al Voth

ACKNOWLEDGEMENTS

I'm starting to discover that every book develops its own 'personality' as it grows from the birth of an idea to published maturity. And although this book is different from its predecessor, one thing has remained the same—the willingness of people to help me make it happen. The list includes Amanda, Kevin and Brad who read and critiqued early drafts of the manuscript; Scott, Mike and many others who helped with technical matters, and Reuben and Penny whose creative talents made the design happen. A special thanks to Sharon—who inhabits the bizarre world of editing—for her numerous trips through the manuscript.

The contributions I've listed above are all important, but the single most important assistance any person can give a writer is encouragement. Encouragement is always the spark that starts and maintains the creative fires. All of the people mentioned above have done that in spades, and none more so than my wife and family.

Al Voth

Destiny is not a matter of chance,

it's a matter of choice.

Author Unknown

CHAPTER ONE

The gunshots in the distance were one possible excuse for distraction, but Nathan Burdett chose not to use them. That wouldn't be credible. His mind processed the environment around him trying to find something that was believable. The blonde kid to his left, barely in his twenties, alternated between scuffing at the gravel with his left foot and cracking his knuckles. Nathan ignored the kid's impatience and fidgeted with a loaded magazine, pretending to concentrate on what he was facing.

The magazine in Nathan's hand was his primary reload; another just like it was locked in the holstered pistol worn on his right side, just forward of the hip. He flipped the stainless steel cartridge holder over and over, blue eyes darting out across the graveled surface on which he stood. His mind working rapidly, but in a way no one could have guessed. This opponent and all the other competitors were concentrating on how to win. But the only thing of concern to Nathan was the rapidly vanishing day and this, his last good chance to lose.

The late afternoon sun cast long shadows and the warmth of the day was at its climax, and holding, waiting for the sun to retreat entirely before surrendering itself to the coolness of a Colorado evening. Here, the mountain air was always clear and now in late October it carried a crispness that made everything seem brighter and closer, giving it an intensity similar to the image seen through a high quality rifle scope.

In the hushed crowd of spectators behind Nathan, Danny Forbes whispered to Kim Corel. "Any guesses as to what he's going to do? He's waited too long."

"You're right," she answered softly. "He shouldn't have let it go this far." She shook her head in frustration, the movement tossing red hair to the sun. She'd seen him do this before, and with more at stake. He'd done it to her in a hellhole of a prison. Waiting until the last

1

possible moment; waiting for circumstances to mold themselves into the exact shape he needed to give himself an edge; waiting for the perfect opportunity before making his move against the cons.

Danny looked around slowly before replying. "One of these days he'll wait too long. I hope I'm not around to see it."

Fifteen yards in front of them, Nathan slipped the magazine into its carrier on the front left of his belt. He pushed it all the way in, brought it back out halfway, then fully reseated the magazine. His right hand was already hanging at his side, ready to snatch at the custom 1911 pistol holstered near it. He moved the other hand down as well, to a position matching its mate. The delay had helped. He knew what to do now.

Nathan thought the kid to his left looked relieved to be getting on with it. What was his name? Josh. That was it, his name was Josh. He seemed like a nice fellow, but his fidgeting indicated he was a little high-strung. His weren't the methodical, controlled movements of a veteran. Josh's movements were quick and darting. There was no plan or intent to them. They were like a fleeting thought, here and gone, only to be replaced by another one, equally fleeting and equally insignificant. Josh didn't have enough discipline yet, but he was fast. Nathan would give him that much, the kid was fast. Once he matured a bit and gained some experience, Josh would be someone to be reckoned with.

From the side of the assembled gallery opposite Kim and Danny, Jerry Mitchell watched Nathan as well. Unlike theirs, his perspective was more detached. He prided himself on that. Detached, professional, analytical; a recorder of the facts, an interpreter of events, a voice of the public conscience; that was Jerry Mitchell. A notepad rested discreetly in the cargo pocket of his safari shorts and the 35 mm Nikon around his neck, while much more visible, was entirely appropriate for the setting and therefore effectively invisible—as invisible as Jerry himself.

Invisibility was one of the things that made him a good reporter. He knew it, and except for the fact he was also invisible to members of the opposite sex, he liked it. At a little over five and a half feet tall, Jerry was close to an average height, but so slimly built that if

2

he wore glasses and carried a laptop computer he'd fit the classic image of a nerd. He knew that and so he diligently avoided both. Being slightly on this side of geek was his lot and he accepted it. He didn't try to be anyone other than himself and he had no intention of trying to change.

Jerry felt out of his element here—a pseudo-nerd with an elemental distaste for firearms in a sea of gunpowder-laced testosterone. Every second man in the crowd wore a pistol of some fashion, as did every third woman. He observed that a woman wearing a pistol was automatically more attractive. Now, why would that be, when he disliked guns so much, he asked himself. Probably the same reason the female police officers he regularly dealt with were more attractive to him because they wore a uniform. And he still hadn't figured out why that was so.

As he watched, Nathan's and Josh's hands dropped down into a ready position. A teenage girl behind them, as blonde as Josh, held up a squeeze bulb bicycle horn in her right hand. Both shooters stood in their respective shooting boxes, four foot squares outlined on the ground by narrow wooden boards. The command to load had already been given. "Are you ready?" she called in a clear strong voice. When no one replied to the contrary, she called louder, "Standby!" Two seconds later she squeezed the bulb firmly. For the umpteenth time that day the blare of a bicycle horn bellowed across the ranges, followed by the rapid-fire booming of semi-automatic pistols.

The response to the horn was immediate and too swift for the eye to follow. Two men snatched pistols from their holsters in a test to see who could shoot faster and straighter. The movement that brought two guns to bear was a blur, but those observing were not watching the shooters as much as they were the targets. Various shapes of steel plates, the intended victims of the shooters' bullets, were what one hundred pairs of eyes in the gallery focused on. A similar bank of targets faced each shooter, and to win they had to slam their targets over before their opponent could do the same to his.

Nathan fired twice in rapid succession and was rewarded by the ringing sound of high-velocity impacts. Like all accomplished shooters, he knew the hits were good because the sight picture had been perfect

3

each time the hammer dropped. He didn't have to watch the targets fall, he knew they were going down. Instead, he was already moving to his second shooting box, dumping the gun's partially expended magazine to the ground as he propelled himself to the right.

The rules said, shoot two targets from the start box, then move to the second box. There you could engage the remaining five targets. Fastest time wins. The distance between boxes wasn't far, only about four paces, but the stage specified a mandatory reload between the two positions.

Nathan's first ejected magazine was still falling to the ground as he snatched a reload from the holder on his belt. Still moving, he slammed it into the empty pistol in one blurred motion, clamping the now empty hand around his right to perform its support role. The gun was fully extended by the time his leading foot hit the ground inside the second box. The glowing red dot of his electronic sight found the first target and he triggered the shot, covertly punching the magazine release button immediately after the gun fired. Pretending not to notice the magazine that fell to the ground, he traversed to the next target. The slide had picked up one more round before the magazine dropped, and now with a missing magazine he fired that last round. For effect, he swung to the next target and dropped the pistol's hammer again. The click was expected. Feigning surprise and puzzlement he stuffed in a spare magazine, pulled back on the slide to chamber a round and mowed down the remaining targets in a furious burst of gunfire.

Danny buried his face in his hands and moaned.

Kim looked skyward, throwing her hands up in helplessness. Nice move, Burdett, she thought. Too bad it didn't work. She would have said it aloud but there were too many ears nearby.

Nathan thought he had pulled that off rather well. Fake a partially seated magazine on the mandatory reload, it bounces out when the first shot is fired, and the now necessary second reload eats up so much time the kid wins. Nice touch. He cleared his gun and glanced at the targets before walking over to Josh to congratulate him on his win. Josh's last three steel plates were still standing. Nathan turned and looked incredulously at his opponent. The young shooter stood there

4

still holding his gun, casually pointing it down range at waist level, the slide locked back.

When he saw Nathan's expression, Josh pointed at his pistol and shrugged. "Major jam," he called out in explanation. "Looks like you win."

Nathan's mouth sagged open. This was not going well. In the top ten of the match now, he had progressed as far as he dared. It was time to fold up the tent and go home. For him, winning was not allowed. His eyes panned the crowd looking for which of his fellow competitors may have witnessed this fiasco, and a blaze of red hair on the gallery's right fringe stopped his search. Kim. Danny stood with her. What were they doing here? Danny had given him a week off to take in this shooting competition. They must be here for a reason. A call-out? He glanced down at his pager. It was blank. Danny glared back at him and Kim giggled uncontrollably. The young Range Officer cried, "Right side wins!"

That snapped him out of the errant thoughts Danny and Kim had generated.

"Wait!" Nathan yelled, holding up his right hand and stepping toward the official. "That's not right." He knew he had to do something, but what? His win had been so blatant it wasn't contestable.

"Mr. Burdett," explained the pretty Range Officer, "you are the winner of the bout and of this stage. Do you have a problem with that?"

"Well, no," he hesitated. "But, it's not right. This isn't fair to Josh . . . I mean, he really didn't have a chance. His gun jammed."

"There are no alibis for a malfunction," said the R.O., "and," she reminded him, "your magazine fell out halfway through your last string." Nathan didn't reply. "Do you have a problem with my ruling?" she questioned, sounding puzzled. Nathan still didn't respond. She probed further, "Are you saying you wish to forfeit Mr. Burdett?"

That was it, thought Nathan. This was the way out. "Yes," he said, with as much compassion for Josh, as he could squeeze into his voice. "I wish to forfeit. I don't want to win that way. I don't want to win because Josh's gun jammed. I win clear, in a fair contest, or I don't win at all. I forfeit."

The crowd heard all of what Nathan said and responded with a sudden subdued muttering that quickly changed to appreciative applause. Jerry took the opportunity to question a woman beside him. In her early thirties, she appeared to be close to his own age. Although she wore no gun, there was an empty holster rig around her waist that indicated she knew the sport and probably some of the people in it.

"Pardon me," he said. "I'm not very familiar with what's going on here. Could you explain what just happened?"

"Oh sure," she replied, smiling. "I'm Laura, by the way," she introduced herself with a firm handshake. "Nathan there," she pointed with her left hand, "did what he always does. He totally whips everyone all through the match and then chokes up at the end and blows it. Only this time his opponent blew it worse than he did. So he won. I've never seen anyone so surprised at winning."

"This Nathan fellow never wins then?" Jerry asked.

"Never." She shook her head as if to emphasize the point. "He always chokes."

"But, even though he won they shoot again?"

She shrugged and looked off to where Nathan stood talking to the Range Officer. "Yeah. He wanted to give the new guy a fair chance. I've only ever seen that done once before."

"Isn't there a lot of money at stake here? Why would he do that?"

"Sometimes his shooting may stink, but there's never anything wrong with his character."

Jerry didn't see how that answered his question, but she apparently thought so and now seemed to be waiting patiently for a clue as to what else he wanted to know.

"Where's he from?" Jerry knew the answer better than she did but the question was a filler to keep her talking. Always keep them talking. He admitted to himself that information gathering was only part of his reason for talking to Laura. Any excuse to look into those brown eyes would be a good one.

"Calgary. He's a Canuck."

Jerry nodded and pointed a thumb in Nathan's direction. "I've heard stories about a Canuck pistol shooter who killed a truckload of bad guys last summer. Is that him?"

Laura didn't answer right way. She'd heard the same stories. Glancing at the camera she mentally added in the questions. One plus one is two, and in this case camera plus questions could mean media. "I have no idea. I've never heard that, and it sounds pretty far-fetched anyway." Turning her back on the skinny guy with the camera, she watched what was happening on the range.

The Range Officer directed the resetting of the targets and when it was safe, gave the command to load. Nathan pretended to go through his concentration ritual again as he prepared to shoot. Nothing left to do now, he thought, except miss the old-fashioned way. He picked two spots on the horizontal steel rack just below the last bank of targets. These would be his aiming points. Okay Josh, he thought. Keep it together pal. Don't let the pressure get to you. It's sight picture and trigger control, that's all. Place the dot and press the trigger. You can do it. And if you don't I'll cross over and shoot your targets for you. This has gone on long enough.

"Are you ready?" called the R.O. "Standby!"

The horn's blast jolted the two men into action with Nathan taking his first two targets cleanly. Once again he performed the mandatory reload on the move, doing it smoothly and efficiently, but more slowly than he was capable of. The third and fourth targets of the last bank he missed low, returning with his sight to pick each of them up on the second try. Nathan tracked to the last target, a three and a half foot tall piece of lollipop-shaped steel plate known as a pepper popper. Two of them were set close together and situated so that when they fell, they would overlap. The winner clearly indicated because his target, having fallen first, would be on the bottom. Josh's popper was already going down as Nathan's dot arrived, and so Nathan triple-tapped his own in a mock display of frustration.

Josh whooped in triumph as he realized he'd won and once the guns were cleared, hurried over to where Nathan stood and shook his hand. "That was great of you to give me another chance," he said. "You didn't have to do that."

7

"I know," replied Nathan. "It just seemed like the right thing to do under the circumstances. You get on to your next bout and I'll come watch once I get my gear stripped off. You've got a long way to go yet."

"Thanks, Nathan," called Josh as he hurried off the range to the applause of the crowd. Nathan, too, left the field of contest to applause—applause considerably greater than that given Josh. He doffed his blue Dillon Precision cap to the crowd and walked to where Kim and Danny stood.

Kim was just recovering from her giggling fit. Danny apparently hadn't seen anything funny. "Left that a little late, didn't you?" he said. His tone indicating he didn't expect an answer, that this wasn't a question—it was a reminder.

"Hey, no problem," countered Nathan. "I should end up in the bottom end of the top ten. No problem," he repeated, as he pulled magazines from his belt and deposited them into a green Waller shooting bag. "What are you two doing here?"

"A bit dramatic with the forfeiting business," said Danny, unwilling to let it go.

Kim spoke up in Nathan's defense. "Come on Danny, it was a tough break when the other guy's pistol choked. I thought he made a good recovery."

"If he hadn't left it 'til the last possible minute he wouldn't have had to make *any* recovery, or such a scene."

"You suffer from excessive worrying," said Nathan. "Is that what happens when you get close to forty?" he prodded.

"No. That's what happens when your job is nursemaid to the world's best pistol shooter."

Nathan didn't reply. He busied himself emptying the magazines, thumbing the rounds out one by one and dropping them into a container.

"Look," said Danny, "it turned out okay. You did well. You threw the match when the time came. It's just that maybe you left it a little late, that's all. And I get paid to worry."

"Sure," drawled Nathan picking up the shooting bag. Another bout was about to start and he wanted to move someplace quieter. "I'll swing by the safe area and case my gun. I know you didn't come here to watch me shoot. So, where's your car? I'll meet you there."

"I'll go with you," volunteered Kim, tagging along.

Nathan waited until Danny was out of earshot. He inhaled a deep lungful of mountain air and let it out slowly as he shifted the heavy bag to his other hand. "He doesn't understand how tough it is to lose."

"No," Kim disagreed, "he understands exactly how tough it is, for someone as competitive as you, to lose. That's why he worries."

Nathan said nothing until he was in the process of casing his gun at the safe area. "I suppose there's no point in asking why you're here?"

"No. Danny will fill you in."

"You know, Kim, if it was only you that showed up unannounced, I'd welcome it. When Danny arrives suddenly, I know it's bad news. Now, when you both drop in unexpectedly I know it's *really* bad."

Kim was supposed to laugh, it was a joke, thought Nathan. She didn't even smile.

They walked in silence to the parking lot, the rapid-fire staccato of the day's remaining bouts fading further into the distance. When they reached the stairs that descended to the vehicles Nathan saw Danny waiting for them, leaning on the trunk of a white Chevrolet Lumina. The car had a sticker on the left rear bumper, and although he couldn't read it from this distance he guessed it was the name of the rental company that owned the car. It reminded him of the first time he'd met Danny.

A year ago a stranger driving a rental from the Calgary airport had shown up at Bob Coombs' rural gunsmith shop near Cochrane. The driver had been Danny Forbes, an FBI man with a vision. Find an up-and-coming action pistol shooter with the potential to be the best in the world, train him to the absolute limits of his ability and then make him available to whatever agencies required his specialized skills. That was Danny's dream. He'd labeled it The B-Zone Project. It had worked, too. After going through the selection process and then the training at a shooting ranch in Arizona, Nathan proved it. He'd proved it on a deserted airport runway; in a foul smelling New York State prison; then ultimately when the lives of his friends, the Coombs, had been endangered.

His mind replayed the images. They weren't pretty, but creating them had been necessary to keep good and innocent people alive. That was the only reason he could live with them—even when they came back. But he didn't ever want to live with *unnecessary* images like that. He wondered if he could.

When the bodies had been cleaned out of Bob's shop, Danny had given him most of a month off to recover from the beating he'd taken. At least that had been the official line. Nathan suspected the doctor they'd assigned was reporting on his mental condition as well. He must have passed, because when the doctor pronounced him fit Danny called him back to the ranch. Four more jobs had come his way over the last month. He hadn't fired a round on any of them. Everything had been resolved peacefully. No hits, no misses and everybody left standing. It had been a good month.

Today's misses, however, had been deliberate, the loss intentional. Winning an event like this would bring too much attention, and attention was dangerous. Even Nathan conceded no one else in the world could do the things with a handgun that he could. Never had he dreamed his skill level would be where it is now. And it wasn't just training that kept it there. Active shoulder-to-shoulder competition with the best in the world maintained his skill and pushed him to continue improving.

Danny straightened as they approached the rear of the car. Nathan spoke first. "Well, I'm going to guess this isn't a call-out."

"You're right. Things are still quiet. I did get a call from Miami the other day. Otto said to thank you for the day you spent on the range with his team. Said they've never been shooting better. Wants to know if you'll come back for a week of instruction."

"I don't think you want me to be a firearms instructor. Do you, Danny?" Nathan deposited his shooting bag on the ground near the bumper.

10

"You're right. And I told him that. There are lots of good ones out there and I gave him the names of a couple of freelancers that can follow up on what you showed them. It was a good idea on your part."

Nathan nodded. "It seemed like a worthwhile pastime while we were waiting for that phantom drug shipment to come in. I got to know the team that way, and a range is someplace I feel comfortable anyway. Too bad we never got the shipment."

"Too bad we won't be able to do it again," said Danny, looking knowingly into Nathan's eyes for a reaction. He got it as the blue eyes narrowed.

"What's that supposed to mean?"

"You've been recruited."

"Yeah, I know. You did it. Remember?"

"No. I recruited you from competitive shooting. Now, you've been recruited from me."

Nathan's eyes flickered to Kim, looking for a straight answer. Two shooters came padding down the wooden stairs from the upper level and onto the parking lot where conversation at the back of the Lumina came to a stop as the trio waited for them to pass. Another man remained at the top of stairs, looking bored, checking his watch frequently as if waiting for someone. Nathan didn't recognize him as a competitor. The camera around his neck made him look like a tourist or a friend of a shooter, come to check out the sport of action pistol shooting.

Nathan nodded to the two competitors as they walked by on the way to their vehicle. "See you tonight at the pig roast," said one.

"Looking forward to it," replied Nathan. When they were out of earshot, he turned back to Danny. "I didn't know it was possible to be recruited from you."

"I've always known it was a theoretical possibility," acknowledged Danny, "but realistically I never expected it to happen. They're stuck in one way of doing things and what we're doing with you is just too different."

"Who's they?" asked Nathan, crossing his arms.

Danny slumped back against the Lumina's trunk and lifted his right foot, hooking the heel onto the bumper. "Remember the last day

11

of your formal training? When I brought in all the backers of this project to watch you work some scenarios on your own and with our Hostage Rescue Team?"

"Sure. There were military types, some suits and her scar-faced Israeli friend." Nathan pointed a thumb at Kim, who had removed her sunglasses and was chewing on one of the plastic arms.

"Remember the best dressed fellow there? A Brit. named Kent? He was at my elbow most of the day."

"I do. He gave me some strange vibes."

"Probably well deserved. He's the one that wants to borrow you."

"Like I said, I didn't know I was available."

"Well, you *are* available. Call it a loan or a secondment, whatever you like. Actually, the only thing changing is the person calling your assignments. The formal contract with us still stands. Your employer is the same, your paycheck is no different and your mission hasn't changed. It's still hostage rescue, protection duties, technical expertise, high-risk arrests and operations, anyplace someone with your talents can be used."

"You've been doing domestic work 'til now, Nathan," said Kim, speaking for the first time. "Kent works in the international arena. That means you can add terrorists to your job description now."

"So, you both came out here to see me off and wish me well?" Nathan asked sarcastically. He had an uncomfortable feeling about this.

Danny scratched the back of his neck. "Not exactly. For starters, this isn't the kind of thing to tell you over the phone. And, besides I brought your stuff." He tapped the trunk. "I took the liberty of packing you some essentials. Your plane leaves Denver tomorrow morning for New York. If there's anything more you need from the ranch, call George and he'll ship it out to you."

"What's Kent's hurry?"

Danny shrugged. "I don't know. He's got some high level strings, and he pulled them all to get you. I said you weren't ready, needed more operational experience. But it didn't wash. The Director says you're temporarily assigned to Kent, so that's it. His operation is a

12

combination Interpol-UN office that deals primarily with international criminals and terrorists. Have a nice time in New York city, Nathan."

"I think you know, I've got some contacts in that world," volunteered Kim. "I've asked a few questions about him and everything I hear is the same. He's only had his shop in operation six years but already he's thought of as one of the best people in the business. We're lucky he's one of the good guys, Nathan. He's got a mind like a steel trap and the small group of people working for him have put more nasty life forms out of business than a truckload of bug killer."

Danny picked up Kim's explanation. "I've heard things too, Nathan. I've heard he's ruthless."

"Probably because the stakes are higher over there," suggested Kim.

"We're not going to have to go through this hired gun thing again, are we?" asked Nathan. "Danny, I hope he doesn't expect me to go around being his own personal avenging angel of death. You and I have come to an understanding about my capabilities and what I choose to do with them. I won't kill unless I have to, and I've got more leeway in that decision than most people. Does he realize that?"

Danny was already nodding his head. "I talked to him on the phone yesterday. That was one of the things we discussed. He assures me he'll give you a long leash."

Nathan looked at Kim. "What about you?"

"I'm going back to Israel for the time being. Kent has his own people to help you out. When you come back from this loan maybe they'll let me back in too." Then in answer to Nathan's unasked question, "I just came to say goodbye."

Nathan still hadn't taken off his safety glasses. He removed the Oakleys now and bent down to tuck them away in his range bag. He substituted them for a pair of sunglasses but didn't speak until he straightened up. His question wasn't directed to anyone in particular. "If I'm just going out on loan, why does this little meeting have such an air of finality to it?"

Danny and Kim squirmed. Danny spoke first. "I doubt you're coming back, Nathan. I've seen others go to work for the spooks and I've never seen anyone come back. They drop into a black hole."

13

"Never to be seen again?" mused Nathan.

"No. That's too melodramatic. I wouldn't say that. It's just that there's a fence dividing the spooks from law enforcement, and the only way through is a one-way gate. Not officially, mind you. It just seems to work out that way. I've never seen anyone come back through, that's all. I don't know if the grass is that much greener over there or if it's something else." Danny shrugged.

"It's probably all the frequent flyer points you can earn over there," volunteered Kim.

Nathan laughed. "Kent is a spook?"

"He fits my definition," said Danny.

"Well, I only have a year and a half left on my contract. He may be able to keep me out of circulation for that amount of time, but that's it. If I don't like the spook side of the fence I'll come back. At least, if you'll still have me?"

"No fear of that, Nathan. I'll take you back in a heartbeat. Just watch yourself over there. That side has its own peculiar brand of animals roaming around. And Kim won't be around to look after you." He slapped Nathan's shoulder.

"How about it, Kim?" asked Nathan, smiling again. "Pull some of your own strings and come look after me."

Kim didn't smile. She had eased Danny away from the back of the vehicle and was opening the trunk. "Let's get these bags into your car, Nathan. You have a plane to catch."

Jerry Mitchell lowered his camera. From where he stood, he could tell the conversation had been private and intense but had no idea what it was about. He'd taken a few pictures and they might be helpful. The license plate on the rental car would be readable and he should be able to get one of his contacts at the Department to check with Budget and see who they rented it to. That might be interesting.

If there wasn't a story here he'd eat his notepad. He had no idea what it was yet, but it was here. And he was only in Colorado because he'd managed to convince his boss of that possibility. Frank had given him authorization for a return plane fare from Calgary and two days on the ground in Denver to snoop around. Working for the biggest daily in Western Canada did have its advantages. There was a budget for this sort of thing, and as the paper's senior crime-reporter he was given the nod.

But then he'd been assigned the story in the first place. The violent deaths of eight known criminals had been the natural domain of the senior crime-reporter. Nathan Burdett's name had come to Jerry's attention for the first time back then, both officially and unofficially. Officially, Burdett was one of the civilians in a gunsmith's shop when the 'alleged criminals' had tried to liberate the firearms it contained. The crooks all ended up dead for their trouble, and the entire metropolis of Calgary was still enjoying a massive reduction in robberies and burglaries. Speculation in the city was that a new-found fear of finding an armed proprietor or homeowner waiting in the shadows was keeping the thieves home at night.

Unofficially, Jerry's contacts with the city's law enforcement sector told him things were more complicated. All he had were rumors and speculation, and there had been enough that his professional story-detecting senses had gone into full alarm mode. Most of the police contacts hadn't known anything other than the official version. Others had stonewalled him—like Laura had—and done a poor job of it in the process. The stonewalling alone meant something was going on, and the rumors never stopped.

They'd centered around a good-looking redhead and Nathan Burdett, a local competitive shooter who'd leave town for months at a time, and come back with a tan just in time to be around whenever bullets began flying and bodies falling. And here he was, in Colorado. The shooter was here and the bullets were flying. The redhead was here too, whoever she was. So far there weren't any bodies.

CHAPTER TWO

The next day, Monday, Nathan's airplane took him half a continent east. The elevator on Tuesday took him twenty-nine floors up. When the door finally slid open, Nathan followed instructions and turned right down a nondescript hallway. He passed three unmarked doors and stopped where the hall made an abrupt right at a door marked *UNOG*. The door was open and inside was a waiting room with a receptionist seated behind an oak desk. The words *Universal Nexus Operations Group*, in tasteful brushed chrome lettering, hung on the wall behind her. The nameplate on her desk read *Jenny*.

She appeared old enough to be nearing retirement, with the detached manner of someone who had been working a job like this all her life. Nathan smiled at her as she looked up from a scattering of papers in front of her. "I'm here to see Mr. Kent," he said. Then, in response to her expectant look, he added, "I'm Nathan Burdett."

"Oh, yes," she nodded, abruptly smiling. Behind her eyeglasses were eyes that looked friendly. Her hands darted across the desk, performing tasks while she spoke. "He's expecting you. If you'll have a seat, I'll tell him you're here."

Jenny disappeared around a corner but Nathan remained standing. He studied a painting hanging on the wall to his right. An original oil, it was an African scene featuring a species of antelope in various poses of feeding or watering. Nathan couldn't put a name to the species but he had seen pictures of them before. An orange African sun hung low in the sky, and laying in the foreground grass a cheetah watched the plain. The cat wasn't stalking or making any pretense of hiding; it just rested on an open knoll surveying the field. Nathan guessed it had fed recently and wasn't hungry. Somehow the antelope sensed this as they seemed completely unalarmed. He was marveling at how the artist had managed to draw him into the setting, making him

16

think about what was happening in the scene, when movement to his left and a friendly voice with a distinctly British accent caught his attention.

"Nathan Burdett, good of you to come. Welcome to New York city."

Nathan recognized the immaculately tailored Mr. Kent immediately. A year ago in the Arizona desert his conservative pinstriped banker's suit with the blazing red tie had made him stand out garishly among the uniformed and casually dressed observers. Here, however, in an office tower in New York city, Kent looked like he belonged and Nathan felt out of place.

"Good to see you again," said Nathan as they shook hands. Kent, he observed, hadn't changed much. The suit still looked expensive and immaculate, except today it was gray instead of blue. The tie was still red but of a slightly different shade. Kent's face was a model of sincerity and wisdom, with a grandfatherly look imparted by eyeglasses, a modest mustache and a horseshoe of gray hair around a balding head. When Nathan first met him, there had been a sense of encountering an unusually capable mind. He felt it again now—an impression of mental strength and intellect that was inescapable.

"Come into my office," said Mr. Kent, ushering Nathan ahead of him. Then he addressed Jenny. "Would you fetch us a spot of tea, Jenny? Is tea all right with you, Nathan?"

"Tea is fine."

"That's the spirit, Nathan, keeping up the British tea tradition. These colonists here in America certainly don't. And I hate coffee!" he laughed.

Around the corner from Jenny's desk a door stood open and Nathan was escorted through. The resplendent view afforded by the corner windows captured his attention immediately and he paused to explore it. Floor to ceiling windows revealed he was halfway up a canyon wall of glass and steel, standing at the edge of a precipice with a panoramic view to the rising sun in the east and rows of man-made pinnacles to the south.

He dragged his eyes away from the view, intending to refocus his attention on Mr. Kent. Instead, upon turning Nathan became aware

17

of the remainder of the room. The colonial British décor he observed, suited Mr. Kent and came as no surprise. The computer next to the desk was an essential. The zebra skin on the wall, however, was unexpected. Immediately, other items in the room caught his attention as well.

A photo of a younger Mr. Kent hung on a paneled wall. He was kneeling beside an enormous cape buffalo, a double rifle in his hands. Tastefully mounted to the bottom center of the frame was an expended cartridge case, and beside the case, a full metal jacket, round nose bullet. The bullet, a solid, looked as big around as Nathan's thumb. There was a dent in the nose and a slight bend to its length. Easily visible rifling grooves engraved its coppery surface.

Tusks lay on a small table below the photo. Nathan's limited knowledge of African animals prompted him to guess a species of warthog. A display of native art in the nearby corner featured a spear and intricate ivory and wood carvings. A boomerang, in brightly painted colors, represented the other side of the world.

Beside the desk, on a stand of its own, was a stone carving of a massive polar bear. The bear was up on its hind legs, in full fury, facing a parka-clad Eskimo hunter armed with a spear carved of bone. Two huskies crouched with the hunter, defending their master against the monster bear; which in this rendering stood a full eighteen inches high. The battle was locked in time, frozen in basalt stone, the outcome never to be determined.

Nathan was aware that Kent was standing quietly behind him while he surveyed the artifacts and trophies. After what seemed a polite pause, and with obvious pleasure, Mr. Kent said, "As you can see, I too am a hunter."

"I would say you're considerably better traveled than I am."

"Yes, I dare say you're probably right. But due to circumstances beyond my control I don't get out as much as I'd like to anymore. You could say I'm in a forced state of semi-retirement."

"I can understand that," said Nathan, sensing a kindred spirit. "But once it gets in your blood it never leaves, does it?"

"No, never."

"You can't fly in an airplane or drive across a piece of land without looking out over the country and evaluating its hunting possibilities," said Nathan, thinking of the view behind him. This was a hunter's perch, a place to look out over the world and watch. A place to sit and wait; to watch the game moving in the distance and select the trophy; then to plan the stalk or the shot. Which choice a hunter made depended on the nature of the man. Some men stalked because it was the sporting thing to do—others just shot. Collecting the trophy was all that mattered. He wondered what kind of hunter Kent was.

"Exactly. Being a hunter is not something we do, it's who we are. It changes our outlook on the world, doesn't it?"

"It does," replied Nathan. "I think it helps us understand it more realistically and it helps us appreciate nature—its balance and the value of life."

"Yes, balance. Interesting you should mention that. I'm actually working on a magazine article on that very topic. Under a *nom de plume*," he added, with a conspiratorial wink. "It's something I've been giving some thought to lately. Have you ever noticed, Nathan, how in a park setting, I mean a wilderness park setting, where no hunting is allowed, the animals have no fear of man?"

"Absolutely. In Banff, near where I grew up, all kinds of animals roam the townsite. They're a major nuisance and a tourist attraction at the same time, but the local philosophy there is, the animals belong and people don't."

"Now is that balanced, Nathan? I ask you, is it?"

"Interesting point, Mr. Kent. It's not totally natural, I suppose. It's certainly an artificial balance that has been worked out for those settings."

"It's totally unbalanced, Nathan, and it's completely unnatural. Man is at the top of the food chain and the animals are below us. For them to have no fear of us, especially animals that are our legitimate prey, is unnatural and completely unbalanced. That's a hierarchy that exists in the entire world, at all levels, and you'd do well to learn that early in life, Nathan."

"I'll keep it in mind." Pointing at another photograph of Kent, again much younger, and this time with a polar bear trophy, he changed the subject. "Taken in my part of the world, no doubt?"

"Well, certainly your country but probably a thousand miles from your home."

"Of course," agreed Nathan as he stooped to look closer at the photo. "Looks like you left your British double at home on that hunt."

"Yes, I did. It would've served me well, I'm sure of that. It just didn't seem to be the right rifle."

"It's a bolt action of some description?"

"Correct, a Rigby built on a Mauser style action. That's a Swarovski scope on it, in a quick release mount with express sights for backup."

"A wise precaution in that sort of environment. What caliber?"

"One of your North American calibers, .338 Winchester Magnum. I loaded it with 250 grain Nosler Partition bullets."

"Looks like it did the job."

"It certainly did, but then I wouldn't expect anything less from Nosler bullets."

Nathan pointed to another photo, this one of an unshaven and tired looking Kent posed with a full-curl bighorn sheep. They seemed precariously balanced on a rocky slope with jagged peaks breaking up the horizon behind them. "I'll bet that's closer to my home," he suggested.

"Very true, British Columbia that one. A tough hunt."

Nathan grunted in response and turned away from the wall. "Have you ever tried competition shooting?" he asked.

"No. Goodness, no. Nothing formal certainly. There are always the informal competitions that break out on ranges and in hunting camps. I'm sure you're familiar with those."

Nathan nodded as Mr. Kent pointed him to a chair in the sitting area of the expansive office. As he sat down, Jenny walked in carrying a silver tray filled with a china tea service.

"Just set it down over there," said Mr. Kent, indicating a low table amidst the group of chairs. "I'll look after serving our guest. And would you be so good as to let Leith know that Nathan is here? I believe he's in his office."

"Certainly," Jenny replied, as she made her way out the door.

20

As she left, Nathan noticed another smaller door set into the wall opposite the large walnut desk. A private bathroom, he guessed. "Now then," said Mr. Kent. "Let us enjoy some tea. I'm going to guess that you don't like your tea in the British fashion with large quantities of milk."

"Just a little sugar is fine."

"The colonies must always find their own way of doing things, even drinking tea," laughed Mr. Kent.

Nathan lifted his cup. "To the colonies," he toasted.

"Jolly good," came the reply. "To the colonies."

As they drained their tea and consumed the dainty biscuits Jenny had added to the tray, Mr. Kent kept the conversation focused on hunting and firearms. When the tea was done it signaled a change of topic.

"How do you feel about coming to work for me, Nathan?"

"I don't really know. I just barely started working for Danny Forbes and now I'm in your employ, apparently."

"Yes, from your perspective things have been moving rather rapidly, haven't they? Be aware, Nathan, that you have some unique abilities. There are people and agencies that want to use those talents, especially in these difficult times. What's happened now is that the international interests have taken precedence over the domestic ones. I know you don't have any military experience, Nathan, but I'm equally sure the term *pulling rank* is clear to you. To be brutally honest that's what we've done."

"I don't think Danny is too pleased."

"I *know* Mr. Forbes is not, and I can sympathize with his viewpoint. He, after all, initiated the project, discovered you and trained you; now we've effectively stolen you away from him. I'm sure I wouldn't be pleased either. It's a matter of understanding and appreciating the big picture, and intellectually I'm sure he does that. He is a professional, after all. But emotionally, it's difficult for him to see you spirited away."

Mr. Kent pointed an emphasizing finger at Nathan. "The work you were doing for Mr. Forbes was certainly valuable and important, but you can expect the bar has been raised here. As an agency with

21

direct ties to the UN and Interpol, we operate, as I'm sure you expect, in an international environment. What that means is, rather than dealing with domestic or petty criminals, or deranged individuals in a local setting, our focus tends to be on the more sophisticated international criminal. There are two broad categories of those, Nathan. There are plain vanilla-type criminals, who operate simply to acquire illegal gain, and there are those who operate with a political motivation—terrorists." Kent pointed in the direction opposite his vast windows. "All you have to do is look at how the skyline has changed on the other side of this building and you're reminded of what they are capable."

"I saw it yesterday from the airplane," said Nathan. "If those are the people we're going after, this is where I want to be."

"You'll have your chance, Nathan. Not just yet. You're not starting there. But you'll have your chance. I do hope you have your bags packed and your passport in order. You *are* going to be doing some traveling."

"'Go to work for Mr. Kent and see the world.' That's what Danny told me."

Mr. Kent clapped his hands together. "Very good and likely quite true. We won't take you too far initially, Nathan. We're going to team you up with one of my senior operators and that will give you a chance to learn the ropes and see how we do things—what's expected of you and what isn't."

"Exactly what is it you do here?" asked Nathan, opening his arms in a questioning gesture. "What's your mandate? I don't know much about the UN, but the picture I have in my mind is one of diplomats and government officials sitting around and living the high life, conducting meetings and not doing much of substance."

"Generally speaking, that's a commonly held view and it's all too often an accurate one. It's also one of the reasons I created my little group. You may not be aware that the UN has many agencies under its umbrella, agencies that do take direct action in their specific fields. Disease and health issues are an international concern and so they have people that deal with those, and not just diplomats, as you say, who talk. Certainly, most of what people do around here is talk. And most times that's about as useful as a London fog. They've begun to realize

22

that, and are moving more and more into a mindset where action is taken as well."

Mr. Kent repositioned himself in his chair and moved the tea tray on the table between them an inch to the left. "So, now there are UN agencies which intervene in health crises and provide assistance to domestic authorities. We have similar agencies that assist in natural disasters, providing aid and expertise wherever they are needed. Of course the UN intervenes militarily as well. There are no standing troops, as you know, but coordinating the movements of member nations' troops is something they've always done."

Nathan nodded. "My country has regularly sent troops on UN peacekeeping missions."

"These days more is being done," said Mr. Kent. "An international punitive action against a rogue nation, such as what occurred during the Gulf War, is an example. But on a smaller scale, they're bringing war criminals to justice in the Balkans. Similarly, we are a direct-action agency targeting the international criminal and terrorist. When these people start to cross borders, thus making it difficult for national law enforcement to deal with them, then we can become involved. We will also assist with domestic situations, if the host country requests our assistance and expertise."

"I take it you'll only operate in a country with the permission of the appropriate authorities and under their umbrella?"

Nathan noticed that Kent's gaze left him and wandered briefly out the window before returning to look at him again and answer the question. "That's correct, Nathan. But not in the way you might think. You're used to working with the local authorities as part of their operation, and 'under their umbrella', as you put it. That's not our method. In most cases the local authorities don't even know who we are or what we're doing. Our authority to be there comes from the highest levels of the national government and they often don't want to admit that we're there or that we even exist. So you see, you'll always have the authority to be where you are and to do what you're doing, but you'll be working alone or with our people. Generally, there will be no liaison with local police or military."

23

"Then, what exactly will be my role?" asked Nathan. "I don't think you hired me to be an intelligence gatherer or an investigator. I'm a shooter, I know that."

Mr. Kent nodded his head. "Yes, yes. You're a shooter. That's what you do. That's part of who you are, just as we are hunters. Your work will be much the same as it was with Mr. Forbes. You'll provide security for my operators, firearms expertise where required, assistance in hostage-takings or international terrorist incidents and, occasionally, direct action against specific targets."

Nathan frowned. "Direct action? That's another one of those code phrases for killing."

"Killing is what we do, Nathan. We're hunters."

"Granted, but there are rules to the hunt and there are rules to the kill. I'll kill only when it's necessary. I'm sure you know that. If you're counting on me to be some kind of hit man for your organization, you'll be disappointed."

"Indeed. I've followed you from the beginning, Nathan. I know you very well. In any case, I can assure you we won't ask you to do anything your conscience won't allow you to."

"As long as we can agree to that, I'm sure we can work together," acknowledged Nathan.

"Splendid," exclaimed Mr. Kent, smiling warmly and spreading his arms wide in a gesture of welcome. "I'm sure you'll enjoy your time with us. It's very important work we do. Think of it as simply another kind of hunting, Nathan. I believe that's why I enjoy the work so much; studying the quarry, learning everything there is to know about him, developing a strategy and then completing the stalk. It's part of why I believe you belong here with us."

"Do you ever take part in operations yourself?" asked Nathan, noticing a touch of sunburn on the balding head.

"Not directly," came his reply. "At my age I can do more good here by coordinating and providing information and intelligence. But occasionally I still like to venture out into the field and watch what goes on. I take no direct part in it myself, not any more.

"However, enough of that," said Mr. Kent ending the topic. "I want you to meet the gentleman you'll be working with initially." As he

24

spoke he strode across the room to his desk and pushed an intercom button. "Jenny, would you send in Leith, please."

A moment later, a man Nathan guessed to be in his late thirties walked into the room. When Nathan rose to meet him he found him to be slightly shorter than his own five feet ten inches. The man looked hard and muscular and the strength of his handshake confirmed that appearance. Kent introduced him simply as Leith, and after first hearing him speak Nathan made what seemed to him a reasonable deduction. "Oh, you're British too."

"Not bloody likely, lad."

"Don't call him English," injected Mr. Kent. "Leith is Scottish and they take great offense to being called Englishmen. And, trust me, you don't want this Scotsman mad at you."

"Sorry about that," apologized Nathan.

"No offense taken, lad. You're new here. Glad to have you on board."

Mr. Kent pointed Leith to a chair and when he sat down himself, everyone else followed suit. "Leith's background, Nathan, is military; more specifically SAS. You're familiar with their reputation I take it?"

Nathan nodded. "Special Air Services. Britain's elite soldiers, very impressive."

Kent carried on. "I recruited him two and a half years ago when he came up for retirement and I had a vacancy. You'll be working with him as we get your orientation out of the way. Your first few jobs will be with him as well."

"Is the flat I found for you to stay in satisfactory?" asked Leith.

"Yes, it's fine," replied Nathan. "I didn't know it was you that had reserved it. Thank you."

"They seem to give good service there. A lot of people in this part of town stay in New York for months at a time doing UN business and they cater to that crowd. You can call that home for the next while. Don't get too comfortable, though. We may have to leave in a few days." He looked at Mr. Kent. "I understand Anton is ready to meet with me."

Nathan saw Kent's eyebrows rise. "Good, that's moved faster than we anticipated. Nathan, you can go along with Leith when he meets with a chap called Anton. It's an information exchange and should be quite routine, but you can provide some security and watch over him. It'll give you a chance to see some of the work we do."

Nathan nodded. "Great. I'm anxious to do something constructive."

"That's still a day or two away," said Leith. "In the interim we'll get you set up with a satellite phone, money, credit cards, all the necessities." Nathan nodded. "Have you used a satellite phone before?"

"No, I haven't. Are they any different than a cellphone?"

"Not much," replied Leith. "We use the Motorola 9505 with an added U.S. government-class encryption cassette. When you pick it up, mention to Jenny that you need some basic lessons."

"Jenny has a lot of that already prepared," said Mr. Kent.

"You can pick everything up on your way out then," added Leith. "And take the rest of the day off. I'll pick you up in front of your hotel at 0730 tomorrow. Bring gym gear and your pistol, we'll spend the morning at some places where we can use both."

"That's wonderful," said Kent. "Sounds like you're all set then, Nathan. Why don't you go out and see Jenny and as Leith suggests, take the rest of the day off. Start to learn the city a little. There are a few matters I need to talk with him about."

Nathan shook hands with both men and left the room. When Jenny saw him leave the office she motioned him over. On her desk were an assortment of small boxes; one of them marked *Motorola*.

Once the door had latched behind Nathan, Mr. Kent turned to Leith. "Anton is already here?"

"He is."

Kent stroked his chin in thought. "Interesting development; but Nathan first. Did you catch most of our conversation before I called you into the room?"

"I did."

"Can you work with him?"

"Aye. I'm sure I can. He doesn't seem to be quite as naive as we were told, though."

"True. I expect that's changing."

Leith helped himself to tea. He used Nathan's cup. "I see a lot of changing, shaping and molding left to do."

"Agreed. But remember, we both come from military backgrounds. The order of the day there, being to strip people of their identity and then rebuild them in the shape the military wants. That hasn't happened with Nathan. You won't be able to tear him apart and rebuild him, Leith. You'll just have to shape what is there so we can use his talents."

"No problem, sir. But I'm still not convinced he's worth it. He's just a civvy target shooter. That's all he is. When things get nasty he'll never make it. And then there's this episode you have planned with Anton and his people, that could get *me* killed too."

"Anton will make Nathan perform, and that will take him another step down the road towards making him useful to us. I concede some work is necessary to make him fully operational, but he can do some things already, and he most certainly is worth the effort, Leith. I concede, there's a risk. You've seen Nathan's tapes. You know what he can do."

"I've seen them, but it's still hard to believe. That's why we're going to the range tomorrow morning; I want to check out his abilities personally. I plan on springing some form of the SAS hostage drill on him."

"Good idea, I'm sure it'll make you feel more comfortable about Anton. Why don't you give me a ring when you get to the range? Perhaps, if I'm not too busy, I can slip down and join you. I must say I wouldn't mind watching him myself."

Leith shook his head in reply. "Watch nothing, sir. If you show up you get to stand in, too."

Mr. Kent winced visibly. "Stand in it is then." He walked to his desk, opened a drawer, extracted a file and came back to where Leith sat. Opening the tan colored folder, he pulled out two sheets of paper. "Now, let's review the Anton matter shall we. Our German friends are very concerned about his trip to America."

27

Jerry Mitchell typed the last sentence of the story he was working on, in his usual brisk and efficient keyboard manner. Then he tapped the final period key with a flourish that would have made a concert pianist proud. The flourish indicated the end of the story and communicated the completion of another dreary assignment. He had spent the day at the Calgary Queen's Bench courthouse following his usual routine of bouncing back and forth between a number of ongoing trials. That way he could keep tabs on what was happening in most of them and still pick up the rare dramatic moments that occurred behind the massive polished brass doors of that structure. In Jerry's opinion, most of the court proceedings were painfully boring. High drama in a courtroom was normally limited to TV and the movies.

Today had been no exception. He'd sat through various parts of a sexual assault trial, an impaired driving case that a wealthy businessman was fighting to the last breath and a murder in which a young man had been stabbed on the strip in Calgary. Nothing of significance had happened at the first two, but the latter had been a sentencing and warranted a story. Second-degree murder, the judge had decreed and imposed a ten-year prison term. Not bad in the grand scheme things.

After sentencing, as he usually did, he'd approached the detective in charge of the investigation and talked to him briefly. Jerry had agreed politely with his mutterings about sentences being too lenient and this being another example of why there would be more stabbings rather than fewer. And then after the accused had been led away, he approached the defense counsel to garner a quotable reaction from him. Jerry had nodded sympathetically when he'd commented on the young man being sent to jail and how it would ruin his career and devastate his family. But he had his quotes, and the story was done.

Jerry ran a spell-check and found no mistakes. A word count was next, and as usual he was right on for a story of this type. Three more mouse clicks on the computer and the story was off to the editor. Jerry checked the time. Almost 4:30 p.m. If Murray was going to call back today he should be doing it soon. He'd give him another half-hour, then call it a day.

Jerry had flown in yesterday from Colorado and was back at work on Tuesday. A briefing to his editor had been accomplished that afternoon. By the end of the day his photos had been developed and he was able to show Frank the pictures of Nathan in the parking lot with the unknown man and the mysterious good-looking redhead. The license plate had been easy to read with a magnifying glass, and that morning Jerry had called Murray, his primary contact in the Calgary Police Service and suggested they may want to see who had this car rented over the weekend.

The story he'd given had been the truth—just not all of it. He told Murray about this car he'd seen in a parking lot, with three people clustered around the back of it, and there had been guns. Jerry knew that would be enough to generate the necessary motivation to make the inquiries but it wasn't enough information to give away what he was looking to get. The role played in this case was that of reporter and concerned citizen. And he made a point of never asking for classified or confidential information, at least not directly. He was just reporting this to his friends within the police service, in his capacity as a responsible journalist. Scooping up his cup he headed for the coffee room for a refill.

When he returned to his desk he called up tomorrow's schedule on the computer and started to plan the day.

Jerry was draining the last of the coffee when his phone rang. As always he checked the call display screen before answering and the words *Blocked Call* suggested Murray was calling back.

"Calgary Tribune. Jerry Mitchell."

"Hi Jerry. It's Murray."

"Hey, Murray, what's up?"

"I checked out that Colorado rental you gave me the lead on, that's all."

"Oh, yeah. I'd almost forgotten about that," Jerry lied. "Anything interesting for you people there? Have we got some real nasties snooping around?"

"No such luck, Jerry. Thanks for the tip, but this is just the opposite. These are the good guys. I can't imagine what they'd be doing in Calgary. I checked with the Chief's office and we have one exchange officer from Czechoslovakia, but that's it."

"What do you mean?"

Murray laughed. "The FBI in Colorado rented that car three days ago. Somebody's done some serious driving to get it up here in that time." Murray was still laboring under the impression Jerry had seen the car in Calgary and Jerry had no intention of correcting him.

"FBI?" Jerry decided to push it. "Do you have the name of the person who rented it?"

"Sure. Sure I do. But I'm not . . . . Do you really need that?"

"No. No, just curious. That's all. As long as nothing illegal is going on. If it was the FBI then there's no problem. Right?"

"No problem. But listen, do you mind telling me where you saw this car?"

Jerry was looking at one of the photo's that showed Nathan in conversation with a redhead and a middle-aged man leaning against a car, the redhead was chewing on her sunglasses. "Hey, Murray," he said plaintively, continuing to examine the photo, "leave a reporter some dignity—some confidences—will you? If you really needed it you know I'd tell everything. Unless it's necessary can we just drop it?"

"Okay, Jerry. That's what we'll do then."

Jerry hung up without saying good-bye. His mind preoccupied with the implications of what he had heard. He studied the photo for another minute and then peeked over the top of the divider that delineated his cubicle in the reporter's bullpen. His boss's office was on the other side against the far wall. Frank was just stepping out of it, jacket in hand, sunglasses perched on the end of his nose. His route would take him by Jerry's desk anyway, so he just waited, holding up the picture as Frank walked by.

"FBI," said Jerry.

Frank stopped. "Say what?"

"The car was rented by the FBI. Nathan Burdett is hanging around with the FBI. What do *they* want with a hotshot Canadian pistol shooter, Frank? Something smells."

Frank peeled off his sunglasses and took the photo. He'd seen it before, but like Jerry studied it again, evidently hoping that this new information would somehow extract something fresh from the colored image. Abruptly he tossed it onto the desk. "Come see me first thing tomorrow morning. We'll talk about giving you some more time on this."

The next morning in New York was sunny and unseasonably warm. The combination drew Nathan out of his hotel's busy lobby to a perch on a concrete planter in front of the building. Two bags, a black gym bag and a green Waller range bag, were piled at his feet as he waited for Leith. By seven-thirty the Scotsman hadn't appeared as promised. Fifteen minutes later he was still a no-show. Nathan had a comfortable spot in the sun, and was in no hurry to go looking for him.

As he sat, he watched the street traffic and the sidewalk pedestrians. Most carried briefcases. An occasional person carried what could have been a gym bag, but he saw no one carrying an identifiable range bag. Not that he expected it and not that the green Waller bag at his feet looked like it contained firearms or shooting gear. To the uninitiated it was just a rectangular green bag of heavy Cordura fabric, perhaps a modern version of the salesman's sample bag. There was a time when Nathan's bag used to be decorated with patches and match pins with his name prominently displayed on the exterior. Those times were over and now anything that drew attention to him was unwelcome. Keeping a low profile had become a way of life.

He thought about Kim. He'd called her last night, but there had been no answer. Same thing this morning. That wasn't unusual. He could've called her pager but he was reluctant to do that just to talk. By eight o'clock Leith still hadn't shown so he checked his phone. The display indicated it was on and seemed to be working. Nathan slid down from his perch and started stretching. He had one heel up on the four foot high planter and was working his left hamstring when a dark blue Ford Explorer pulled off the street and braked sharply in front of the lobby doors. Nathan recognized Leith behind the wheel and extricated his foot from atop the planter. Grabbing both bags, he tossed them into the vehicle behind the front passenger seat.

"Morning, lad," said Leith as he put the vehicle in gear and started it moving before Nathan had the door closed.

"Morning, Leith," replied Nathan, barely getting the door shut as the Explorer reached the street.

"Sorry about the delay, but my phone started ringing at about six this morning and hasn't stopped since."

"Do we need to change our plans for this morning?"

"No, everything is looked after for the time being, so we've still got the morning clear." Leith negotiated his way through traffic, driving aggressively and confidently. The traffic was heavier than anything Nathan had ever seen, but considering it was New York city he told himself he should have expected it. They exchanged small talk for about twenty minutes until Leith made an abrupt right and parked on the second level of a multi-story parkade. A walk down four flights of stairs and half a block north took them to the door of a Gold's gym.

Two and a half hours later, after forty-five minutes of running a fast treadmill and an equal amount of time with free weights, they were throwing their gym bags back into the vehicle. Nathan's assessment of the Scotsman's strength had been correct. He'd never seen anyone getting ready to run a treadmill with a backpack before. Nathan had been about to ask him what it was for when Leith had picked up one ten and one twenty pound iron plate and deposited them in the bag. He'd run the full forty-five minutes with a thirty pound pack on his back. And then he out lifted him on the free weights and still didn't look tired.

"What've you got in the green bag?" asked Leith as they climbed back into the four-wheel drive.

"That's my range bag."

"What's in a range bag?"

That seemed a silly question to Nathan, like asking what's in a peanut butter jar. "My gun , . . uh   ammo, magazines, a training log, you know the usual stuff."

"A training what?"

"A training log, a training diary, if you like."

Leith muttered something under his breath, then announced in a louder voice, "I guess I should have told you. The range we use has ammo available and when you rent a bay, such as we do, you get

32

earmuffs and safety glasses supplied. You don't need to bring anything but your gun."

"Sure," said Nathan, pausing, "I think I still prefer to bring my own stuff."

"Suit yourself." Leith retrieved a satellite phone from the center console and dialed. "Hello, Jenny. Can you tell Mr. Kent that Nathan and I are on our way to the range? If he's able, we'd love to have him meet us there . . . thank you."

Half an hour later they parked across the street from a concrete-block building in a part of the city Leith called Woodhaven. The doors and windows were heavily barred and a large sign across the front proclaimed the establishment to be *The Shooter's Haven Indoor Range*. A smaller sign on one of the windows boasted this was *New York City's Largest Indoor Range*.

Leith threw the shift lever into park and reached into the console again, this time pulling out a pistol tightly secured in a clip-on leather holster. Nathan recognized the classic shape of a Browning Hi-Power. Leith snapped it onto his belt, found a loaded spare magazine in the same compartment and put that in his pocket. "Let's go," he announced.

Nathan grabbed his range bag and followed Leith across the street. As soon as they entered the building Nathan felt relaxed for the first time since arriving in New York. He'd never been here before, but had been in numerous similar clubs, and that gave him a comfortable feeling. It was a case of being familiar with the products, services and layout of an operation such as this. And though he didn't know the people in the store, they gave every indication of being like him— fellow students of the gun—and that made them familiar too.

"Morning Phil," said Leith approaching the front counter. The man on the other side was slender with coal black eyes and neatly trimmed hair and goatee of the same color. "Have you got my usual spot reserved?"

"Sure do." Phil pushed a sign-in book toward the Scot.

Leith spoke while he wrote. "This is Nathan, Phil." Leith pointed a thumb over his shoulder. "We're going to hang out together for a while. He's authorized to put stuff on the company tab, the usual, no restrictions. We trust him." That generated a large smile.

"Nice to meet you, Nathan."

"Good morning."

"Need anything today?"

"No," Nathan answered lifting his bag slightly. "Nothing today, I brought everything with me."

Phil nodded, addressing both men, "Your nine mil. ammo's out on the range. Muffs, glasses and targets are there too. Here's some forms for Nathan to fill out," he added, sliding three sheets of paper across the counter to him. Then in response to Nathan's questioning look added, "We're a private club. You can't just walk off the street and shoot here. You need to have police or government ID, or have a City Pistol License or a Firearms Control Section License."

After he'd filled out the forms Nathan followed Leith into the back, beyond three other range bays and into the fourth. Nathan dug into his bag and readied gear while Leith busied himself putting up a target. Leith finished before Nathan and watched him quietly for a minute as he extracted and prepared equipment.

"I didn't know that much stuff was necessary to go shooting," he teased, scratching his head. The short brushcut that lived there looked entirely in place on the ex-military head.

"These are all essentials," responded Nathan, checking the battery on a shot timer.

"Besides hearing protection and safety glasses, I manage to get by with a gun, ammo and targets. What am I doing wrong?"

Nathan didn't bite. "Go ahead and start," he suggested, "I'm almost ready." He put on his own earmuffs to signal the conversation was over.

Leith took a step closer and cocked his head while examining Nathan's earmuffs. "I've never seen muffs like that," he said. "Why in blazes are there on-off switches on a pair of hearing protectors?"

Nathan removed the dark gray muffs and handed them to Leith. "They're electronic muffs. They protect from gunshot noises but allow the wearer to hear all normal conversation at the same time. That's possible because there's a microphone and speaker built into each ear cup that amplifies all sounds below a certain decibel level. If it hears sounds above that level it shuts down and protects the wearer."

The Scot donned the hearing protectors and repeatedly snapped his fingers. "Bloody amazing."

"Watch this," said Nathan as he reached over and turned up the volume on each cup. Then he pulled a quarter out his pocket and tossed it into the far corner of the range behind Leith's back.

"Incredible." Leith looked back and went off to find the coin. "I heard it hit the wall and clatter onto the floor, as if it were in front of me. They're like a bloody giant hearing aid!"

Leith returned with the quarter and gave it back to Nathan. When he handed the muffs back, Nathan declined, "Use them today. I'll use yours."

Leith accepted, and returned to the firing line where he ran a motorized target holder fifteen yards down range and started shooting. He emptied both of his magazines and just finished reloading them when Mr. Kent entered the range. The three men exchanged morning greetings, then clustered around where Nathan was now loading his magazines.

"Leith, I've read that the SAS have a real love affair with the Hi-Power," said Nathan, nodding towards the Scotsman's holstered Browning. "I guess it's true then?"

"Pretty much the only handgun I've ever used. And I've worn out half a dozen, probably two hundred thousand or more rounds through them. How about you?"

"Always some version of the 1911 for me. I've tried most every other design but in my book Browning got it right the *first* time."

A puzzled look appeared on Leith's face.

Mr. Kent smiled patiently and put a hand on the Scotsman's substantial shoulder. "John Moses Browning designed the 1911 pistol and many years later the Hi-Power. Both designs were purchased from him, the first by Colt and the later one by Fabrique Nationale. His name is still associated with the Hi-Power but curiously not with the Colt, although he did design both."

Leith shrugged. "Whatever. I just know what works for me. So, your gun is a Colt, Nathan?"

"No. Colt was the first, and the most famous manufacturer of 1911's, but now there are lots of other companies making versions of the same gun. This," he slid the pistol at his side out of its holster, "is a highly customized Para-Ordnance. It's a smaller version of their full-sized 1911." Nathan pointed to the abbreviated barrel and butt. "These dimensions are shorter than the full-size gun to conceal it more easily. That's what it was designed as, a concealed-carry gun."

Leith accepted the empty pistol. Nathan had locked the slide back before handing it to him and now Leith thumbed down the slide release allowing the slide to slam shut on an empty chamber. Nathan winced. Do that to a match gun, he thought, and watch an angry owner with a now ruined trigger job, smack you and snatch it promptly out of your hands.

"Got an empty mag, lad?" Leith held out his hand. Nathan located one in his bag and handed it to him. After locking it in place in the gun, Leith stepped to the firing line, drew a bead on his already perforated target and the empty pistol clicked as he pulled the trigger. It was Nathan's turn to look puzzled. What was the point in putting an empty magazine in the gun to test trigger pull, he thought.

"Magazine disconnect," whispered Mr. Kent, in Nathan's direction, with a smile and a wink.

Leith dry-fired the pistol several more times. Nathan was about to step over and point out to him that the 1911, unlike the Hi-Power, has no magazine safety, but stopped himself. Mr. Kent found it amusing, so why embarrass Leith in front of the boss. If he wanted to believe Nathan's gun operated like his beloved Hi-Power and would fire only if a magazine was latched in place—that a missing magazine, in effect, rendered it inoperable—it did no harm.

"Light trigger," commented Leith.

"Four pounds," said Nathan. "Not light by competition standards but probably lighter than your Hi-Power, unless its been modified."

Leith shook his head. He locked the Para-Ordnance's slide open, popped out the empty magazine and handed everything back. "I'm sure it works for you lad, so you ought to stick with it. I'll stay with my Hi-Power."

"Leith's not like you and I, Nathan," said Mr. Kent. "To him, firearms are just tools of the trade. To us they're much more, aren't they? Art, history, craftsmanship, mechanical ingenuity; they become the sum of all those things and more. Firearms are worthy of study for all those reasons, and that's what we do. We study them, learn about them, their past, how they work, the people who developed them and those who have used them over the years. To us the tool is as important as the use it's put to. But they most definitely are not just 'tools of the trade'."

"I've heard this sermon before," said Leith, "and, Nathan, I'll tell you the same thing I've told Mr. Kent here. In a fight, all the head-knowledge in the world won't help you much. The only thing that matters is how determined you are to stay alive and win. Never give up. Never, *ever* give up. When your long gun goes down, reach for your pistol. When it's empty, pull your knife." He reached into a pocket and with a snap, a black blade appeared in his hand. Done so smoothly, Nathan couldn't tell if it was an automatic or a thumb-opening knife. "And if you haven't got a knife, grab whatever's at hand—a rock, an ashtray, anything you can use as a weapon. But never give up. Your love affair with guns won't help you much when the only thing that matters is your will to survive. That's what'll keep you alive, lad. Not a lot of useless knowledge about who built which gun first."

"Point well taken, Sergeant," said Mr. Kent.

Nathan elected to remain quiet. It was Leith's sermon, not Kent's, that he had heard before. He had learned that lesson in a small classroom, from a bullet scarred veteran with a serious limp. And while he couldn't disagree with the importance of Leith's 'will to survive' versus a high level of firearms technical knowledge, he also couldn't help but wonder why a person couldn't have both. What would you become if you had both? And then Nathan realized he'd heard that sermon, too. Danny Forbes had told him that's who he was and why he was special.

"Enough theory," continued Mr. Kent. "Let's do some shooting." He looked in Nathan's direction. "Leith's never seen you shoot. Would you mind giving us a little demonstration?"

"What would you like me to do?"

"Your option, Nathan. If Leith is going to work with you, he needs to know your abilities. Whatever you can do to demonstrate them is fine."

Nathan thought for a moment, looking at the resources available to him on this range. No knock down targets, steel or otherwise, no useable barricades other than the shooting stalls and their fold down tables, and only paper police training targets to shoot at. He did have his timer.

"Have you ever used a shot timer?" he asked Leith. A blank look was his reply. He explained, "It's a high speed clock, used in competition, that gives the shooter a start signal and then senses the sound of gunshots to tell the shooter how fast he's completing a particular exercise or drill." He held up the hand-sized, box shaped timer and pushed *START*. Shortly after the loud buzz of the go signal he slapped the side of the box to simulate a gunshot and showed the digital display to Leith. It read 2.17 seconds.

"We'll try a classic competition drill, Leith. With hands raised up above shoulder level, the shooter stands with his back to three targets ten yards away. When the buzzer sounds you turn and fire two rounds at each one, reload and double-tap each one again. The timer records how long it takes you to do that by sensing and displaying the time of your last shot. The drill is called *El Presidente*."

"That's twelve rounds. I won't need a reload, lad. My Hi-Power holds enough in a single magazine."

Nathan shook his head. "No deal. The reload is mandatory, it's part of what the drill is designed to test."

Leith shrugged. "Show me how it's done then."

Nathan took a few minutes to set the targets at the far end of the twenty-five yard range. Then he walked back ten paces and loaded his pistol, settling it into the holster. Next he did a quick check of his magazines, perched in belt mounted holders on the other side of his torso. He'd already shown Leith the timer's simple controls, and when he was ready Leith pushed the start button.

A spin and simultaneous draw to face the targets, six fast shots, reload and six more shots, gave Nathan a time of 4.22 seconds for the exercise. "Your turn," he told Leith.

After patching the target holes, the Scotsman ran the same drill. The timer read 11.13 seconds. "That's three times as long, Leith," chided Mr. Kent.

"A decent time for anybody," countered Nathan. "And the hits are good. From what I saw, Leith, I think we can make a few changes in what you're doing that'll improve your speed significantly."

"That's good of you to offer, Nathan, but I have no interest in being a competition shooter. I'm plenty fast enough for the real world." A gleam came into his eyes. "You've shown me how it's done in competition, maybe I should show you how we would do this little exercise where I come from."

"By all means." Nathan lifted his hands in an exaggerated shrug.

Leith patched the targets and then waved Mr. Kent forward. "Stand there," he said, pointing to a position between the first and second targets. Mr. Kent did as he was told, planting his feet and standing shoulder to shoulder with the paper humanoids, his arms crossed. Leith took up a similar position between the second and third targets, so there now stood an alternating left to right row of targets and humans.

"Okay, laddie. Have at it."

"Have at what?"

"Shoot your *El Presidente* drill again. Like this, with us standing between the targets."

Nathan froze and the range went quiet. The rushing hum of exhaust fans removing the lead and smoke contaminated atmosphere and pumping in fresh air was the only noise. He could see they were serious. "Not on your life, Leith! That's crazy! Mr. Kent, both of you, get out of there."

"We're not going anywhere," observed Leith calmly. "Shooting paper targets with your teammates standing next to them is a standard SAS drill. If I don't trust your abilities enough to shoot someone out from beside me, we won't be working together."

"He's right," agreed Mr. Kent. "Besides, we have ear protection and safety glasses, that's all we need because you're not going to miss. Are you? You *are* the best in world. Right?"

"This is nuts!" yelled Nathan. "Where do you get ideas like this? This goes against every safety rule I've ever been taught."

"War violates a lot of safety rules, lad."

"Well, I'm not going to war," said Nathan, folding his arms and glaring alternately between the two men standing amidst the targets. "Forget it, I'm not playing your game."

Mr. Kent replied first, "It's not a game, Nathan. We're serious. This is standard procedure, you have to do it."

"I'm serious too. I've done it for real. I'm sure you know that. Doing it as training isn't worth the risk. It's crazy."

"We're so serious, that after you've done the drill as the shooter, you'll come stand here with me while Leith shoots it."

Nathan was speechless.

"No need to break any speed records, lad," negotiated the Scotsman, "just do the drill and hit the right targets. Take your time."

"Don't do it," said Mr. Kent, "and there'll be no second chances—ever." Nathan's hands moved to his hips and he looked at the floor. Kent, still standing beside the targets, continued, "Remember what I said yesterday? I told you the bar has been raised, that the level of opposition you're likely to face will be more sophisticated and better trained than anything you've encountered to date. That means you have to be better trained as well. This is part of that." Nathan looked up. "You didn't think your training was over, did you?"

"Training is never over. I know that," he snapped back.

Kent didn't respond in kind. His voice remained gentle and persuasive. "And we wouldn't be standing here if we didn't have every confidence that you could do this. And do it well. Like you said, you've already done it for real. This is just a training exercise."

Nathan pulled a loaded magazine from the holder on his belt and studied it.

"There's a good lad. Now let's get on with it," said Leith. "It's all in the focus, that's how it's done. Concentrate on what you want to hit and ignore us. We don't exist."

With a free hand Nathan pushed his safety glasses up above his hairline and massaged his eyes and face. He muttered something, but above the drone of the range's exhaust fans neither Kent nor Leith

40

could make out what it was. Once the glasses were repositioned he loaded his pistol, exaggerating the standard safety precautions of keeping the muzzle pointed in a safe direction and the finger off the trigger. Nathan said nothing as he once again faced away from the targets and, with his .45 holstered, raised his hands to the required shoulder height.

Leith pressed the timer's start button.

Avoiding 'no shoot' targets was nothing new to Nathan. As a standard part of competitive action pistol shooting he encountered many different variations on the theme. He tried to tell himself this was just another twist. Leith was right about the technique, he knew that too. The key was to focus on what you wanted to hit, not what you wanted to miss. And it wasn't that long ago he'd done this for real, when Bob and Frankie Coombs had ended up on the receiving end of a revenge directed at him.

The front sight was clearly in focus as he fired two shots at the first paper target, then lifting his finger off the trigger he swung by Kent and shot the middle paper. Finger off the trigger again as he came past Leith, and then the last target received two shots. Dump the magazine and reload. Back to the first target, double-tap, swing, double-tap, swing, one last double-tap and done. Again he exaggerated the safety movements as he cleared the pistol and when he looked up it was to see a smiling Leith reading the timer.

"Twelve point zero seven seconds, a decent time. The hits are good. With a few changes we could improve your time significantly." He laughed at his own mockery.

Nathan felt his face reddening.

Leith stepped out of the target row and tossed the timer to him. "All right, lad. My turn. Places gentlemen," he commanded, checking the Hi-Power's load. Kent hadn't moved, the 'places' comment was for Nathan who slowly took Leith's vacant position. The short Scotsman never checked behind him to see if the 'hostages' were ready, he merely raised his hands and tensed, waiting for the start signal.

Nathan wasn't as broad as Leith so he didn't take up as much horizontal space between the targets, but he pulled his elbows in tight anyway. He checked his earmuffs and reseated the safety glasses firmly.

With his finger on the start button he looked over at Kent. The man was still standing with his arms folded, looking impassively straight ahead. Nathan clenched his teeth and pushed the button.

In response, Leith whirled, snatched the gun from his holster and hammered three fast double-taps. Nathan heard but didn't see them. With his eyes closed he didn't see the reload either. Three more double-taps and Nathan opened his eyes and breathed. As far as he could tell there were no new orifices in his body. He had expected to feel burning powder pepper his face but there had been none. Being in front of a pistol had been only slightly noisier than being behind one.

"What does your fancy timer say, Nathan?"

"Oh. Sorry." Nathan looked at the timer. "Ten point two one." Leith had done it faster with live targets, beating him.

Mr. Kent stepped out of the target line. "Good job, Leith." He looked at Nathan. "I'm going back to the office and I'll take Leith with me. If we leave you the keys can you find your way back alone in this New York traffic?"

Nathan fingered the timer in his right hand and nodded. "Sure. No problem."

"Good. We'll be off then. Come by the office about half past one will you, Nathan?"

"This bay is ours until noon," added Leith, dropping the keys beside Nathan's range bag. "Put it to use and get in some practice."

When the range door closed behind the two departing men, Nathan still stood between targets two and three. His first step out of the target line was with his left foot—the kind of step a baseball pitcher takes as part of his wind up. The timer's impact into the far concrete wall spread microchips and circuit board pieces over most of the range floor.

42

CHAPTER THREE

The next day, Thursday, Leith and Nathan drove through the heavily treed countryside northeast of New York city, looking for a rest stop on Route 17. The presence of the particular one they needed was announced by a white on blue road sign. Intended as a stopping point for weary travelers in need of a break from the mind numbing monotony of a long drive, this rest stop was now closed for maintenance—at least that's what the sign at the entrance indicated. At the same time, orange sawhorse barricades physically blocked the access road.

Leith stopped the Ford Explorer in front of the center barricade, "Go pull it aside," he told Nathan, "and close it behind me again."

Nathan complied. Upon dragging the right side of the barricade aside, he noticed faint scrape marks on the pavement suggesting someone else had done the same thing recently. The heavy foliage was turning color, but little of it had yet fallen and therefore it prevented him from seeing into the rest area. The noise from midafternoon traffic on the freeway masked any sounds. Leith drove through and Nathan closed the barricade behind him. "They might be here already," he said, climbing back into the vehicle.

Leith ignored him. Staring straight ahead he followed the short winding roadway until it opened into an expansive parking lot. A squirrel scampered out of their way into the dense underbrush. At the far end, stood a cinder-block building with exotic roof angles and the requisite picnic tables. Half a dozen trashcans completed the scene. Beside the building Nathan saw a green Buick and four men hanging around the front of a white pick-up truck. As soon as Nathan and Leith pulled into view they straightened. One tossed away a cigarette.

"Looks like we're outnumbered," commented Nathan.

43

"No problem," replied Leith, "this is going to be simple. There won't be any difficulties from these characters. They're Russian gangsters and this is business. Russians know how to do business."

Then why am I here, thought Nathan, not feeling as confident as Leith sounded.

The men looked docile enough. No overt signs of hostility were visible, but there seemed to be a certain tension in their movements, the kind bred by uncertainty about surroundings or events. Nothing concrete, just something that tugged at the edge of Nathan's senses, telling him to be careful. He was going to mention something to Leith but decided not to. He's supposed to be the expert, Nathan reminded himself; one of the best operators in the 'business'. Who am I to tell him anything?

Leith stopped the Explorer broadside, eighty yards from where the car and the pick-up were lined up nose to tail in front of the building. As they braked to a halt the largest man in the group walked forward, followed by one of the others, half a pace behind. Both were large men but in different ways. The man in the lead was obese-large while the one behind him was solid-large. The two remaining moved to the far side of the open pick-up and leaned on the edge of the box. The smoker lit another cigarette as Nathan, following Leith's lead, stepped out of the Explorer.

Nathan scanned the line of orange and yellow foliage around them that formed the edge of the parking lot, trying to penetrate the dappled pattern of leaves, shadow and sunlight. The rectangular shape of the lot made that multicolored line anywhere from a hundred to a hundred and fifty yards distant. The combination of the two, distance and pattern, meant he saw nothing suspicious. That didn't mean there wasn't something there, he told himself. All it meant was he couldn't *see* anything.

The fat man and his partner stopped halfway to the Explorer. Nathan followed Leith, a similar half-step behind, walking to where the men waited.

"Good morning. I am Anton," greeted the fat one. There was an accent but the English was good.

Leith didn't respond for a long time. The hum of freeway traffic in the distance was the only sound. He stood in front of the man and looked him over carefully, eventually shifting his inspection to the bodyguard behind him and then to the two men standing on the other side of the pick-up.

Nathan spent the time of strained silence examining those men he could see. Anton was over fifty and considerably overweight. His nose showed the prominent blood vessels of a man who had consumed too much liquor during his life. Nathan wondered if it had been vodka, like in the movies. Did Russians really like vodka that much or was it just myth? If he ever got to know a Russian he would ask him. Anton's nose was bent slightly and the bulge of a shoulder holster was visible under his too tight suit. Nathan's conclusion was that whatever power Anton possessed hadn't been inherited from anyone; this was someone who had taken it himself.

The bodyguard, if that's what he was, was about Nathan's age but bigger and no doubt stronger. His size and strength looked like it hadn't come from a gym or a bottle of steroids but rather had grown as the product of solid Russian stock. Like Nathan he wore a thin jacket. The weather was far too mild for a jacket, but jackets had other uses besides providing warmth.

If things fell apart, he saw nothing about these two he couldn't handle, especially with Leith's help. The two at the truck bothered him. He could only see them from the chest up and had no idea what was behind the truck or even inside the truck box in front of them. And then maybe, just maybe, there were more than these four. That worried him.

Leith finally spoke. "Sure."

Anton wasn't happy. "You are late," he complained.

"Oh yeah?" Leith snapped back.

Nathan cast a brief puzzling look at the two conversing men. Hadn't he and Leith arrived a good ten minutes early?

"You should have been here one half hour ago," scolded Anton. "I do not like to wait."

Leith glanced briefly at his watch and then back at Anton. His voice was conciliatory when he spoke. "Well it's obvious there's been some kind of mistake, Mr. Anton," then suddenly his voice changed to one dripping with sarcasm, "you've mistaken me for someone who cares."

The pinkish blush residing across Anton's nose spread over the rest of his face. "You insolent Englishman," he clipped out the words, "we will do our business and we will go, but I doubt we shall do business again."

Leith shot back, "Who would want to do business with a Jew-lover like you, anyway?"

Anton bristled visibly and took a deep breath, sucking in through his teeth. He looked behind him, first at the bodyguard and then the men at the truck.

Nathan stole a glance at Leith. Jews? The 'Jew-lover' crack had sounded like an insult. This certainly was a unique way to conduct business. Was there something about Russian culture that required you to insult your prospective partner as a greeting?

Before the Russian could respond to the insult, Leith spoke again, "I'm here because I have to be. I don't have to enjoy this, just do it."

Anton relaxed a little, "You are a rude man. I should have you killed, but I want what you people have and so I will let you live."

The tension was draining from the encounter when Leith replied. "What's that supposed to do, scare me? You're just a fat alcoholic who terrorizes old women and children. If you had to do something dangerous yourself, you'd probably wet your pants." As he spoke Leith reached into one of the pockets of his vest and Nathan's head snapped back to the bodyguard who stiffened at the move.

"Cigarettes, you moron," Leith explained, slowing his movements until he had extracted a package of Players. The big guy behind Anton relaxed only slightly. When did Leith start smoking, Nathan asked himself.

The fat man stood frozen in rage, his face turning a deeper shade of red. The bodyguard said something to him in Russian and Nathan understood the *Nyet* reply but not the question.

Leith lit a cigarette and took a very shallow drag, just enough to light it, then shook out the match. He held the extinguished match between his thumb and forefinger and flicked it at Anton. It bounced off his protruding stomach and tumbled to the pavement still smoking lightly. A small black smudge on the tan colored suit jacket showed where it had hit.

Anton didn't move. Nathan wasn't sure if it was discipline or if he was just so shocked at the deed he didn't know what to do in response. As the insult sank in, Nathan saw his jaw muscles and his fists clench. He wasn't far from losing control. The bodyguard was in a similar state but staying disciplined. The two men at the truck were speaking animatedly to each other but Nathan couldn't make out the words. A blind man could see things were spiraling out of control. And it was Leith's fault—he was doing it all. Whatever Leith was trying to do, he was going too far.

Anton spat downward, toward Leith's shoe. Nathan didn't look to see if he actually hit it. He kept his eyes on the two men in front of him. "Our business is finished!" Anton yelled, shaking a fist at Leith.

The Scot didn't react to the spit, any more than Anton had to the match. He merely took a longer drag on his cigarette. The Russian had started turning away when Leith flicked the glowing cigarette at him, catching him squarely on the side of the head and cascading glowing embers into his left ear.

The reaction was predictable. There were howls of rage from Anton as he clawed at his ear. The air filled with unintelligible words, undoubtedly Russian curses.

The bodyguard stepped forward, inserting his body between the boss and these new enemies and pushed Anton forcibly backwards. The move told Nathan he knew his job—completely disciplined. He still hadn't reached for a gun. No simple thug here, he'd been trained somewhere.

This meeting was a bust. Leith had seen to that. With at least two to one odds, they were in deep. Nathan, positioned a half-step behind Leith and to his left side, waited. He could move first and take both of these guys but Leith was still in charge. He'd let him make the call. From here he could see him in his peripheral vision while still watching the opposition. He thought that if this went *really* bad he might have enough ammo left to use some of it on Leith.

47

Anton's words were initially the unmistakable, short, guttural outbursts of profanity and pain. He recovered quickly though and as the bodyguard pushed him away, the wave of an arm was followed with a complete phrase, screamed once, loud. Nathan couldn't understand the words but the action it generated left no doubt as to the meaning. The bodyguard clawed under his coat.

A blind deaf man could have seen this coming. Nathan groaned inwardly, but he was ready. There was no more need to wait for instructions from Leith. Now it was survival. His fingers wrapped around the comforting grip of his .45, and he snapped it clear of the Blade-Tech holster that cradled it. He had time to hope that Leith would be a better shot than a deal maker.

The Russian had good skills, for a bodyguard. His training was going to get him killed, though. He was doing all the right things, getting between the principal and the threat and moving out of the kill zone. Ironic that this time, increasing the distance between the principal and the threat was going to get them both killed.

At fifteen yards and still moving backwards Nathan knew he couldn't risk a disabling shot. They were too far away and moving, and Nathan's gun was an iron-sighted Para-Ordnance compact—too risky.

The training had been military or police Nathan guessed, but he wasn't in Nathan's league. Not even close. Nathan's sight picture came together, top of the front sight level with the rear, equal amount of light on both sides, and he pressed the trigger. Twice. He didn't wait to see the result; his sight already tracking to Anton. The fat Russian grabbed for his shoulder holster but was incredibly clumsy about it. And he started moving laterally. Nathan's sight picture came together again with the Russian's chest superimposed on the front sight. He put on two inches of lead as his trigger finger began its rapid controlled press. At 4.2 pounds of trigger weight the sear pivoted out of the hammer notch and the .45 bucked in recoil. Then it fired again.

The .45 tracked back to the bodyguard. He'd stopped moving but was still standing. Two hits in the chest had staggered him but hadn't put him down. Dead man standing, thought Nathan. Like a fatally shot deer that can still run a hundred yards, this man had a will to fight. The shots had been good—he'd be dead in two minutes. Two minutes during which he could still use his gun. So Nathan put the pistol's front sight on his nose and a 230-grain hollow-point short-circuited his central nervous system and sent him to the pavement.

He shifted back to the fat man and saw him falling. Anton would beat the bodyguard to terra firma, but not by much. At least two men left and now it was Nathan's turn to move out of the kill zone. That meant the Explorer as a destination, a good thirty yards back. His eyes swept the remaining two men by the back of the truck and he turned to run. He saw movement there, but was moving too fast to register any detail.

Leith, ahead of him, sprinted for the Explorer as well, unholstering his Browning Hi-Power as he ran. Rounding the back of the Explorer he crouched at the front wheel; the vehicle's engine block between him and the remaining men. At least he's got good cover, thought Nathan, as he too crouched, but at the rear wheel.

Nathan's left hand reached for the spare magazines on his hip and snatched out a reload. He popped the partially empty one from his gun and replaced it with the full one. The magazine that had been in the gun went into his rear pants pocket.

He poked his head up to try and see through the glass but found it too darkly tinted and, with the sun behind him, acted like a mirror. On a February afternoon in Calgary that trick of glass on the window of a pizza joint had saved his life. There it had revealed an unseen professional killer closing in on him. Here it hid those who intended to kill him.

Crouching again, he looked at Leith, coming down from his own pop-up-and-peek. Leith caught his eye and waved him over. Nathan shuffled to him and two grown men tried to hide behind one truck wheel.

"I saw them pull two long guns out of the pick-up's box," Leith said. "One was an AK of some type but I couldn't tell the other."

The boom of a center-fire rifle added an exclamation point to the observation and a bullet's smack into the front of the 4X4 was felt by both. Another boom followed, and Nathan, who now faced the rear of the Explorer, saw a sharp jagged hole appear in the metal just above the rear wheelwell, a spot he had occupied a moment ago.

Another boom and another bullet impacted the front, then another and one more hole in the rear.

"One's working the front and one the rear!" yelled Leith.

"It's the same shooter," disagreed Nathan. "He's alternating between front and back."

Another round smashed into the engine block and Nathan immediately bobbed up to peek and came back down.

"I only see one," he reported.

A bullet ripped through the back of the vehicle and whined off into the distance, its flight no longer stable after a high-velocity trip through metal and plastic.

Nathan braced himself.

Another bullet slammed into the engine block. Nathan waited half a heartbeat and came up over the hood, bracing himself on the warm metal. He exposed only what was necessary, the .45 in his hands and enough of his head to find the other shooter and see his own sights.

He'd guessed right. The operator of the AK was sighting at the rear of the Explorer. Amateur, he thought. Too exposed. Both elbows were on the hood of the truck—the thirty round mag of the AK wouldn't let him get low enough in that position. A pro would have pulled back half the length of the gun and gone lower.

As his sight picture settled on the distant shooter Nathan told himself eighty yards wasn't that far. He could make this shot every time on the practice range. Only this wasn't practice. Now the target was shooting back and this shot would take all the self-discipline he had.

He willed his eyes to concentrate on the front sight and in response the target drifted out of focus as he began his trigger squeeze. His own gun was about to fire when he heard the AK boom again and the smack of bullet on steel to his right told him the rifleman would be swinging his gun to Nathan's end of the vehicle once again and would no doubt register him. He fought to maintain control as he finished the last portion of the squeeze. Focus on the front sight—squeeze the trigger. The .45 roared and twisted again. The sight picture had looked good and Nathan heard the solid plop of a distant bullet impact.

The target was still there, so he reacquired the sight picture and fired again. The AK boomed, but the shot seemed wild. Once again

Nathan fired, and in response the rifle slipped from the shooter's grasp and slid from the hood on Nathan's side of the truck. The shooter sagged out of sight on the opposite side.

"Got him," yelled Nathan, recovering from his shooting position and squatting down beside Leith. He performed another reload, adding one more partially empty magazine to his left rear pants pocket. The magazine in his gun was his last full one. There were no more on the belt.

Since Leith didn't seem to be taking any kind of a leadership role he made his own suggestions while executing the tactical reload. "Let's get out of here. See if this thing will start. I'll watch for number Four, he's still out there."

Leith stayed low as he opened the door and reached in to turn the key. They heard a faint click from the engine but nothing more. Leith slid back out and closed the door. "We can't stay here."

"Let's go for their vehicles," suggested Nathan.

"Lead the way."

"I'll swing wide to the left. You come straight in."

"Okay. Don't stop moving 'til you get some cover."

Nathan sprinted out with Leith on his heels. As they'd agreed, Nathan ran in a sweeping circle to the left, and as he swung towards the two vehicles he saw Leith making a zigzag path in the same direction. Their timing was good, for as Nathan approached the still form on the ground behind the truck, Leith had finished clearing the car and was covering the rifleman from the corner of the truck.

The rifleman lay on his back by the front wheel. His open vacant eyes and the palm-sized cluster of three bullet holes in the chest told Nathan what he needed to know. Leith came around the front of the truck and bent down beside him. Leith retrieved the AK and checked its load, eventually holstering his pistol in favor of the rifle. He scanned the surrounding area, speaking as he searched, "Nice shooting. You didn't even hit the rifle."

"He was holding it way too high. That meant I could slip the bullets in low."

"No sign of number Four?"

"Nothing," replied Nathan.

51

"There's two empty long gun cases in the back of the truck."

The distant tree line and the thought of a hidden rifleman out there made a chill run through Nathan. "Let's get out of here." He nodded toward the vehicles.

"Not quite so easy. No keys."

Nathan started going through the dead man's pockets. "No keys here either. Can you hot-wire either of these?"

"Not a chance, laddie. How about you?"

"No."

Both crouched near the front wheel again. Only this time they were sharing the space with a body. The cinder-block building protected them to the north but that still left exposure on each side. Back to back, they covered this area while their minds worked.

"What do the gun cases look like?" asked Nathan. "Are they hard or soft?"

"I guess you could say they're hard. Both are a brown color and hinged along the entire length. Like a long flat suitcase."

"Foam interiors?"

"Yeah. One is open and the other has the lid closed but not latched. I popped a look inside but it's empty."

"Can you reach into the box and grab them?" asked Nathan.

"I can if you really need them. That exposes me to whoever's left out there though. They *are* empty."

"It's important."

"Bloody great," muttered Leith as he duck walked forward, stopping at the rear wheel where he laid down the AK. He reached into the open box with both hands and came out with two cases, which he tossed unceremoniously in Nathan's direction. As quickly as possible he crouched down, once again filling his hands with the rifle.

Nathan reached behind him and pulled the cases closer, rearranging them so they lay open before him. His eyes alternated between the open space in front of him and the foam-filled gun cases at his feet.

"And just what is it you're doing?" Leith asked, working his way back to the front wheel.

"If you store only one model of rifle in a case like this, the foam eventually takes an impression from it. I thought it might be possible to figure out what the other shooter has with him, that's all. If it's a rifle, he's a threat at long range. If it's a shotgun, we should be a lot safer."

"Bloody clever," nodded Leith, taking the time himself to look at the foam. He pointed at the furthest case. "That one had the AK in it, I'd wager."

"I agree. And it wasn't an AK in the other one."

"Right. But I'm not getting anything from it. How about you?"

"See the stab mark on the lid from the cocking handle?" Leith nodded. "Where it's located, the overall length and what I can see of the stock suggests a Mini-14. At least there's no scope." A puzzled look passed across Leith's face. "Made by Ruger," explained Nathan. "Semi-automatic rifle, .223—sorry 5.56 mm."

"Got it," Leith turned back to cover his side of the parking lot. "Probably moved out to try and flank us. He would've run off behind the building here, to pick up the bushline and then circle behind us."

"Which way would he go when he hit the trees?"

"We're about centered. He could have gone either way."

"Any suggestions?"

"We hit the bush ourselves; I'll go left, you go right. If we follow the treeline one of us will see him. Hopefully before he sees us."

"I'm right behind you," prompted Nathan.

With a last check of the parking lot, Leith sprinted around the corner of the building. Nathan was half a dozen steps behind and found the exposed run to the trees was mercifully short. Ahead of him Leith went left so he veered right, stopping briefly twenty yards from where they separated. The solid trunk of an oak gave him some comfort as he squatted, planning what to do next.

Nathan felt safer here, closed in and concealed by the surrounding vegetation. He had to remind himself that it concealed his prey just as well. Or was he the prey? Best not to forget that. Almost like deer hunting, but only in the sense that he held a gun and was stalking through the woods—now the prey was hunting him too.

The rifleman had probably done the same thing he and Leith had; run madly for the trees and then moved quickly in a large circle. Once the shooting had stopped he probably got curious and worked his way to the edge of the parking lot to see what happened, especially since his partner wasn't yelling the Russian equivalent of 'got em'. Had he seen them run for the trees too? Was he making an escape now or was he going to stand and fight?

The foliage here wasn't as thick as that bordering the edge of the lot, the result of sparse and filtered sunlight on the forest floor. Nathan studied his surroundings, noticing he'd separated from Leith at a natural thinning amongst the trees. On the ground, littered with decaying vegetation and the odd bit of tourist trash, were two sets of scuff marks. One led to where he crouched behind the tree and the other carried on past and disappeared from view. Definitely a lot like deer hunting, thought Nathan. And this guy's eyesight, hearing and smell aren't even a tenth as good as the most inept whitetail in the Rocky Mountains.

With a deep breath, he stepped out from behind the comfort of the tree and jogged to the protection of another trunk thirty feet distant. There he squatted and, after careful examination of the terrain around him, checked the tracks again. On one the sharp edge of a heel was visible. The stride indicated he was still moving fast, with no apparent caution. Nathan felt comfortable enough with that information to move quickly again. Another trunk, another scan, check the tracks and pick out another trunk. He repeated the movement five more times, then lost the tracks on a patch of ground carpeted deeply with leafy humus and discarded squirrel snacks.

After an intensive examination of the area where the tracks were last headed he eased out from behind the protection of the trunk. From what he'd seen here the rifleman was still moving. Nathan took three steps into the relative open and paused to look. Nothing. Three more steps. Nothing visible ahead or on the ground. Three more steps and he picked up the tracks again. Still moving, but the stride was shorter. He'd slowed down. Nathan picked up the pace as much as he dared.

On his right the thinning trees indicated the edge of the parking lot, and soon he picked up the right angle that formed the corner of the pavement. There was a little more tourist garbage here, either deposited by those seeking privacy or carried by the wind. Shortly after making a turn that skirted the corner, the pace of the tracks slowed to a careful walk and became impossible to follow.

This is where he got suspicious, thought Nathan. The rifle shots have stopped and he's not hearing from his partner. 'Maybe he's reloading' would have crossed his mind first. Then 'maybe he got them', and when nothing was heard for a long time 'maybe they got him'.

The smell of the fall woods, the gun in his hand and the stalk dragged Nathan back to an early hunting lesson. On a crisp autumn day of the first year he'd known Bob Coombs, the gunsmith took a teenage Nathan hunting. The game was whitetail deer in heavy cover. 'Might as well start with a tough one,' Bob said. Nathan absorbed everything the gunsmith taught him that day and went on to learn more each time they went out. Now he reverted to those lessons; slowing into his best Bob Coombs' taught 'there's a ten-point buck somewhere ahead of me in this patch of bush' still-hunting mode.

Nathan picked a spot on the ground on which to place his foot and carefully took one step. His eyes hunted the terrain ahead of him for anything that didn't belong. Seeing nothing, he slowly lowered himself to a squatting position. The eyes hunted again. Not for a full human shape—'never look for a full deer' Bob had hammered home, 'scrutinize for a patch of wrong color, a line too straight, a twitch of movement, a texture that doesn't belong'.

Finding nothing, Nathan picked a spot for his next footstep. When he'd placed the foot his eyes hunted again, first upright then crouching. Still nothing. One more step. Search. Step. Search. Step. Search. Step . . .

Each step took a full minute. At this rate, it would take two hours to reach the far end and the highway. The temptation to hurry, to get it over with, to take a quick extra step and thereby gain the protection of a tree trunk sooner, was overwhelming. Nathan gritted his teeth and steeled his mind. Discipline was the key, hard cold discipline.

He hadn't hunted in almost two years but he was familiar with discipline. Discipline kept the calluses on his hands from long hours of pistol practice; discipline made the body ache from lung-busting runs and grueling weight sessions; discipline focused his mind—a focus he needed now.

A flicker of movement to his right stopped him in mid-stride. Was it a falling leaf or something more? It didn't repeat, and after five minutes of standing in an awkward position without moving, he wasn't sure it ever happened. Then, movement again. The slightest twitch of a shadow from under a willow ten paces away. It was darker under the willow's overhanging branches. A shade darker than the shadow. Gray on gray. There and gone. No sound.

Nathan held his position. His heart pounded faster, breathing became ragged. He had started to calm down during the stalk but now the adrenaline was flooding back with a vengeance. His visual focus began narrowing and he forced himself to keep his eyes roaming and scanning. Moving his head was out of the question. Breath came in short pants. Hearing was shutting down. Nathan caught his trigger finger creeping off its position along the side of the .45's frame and slipping into the trigger guard. No need for that. It was buck fever, that's all. There was no target. He was losing control. Remember—discipline. Focus.

A sound broke through his adrenaline-induced shutdown. A rustle. Only a small movement. Was it precursor to a major one? Finger back to the trigger. The shadow didn't fit. It moved. He's coming out!

A dark shape bolted from the under the willow, feet clawing for traction, zigzagging through the trees, angling across his front. Nathan jammed the safety down as he brought the pistol up to eye level. Like a million times in practice, his eyes found the front sight and he tracked the runner while his finger pressed the trigger. Follow and press.

A squirrel! The darting animal hit the base of a large cottonwood in front of him and scampered four feet up the trunk before it stopped. So did Nathan's trigger squeeze. Just in time. He was easing his finger off the trigger when the squirrel reversed direction, ran down the trunk and hurried out of sight to Nathan's left.

The squirrel induced adrenaline dump started a tremble in his hands. Nathan squeezed the pistol harder to try and control it. Discipline. Focus. Why had the little nutcracker run four feet up the tree and then back down? He saw me, thought Nathan. Why not climb the tree and get out of danger? Unless—? Nathan looked up.

He was there. Twenty feet up the tree. He sat, at the crotch of a large branch, facing the parking lot, his right side to Nathan. The Mini-14 was pointed towards the lot but starting to move. The squirrel's sudden rush causing him to look down towards the noise an instant before Nathan looked up. But the shooter was right-handed and with Nathan on his right side and an awkward position in the tree, it was taking an extra second to bring the rifle around. Nathan's safety was already off as he snapped the pistol up once again. He fired four rounds before pausing to evaluate their effect.

The rifle fell first, bouncing off small branches and landing with a metallic whack. When the man fell he crashed through the branches and landed with a dull and terminal-sounding thud.

By the time the body hit the ground, Nathan was thirty feet from where he'd been standing when he fired. A tree trunk, too small for his liking, was between him and the still form on the ground. He watched over the top of his pistol's sights, looking and listening for any indication there was still a threat present. The man lay on his chest. The face wasn't visible, nor were the hands. The Mini-14 lay on the leaf-covered earth six feet to the man's left.

After five minutes there had been no movement. If that were a deer I'd move in closer and check the eyes, thought Nathan. Open and vacant usually meant dead, but he would have brushed at the eye with a stick to make sure. Lack of response was guaranteed dead. That worked with animals and with people. But people are more deceptive than animals, and trying to get close enough to do the eye test on a human could get you killed. That had been one of Danny's tactical lessons.

'Unless someone is covering you, never approach a downed adversary; and when you do never approach armed. Void yourself of weapons before you go in, lest he overpower you and thus, inadvertently, you arm your enemy. If he's playing possum, waiting for you to get closer, and when you do, he attacks; your job is to get out of

57

the kill zone. Your covering partner's job is to fill the air with lead and put him down.'

And therefore Nathan waited. He whistled twice, sharply, then readjusted to a more comfortable position. Twenty minutes later he heard movement from the way he'd come. He tried to think of something Scottish to whistle and *Danny Boy* was the only thing that came to mind. He whistled the first few bars and paused. The tune was picked up and a silent shadow appeared through the trees moving from cover to cover. Nathan raised his left arm and the motion froze the shape to a distant trunk. A moment later it moved closer as Leith maneuvered in his direction, stopping when he saw the body on the ground. Pausing briefly to analyze what was before him, he made two more moves that took him to a covering position. Leith shouldered the AK firmly, sighted on the still form and nodded.

Because moving forward from his position would take him across Leith's line of fire, Nathan slid backwards from behind his tree. A crouching jog carried him to a position behind Leith, who never took his sights off the still form while Nathan stuffed his .45 into Leith's belt at the small of his back. Moving out again, without his pistol, he took a route that would place the trunk of the large cottonwood between himself and the body. With Leith covering him, he moved in alertly and confidently, stopping when he reached the trunk and then darting out only far enough to snatch the Mini-14 off the forest floor.

After removing the rifle's magazine, he pulled back on the operating lever to extract the single chambered round. He left the ammunition on the ground and flung the now empty rifle as far as possible behind him. With a confirming glance toward Leith, he again left the protection of the trunk. Staying as low as possible, he reached across the body, grabbed the opposite shoulder and rolled him onto his back. The movement caused a gurgling sound in the chest cavity and the head flopped lifelessly. Bits of earth and vegetation clung to the face and adhered to the moist corneas. Seeing that, gave Nathan the confidence to crouch over the man and go through his pockets. There were no more weapons but he did locate keys. By the time he stood up with them and walked to where Leith waited, the tension had begun to seep away.

"Anything on your side?" asked Nathan.

"Nothing." Leith pulled Nathan's pistol from the back of his jeans and handed it over, butt first.

"He's the only one that went this way." Nathan nodded his head toward the lifeless form as he pulled the two partly empty magazines from his pocket. Extracting all the rounds from one, he reloaded them into the other two magazines. A full one went in the gun, the other he reseated into his belt pouch. That left one empty, so he tucked it back into his pocket. Satisfied he was as fully loaded as he could be, he addressed Leith. "Well, that was pretty much a total disaster. You're apparently better at starting fights than you are at ending them."

Leith was crouching, peering off towards the parking lot, trying to find a sparse spot in the foliage so he could spot the vehicles. "Did you know *Danny Boy* was actually written by an Englishman? And the Irish claim it as one of their songs?"

"What? Who cares! Leith, what exactly were you trying to do?" continued Nathan. "Were you *trying* to start a gunfight?"

Leith ignored the question. "You're shooting was spot on," he said, straightening up.

"Lucky for both of us it was!" Nathan stepped in front of the Scotsman, almost nose to nose. "Just how are you going to explain this? I hope you can treat the cops with more tact than what you've shown here. Maybe I should make the call instead of you. With your skills you'd probably bring a squadron of Apache helicopters down on us." He was within a hair's breadth of giving him a shove, but reconsidered in time to stop himself.

"Nobody's calling the constabulary, lad."

"Oh really. And just what is it we're supposed to do with all this?" Nathan waved an arm in a semicircle encompassing four bodies and a shot-up Explorer.

"We sterilize, laddie. This, is where I teach you how to sterilize."

CHAPTER FOUR

The taxi driver looked Lebanese. At least, that was Nathan's best guess, and it was only a guess. His dark skin, hawk nose and black hair certainly indicated a Middle Eastern heritage. Baubles hanging from the rear-view mirror and the statuette on the dash were a clue as well, but Nathan had no idea how to read them. Hot-tempered and an aggressive driver, he maneuvered his taxi through choking New York traffic with the assistance of frequent curses in a language Nathan didn't understand.

The disagreeable taxi ride to Kent's office wasn't doing anything to help Nathan's mood, but it did complement it. His black disposition hadn't changed much since the previous day when he and Leith had left the rest stop. They'd left together, Leith driving the Buick and Nathan the truck. Nathan hadn't seen him since.

Leith's idea of 'sterilize' was to erase anything concrete that might link them to the events there. He'd used his knife to puncture a hole in the disabled Explorer's gas tank, caught some of it in a discarded paper soft drink container and poured enough around the interior, tires and engine to initiate a fire that would destroy the vehicle. The plates, serial number and registration, Leith explained, were not a problem as they belonged to a non-existent person at a non-existent address. He took Nathan's gun, stating his intention to dump both it and the Browning in the East Branch of the Delaware river. His last task was to give Nathan explicit instructions on where to park the truck in New York city. "Leave it unlocked with the keys in the ignition," he'd said, "then walk two blocks and use your phone to call a cab. The truck will be gone before your cab gets there, and within three hours it'll be in parts. I'll do the same with the Buick."

Nathan got lost twice but eventually did exactly as instructed. The whole procedure left him with the nasty feeling that he was covering up after a crime. It was unfounded, he knew that, but it didn't change the way he felt. He wanted to be one of the good guys, and to him that meant working in the open, not skulking around in the shadows hiding from the law. He'd said as much to Leith who immediately dismissed his concerns and countered, saying they had complete authority for everything they were doing. Even if what he was doing was legally and technically right, it still left Nathan feeling dirty.

Nathan didn't know the reason for the taxi driver's foul mood, but now the final straw for the dark-haired man seemed to be arriving at his destination and finding the designated taxi zone occupied by a dark blue Mercedes limousine. The irate cabby braked to a stop so close alongside the illegally parked limo that Nathan had no hope of exiting on the right side of the car. So he waited while his driver berated the chauffeur in an obscure and unknown language. The limo's driver was a large black man whose massive arms and imposing jawline were doing little to temper the taxi driver's remarks. It occurred to Nathan that his cabby should probably keep any opinions about the black man's driving or ancestry to himself—as the chauffeur looked entirely capable of feeding the cabby that dash statue. He refused to let up, however, and before easing forward to where Nathan could open his door and exit the cab, he gave the black man a one-fingered salute. To Nathan's surprise he received nothing in response. The chauffeur remained silent and his face expressionless behind dark sunglasses, not even the usual return of the gesture.

When the building's elevator deposited him on the twenty-ninth floor, Nathan strode purposefully through the outer door of UNOG. He took a deep breath before addressing Jenny. No point in taking her head off. "Is he in?"

"Yes, he is, Mr. Burdett, but I'm afraid he can't be disturbed."

Nathan ignored her, walked around behind the desk and reached for the door handle. An audible click emanated from the latching mechanism just before Nathan's hand hit the bar-shaped lever. He jammed down on it anyway, but it wouldn't budge. Giving the door a frustrated open palm punch Nathan stepped back around the corner to where Jenny sat, and gave her his darkest scowl.

"I'm sorry. But . . . ." Her telephone emitted a pleasant beeping tone and she looked away from Nathan to answer it.

"Yes, Mr. Kent," she said, into the receiver. "That was Mr. Burdett, sir. He's, um, anxious to see you . . . no, I didn't, sir . . . yes, I'll do that . . . thank you."

"If you'll wait just a moment, Mr. Burdett," said Jenny replacing the receiver, "Mr. Kent will see you."

Nathan didn't move from where he stood, but merely leaned against the wall looking down on Jenny who squirmed uncomfortably as she returned to shuffling papers on her desk. Exactly two minutes later, she reached under her desk and caused a muffled click to come from the door again. "He'll see you now," she said without turning around.

When Nathan entered the office, Kent was standing behind his desk. This time Nathan ignored the view and the assembled artifacts from a lifetime of hunting, and took up a similar position across from him. Kent opened his mouth to say something—a greeting of some sort, or perhaps congratulations for a job well done—but Nathan cut him off. "Was that a demonstration of how all your people work?" he demanded.

Kent was about to answer the question when Nathan interrupted him again. "That was the most blatant example of goading someone into a fight I've ever seen. Did Leith do that on his own or did you put him up to it?" Nathan pointed an accusing finger at Kent and a fleck of spittle flew out of his mouth and arched onto the polished desktop. Both men ignored it and Nathan vented further. "I thought you people were professionals. What is it you're trying to do? If I hadn't been there Leith would be dead three times over. Who bails you morons out when I'm not around?"

"Nathan, please sit . . . ."

"What did you do before I came along, pray for thunderbolts?"

"Nathan, I understand you're upset." Kent finally managed to speak, as Nathan stopped to catch his breath. "It was a strategic maneuver on Leith's . . . on our part, to treat Anton like that."

"And a stinking poor one wasn't it?" Nathan's voice lost none of its censure as his eyes bored into Kent.

62

"It was. It was," said Kent, nodding sagely. "We did the wrong thing. We approached it the wrong way." He threw up his hands and shrugged. "You're right, Nathan. And the only explanation I can offer is that we had bad intelligence. And I don't offer that as an excuse. I accept full responsibility for everything that happened."

Nathan felt the anger draining out of him. He had come for an argument and he wasn't getting it.

Kent came around the desk, put one hand on Nathan's shoulder and looked into his blue eyes. "I thank God you were there Nathan. You saved Leith's life. It's exactly why I need you on my team. You're the only person who could have done it."

Nathan avoided the old man's gaze and looked out the window.

"Come over here," continued Kent, directing Nathan to the floor-to-ceiling glass. The panorama today was available for only half a mile. After that, smog was an ever-thickening cloud filtering away the view. "See how bad the smog is today?" asked Kent, gesturing out into the distance. "That's how intelligence works. We generate very little of our own, by the way. We import all of ours from other agencies. But, the further away you are from something, or someone, the murkier it is. However, the closer you get, . . . ahhh, then you can start to see through the pollution and discern what's out there."

Nathan stood silently, his hands in his pant pockets.

"That's how it was with Anton. Leith's approach to him was what we were told would be most effective. Obviously it was wrong. He didn't knuckle under and cut a deal like we had been told to expect. He came up fighting. And, well, as you saw, he came ready to fight."

"And all four of them are dead because you got bad information," added Nathan flatly.

"Unfortunate. Yes. But unavoidable." Kent drew his eyes back from the view and looked at the young man beside him. "It was unavoidable, wasn't it?"

"With the gun I had, and the way the targets presented themselves? Yes." Nathan paused for a moment. "But from now on I'm going back to a bigger gun and a dot sight whenever possible. I should have had one yesterday instead of that compact. With a match gun I

63

could have disabled both Anton and the bodyguard. The other two would still have died."

"I see." Kent moved away from the window to sit on the corner of his desk, studying Nathan from there.

Nathan glared back, a combination of steel and ice. "And that would have been two less deaths I now need to justify to myself."

Kent looked at the floor briefly and Nathan saw his hands tighten and relax their grip on the desktop before he looked up again. "It's unfortunate you had to kill them, Nathan, but it is an acceptable outcome. No need to torture yourself over it. They brought it on themselves. They tried to kill you, remember? Certainly Leith prodded them a little, but they made their choice as to how to respond. It turned out bad for them." Kent shrugged, and after a minute of silence with no response, added, "You'll get used to it."

Nathan snapped out of his reverie but didn't look at Kent. He continued to stare out the window. "That's precisely what I'm afraid of. I'm afraid I'll get used to it. Like water running down a hill. Killing will eventually erode a part of me away until it's cut a groove, a channel, right through me, just as if it belongs there. Just like it's always been there. But part of me will be gone and there won't be any way to get it back." He looked at Kent, adding quietly, "Will there?"

Nathan moved away from the window. The anger still burned, but he had vented its critical mass and was starting to calm down. Bitterness was replacing it. "Maybe it would be best if I just went back to work for Danny. What you're doing here may not be what I'm cut out for."

"Nonsense, Nathan. It's far too soon to determine that. You've only seen one operation, and it went badly at that. Don't judge all of our work on the basis of one task. Besides, how much sleep have you had in the past twenty-four hours?"

"Not much," conceded Nathan.

Kent clucked his tongue and wagged his head from side to side, taking on the air of a concerned father. "As I thought." He clapped his hands together and rose from the desk. "Off with you then, young man. Go get some sleep. Rest over the weekend and come back here Monday morning. You and Leith can debrief on the matter and he will then assemble his written report." The hand went back onto Nathan's shoulder as he ushered him to the door. "The aftermath of events such as these can be difficult to deal with and we'll help you any way we can. But you have to help yourself, too. So go back to your flat, relax and get a good solid sleep. And don't come back here until that's done."

Nathan knew Kent was right. He felt drained. Anger and remnants of adrenaline were keeping him going. So he allowed himself to be herded from the office, walking out without replying to the soothing words of the kind-looking man who quietly shut the door behind him.

"I don't believe it," said a female voice behind Kent after the door closed. "Am I a witness to the fallibility of the mighty Mr. Kent?"

A sour look was her only reply.

"I'll hide in a bathroom for hours to listen to a performance like that," she prodded. When Kent walked back to his desk and sat down without responding, she tried again. "You're not going to be able to control him. Do you realize that?"

"You're wrong. It'll just take more work. But he's worth it."

She shrugged, dismissing his comment, and walked to the window where she looked down to see the roof of her limo. She strained to see if she could pick out someone leaving the building who might be the man she'd heard but had not seen. "Who is he? You've never told me about him."

Kent slipped off his glasses and laid them on the desk. Then he leaned back in his chair and put his feet up on the polished top. "He's a civilian, a competition shooter." That made her turn around. He knew it would. Once she was looking at him again he said, "And why is it, my dear, that you think I'll never control him?"

The question went ignored as she asked one of her own. "What's he doing working for you?"

He let her change the topic. "He was recruited out of civilian sport shooting by another agency and given training in a number of vital areas. I borrowed him and now here he is, working for me."

"You make it sound simple."

"Believe me, it wasn't."

"I do. I do believe you . . .," she affirmed, the words trailing off as she returned to the window and looked down at the street.

"There's nothing in him for your agenda," Kent said, looking at her back. There was the slightest stoop to her back. Other than that she looked much younger than her fifty-six years.

"You're sure of that?"

"Yes. He's working for me. He has phenomenal skills and I've invested a lot in getting him here."

"You don't know everything I'm doing, dear. With a background like that I may be able to use him sometime. Right now I can't imagine how, but you never know."

"And you don't know everything I'm doing. If you think you might have a use for him let me know and we'll discuss it like we always do."

"Of course, dear." She pivoted to face back into the room, giving up on what she now realized was a foolish attempt; to spot someone who looked like he fit the voice she had heard. "Before I go, we are agreed on the Canadian event? You'll send one of your people to . . . what's the word you use?"

"Sterilize."

"Yes, that's it. But only if it's necessary. The usual requirement, the target mustn't survive." She paused. "Why don't you send him?"

Kent shook his head. "No. He's not ready for that."

"Didn't I just hear that he killed four men for you?"

"And you also heard how he felt about that." Kent issued a long sigh and rubbed his temples. "He's proving most difficult to deal with. The skills are there but he won't commit himself to doing what's necessary."

"So I heard."

"Before he came to work for me, I manipulated some, shall we say, 'circumstances' so that he would be forced to overcome this apparent aversion he has to killing. Either that or die himself. I was sure that was all it would take, but now it appears more work is required."

"So send him to Canada," she said insistently.

"And when will that finally happen?"

"These things are difficult to predict but probably within a week. You'd send more than one person anyway, wouldn't you? The irony of sending him would be just too delicious."

"True." Kent put his glasses back on, thinking through the possibilities.

"I insist." When no response was forthcoming she walked over to the desk, put her palms on its surface and leaned over sufficiently to guarantee his attention. "I insist," she repeated firmly.

Kent looked at her for the first time in several minutes. "Well, if you *insist* than that's what must happen, isn't it?"

She didn't give him an inch. "Yes, it is."

Kent broke their locked gaze first. He could easily have stared her down and enjoyed doing it. She was wrong but it was best in this case to give in. "Very well. He'll be there. But you must realize this is the most disgusting thing I'm involved with. And I do some revolting things."

"It's only what we have to do. We've talked about that, darling. Why, what if . . ." Holding up his hand, Kent cut her off. She walked around the desk and leaned over him, kissing him lightly on the lips. His heels remained firmly planted on the desk. "See you at the Secretary General's reception tonight?" she asked, straightening.

"I think so. There's nothing on the stove at the moment so I should have the evening free."

"Try and make it. I'll buy you a drink and introduce you to someone from the Japanese delegation I want you to meet."

Kent stretched out his arm and pushed an intercom button. "We're ready to go here, Jenny."

"The front is clear, sir," was the reply.

"I'm off then," she told Kent cheerily.

She was almost to the door when Kent repeated the question she had dodged earlier. "And just why is it you think I won't be able to control him?"

She stopped, her left hand resting on the door handle. "Because he's someone with integrity. Something you have difficulty understanding or appreciating. As good as you are at manipulating people you still haven't figured out how to control an honest man. I

67

don't know if you can." She pulled her hand away from the door and pointed out the window. "Too many of them are like him. I should know. That's one of *my* biggest problems. It's why we've moved our focus. There's an old saying: 'You can't cheat an honest man.' Well, I think you can't *control* an honest man either. Direct your energies at those you can control. It's what we do." She pointed at Kent, "You'd do well to learn that, my dear." Then, with an emphatic nod of her head she was gone.

Mr. Kent removed his feet from the desk and rolled his chair to the window so he could see down. While he waited, another old saying popped unbidden into his head, but he couldn't remember entirely how it went. Something about sleeping with the devil, beyond that he couldn't recall. Three minutes later his random thoughts disappeared when he saw a blonde head of tightly curled hair atop a pale green suit get into the limo. "Well, my dear," he said to the empty room, "if it's only possible to control a dishonest person I should have no trouble with you, should I?"

Multiple time zones made it two hours earlier in Calgary, where Jerry Mitchell also stared out a window; one of a west facing bank in the Calgary Tribune's research library. Like most libraries it was a quiet place and that made it ideal to sit and think. His thoughts were interrupted when the door opened and Barbara Latoski swept into the room with her typical aggressive stride.

Seeing Jerry seated by the window, a coffee cup on the ledge in front of him, stopped her. "You're up early for a crime reporter. I thought you guys always worked late and never came in before noon."

"And I thought you star reporters had peasants to do all your research for you." Jerry turned back to watching the sunrise and drinking his second coffee of the day.

Barb walked over to where he sat and tried to sit on the tiny window ledge that had held his cup. "From what I hear you're the one becoming a star." When Jerry just shrugged she pushed further. "Come on, Jerry. What's going on? I heard you got some juicy stuff on that Burdett story you've been chasing."

Jerry looked at her for a moment before replying. No winners today. The guys in Sports had a pool going as to when Barb would first wear a dress to work. No one had ever seen her in one and today was no exception—blue slacks and a white blouse. No winners.

Barb was okay, maybe a little conceited, but she had some of the best instincts in the building. She just knew it as well as everyone else, that's all. "Frank gave me official approval to follow up the Burdett story on an increased time basis. And he gave me an assistant to be shared with some other projects, as well as a modest budget. It'll get me started."

"How are you going handle it?"

Once again Jerry shrugged. "That's what I'm trying to figure out."

"Want some help?"

"Sure," replied Jerry. As long as she doesn't try and steal my story, he thought.

Barb gave up on the ledge and pulled a chair over. "It's a complicated one, right?"

"Sure is."

"So, it's unlikely you're going to get to the truth in one deft strike. It'll take patience, like peeling an onion, one layer at a time. The question is, where to start peeling."

"Easy. The people involved, and the groups they belong to, are the key. That's where the story is. I'm sure of that much. The police are one group, in this case the FBI and probably some local cop connection as well. The second is this gun-owning group of shooters that Burdett belongs to."

"Who are you most likely to get something out of?"

"The shooters," answered Jerry, without hesitation.

"Then try there first." She saw Jerry wince. "Is that a problem?"

"I hate guns," he said, matter-of-factly. "Guns are only used for killing. And personally, I can't stand to be around them for very long. Oh sure, they're fascinating in a macabre sort of way but if I had to go into that world and pretend to like them . . ." He shook his head. "I don't think I could do it."

"I feel the same way you do, Jerry. But you know as well as I do that a good reporter goes where the story leads. Even if it's out of your own comfort zone."

Jerry looked back out at the rising sun. When he had started associating with the police as a rookie crime and court reporter, the presence of a holstered pistol was enough to make him uneasy. He'd managed to overcome most of that, but it was still his opinion that there was no need for civilian ownership of firearms. Whenever the opportunity had presented itself, he'd voiced that opinion. But that had been when he was still young and idealistic. He'd quickly learned that doing so was a good way to start an argument, alienate a lot of people or just get himself branded as an 'Easterner' who didn't understand much about life in the West. Now he largely kept his opinions to himself and only brought them out when he was sure the people around him were like-minded.

"I could never pull off the pretense of being a gun nut anyway," said Jerry, "I don't know enough."

"You might as well pretend to be a professional wrestler," agreed Barb, smiling. "How about going in as somebody who's interested in learning about guns? Would that work?"

Jerry took a minute to think about it. "That might do it. I could be your typical middle-aged bachelor yuppie with some time and money who's looking for a new hobby."

"Great."

"Tell them I've never owned a gun but I'd like to learn. Say that I've seen all these guns on TV and the movies, now show me what it's all about in the real world."

"Perfect," said Barb. "Just keep your opinions to yourself. Do that and from what I've seen of the people in the gun culture they'll be only to happy to share their bizarre knowledge and strange ideas with you."

"There wouldn't even be a need to conceal being a reporter," suggested Jerry. "Everyone has a day job anyway. I just won't flaunt it, no notebook or camera. It could work."

Barb slapped him on the back as she got up and kicked her chair, returning it to its place. "Go get 'em Jerry. Call me if you need any help." Barb stopped in mid-stride. "Now, why did I come in here?" She looked down at Jerry. "Do you know why I came in here?"

"I have no idea?" She wandered towards the door still looking puzzled. "Thanks, Barb." Jerry called after her with a chuckle. He stayed in the library another ten minutes. When his coffee was gone he crushed the empty paper cup and tossed it into the nearby garbage. He even knew where to start.

Two hours later, Jerry walked casually into Gunsport Ranges. He'd been here before, shortly after word of the shooting in the Cochrane gunsmith shop of Bob Coombs had filtered out. Back then, he'd come in as a reporter looking for information on where to find the mysterious Nathan Burdett. A quick "never heard of him" followed by a masterful job of ignoring all other questions had been the response. But that had been months ago and, as with any other busy retail establishment, it was doubtful that the owner would still recognize him. Jerry allowed a faint smile to appear on his face today, because the person behind the counter wasn't the same one he'd questioned two and a half months previous. After a short wander through the displays he approached the counter and began looking at pistols under the glass top. It didn't take long.

"Can I help you?" asked the clerk, diverting his attention from boxes of ammunition he was arranging on shelves behind the counter.

"Maybe," replied Jerry, "I've been thinking of buying a gun and I just thought I'd wander in and get some information. You know, see what I can learn. Think you could help me out?"

"I'm sure we can. Do you have any particular kind of gun in mind?"

"No, not really."

"That's okay. If you can tell me what you'd like to use the gun for, maybe I can recommend something. What do you want to do, target shooting, plinking, collecting . . .?"

"Plinking? What's that?"

"Plinking is informal target shooting. No competition. Just shooting targets or knocking over soda cans."

"I've seen some pistol shooting, where people run around and over barricades shooting at targets as they go. It looked like fun. I think I'd enjoy that."

The clerk smiled patiently at Jerry's ignorance. "That's called action pistol competition and the International Practical Shooting Confederation is the governing body for most of that sport. You're right about it being fun. It's easily the most popular handgun sport in the city."

Jerry shrugged his shoulders helplessly. "Where do I start?"

"You came to the right place," said the clerk leaning on the counter. "Because you start here. But I have to warn you, by the time you've jumped through all the bureaucratic hoops the finish line is far away."

"That's okay," said Jerry. "I'm serious about doing this."

An hour later he left the store with a handful of government forms, two rental videotapes and a book he'd purchased. He also had an appointment to come back at 4:00 p.m. and do some shooting with a rental gun under the supervision of an instructor. That bothered him a little. He'd known he was going to have to shoot a gun sooner or later but he'd been hoping for later. It was going to be noisy, painful and violent and he detested all three, but a professional reporter did what was necessary to get the story and Jerry told himself he was a professional.

Walking back into Gunsport Ranges at four o'clock, he estimated he'd told himself that seven million times.

When the instructor turned out to be female he almost left. Over the course of the day he'd developed a mental image of his firearms instructor as an old grizzled army veteran. Someone who was nearly deaf and called him 'son.' Not that he thought a female would be a bad instructor, but she didn't fit the image—and now the thought that she might see his fear of guns bothered him almost as much as the fear itself.

By the time he shook hands with her and learned her name was Sue, his palms had started to sweat. By the time they made it into one of the ranges and were putting on safety glasses and earmuffs his hands were shaking. The shakes weren't bad, but Jerry could feel it. He hoped Sue didn't notice.

"First time you've ever shot a gun?" asked Sue.

Jerry grimaced. "It shows, eh."

"Oh yeah. But it's not a problem. There are a lot of people like you who never even try. Instead, they carry a fear of guns around with them all their lives and do nothing but try to infect others with it. You're a brave person to be doing this. Braver than most."

"Thanks. You're very kind."

"Hey, I'm here to help you. And I do this part-time because I like it."

Jerry took a deep cleansing breath and tried to calm down. "Okay. Where do we start?"

"We'll start you off with a small, easy to shoot gun, and work up from there," Sue explained, opening a case she carried and pulling out a black pistol. It didn't look that small to Jerry. "This is a Ruger 22/45. It shoots a .22 Long Rifle cartridge, about the smallest, cheapest round available. It's also very light and that makes it great for beginners. I'm going to shoot a magazine full and you can watch me."

Jerry did as he was told. So far so good, he hadn't even had to touch a gun yet. When Sue was done he expressed surprise at how little noise and recoil he'd observed.

"You're right," she said. "Remember it's close to the smallest cartridge available. But you have to respect it. It can still kill you very dead." Jerry nodded, trying not to reveal what that last statement had done to his guts. Sue started in on a short safety lecture and Jerry paid as much attention as he could, consumed with the thought he was still going to have to shoot that thing.

"Okay Jerry," she said when finished. "It's your turn. You paid money so you could shoot, not so you could watch me."

"Watching you is okay with me." Jerry laughed nervously. He did mean the watching part. Sue was close to his own age and Jerry found her easy to look at. Sure, maybe she carried a few extra pounds but she had a kind and pleasant face. And so far she'd lived up to the face. He drew a deep breath and took the gun from her, trying to remember the safety rules she had outlined. "Hey, you're right, it's not very heavy."

Sue had him work the pistol's mechanism and controls, and practice aligning and firing the pistol without ammunition. Eventually she asked him to load. His first shot was with eyes closed and teeth gritted, but by the time he'd reached the end of the ten shot magazine he shot with his eyes open. The teeth, however, were still clenched. Sue stayed by his side and kept a hand on his shoulder while he fired, encouraging him between shots; "take it slow . . . good grip . . . you're doing great."

Beads of sweat had blossomed on his forehead by the time he put the gun down. "That wasn't bad," he said.

"The first response from most people is that it's fun," chided Sue gently.

"I wouldn't go that far yet, but I *will* try again."

The hour he'd paid for passed quickly and when it was gone Jerry Mitchell conceded that near the end he had almost been having fun. Making a second appointment in two days time came easily. There was little need to convince himself it was a necessary thing to do in order to get the story. He was careful to book a time when Sue would be there. She was way better than the grizzled, old, mostly-deaf drill sergeant.

CHAPTER FIVE

Nathan Burdett stood in front of the bullet trap, at the far end of a poorly lit indoor range, and let someone shoot at him. It didn't take long to realize that this was a dumb idea. The only reason he was still alive was because the bullets were going slow enough that he could dodge them.

The concentration required to pull it off was extreme. Muzzle flash announced the bullet was on its way; then it became a matter of picking it out of the swirling clouds of black powder gunsmoke and making the dodge. Nathan wouldn't have believed this was possible, but here he was doing it. The bullets were big—that helped. That and the thumb cocking required of the revolver meant the gun was probably an old Colt in .45 or .44-40.

Whoever the shooter was, he was good—the fastest Nathan had ever seen at thumb cocking an old cowboy gun. The face was a shadow behind the smoke, as much an enigma as the gun that never ran out of ammo. This guy would fire three or four shots at him, there would be the briefest pause, and then he'd shoot again. Never a reload.

The shooter fired four bursts before Nathan woke up and realized the 'shooting' was someone pounding on his hotel door. He looked at the digital alarm and blinked his eyes until they focused clearly on the numbers—10:46 a.m.

Grabbing the pistol that lay beside the clock he negotiated his way through the two-room suite. By the time he made it to the door's peephole, reality had fully returned. The optically distorted face of Leith looked back at him from the other side of the viewer. Nathan pulled his security wedge from the bottom of the hotel's door, hitched up his boxers and unlatched the deadbolt. Letting the pistol drop to his thigh he allowed the door to swing open and an animated Leith to burst into the room.

75

"What are you doing still sleeping? Get your clothes on lad, we're going to work."

Nathan scratched his tousled head and placed the .45 on a low table by the door. "A friend of mine from the ranch, Aaron Crantz, landed a job with the Spokane Police Department after Danny sent us all packing. I was out late on a ride-along with him. Is this the call we came here for?"

"No. Something else has popped up."

"Didn't I ever tell you I'm not very good at mornings," Nathan said, disappearing into the bedroom where he threw on a shirt and began pulling on jeans.

Leith called after him. "As a matter of fact you didn't. But since I don't care, it really doesn't matter. Does it?"

"You sound like my mother waking me up for school. So, what do I need?"

"A gun."

"Oh, you're a big help." Nathan came out of the bedroom. "Can you at least tell me what the call is?"

"Once we're rolling. Where's your call-out bags, lad?"

Nathan pulled on a coat before reaching behind the couch and extracting two bags. "One for me," he held up the right hand bag. "And one for my tools." He indicated the left bag which was the same size but heavier. Skirting the TV as he walked to the door behind Leith, he scooped the STI .45 from the table and tucked it in his waistband. This gun was the replacement for the Para-Ordnance that was now at the bottom of a river. Checking the clock on the microwave was the last thing he did before leaving the room. It read 10:49 a.m. It had taken him three minutes. On two previous occasions he had set an alarm as a dry run to wake him from a dead sleep. He'd never beat four minutes. The reason for the improvement this morning was, he suspected, motivation. He slammed the door behind himself and twisted the knob to ensure it was locked. Leith was already halfway down the hall.

They tossed their gear into the trunk of a cab parked in front of the hotel. Moments later, the driver had the car dodging through Spokane's morning traffic. They'd been waiting here for eight days.

Waiting and training. Training and waiting. Nathan didn't know what for and Leith claimed he didn't either. When Nathan first complained about it he got another 'soldier' lecture from Leith. After that he kept his complaints to himself.

Since the incident with Anton, the relationship between Leith and Nathan had come full circle. Initially, Nathan had berated both Leith and Kent yet again with his misgivings. They had, however, been uniformly contrite in their response; both acknowledging their error in approaching Anton in such an aggressive manner. Blaming the blunder—for which they accepted full responsibility—on poor and incomplete intelligence. Despite the words, Nathan observed that neither seemed too upset about how the encounter had ended and never missed an opportunity to thank Nathan for his courage or compliment him on his skills. Nathan's anger and disappointment slowly faded and so did the compliments, both of which suited him fine. Now, he just wanted to forget the entire episode and there seemed to be a unspoken three-way willingness to do that. Within four days it was never mentioned again. Then they left for Spokane. Workouts at a nearby gym, shooting practice, equipment preparation and tinkering filled their mornings. After lunch they would go their separate ways and Nathan wouldn't see Leith again until breakfast.

One morning, a Friday, Leith told him there was a 'fifty-fifty' chance of being called out that night and to 'stay available'. As far as Nathan was concerned, with both a phone and a pager he was always available anyway, so he didn't see the need for the standby status. The only thing it had seemed to accomplish was to keep him in his hotel room on a Friday and give him a restless night's sleep. In the end he wondered if it hadn't been a training exercise too.

This, Nathan trusted, was not an exercise. As the cab pulled out into the mid-morning traffic of North Division Street and the driver accelerated, Nathan looked at Leith. There was an excitement in his eyes. He wasn't about to ask Leith for specifics with a cabby within earshot but the Scot broke the silence.

"You should fancy this trip Nathan, we're going home."

"Home? Like in Canada."

"Exactly. A place called Jasper. Do you know it?"

"I do. I've been there half a dozen times. One of our national parks. A beautiful place."

"I've heard of it, myself. That's all. The Gulfstream's pilot will have a flight plan by the time we get to the airport."

"Gulfstream? Well, if he gets lost I'll give him directions. That is if I can see any landmarks from thirty thousand feet." Leith's laughter came easily. He's got some adrenaline in him, thought Nathan. It's a real call.

After they'd been dropped at the terminal and when no one was within hearing distance, Leith spoke up. "We're a touch shy on details yet," said the Scot. "The basics are a nut case with a gun and hostages."

"Why us? Sounds like something the locals should be able to handle."

"On the surface you're right. It sounds like a local matter but I suspect there are international political ramifications to this one. Remember, I'm just a small cog in a big wheel too. I never get all the details. Like I said, I only have the basics so far. You'd do well to keep in mind that we're only soldiers following orders. We don't always know what's really going on."

"The last time I checked we weren't in the army."

"We're still soldiers, lad. A different kind, but still bloody foot soldiers. They feed and clothe us, give us training and equipment and send us out to fight for them. That's a soldier by anybody's definition."

Nathan didn't reply immediately. He thought about what Leith had said. It was the closest thing to a murmur of complaint he had ever heard from the man. "Doesn't it bother you, not knowing why you're doing a job? I don't necessarily mean this one. Any job."

"Aye. It did when I first joined the Regiment, but no longer. You get used to it. You can get used to anything, Nathan. Bad food, no sleep, heat, cold and no information, it's all the same. The lot of a soldier."

A noncommittal grunt was Nathan's only response.

"You don't have to like it, lad. But that's the way of the world. Fortunately it's not like that all the time. This job gives us more freedom and information than I ever had in the Regiment. Here, I know far more about *why* than I ever have before."

"But this job may still be one of the blank ones?"

"Not blank, Nathan, black. From what I see so far, there's no doubt. This job is one of the black ones."

It took ten minutes to find the route out onto the tarmac and the waiting steps of a Gulfstream IV. The co-pilot offered to help with their bags but they declined.

"Who owns the jet?" asked Nathan, as he buckled in. He'd seen no insignia on the aircraft's tail or fuselage.

"No idea," replied Leith. "Usually these birds are owned by private companies that contract regularly to the UN. Sometimes it's a good idea not to ask too many questions. People remember you if you chat them up or ask a lot a questions."

The pilot stepped into the quiet cabin and looked alternately from Leith to Nathan, not sure who to address. He chose the oldest. "I have a flight plan filed for the Jasper-Hinton Airport, Alberta, Canada. Flying time one hour. Is that satisfactory gentlemen?"

Leith answered, "Fine. And anything you can do to get us there quicker would be appreciated."

"I'll let you know how we're progressing. If you need anything push the call button on the panel. The cooler is stocked with drinks and food. Enjoy the flight, gentlemen." He squeezed back through the narrow cockpit door and closed it.

In New York, Kent waited till the clock on his desk said 3:30 p.m. He'd been putting off making the call but he couldn't procrastinate any longer. He folded the newspaper he'd been studying for the past half-hour and dialed. "They're on the way," he told her. "Likely been in the air forty-five minutes already."

"They'll be there on time?"

"Probably ahead of time from what I can see. I've been checking CNN occasionally for the last hour and it hasn't been mentioned yet."

A small laugh. "My dear, you're such a worrier. Everything is fine. Just a touch behind schedule but not bad considering."

"As soon as you hear something call me. I'll do the same."

"And in between we'll both watch CNN, right? Dinner tonight?"

"Not until it's over and my people are out."

"You did send that Burdett fellow, didn't you?"

"He's one of them."

"And that's why you're worried?"

Kent didn't reply immediately. He looked out the window and watched a crew of window washers on the building next door. They'd been working the building all day. They'd anchor their trolley at the top, then winch down, cleaning on the way. Then go up and start over. That was their routine. Like an ancient sailing ship, a bewildering array of ropes, slings and harnesses connected everything. He noticed for the first time that there was no one on top of the building raising or lowering them. They could control everything from where they worked. Essentially, they pulled their own strings. The thought of it made him smile. "Between the three of them, they'll do the job."

"I'm sure they will. Thanks for calling, dear. Stay in touch."

Kent hung up without replying. His gaze moved from the view to the muted TV screen on the shelf. Still nothing. He'd give it another hour. If it wasn't on the air within an hour he'd call them back. It was out of his control now. Setting the newspaper aside he saw the ink had, again, left black smudges on his hands. He was halfway out of his chair and on his way to the small private washroom at the other end of the office when, thinking better of it, he sat down, extracted a hankie from his pocket and wiped his hands clean. A trip to the washroom meant he'd have to look at himself in the mirror. Right now the prospect of that made him uncomfortable.

The flight was uneventful. They ate and read. Leith found a current issue of *People* magazine, thoughtfully supplied by whoever had prepped the aircraft for flight. Nathan started one of two paperback westerns in his travel bag but couldn't get into the story. Seeing a first aid kit he rummaged in it until he found a small Band-Aid, which he tore in half, pasting each piece on the wall of the fuselage. Then he sat down on the other side and looked at them.

Leith watched as Nathan's eyes flicked back and forth between the two pieces of tape, then he asked, "And just what is it you're doing?"

Nathan broke eye contact with the opposite wall and swiveled to his left to look at Leith. "Training. It's an exercise designed to increase eye speed." The look on Leith's face indicated a further explanation was necessary. "The eyes are the fastest part of the body and they lead everything. If you want to shoot something you have to look at it first, then the hands and gun follow. Exercising eye muscles decreases the time it takes to transition between multiple targets."

"Horse feathers," snorted the Scot, turning back to his magazine. "You'd be better off doing push-ups. Now that's training."

The comment generated a knowing smile on Nathan's face. But his only response was to get up and readjust the dots so one was significantly higher than the other. The horizontal exercise was done, now he'd do the vertical component.

It was early afternoon local time when they landed at the Jasper-Hinton Airport. A shaved and reasonably well-rested Nathan walked down the aircraft's steps onto the ground of his native Alberta. Leith came down behind him. The temperature hovered near freezing as the sun did its best to melt the traces of snow that hadn't been scraped and swept from the runway. It shone valiantly, but the late November position it occupied provided little real warmth. A light breeze blew away the remnants of jet fuel that lingered in the air. When the kerosene-like odor was gone Nathan filled his lungs with mountain air. It smelled of spruce and pine in deep snow. "Have we got a ride?" he asked, pulling on his coat.

Leith snorted. "No one knows we're here. How could we have a ride?" Then in response to Nathan's questioning look he added, "There's a rental waiting for us. Jenny set it up, as well as rooms. Go find the car and I'll call in to see if anything has changed." Nathan nodded and left.

By the time Nathan returned with car keys, Leith was turning off his phone and studying notes on a small paper pad. "My gear's loaded," Nathan said, holding up the keys. "Anything new?"

81

"Looks like we're in business," replied Leith, picking up his bags and following Nathan. "We're now here officially. We've been training with the Canadian military at a large infantry base called Wainwright. Right now we're on holidays and just happen to be in this area. We've been made available to help out wherever we're needed."

"The local authorities are going to believe that?"

"If this is a nasty one I doubt they'll have time to question it. They'll be only too happy to get some help. But that's not the only thing they have to believe."

"And what's the rest?"

"You're SAS too."

"Oh come on, that's ridiculous!"

"That's our cover lad, ridiculous or not. We're both active SAS specialists in hostage rescue operations. You're just another of Her Majesty's subjects who crossed the big pond to join the fabled Regiment. It's happened before." Leith waited for Nathan to open the car's trunk and then tossed in his bags. "These are local police only, with an Emergency Response Team on the way from Edmonton. There's no one within three hundred miles to effectively question who we are. They have no choice but to believe whatever we tell them. And if they happened to get a Federal phone call that tells them to bring us into the operation, well, that just settles it then. Doesn't it?"

Nathan slammed the trunk, shaking his head and didn't respond until he'd positioned himself behind the wheel. "Where to?" he asked, starting the car. "Where's our psycho?"

"The public library. Know where it is?"

Nathan groaned, "Roughly. It's north of the downtown core, a small heritage building set off by itself, very quaint."

"Quaint is nice. I like quaint. It reminds me of Scotland."

"The lower half of this quaint is made of solid stone, probably two feet thick. There's good visibility all around with high windows and narrow doorways."

"I hate quaint."

"Yeah, me too."

82

Nathan's recollection of the small town of Jasper was sufficient to get him to the area of the library with only one wrong turn. It had taken forty-five minutes from the airport. As they approached from the north on Geikie Street an RCMP constable was stopping all traffic and directing it away from the scene. The curious and the concerned were gathered on the sidewalks and steps of a red brick church dominating the intersection. This was as far as the public was being allowed in on this side. The constable approached Nathan's open window but before he could speak Leith leaned over and addressed him.

"Afternoon, Constable. We're the Brits. Staff Sergeant Martin is expecting."

The officer's return look was the cynical stare of a veteran who's seen and heard it all. "I didn't know he was expecting any Brits," he said, standing back from the car and folding his arms.

"He is indeed," replied Leith. "Give him a ring on your two-way there and ask him. We'll wait." Nathan just looked from one to the other and smiled.

The constable took a step back and spoke into the microphone clipped to the front of his dark blue coat. In a minute he stepped back towards the car and knelt down beside the open window. "The command center has been set up over there." He pointed to the south, at the back of a school. "Park along the chain link fence, behind that last patrol car. Stay on the sidewalk to your right, tight to the fence, and you won't be exposed. Slip through the gate and go in the school's back door. We're setting up in one of the classrooms. You'll find him in there."

"Aye. Thank you."

Nathan gave him a polite nod and drove off.

They followed instructions and entered the school via a door that, on a better day, would have served to empty laughing students out onto the playground. The hallway it led to was empty except for the sound of static-filled police radios and the scattered remnants of students' possessions. A brightly colored backpack shaped like Winnie-the-Pooh rested beside the door from which the voices came. Beyond it lay a three-ring notebook, its chrome rings snapped open, white papers strewn across the hallway, most of them showing the shadowy

83

footprints of small feet being hustled out of the building. A single white running shoe lay in the middle of the floor at the end of the hall.

Nathan imagined the puzzled looks on the children's faces, the buzz of their questions and the quiet firm answers of adults. Teachers, whose own faces mirrored the grim reality of which they understood only the shadowy basics—an understanding that violence was nearby and their charges needed to be protected and evacuated.

They followed the sound of static and unintelligible conversation to the second classroom on their right. Considering the individuality of each room and situation, this command room, at first, didn't look much different than any other Nathan had seen. The rooms tended to be like the people caught up in these things—intended for more peaceful pursuits. But now their lives and spaces had been hijacked and rearranged by desperate people in a circumstance of time and place.

Nathan and Leith stepped into the bustling room and waited politely for an opening to ask for their man. Two people were talking on phones and one on a radio. A burly police officer with a shaved head sat in a corner, on top of a child's desk, writing in a notebook. A cluster of three people stood around a tall middle-aged man in a uniform who wore the chevrons of a Staff Sergeant, their conversation intense. A female constable was furiously writing on a flip chart, a portable radio clutched in her free hand. Tears rolled down her cheeks.

Something's wrong here, thought Nathan. A profound change has occurred from the norm. Every command post had an emotional undercurrent to it. That came with the nature of the work. Life and death were the currency this room traded in and that caused emotion. This was no undercurrent. It was a riptide of emotion. From the buzz of conversation in the room he hadn't yet deciphered a single understandable word, but he understood the electricity in the air. It hit you like a load of buckshot that drags a man's soul out of his body. Only, instead of your soul, this—this hit you and grabbed your emotions, wrenching them out through your pores and into a wildly spinning vortex that threatened to turn the people it caught into useless debris. Nathan took a sharp breath as the impact of it hit him and then immediately looked to his left at Leith. He saw him swallow. Other than that there was no visible reaction. They waited quietly.

Billy punched the magazine release button and took out the pistol's magazine. Immediately he reseated it in the gun. Then he did it again—and again. He wasn't sure why. It was just something to do to kill the time. Sometimes Billy wasn't sure why he did anything any more. But if he kept his hands busy his head didn't hurt as much and the demons that danced under his skin were bearable. Coming in here had helped the most, at least for a few hours. They had been good hours. He'd stayed focused, his thoughts clearer and more logical than they'd been in months, and it had worked, just like Chris said it would. It had been a long time since he felt this good about doing anything. It had been a long time since he'd done anything useful. Six months? A year? He wasn't sure anymore. Time was a funny thing. How long had it been since he last felt good? He couldn't remember that either.

Billy sat on the floor and rocked back and forth. He had always been sick. He knew that. But these last six months he'd felt better and better about his problem. Poor little sick Billy, who'd never amount to anything. This would change all that. Now he'd do something important, he'd be remembered. But to get this done he had to keep the demons quiet. They were back, with their claws digging into his brain and their shrill voices screaming in his ears. If he kept his hands busy, though, he could ignore them. He knew he could do it. Chris had told him how. All he had to do was concentrate on the end, on the greater good. He could do it. There was strength within him now, strength to finish this.

Jerry Mitchell found out about the hostage taking eleven minutes and forty-five seconds after word of it first reached the Calgary Tribune building. It took Jerry fifteen seconds more to think about it and then he sprinted for the assignment desk. When he learned Barb Latoski had the job and was already heading for the airport he grabbed his notebook and camera and made a run for the parking lot. All he saw was her car turning out onto the street heading east.

Jerry ran for his own vehicle and thirteen minutes later caught up with Barb and a photographer as they reached the Shell Aerocentre in Calgary's northeast corner. But he was only in time to see them disappear through the terminal doors. He parked illegally and then dodged his way through the people in the small terminal, until he finally caught her walking across the tarmac to where a single engine PC-12 sat waiting, the passenger door open.

"Have you got clearance from Frank to go?" asked Barb, as a breathless Jerry stopped her twenty steps away from the aircraft's door.

"I don't have time," yelled Jerry, over the roar of a nearby takeoff.

"Then stay here and get clearance." She turned her back on him and walked away.

"I don't have to tell you how big this could be," Jerry persisted, putting himself between her and the airplane. "My man will be there, I know it. I'll bet you a paycheck he'll show up. And if he shows up at this, Barb, there *will* be bodies. I'll bet a paycheck on that too."

That made her think. Everyone at the Tribune had heard of Jerry's mystery man. A lot of people thought he was chasing a ghost. A few, Barb included, thought he was onto the story of the year. If Jerry was right, Barbara Latoski, senior reporter for the Tribune wanted a piece of the byline. But that was speculation. This hostage-taking in the tourist Mecca of Jasper wasn't speculation, and if the two combined it would become a career-maker. And besides, she could use the help, especially from someone with the police connections Jerry had. She jerked her head toward where the co-pilot stood waiting by the fold down steps, impatient to close the door on this rush flight. "Get in the stupid airplane!" she finally yelled over the sound of the busy airport. "I'll explain it to Frank."

Nathan and Leith were finally noticed by one of the men standing with the Staff Sergeant. He touched him on the arm and pointed at the doorway where the two newcomers stood. Conversation stopped as the intruders were examined. The Staff Sergeant walked over. He was so tall it took him a good one third less steps to cover the distance than it would an average man.

86

"You fellows must be the Brits we heard were in the area," he said extending a hand.

"Right you are, sir," replied Leith, offering his hand too. "I'm Leith and this is Nathan—22nd SAS." He pointed at Nathan.

"Bill Martin. Thanks for cutting your little holiday short to help us out."

"We're used to it, sir. In our job we're never off duty. Right, lad?" He slapped Nathan on the shoulder.

"Never," added Nathan quietly, shaking hands and trying hard to remember he had an actor's role to play.

The Staff Sergeant, however, never gave him a second glance. He determined that Leith was in charge and he'd deal with him. "I have to tell you, I've never seen such fast liaison with the military. After we called this in to Headquarters, in no time at all our National Operations Centre called to tell us you two were in the area."

After leading the two deeper into the room, he introduced them to the others in the fledgling command center. "It's rather sparse in here at the moment," he said. "We're just a small detachment and when something like this happens we have to pull resources in from everywhere to deal with it. All we can do is contain the situation and set up a command post for when the cavalry arrives."

"How long now?" interrupted Leith.

The Staff Sergeant looked at the woman with the tear-stained cheeks writing on the flip chart. "Penny? Where are they?"

"Still on the other side of Edson," came the reply. Nathan saw she was barely under control. The vortex had sucked her in and she was clinging to the lip of emotional control with her fingernails.

"Way over an hour," interpreted the Staff Sergeant. "I know you fellows are supposed to be experts at this sort of thing, so if you see us doing something wrong feel free to make suggestions. I just want to survive this long enough for the pros to get here."

"We'll help any way we can," said Leith. "But right now we know less than nothing. We need a briefing badly."

"Judd." The Staff Sergeant pointed at the constable in the corner. Judd looked up from his notebook when he heard his name.

"You've been here since the beginning, take these Brits for a walk and give them a briefing."

Judd never said a word as he walked by the newcomers, and out the door into the hall. Nathan figured he had only a slightly better grip than Penny. Any longer in here and he might lose it, perhaps the Staff Sergeant saw that too.

Leith and Nathan followed, stopping on either side of the constable once he reached the school's main entrance. They remained silent, watching as he carefully put away his pen, closed his notebook, tucked that into a shirt pocket and buttoned it precisely closed. Nathan heard him taking slow, deep breaths as he gazed across the street. He followed his stare.

"That's the library there, Leith," pointed Nathan.

"I see what you mean," replied the Scot. "Could be a tough nut to crack." He glanced at Judd impatiently. "What's the story here, lad," prodded Leith. "We need to know. We can't help you unless you give us information."

His comment broke Judd's fixation and turning his back to the library he addressed the two men behind him. "The first calls we got were at 11:30 a.m. A couple of the locals reported hearing what sounded like gunshots from the area. Neither one knew exactly from where. I went to check it out." He shrugged. "No big deal, probably backfiring or maybe fireworks. Hey, this townsite is a national park; firearms are controlled very tightly around here." Judd looked alternately from Nathan to Leith. Both nodded understandingly. "I drove around the area a couple of times but didn't see or hear anything myself, so, just to stretch my legs and make sure I hadn't missed anything, I took a walk through those trees on the south side.

"I didn't find anything there either so I figured I'd go in the library and ask Megan, she's our librarian, if she'd heard anything. When I went around the front to go in, right away I found these on the front step." The constable reached into a pants pocket and pulled out a wad of tissue. He unfolded it carefully on an open palm and two brass cartridge cases glinted in the light coming through the window.

Nathan picked them up. "Both 9 mm," he said, after a quick look. "Probably from a Glock pistol."

"Oh yeah? I mean, I knew they were 9's. It's marked right on them. But how can you tell they're from a Glock?"

Nathan held the cartridge cases so Judd could see the primer. "See the firing pin hit," he explained, "it's rectangular. Most firing pins are round. Glocks are by far the most common pistol with a rectangular pin."

Judd was squinting at the marks when Leith reached out. "That hardly matters," he said impatiently, removing them from Nathan's grasp and giving them firmly back to Judd. "Excuse Nathan, sometimes he gets too caught up in the unimportant details." Nathan ignored the look that went with Leith's words.

Judd continued. "Finding these set off my alarm bells." He refolded the cases in their protective tissue and slid them back into his pocket. "I looked closer then, and from the bottom of the step I could see two bullet holes in the front door. One through the glass, right at the edge, and another through the wood.

"That was all I needed to see. I backed off, called in Murray, the other member on duty this morning, and had him watch the back side of the building while I had Betty, at the office, call the library." He looked from Leith to Nathan. "No sense in storming into who-knows-what. Right?"

"You did the right thing," encouraged Leith.

"Betty called me back in a couple minutes, saying there was no answer. That's when I knew we had something really bad happening here. I mean, Megan's car and one other parked outside in the lot, the library is open, there's two fresh bullet holes in the front door and no one's answering the phone. I don't care where you are, that's not a good start to your day."

"That's not where we're still at, is it?" asked Nathan.

"No. No. I had Betty keep trying while I got a few more guys out and we figured what to do. On her third try Megan answered." Judd turned back to the library. "Billy Cardenas," he said and paused. "Billy Cardenas lives about two blocks to the south. There." His uniformed arm waved in the general direction. "He's in his twenties and has always been a little odd. Never gave any indication of this though." Judd shook his shaved head. "What we've pieced together so far is that

Billy walked up to the library fired two shots through the front door to announce himself and walked in. He was waving a gun around, talking and yelling, none of it making sense. He made sure he had everyone in the building on the upper floor, and then sat them down. Fortunately he's let Megan talk on the phone a couple of times.

"Any demands?" asked Leith.

"No demands. And 'innocent blood' is the only constant. Megan says he wants people to know that this is 'a necessary action to shed innocent blood'. He's gone over the edge. You figure it out."

A grim smile showed itself on Leith's face. "Aye, sounds certifiable. And no demands you say?" Judd shook his head.

"Then he can start the killing anytime," said Nathan.

"We thought of that too," replied Judd.

"Is crazy Billy by himself?"

"As far as we know."

"The crazier they are the more likely they're working alone," added Leith. "How many people is he holding in there with him?"

"Eighteen."

"What? There's eighteen people in that little building with him?" Nathan asked incredulously. "What are eighteen people doing in a small town library on a week day morning?"

Judd extended his right arm to its full length, index finger pointing at a renovated, older white house to the southeast. A wooden sign hung from the picket fence and brightly painted wooden balloon silhouettes hovered above it. Nathan squinted, straining to read the sign's lettering. "*Sunshine . . . .*" But it was too far away and he couldn't make out the last two words.

"*Sunshine Day Care,*" completed Judd. He swung his still extended arm back to the library as he continued. "Two staff walked fourteen kids over for story hour this morning. Crazy Billy has four adults and fourteen innocent, bright-eyed, rosy-cheeked, preschoolers in there, with him and his 9 mm."

"Bloody 'ell!" whispered Leith. Nathan just shook his head slowly.

Judd was silent as he took a deep breath before carrying on, "This is a small town, guys. I know most of those kids and their

90

parents. So does everyone else here." He waved a hand back in the direction of the library. "Those kids have to come out of this okay."

Nathan's mind rushed unbidden into what a disastrous ending would look like. The sights, sounds and smells came easily and it took a massive effort of willpower to pull himself away from that dark image. He looked over at Leith. The Scot had made the trip too. Apparently he had come back sooner as he was the first to respond, his voice slow and deliberate, speaking in bursts, words carefully chosen, pausing often. "We'll scout around the perimeter—do some preliminary work for when your ERT arrives—find the best observation points for your snipers—maybe even get some waypoints and entry spots laid in."

"Can you guys talk to Billy?" asked Judd.

"You have a negotiator coming with the ERT?" responded Nathan.

"Sure."

"Best to wait for him, then. In the meantime make sure there's only one person working the phone. Give the people in the library and out here some continuity."

Judd nodded. "We haven't been able to get any phone response for the last hour, but we'll keep trying."

"Negotiating isn't our field," explained Leith, pointing at the library. "We work there, at the sharp end. Go back inside, Judd. Let your people know we'll be working out here. Whatever we can do will speed things up for your ERT when they get here."

For a moment Nathan watched Judd's broad back as he walked back toward the command center. A tap on his arm made him turn to see Leith inclining his head in a direction that would lead them back to their car. Nathan followed silently. Back at the car, Leith opened the trunk and they were pulling on soft body armor vests when Nathan asked, "Ever had one like this?"

"I've had plenty of crazies but no, no kids if that's what you mean."

Nathan snapped a loaded magazine of hollow-points into a .45 fitted with a C-More electronic sight and racked the slide to chamber a round. "It changes things," he said.

"Only if you let it, lad. Remember what I said before. We're soldiers. We follow orders and then we go home." He spit out the words. "That's what good little soldiers do." Leith loaded a magazine into his Hi-Power, slamming it home with more force than Nathan had ever seen him use on a gun. "Bloody kids! Who would've figured on kids?" He looked pointedly at Nathan, "Some jobs are easier than others that's all. This could be a hard one. In the end it'll be just that much more satisfying cleaning up." He slammed the trunk shut, again with more force than necessary and stalked off toward the library leaving Nathan to hurry after him.

Five minutes later they circled to the library's east, slipping through snowy yards and jumping fences. They found a good observation post for one sniper and talked briefly to a constable armed with a shotgun, squatting behind a patrol car. The man was cramping up because of the cold, but all they could leave him with was encouragement. They were almost finished on the east side when the quiet of the mountain afternoon was interrupted by a muffled gunshot. Subdued and flat sounding it made both men flinch nonetheless. They paused behind a parked car, abandoned on the cordoned off street.

"That wasn't directed outwards," noted Leith.

"I'd rather it were."

There was no reply. Leith was studying the building, a military field message pad in which he'd been taking notes in his left hand. Nathan focused the binoculars he carried on the visible windows. "See anything?" asked Leith.

"No. Nothing."

Leith looked at his watch. "At least a half-hour before the cavalry gets here."

"And then at least another thirty minutes before they get set up and have any kind of plan."

Leith grunted in acknowledgment, "Whatever happens we wait for them."

Nathan didn't remove his eyes from the binoculars. "Whatever?"

"Whatever."

92

Nathan pulled his eyes away from the optics and looked questioningly at Leith. "*Whatever* covers a lot of ground, Leith. I can think of . . ."

Leith cut him off. "Then don't think," he snapped. "Just follow orders. Those are our orders. We do nothing until ERT gets here and then only what they want us to do."

Nathan didn't reply but resumed his examination of the library windows.

Both men were quiet as they continued to wait, neither one sure for what. Perhaps another shot, some reaction from that first one or some unknown and unexpected new development. The tension between them mounted, threatening to grow as solid as the stone walls that formed the foundation of the library.

Leith took an audibly deep breath and broke the silence first, "Sorry I snapped at you, lad."

Nathan uttered a noncommittal grunt, adding, "The kids make it a tough one."

"Tougher than you know. You shouldn't be here. You should've stayed home."

"I'm okay."

Leith readjusted his position and sat down on the sidewalk leaning his back against the car. "We'll give it another couple of minutes. If you don't see anything we'll move to the south side."

Nathan continued to watch through the field glasses but a minute later Leith broke the silence. "Kent shouldn't have made me take you, Nathan. There are things going on here you don't understand. Even I don't understand all of it. But if we're going to get through this I need you to promise you'll trust me and do what I say. Can you do that, lad?"

Nathan didn't answer right away. He could have. The response to Leith's question was obvious to him. How best to express himself required some thought. "Not yet," he said finally. "Especially after Anton and his crew. Maybe in the future after we've worked together for a while."

"Aye, that's what I thought." Resignation filled his voice. "Anything moving yet?"

"No."

Leith rose to a crouch. "Let's move out." He turned to Nathan who lowered his binoculars. "Time to lay out some rules then, lad. While we're here, remember that to me, the mission comes first. The mission is always first. Everything and everyone is expendable for the sake of the mission. And that includes you." He tapped his forefinger on Nathan's chest, emphasizing each point with a tap. "You just follow me and do what I say. Do what I say, when I say it. Nothing more or less. If I had my way you wouldn't be here, so let's compromise with me doing the work and you staying out of my way."

Nathan replied with an icy stare a terse one-word reply. "Whatever."

Continuing to move around the perimeter, they found another sniper perch. The best hidden approach to the library was also identified. Not perfectly blind—but the best to be found. "That could be the place to get the techs up to the building," suggested Nathan. When Leith didn't reply, he added, "We won't know until we try it."

"Right you are," agreed Leith. "Follow me."

In a low crouch they approached from the south, moving slowly and carefully along a low rock wall. A short burst of speed took them across some open ground to a white picket fence, and a final burst put their backs against the cold stone of the seventy-five year old building. As long as they stayed tight against the wall near the corner, the deeply set windows gave them effective invisibility from the inside. Nathan slid silently to the right and peeked around the corner. Leith moved left doing the same. Nothing had changed. They had apparently arrived undetected. The two were exchanging thumbs-up gestures when, from inside the building, a gunshot cracked. The sound drove two hands to their respective holsters. On the right a .45 cleared leather, on the left a 9 mm. A cacophony of screams echoed the shot from inside the building. Multiple screams, high pitched and quavering, caused a tingling sensation along Nathan's spine. He felt his mouth go dry. If terror had a sound, he'd just heard it.

Nathan peered around his corner again. Nothing. He looked behind, up at the windows above them. Nothing. Leith caught his eye and in response to his questioning look Nathan shook his head and

94

shrugged his shoulders. Leith waved him over and Nathan was halfway to him when the stone reverberated with another gunshot. Again screams masked the shot's echo. Abandoning his move toward Leith, Nathan slid back to his corner. Nothing. A moment later Leith shuffled up beside him.

"Time to go, lad. We've done all we can here," whispered the Scot. Nathan didn't so much as turn around to acknowledge him. Leith grabbed his collar and pulled him forcibly back. Three feet from the corner he dragged him down to a crouch and the two men clustered there, pistols pointed towards their respective zones of fire, only turning their heads as necessary to whisper to each other.

"Something's going on in there, Leith."

"Aye, that it is. But there's nothing we can do about it. So we'll be going."

"What if he's shooting them?"

Silence.

"What if he's shooting them, Leith?"

"We don't know that."

"We know he's crazy."

"Aye."

"If we were an ERT wouldn't we go?"

"We're not and we won't be going anywhere except back the way we came."

"He's a nut case, Leith. Come on, you know the profile. He's acting out some warped delusion of his. He's probably done no tactical planning and has no skills. I'll bet he can't hit anything further than five feet in front of him. I say we go. Right now."

The boom of another shot reverberating through the stone walls was Nathan's only reply. It prompted him to maneuver fully around to face Leith. "Well," he hissed, "what if we just lost another one?"

"Then we just bloody well lost another one! But we're not going in. That's an order!"

Nathan returned to cover his corner again. He checked the dot on his C-More sight and pulled the pistol's slide back far enough to verify a round was in the chamber. Pausing a moment he rubbed at something on the side of the slide. His mind raced through the options and the possible outcomes—outcomes for him *and* for those in the building. The decision was easy. "See you inside," he whispered as he jumped up.

Leith lunged at him, catching Nathan's belt with his left hand; stopping cold any progress Nathan made in leaving. At the grab, Nathan spun around, clutched Leith's wrist with his free hand and wrenched loose from its hold. Leith's face was at belt level and he was off balance as Nathan's gun hand swung around, driving the .45's butt and magazine pad onto the bridge of the Scot's nose. The thud of impact dropped Leith onto his back and Nathan sprinted around the corner and up the steps to the door.

The knob turned in his grasp and the door eased open smoothly. The unlocked door gave him confidence that his initial assessment had been right. No tactical planning at all. Nut case all the way. Nathan paused inside the door, letting the hydraulic mechanism shut it silently and turning the knob to prevent the latch clicking as the door closed. He crouched in a tiny foyer, a coat rack and a place for boots were on his right. To the left a window allowed a view into the building's interior. Before him was another door. No lock, and the top half was largely glass. Staying below window level he shuffled silently into position and taking a deep breath, slowly stood. The .45 came with him.

Nothing. He saw a small sitting area in front of an old stone fireplace and rows of shelved books, but no people. Nathan took the opportunity to drop his coat on the floor behind him. He had to shift the pistol between hands in order to slide out of the sleeves. Then pulling the door open he eased through. Mercifully, the hinges were quiet. As he slipped into the room the sound of sobbing reached his ears and the smell of urine drifted to his nostrils. Both were by-products of fear and were to be expected. While his eyes scanned the room he tested the air further, searching for the telltale smell of blood. It wasn't there. At least not enough to be distinguished from the urine. So far so good.

Sobbing filtered down from the upper floor. Beyond the service counter to his right were stairs leading up. Nathan moved in that direction. He'd slid two steps, gun up, ready, searching, when another shot exploded. Nathan started and tucked in behind the counter.

Definitely upstairs. Screams, once again, were the shot's by-product. Seeing the opportunity Nathan moved forward rapidly, using the screams to cover the sound of his steps. The stairs went up in two flights, reversing direction at midpoint. He took the first flight of stairs backwards, eyes and pistol pointing upwards towards the threat. When he hit the landing the stairs reversed direction and he walked up the second flight normally, again leading with the .45. The upper floor became progressively more visible with each step.

Reaching the second floor he saw the bookshelves were set in rows at right angles to his approach. But he could follow the wall to his right, clearing one shelving aisle at a time. Then he smelled it— blood—distinctive, metallic, coppery. If there was enough to smell, it was bad. Clear one aisle, move to the next. Clear that one, then another. He reached the end of the shelving as the screams faded.

He saw a kid's corner. A three foot high pony wall separated it from the rest of the library. The corner was painted bright cheerful colors, mobiles hung from the ceiling and kid-sized chairs and benches were strewn around the area. Against the outside wall, separated from him by the half wall; huddled on the floor and facing but not yet seeing him was a panicked crush of four women and a mass of children. No one else. Nathan stepped out from behind the last shelf and tracked his pistol to the left, already taking up two pounds of trigger weight, sure that the gunman would be there. Empty. No one.

His sudden move brought him to the attention of the terror-stricken huddle and a collective gasp sounded. Nathan looked back at the group, then on a sudden premonition spun around leveling his pistol back the way he had come. The aisle was empty. He pivoted down the last row of shelving. No one. Back to the kid's corner. Nothing. Where could he be? Cold fear gripped his throat.

A movement from the huddle caught his attention and he saw a young woman near the front of the group. She'd been using her arms to shield the children behind her, but now she lifted her left hand and pointed to the low wall separating Nathan from the assemblage. Her eyes met Nathan's and they communicated horror.

A scraping sound on the other side of the half wall reached his ears. Out of sight to Nathan, something or someone stirred. Whatever was on the other side wasn't good. Nathan thought about vaulting the wall. He'd fill whatever it was with hollow-points as he passed over. He was starting to shift his body weight in preparation for the short sprint when a bloodstained hand grasped the top edge of the wall and stopped him. It had been clutching a large kitchen knife but that slipped from the fingers and clattered noisily to the floor on Nathan's side of the wall. A matted shock of brown hair appeared.

"Chris?" called a voice from behind the wall. "Is that you Chris?"

Nathan slid slightly back and left, taking some cover from the last bookshelf and waiting. The advantage was his now. A rack of heavy books for cover. Braced. Ready. The gunman moving, not knowing exactly where Nathan was, or apparently *who* he was. If he came up just a little more, it'd be enough. The shot was maybe twelve feet. If he shot through the wall, he could take him now. But that was too risky, bullet placement too unpredictable. Wait.

A second hand, bloodier than the first, appeared on top of the wall, a Glock pistol firmly in its grasp. And then a full head came into view and Nathan Burdett looked into the face of madness.

Jerry Mitchell arrived with Barb and her photographer in tow and got absolutely no cooperation from the officers manning the barricades. So far they had no one designated to talk to the media and they weren't allowing them any special access. Warnings about not getting in the way were all they got. Barb found the church that had become the place for family to gather and although the two men manning the front doors wouldn't let media in, she elected to hang around the outside. Jerry left to prowl around the perimeter on his own.

He managed to get some long distance photos of the library but there was no sign of anything exciting. Not about to give up, he continued to roam the police barricades, watching and waiting, until the sight of a constable giving first aid stopped him. She was treating a man seated on the curb next to the open trunk of a police car and the unmistakable color of fresh blood was being wiped from his face. They were at the south end of a stone wall, within a stone's throw of the town's hospital, at the edge of police perimeter. Jerry couldn't get any closer than where he stood— with a growing crowd of rubber-necking townspeople a good twenty yards away. A bandage across the patient's nose appeared to be the work of the constable. But as she finished cleaning off blood, the unappreciative patient rose, pushed her aside and hurried off to stand alone.

Jerry watched the man retrieve a phone from an inside pocket and dial. Then he heard a cellphone ring somewhere in the crowd behind him. A reporter's curiosity made him turn around in time to see a woman pull a cellphone from a fanny pack and answer it. She appeared to be the typical mountain country tourist, hiking boots, outdoor clothing and tanned skin. At least what he could see of her— sunglasses, a Tilley hat and long raven black hair obscured most of her features. Speaking intensely into the phone she turned and walked out of the crowd. Jerry watched her go. There was something familiar about her. Had Mr. Nose-Bandage been calling her or was that a coincidence? No. Not a coincidence. A career as a reporter had destroyed any belief he'd ever had in coincidences.

Working to keep them both in sight, he bumped through the crowd. Nose-Bandage lowered his phone and punched what Jerry presumed was the *END* button. Jerry searched for the woman. Yes! She was hanging up too, coming back in his direction as she did so. Jerry stopped, looked down and fiddled with his camera. He stole a glance at Nose-Bandage and saw him trotting off in the direction of the library. A furtive peek at the woman revealed she hadn't noticed him. It was great to be invisible. She pulled off her sunglasses, squinting intently in the direction of the library and for the briefest moment chewed on one of the arms. Jerry almost dropped his Nikon.

Her. The redhead. Now the hair was black, and there was too much of it, like a wig. But it was her. Absolutely. Positively. She too trotted off, but in the opposite direction, leaving Jerry with one of his toughest choices in recent memory. He chose to let her go and stay where he was. If she was here Burdett was too, and Burdett would be where the shooting happened. And that, after all, was where the story would be. He congratulated himself on calling it right. This was going to be good.

Mentally disturbed people were nothing new to Nathan. He'd handled more than his fair share in the five years he'd spent as an EMT before Danny recruited him. But he wasn't ready for this.

The hostage-taker's hair was matted and slick with blood; blood that flowed from short, deep cuts scattered across the face and head. The arms and shoulders came into view and they were cut too. Through the ooze of dripping blood was a face, its features a red-smeared blur except for a pleasant smile.

"Chris. I figured it out." His voice was excited but also plaintive. "I figured it out. I can use my blood instead. See?" He lifted the Glock higher to display the arm and Nathan saw more cuts, all dripping blood. Billy rose to his knees. So far he wasn't threatening with the pistol. Head and shoulders were visible above the wall.

From Nathan's perspective, through the slightly greenish lens of the C-More, a red dot appeared to float on the face. It held steady on a track that would take a bullet through the medulla and—and out the back of the skull into the cowering mass of humanity behind the madman. Nathan cursed his luck. A perfect shot and he couldn't take it because the man's head was exactly in front of the children. The wall two feet to Nathan's right stopped him from changing the angle in that direction. A move left or down would cause the gunman to disappear behind the bookshelf or the low wall. For the moment it was a standoff.

"Chris?" The bloodied face called out again.

Nathan drew a shallow breath and answered. "Yeah, it's me. It's Chris."

"You're not Chris." The smile on the face disappeared. "Where's Chris?"

Nathan's mind raced. He needed more time and he needed Billy to move, changing the angle for the shot. "Chris got tied up. He sent me."

That seemed to make him think. He broke eye contact with Nathan but the pistol disappeared from view below the wall.

"He gave me a message for you," tried Nathan. "He said you're supposed to give me the Glock." It was worth a try.

The eyes came back up. A puzzled look spread across the face. "Give you the what?"

"The Glock," repeated Nathan a little louder. "You're supposed to give me the Glock."

The puzzled look remained. "What's a Glock?"

"The pistol, Billy. You're supposed to give me the pistol. That's what Chris said."

"You're not Chris."

Nathan drew in a ragged breath before answering. Billy hadn't moved. Comfortably planted on his knees, there was no sign he was going to change position. "No, I'm not Chris. He sent me instead, Billy. You're supposed to give me the pistol."

Billy shook his head. "Chris gave me this pistol. He said it's for the greater good. Is Glock its name? I didn't know it had a name. He gave me Glock. I'm supposed to keep it 'til I'm finished and I'm not finished yet." He half turned and pointed the 9 mm at the people behind him. Nathan increased pressure on the trigger. The angle was as bad as ever but he'd do it if he had no choice. "Chris showed me why innocent blood has to be spilled. I understand everything he told me. But you know what? In here I realized it doesn't have to be theirs."

He turned back to face Nathan. "I had to cut myself to let the voices out. I've been trying to shoot them when they come out but it's not working. But they do come out and that's when I realized my blood would work too. I let my blood out for the greater good. That'll work, it doesn't have to be theirs."

"You've done fine, Billy. I'm sure Chris would be pleased. Now just give me the gun and we'll go find him. Okay?"

"No. You don't understand. I can't leave here. Do you think my blood is enough?"

Billy ran his free hand, as best he could, through his clotted hair and looked at the pistol in his other hand. Resting it on the ledge in front of him, he examined it. "What's your name?"

"Nathan. My name's Nathan."

"How do you know my gun's name?"

"It's written on the side of the gun, Billy."

"Does your gun have a name?"

Nathan didn't answer as Billy supported his 9 mm on the ledge and wiped the side of the bloody slide with an equally bloody finger, studying it intently. "You're right!" he exclaimed. "It says *Glock*, here on the side. I never noticed that before." Billy held the Glock at nose level, the pistol in profile to Nathan, finger wrapped tightly around the trigger, reading the markings on the slide.

Nathan saw his shot. He remembered, years ago, watching a news video, of a rifle sniper who'd done the same thing. In the last year he'd thought about it some, even tried it at the range once. Generally it was just too bizarre to even consider. Here, however, bizarre seemed to fit. Nathan checked his grip and repositioned the brace of his support hand on the bookshelf. "Billy," he said softly.

"Yes, Nathan." The blood smeared face looked up, the eyes questioning.

Nathan thought about the shot. At this short range he'd have to allow for the height of his dot above the bore line. Should be one and a quarter inches—probably. Would have been nice to try this on the range first. The very next trip to the range, he told himself while repositioning the dot another quarter inch higher. "My gun doesn't have a name, Billy."

"No?"

He glanced to either side of Billy's head, at the women protecting the children. At least two of them looked like they had enough left to get the kids out without his help. They'd have to manage. "No, Billy. But the bullets do."

"Your bullets have names?"

Billy was fidgeting too much. "If you're really quiet and listen carefully I'll tell them to you. But I have to say them very quietly because they're secret."

Billy stopped rearranging the blood smears on the Glock and strained to hear the words.

Nathan whispered them slowly, praying Billy wouldn't move as he applied force to the trigger and fought to hold the dot on target. "They're called Dopey . . . Sleepy . . . Sneezy . . . Grumpy . . .," he was halfway through 'Bashful' when the sear released and the .45 roared. Nathan knew Billy's head wouldn't stop the just-launched 230-grain hollow-point. But he'd just bet innocent lives the Glock would.

102

As his pistol recoiled, Nathan's mind replayed the sight picture at the instant of hammer fall. The shot was on, he knew it, then the familiar target-range *smack* of high velocity lead on a solid object confirmed it. His tensed leg muscles were already uncoiling, driving him forward as he watched the Glock slam backwards from the force of the blow, bounce off Billy's teeth and topple from his grasp onto the floor on Nathan's side of the low wall. Billy sagged out of sight as Nathan launched himself forward. "Go! Go! Go!" he screamed, urging the terrified women behind Billy to start the children moving. This wasn't over yet.

Nathan sprinted for the wall, intent on vaulting it and putting himself between Billy and the hostages. Three strides got him there. The fourth put his instep on the top edge, pushing him over and giving him a leverage point to start changing direction in mid-air—and in position to put as many more bullets as needed into the madman. But the thick blood covering the wall's top edge was still fluid enough to be slippery. Nathan's right leg spun out from under him and his back bounced onto the edge of the wall with all the weight and speed his hurtling body possessed. Little bursts of light exploded in his brain and he spun onto the floor dazed, looking up at the wall, unsure on which side he had even landed.

His question was answered as a bloody hand gripped the top of the wall from the opposite side, and Billy hauled himself over enough to thrust a pistol into Nathan's face. Nathan's eyes came back into focus enough to recognize the C-More sight. Billy was going to kill him with his own .45.

"You lied to me Nathan," sputtered Billy through broken teeth and still more blood. "Chris didn't send you. You lied to me!" he screamed. "You don't believe in the greater good. Now you have to come with me to Hell!" The .45 twitched in his hand, then twitched again, but there was no sound. A bewildered look crossed Billy's face. Nathan's eyes wouldn't focus well enough to see the gun clearly but he remembered the sight picture when the hammer dropped. The shot had been good. He knew why Billy couldn't fire the gun. With his left hand he reached up and twisted the .45 away, at the same time grabbing a handful of bloody hair and pulling Billy down on top of himself. He

103

rolled the shrieking madman face down onto the floor and pinned an arm behind his back. Between Billy's screams he heard the children's. Nathan yelled again. "Go! Get the kids out of here! Go now!"

This time they responded. A frantic rush of screaming, tumbling arms and legs streamed out the building behind him. Nathan stayed put, pinning a still struggling Billy. Now the troops would come.

Leith reached him first. Judd came in next, standing back a little, a Remington 870 shotgun in his hands. "I've got him, lad," said the Scot, bending down to take custody of Billy.

Nathan didn't move. "I haven't cleared the building yet, Leith."

"Then you two get to it. I'll take out the trash." Leith pulled a Flex-Cuff from his vest, gave a quick wrap around Billy's wrists and snubbed it tight. "What . . . ."

Nathan released Billy, but didn't wait for Leith to finish the question. "He was busy cutting himself up when I got here. By comparison I didn't do much to him at all. I'll fill you in when we're done."

Fifteen minutes later, Nathan and Judd had checked every conceivable nook and cranny of the building and declared it clear. They met Leith and two other shotgun-wielding constables on the steps outside the front door. "I put crazy Billy in an ambulance," said Leith. "He doesn't look good."

For the first time Nathan noticed the bandage across Leith's nose and the bruise spreading through the eyes. He decided not to comment on it. "How about the kids?"

"Nothing worse than some scratches and bruises. And that's mainly from running out of the building," Leith answered.

"Thank goodness." Nathan suspected Leith had other words for him as well but he was saving them for when they were alone. He grimaced as another bolt of pain shot up his right leg. He'd been coping off and on with that for about five minutes. Something had happened in the spill from the wall. Now with the adrenaline starting to wear off it was feeling continually worse. Nathan lifted his pistol from its holster, dropped the magazine and flipped the live round out of the chamber. He passed everything over to Leith. "I better make a trip to an X-ray room myself. I've got something seriously bad going on in my right ankle."

"Come on, I'll drive you," volunteered Judd pointing to a brace of patrol cars pulled up near the front door. "Can you make it to a car?" Nathan looked at the distance and calculated the pain involved in getting to the car. "Yeah, I can do that." In the background he saw a crowd at the eastern police barricades and although he didn't see any cameras, at this distance he couldn't be certain. Taking the offered shoulder for support he kept a hand up near his face and occasionally looked back at Leith. The returning gaze was steadfastly cold and tinged with hate.

Six hours later Nathan rested in a hospital bed with a fresh cast on his ankle and doctor's orders to stay for the night. There was one other bed in the room but, much to Nathan's relief, it was empty. He didn't feel like having a roommate who, considering the afternoon's events, would have more questions than a high priced lawyer. He'd finished a passable hospital meal when Judd walked into his room with the casual stride of an experienced police officer. After inquiring about Nathan's ankle and receiving assurances that it would be as good as new—'in time', Judd handed him a sealed, letter-sized envelope. "Your partner gave me this note for you. I'm supposed to take a formal statement from you as well."

Nathan set the envelope aside unopened, doubting it was praise for a job well done. "I'd really rather not get involved in a court case."

"What court case? I take it you haven't heard then?"

"Heard what?"

"Billy died in the ambulance on the way to hospital. We'll have to wait for the autopsy to be certain, but it looks like he just bled out."

"I didn't think he'd lost that much blood?"

"The doctor who pronounced him dead said there was a laceration along the neck." Judd drew a finger along the side of his shirt collar in demonstration. "It nicked the carotid artery and that's what finished him off. It must have been close to the last cut he made on himself." Judd shrugged and pulled a tape recorder out of his briefcase, setting it up on the table beside the bed. Nathan tried to picture how and when the cut occurred. Certainly there had been no arterial blood flow from Billy's neck while he'd been dealing with him. Could a bullet fragment from the impact on the Glock have cut him? It didn't seem likely.

Judd interrupted his thoughts. "Shall we start?" he asked.

Thirty minutes of questions and answers brought them to the point where Nathan was about to fire his lone shot. He hadn't mentioned the earlier altercation with Leith and Judd never asked. Nathan explained his predicament of innocents behind the target and that the idea of putting a bullet into the pistol itself seemed to be the only option. Judd raised his eyebrows at that but said nothing. The tape recorder continued running as Nathan talked through the shot and his failed attempt to vault the wall. When Nathan related how Billy had stuffed the .45 in his face but he'd remained positive Billy couldn't shoot, Judd stopped him.

"Now hold on just a minute. That's about the most confident piece of instant psychoanalysis I've ever seen."

"No, you don't understand," countered Nathan. "I mean he was physically incapable of shooting me, not mentally incapable." The puzzled look on Judd's face told Nathan he hadn't examined the body yet and it would take some explaining. "Are you a shooter?" he asked patiently.

Judd smiled and shook his head. "No." He patted the Smith & Wesson semi-auto on his duty belt. "This is the only gun I shoot and I limit that to once a year during our qualification shoot. That's all. I'd rather be fishing any day."

Nathan nodded. "First, when you qualify, do you ever fire a shot and just hope it hits where it's supposed to?" A knowing nod was his answer. "That's normal enough, Judd. But it's not what happens with people like me. You need to understand that a shooter like me can call his shot—every time. That means, when I've fired the shot I know exactly where the bullet is going. If I'm going to hit, I know it before the bullet gets there. And if I miss I know how far off and in which direction the miss is, again *before* the bullet gets there.

That made Judd's eyebrows go up again. Nathan continued, "Also, when trying to pull off a precision shot, which this was, the rule

106

is: aim at the smallest possible point. For example: if you're shooting at a deer, don't aim at the whole deer. Pick a spot behind its left shoulder, a third of the way up. That's what you aim at, not the whole animal. In this case I didn't aim at the whole gun."

"Okay," interrupted Judd. "I follow your theory. So what were you trying to hit on the gun? And how did that tell you he couldn't shoot you, especially with your own pistol, which hadn't been damaged?"

"No. No. You still don't understand." Nathan put a hand to his forehead in exasperation. "Not the gun, the hand holding the gun. The knuckle where the trigger finger joins the hand falls naturally in the center of the pistol's grip frame. I put the bullet through the knuckle and into the frame. That way I stopped my bullet from over penetrating, hammered him in the face with his own pistol and that big .45 slug took off his trigger finger at the same time."

Except for the quiet hum of the tape recorder, the room went silent.

"I didn't have much choice," shrugged Nathan. "At least he was only twelve feet away and I was well braced, not really that tough a shot. I figured I needed a fast follow-up though. In the state he was in, his pain receptors had essentially shut down. If he managed to hang onto the gun, I had only until he realized his finger was missing before he used the other hand—or another finger. Fortunately he didn't catch on right away."

Judd stared at Nathan. He blinked, then he coughed. "What kind of drugs did you say they have you on?"

Nathan shook his head. "No drugs. Check the body."

The tape recorder continued humming.

Judd looked at this watch and then back at Nathan. "Right. It's what I'd do. Shoot off his trigger finger. As a matter of fact, I think that's what I'll do to the next druggie who draws down on me. Shoot off his trigger finger. It would make for less paperwork wouldn't it? I mean, wouldn't it?"

Nathan ignored the sarcasm and Judd again lapsed into silence, at a momentary loss for words. Shaking his head he reached out and abruptly turned off the recorder. "I'm going to the autopsy tomorrow,

Nathan. I'll look at the body and then I'll come back. We'll talk more after that." They said their good-byes and Judd disappeared from sight when the door swung shut.

As Nathan opened Leith's note he abruptly heard Judd's footsteps returning. The mustached face appeared back around the corner. "I'm going to take a camera to the autopsy, Nathan. I'll make sure I get good pictures, with lots of copies. You do realize nobody's going to believe this without pictures. And I mean nobody." He pointed a finger at Nathan. "Without pictures, *nobody'll* believe it."

"Sure, Judd. If that's what you figure," Nathan nodded. Then he was gone.

Nathan returned to opening the envelope, unfolded the single sheet of paper inside and read the contents:

> *Nathan,*
> *I've taken the plane back.*
> *Your gear's with the local constabulary.*
> *Kent will call. Expect disciplinary action.*
> *Leith.*

CHAPTER SIX

From Leith's perspective at thirty-two thousand feet, the sun was still an orange ball balanced on the horizon's edge waiting to abandon the earth into the concealing blackness of night. At the other end of his scrambled phone connection, the late-working Mr. Kent, half a continent away, was already wrapped in that black shroud.

"It's over," said Leith, as soon as the line cleared.

Kent didn't reply at first. He turned his chair and looked out the window. At night he sometimes kept the lights in his own office subdued so that he could see out across the city. The only light left out there was artificial, tiny squares and dots of life. In the nearby high rises they were squares, further away they were dots and in the very distance they twinkled like stars. He knew Leith's report wouldn't be good. He'd known it would end this way, the only question remaining was how bad it was.

"Hello. Are you there?" asked Leith.

"Yes. Go ahead."

"You never said anything about kids, Kent."

"That's true, Leith. But it wasn't confirmed at the time of your briefing. They were a possibility I didn't tell you about. I did say it would be extremely unpleasant. And that's why the large bonus. I'm sure you'll agree, in these circumstances, children are included in 'unpleasant'. You know I don't pay bonuses like that for easy work."

"I . . . well . . . next time you tell me if there's kids, or find somebody else to do it."

Kent ignored the comment. "What happened?"

"Burdett, that piece of slime, pulled a John Wayne. He went in and terminated the situation before it had a chance to develop."

"You didn't stop him?"

Leith ignored the question. "He doesn't follow orders very well."

"No, he doesn't," agreed Kent, silently wondering how much damage Nathan had done to Leith. "Let me guess. He took the subject alive."

"Right as usual, sir, but I was able to correct that deficiency."

"I never doubted that would be the case." Kent was relieved. "That is, after all Leith, why I retain you, because you are the best. Just to confirm though, there were no other casualties?"

"No. No others."

"Where is Burdett now?"

"He messed up his ankle in the operation and I left him in the local hospital. He'll likely be out of circulation for several months."

"Just as well, it gives me some time to determine what's to be done with him. And Kim?"

"She's here with me."

"Let me talk to her."

"Standby." Leith passed the phone to Kim. "The man wants to talk to you."

Kim pressed the phone to her left ear and pressed a finger into the right one to drown out the drone of the jet's engines. "Just what kind of a job was this supposed to be?"

Two thousand miles away Kent grimaced. What was this business coming to? Nothing but questions and accusations from people who didn't understand their roles. In the past this had never happened. People realized they didn't understand everything about a mission but they went ahead and did it without asking unnecessary questions. They trusted their superiors. They got the job done. Now second-guessing seemed to be an occupational pastime. "It was complicated and difficult," he answered. "That's all you need to know. You had your orders. If you have any difficulty following them I can simply advise the Colonel."

"That won't be necessary."

"Very well then. You need to understand that things didn't go entirely as planned, but these are fluid and unpredictable situations and we do the best we can. You'll speak to no one about this until we debrief. I'll see you when you get back."

Kim turned off the phone and flung it back at Leith. She looked outside at the sun—half gone at the horizon. That's how she felt, dropping, falling into something dark and unknown. She was used to unexplained missions, operations with no discernible purpose and taking life, or living it, with no meaning. But this was different. She folded her arms, took a last look out the window and then closed her eyes. Maybe she could sleep.

Kent didn't hang up the phone, he merely dialed a new number. "You're still watching CNN?"

"Yes," she said.

"You can turn it off. There won't be anything there." Silence. "It seems," he continued, "that our Mr. Burdett launched an unauthorized pre-emptive strike and terminated the situation."

"I see."

"You wanted irony? You just got it, my dear. And one more thing . . ."

"Yes."

"Mr. Burdett took your subject alive." That generated an audibly sharp intake of breath. Kent toyed with the idea of how long to let her dangle. He waited an enjoyable fifteen seconds before ending her misery. "One of my other people took care of it for you." He pictured the color returning to her face.

"I see."

Kent smiled. "You seem to be at a loss for words, my dear."

"This hasn't gone especially well has it? And from what you're telling me, it seems your people have messed it up."

"Yes, Mr. Burdett 'messed it up'. And if you suggest I owe you a massacre I'll personally come over there and drown you in your pool. Let's not forget who it was that wanted him there, in a desire for irony."

"We had a lot of time, energy and money invested in this."

"Yes, I can understand that. Much like Mr. Burdett and myself. It appears we have both lost an investment."

"I'd still like to talk to you about him. There may be something we can salvage if we work together."

"I'll be sending him back where he came from for the time being. Maybe at some future date, when he has matured a little more, I'll be able to bring him back. But we're through with him for now."

"We'll salvage what we can, too. I'll talk to you tomorrow night."

"Dinner at Chanterelle's?"

"Certainly. Sevenish?"

"And just one more thing . . ."

"Yes."

"No more children."

"But nothing works better than . . ."

"I realize you don't need my service very often, my dear, but henceforth when you do, there'll be no more children," said Kent.

"We can talk about that over dinner."

"No, we can't. This isn't open for discussion. It's final. I will not be involved with any more children." She was saying something else in protest but Kent didn't wait to hear what it was. He gently hung up the phone, turned out the lamp on his desk and watched the lights of the city.

The tall brunette from the Tribune's photo lab brought Jerry's pictures up to him personally. "Take a look at those and tell me which ones you want enlarged," she said, tossing them on the desk. Jerry ripped open the pouches and thumbed through the prints. In seconds he narrowed it down to half a dozen.

"These are the three people I need," he said, circling two heads on one of the prints and a third on another. "Mr. Nose Bandage, the girl with the too big hair and Nathan Burdett, nice and large, all of 'em."

"I'll have them in a few hours."

That was how long he'd been back in the office, only a few hours and everyone was bending over backwards to help him. Even the doubters believed him now. His assignment had been justified and everybody was insanely jealous. Especially Barb. It was great. He dug back into his notes and tried to sort out two days of leg-work in Jasper.

Nathan anticipated release from hospital the next day. With an ankle immobilized by the latest in cast technology and an all-clear from the doctor on a possible concussion he was free to leave tomorrow. That meant he had some phone calls to make this evening. Because his phone had been clipped to his belt when he'd come in, it was a simple matter of retrieving his possessions from the hospital. Strict rules prohibited the use of wireless phones within the building so an inquiry with a nurse at the station down the hall directed him to the outside doorway where smokers gathered to consume their carcinogens.

As he hobbled off in that direction she added, "You've had visitors."

He stopped. "Who?"

She smiled. "You said, 'No visitors', so we haven't allowed anyone in to see you except the officers. We haven't been asking for ID, Mr. Burdett."

"Of course." Nathan turned to go, but stopped when she continued.

"I think they've all been media though. I know the local ones, but there's been others too and though they're not saying, they have reporter written all over them."

"Thank you. That's just who I was trying to avoid." Nathan shuffled around and carried on toward the door.

When he limped out of the building, sudden animated conversations and furtive glances suggested he was the subject of discussion around the smoker's doorway. He should have expected it. This was a small town, not all that different from Cochrane where he'd grown up. He knew how well the rumor mill worked there. Moving out of earshot to keep people from hearing, Nathan dialed.

Two calls later he had assured his mother in Calgary of his good health and informed her of his imminent arrival for an extended visit. Nathan also arranged for Bob Coombs to make the four hour drive from Cochrane to Jasper to pick him up.

Nathan speculated that if he'd been in this circumstance six months ago he'd have called his good friend Paul Simmons instead. But Paul wasn't in Cochrane anymore. On a windy February street in

113

Calgary, Paul had saved his life by killing the gunman homing in on him. In the world of the RCMP, where Paul worked, that meant an immediate transfer—in Paul's case it earned him a desk job in Kamloops. Not bad as far as transfers go, and by all accounts his leg was healing well enough that he'd be back on the street soon. Nathan resolved to call him once things settled down and compare injured-leg stories.

Bob knew better than to ask a lot of questions over the phone. The next day he merely hung a *CLOSED FOR THE DAY* sign on his gunsmithing shop's door, settled his six-foot frame behind the steering wheel of his truck and made the trip north. He saved the questions for the drive home. "When I heard the first radio reports I thought you might be in on this," he said.

Nathan looked over at his friend and mentor. Even in profile you could tell Bob's nose had been broken. The bruises and cuts had all healed but the nose still showed the effects of being stiff-armed with a shotgun. The images returned. That shouldn't have happened to a man and his wife pushing sixty. It shouldn't happen to anyone. "We were there before the ERT," said Nathan.

"That's pretty good from Spokane."

"In all fairness, they have a long response time. Figure they don't get called until a half-hour after the locals become aware of the situation, then maybe an hour to assemble everyone and then a three hour drive into the boondocks. They aren't going to get there quickly. Still . . ." Nathan paused. "It was too fast."

"What do you mean?"

Nathan looked over at his friend. "Jasper detachment got the first calls on this at 11:30 a.m.. That's 10:30 in Spokane."

"So?"

"I didn't get to bed until two in the morning, so, I was still sleeping when Leith rousted me at 10:46. That's 11:46 a.m. Jasper time. I knew about it fifteen minutes after the local cops did, and the people who woke me up, knew about it before I did. It's all too fast. Things don't work that fast."

"How do you explain it then?"

114

"I have no idea, but something's not right."

Bob was silent for a moment trying to work out the information Nathan had given him. It didn't make any more sense to him. They drove for five minutes before Bob broke the silence. "Have you seen today's paper?"

"No."

Bob reached under the seat of the truck and extracted a folded copy of the Tribune. "I stopped at a Tim Hortons donut shop for coffee on the way up and saw this."

Nathan took the paper, unfolding it enough to read the front page. A color picture of the Jasper Library predominated, showing a few police officers milling around the front steps. Filling in the corner of the page was a head-and-shoulders photo of a broadly smiling Billy Cardenas. Billy was wearing earmuffs and yellow tinted safety glasses. With the muzzle of a Glock pistol he was proudly pointing at a target with ten rounds neatly centered in the black. The headline read, *Jasper Target Shooter Goes Berserk*. "What's this supposed to be?" exclaimed Nathan.

"Read it for yourself," said Bob.

It took Nathan ten minutes to read how the 'expert target shooter and gun nut' Billy Cardenas had gone over the edge and taken one of the firearms from his 'legally owned, personal arsenal of weapons' and tried to massacre 'eighteen people, mostly innocent children' until stopped by an RCMP Emergency Response Team.

"Did you know he was a shooter?" asked Bob.

"If he was an 'expert target shooter' I'll personally eat his Glock, Bob. Crazy Billy didn't even recognize the Glock name as a manufacturer; he thought it was the personal name of his pistol. He went over the edge all right, but he knew so little about his gun he was surprised to find Glock marked on the slide. Where do they get this stuff, Bob? Do they just make it up as they go along? Don't they check out their stories? Do a little research?"

Bob reached out and put a hand on Nathan's arm to stop his rant. "Slow down there, youngster. I agree with everything you're saying. You know that. But we've all seen it before. The gun-owning sportsman gets vilified at every opportunity. That seems to be one of

115

the rules of journalism. And this is just another opportunity. An incredibly juicy one at that."

"And there's nothing we can do about it?"

Bob shrugged. "I don't know." Then with a facetious smile he added, "You could call that reporter and straighten her out. Tell her how you were there and what really happened. Give her an exclusive interview. Explain to her you're really a gun-owning sportsman yourself and it was you, using the skills you learned in competition, that saved those kids—not a professionally trained ERT."

Nathan refolded the paper and threw it down on the seat between them in disgust. "Right. And that'll be the end of my career."

"Uh-huh."

Nathan stared ahead, saying nothing, thinking to himself that if a person really did want to shut the door this could be a way to end it. He picked up the paper again and opened it to the reporter's name. Barbara Latoski. He memorized it. Right now he had no intention of calling her. Perhaps one day, though. If it ever came to it, he just might make that call.

"What's the 'greater good', Bob?"

"Pardon me?"

"Billy said what he was doing was for the 'greater good'. Does that mean anything to you?"

Bob scratched his head. "No. Should it?"

"I guess not."

"He was insane, Nathan. That's a given. I wouldn't be trying to figure out the meaning of *anything* he said."

"Yeah. You're right." Nathan reached down and readjusted his foot to a more comfortable position. "Poor Billy. He was as crazy as it's possible to get."

Nathan decided to stay with Bob and his wife Frankie until the weekend and then move to his mother's place in Calgary for the remainder of his rehabilitation. Not that there was anything wrong with his mother's apartment, but Bob and Frankie's was the only place he knew where a person could smell gun oil and fresh baking in the same building. Bob's shop was attached to his house and when the adjoining door was open the mixture of smells was unique. And beside the county road, in the small valley northwest of Cochrane where Bob's place was located, the scenery was superior to anything found in the metropolis of Calgary.

The next day Nathan sat and watched TV in Bob's living room. With his leg up on a padded stool and remote in hand, he was alternating his attention between the tube and the rolling parkland visible out the window when his satellite phone warbled.

"Hello, Mr. Burdett. Jenny here. Just calling to make sure you're looked after," said the ever-efficient secretary of Mr. Kent's.

"Am I still working for you?" asked Nathan sarcastically.

"I haven't been told any differently."

Nathan turned off the TV and checked his attitude. "Sorry, I didn't mean to growl at you. I've been expecting Kent himself to phone. I'm afraid it could make for a bad day around the office when that happens."

"I understand. But we need to work out the administrative details of you being injured. You know, how long you'll be off, medical insurance, rehabilitation, that sort of thing."

"Sure. In a nutshell, it's six weeks with my cast and then about four weeks of physiotherapy."

"Okay. Here's what I need you to do . . . ."

They talked for fifteen minutes and when Nathan sensed everything was covered he changed the subject. "Have you seen Leith around?"

"He's in the office today. Would you like to speak with him?"

"No. Just tell me, is he still mad?"

"No comment, Mr. Burdett."

"I understand. That's very diplomatic of you. So what does he look like?"

Jenny paused a moment. "Sort of like a raccoon. He wears sunglasses a lot."

Nathan smiled to himself. "Well, he's got my number. He can call me if he needs anything. What about the big guy?"

"Mr. Kent is out of the country. I'll be giving him this update on you later in the day. He may call you after that."

117

"I can hardly wait."

"Good-bye, Mr. Burdett."

"Good-bye, Jenny." Nathan turned the phone off and the TV back on. Inside the cast his foot was itching, so he grabbed a pen and poked around under the hard fiberglass, doing the best job of scratching he could. The itch distracted him from thinking about what would happen when Kent called. For that reason the distraction was welcome but he knew he'd have to deal with it sooner or later. So he turned the TV off again and thought about his options.

The phone call and the on-off of the TV attracted Frankie's attention in the kitchen and she came in to check on him. "Can I get you anything?"

"A new life," he laughed.

"Sorry, I'm out of those. I gave out my last one two days ago. How about an ear?"

"Sure, that'll do. Sit down."

She did and they talked. It occurred to Nathan that except for the location, not much had changed. The living room was a switch; usually they talked in her kitchen, over coffee and goodies. Frankie's bright disposition and sunny smile were the same. So was the way she always asked more questions than she answered, at least directly. You spent all the time answering her questions but she rarely gave advice. And yet, when you were done you always knew more than when you'd started. How did she do that? The perky little lady, old enough to be a grandmother but with no kids of her own, got you like that. Weird.

They talked for most of an hour and it wasn't until a half-hour after she left that Nathan called her back into the room. "Can I borrow your car, Frankie?"

"Sure, but who's going to drive it."

"I am of course."

She looked at the cast. "Not my car you're not."

"Frankie, it's an automatic transmission for crying out loud. I only need one foot to drive it."

"Then you'll use my foot, young man. Where do you want to go? I'll drive you. Bob's too busy."

118

Nathan knew better than to argue. "Into Cochrane, the RadioShack store. I'll buy you an ice cream at Mackay's," he volunteered.

"Deal. Get your crippled body out the door and I'll go tell Bob I'm going out for ice cream with a much younger man."

Kent called Nathan's satellite phone on Friday afternoon. When it rang, Nathan was sitting in the customer area of Bob's shop, his foot on a low table, propped up still higher with a dozen gun magazines. He was passing the afternoon talking with Bob and wishing his ankle would last more than forty-five minutes with weight on it. Rebarreling a Martini single shot rifle to .17 Ackley Hornet was Bob's current personal project, and Nathan had been giving moral support to the difficult task of cutting the barrel's extractor relief.

"I was expecting you to call before this," said Nathan, while waving frantically at Bob. The gunsmith dropped his file and trotted through the door connecting the house to fetch Nathan's most recent purchase.

Kent ignored the comment. "And how is your leg?"

"A lot like the report I gave Jenny," said Nathan coolly.

"I see." Kent paused. "You don't sound much happier with me, Mr. Burdett, than I am with you."

"That's probably about right." Nathan accepted the package from Bob and busied himself setting it up while trying to maintain a conversation.

"Your treatment of Leith and your response to his orders was less than exemplary. That sort of behavior is not acceptable, Mr. Burdett."

"You'd find my behavior more acceptable if the orders made sense. But we've had a conversation like this before, haven't we?" Nathan's voice was getting louder.

"In this business, Mr. Burdett, you'll find you don't always have the big picture. All you can see from your perspective is a small slice of it. You simply must learn to trust your superiors and follow orders in faith that they are doing what's right."

119

"Sure. And trust takes time. You have to build it on something. Starting with Anton and his crew, you and Leith haven't been building anything with me. All you've been doing is digging a hole that keeps getting deeper. When are . . . ." Nathan felt himself losing control and stopped.

"If we can't come to a working agreement I may have to terminate your employment with us."

"That's fine with me," he spit back. "I'll go back to working for Danny Forbes, or maybe I'll just retire."

"I caution you to avoid any rash decisions, Mr. Burdett. You have valuable talents that could be put to good use but you must understand that I simply cannot have my people operating on their own impulses or agendas. The stakes at this level are much too high. Unfortunately, I must inform you that your work with us is finished." Kent paused to see if Nathan would respond. There was no reply, so he continued. "I'll advise Mr. Forbes of these developments and if he wishes to take you back, then that's his affair. Any questions Mr. Burdett?"

"What about my stuff?" growled Nathan.

"Once you know where you'll be staying, call Jenny and have her make arrangements to ship it wherever you like."

"I'll do that."

"Good day, Mr. Burdett."

"Kent, you pompous English weasel, why don't you . . . ." Nathan stopped as he realized Kent had clicked off and he was talking to static and Bob. Nathan turned off the phone, disconnected the suction cup from the back of its plastic body and turned off the tape recorder. Then he replayed it for Bob who had only heard his half of the conversation.

"That wasn't very useful."

"No, it wasn't."

"Just what did you think he was going to say?"

"I don't know for sure, but I'm keeping this rig around if I ever have to talk to him again."

"Still think he's up to no good?" Bob moved back toward his lathe and tried to figure out where he had left off when interrupted.

120

"Bob, this guy stinks worse than a two week old piece of coyote bait. And he's about that slimy too."

"Now that you're fired do you need to worry about him?"

"No, you're probably right. But somehow I don't think I'm finished with him."

"How do you figure that?"

"I don't know, it's just a feeling I have. Somebody should do something about this jerk."

"So . . . what are you going to do then?"

"Hey, I didn't say me. I said somebody. I'm just glad to be rid of him with nothing worse than a busted ankle. Now, at least I have time to think about this. Looks like I've got more than two months to decide."

Bob gave up on the extractor and went over to a bulletin board on which dozens of business cards were pinned. He pulled one off, brought it back to Nathan and tossed it into his lap. "There's an option for you."

Nathan read the card. "Jerry Mitchell, The Calgary Tribune."

"He came by here shortly after our problems with the Riders. Wanted to do a story on the whole thing but I showed him the door pretty fast. He left his card but I threw it out. He's come back twice since, always asking politely if I've changed my mind. I haven't, but as you can see I'm at least keeping his card now."

"I don't think . . ."

Bob held up a hand and Nathan stopped. "About a month ago Sue was in. Do you remember her? She does some competitive shooting and is doing quite a bit of instruction at Gunsport Ranges these days." Nathan nodded. "She was in here to get a slide milled for a dovetail front sight and happened to see the card while she was waiting. Says Jerry Mitchell has taken up shooting, is getting lessons from her and is even thinking of buying a pistol."

Nathan's eyebrow's raised in response. "That's pretty radical. Jerry Mitchell better watch himself. He could get fired from the International Brotherhood of Left Wing Journalists."

Bob laughed, "Hey, there are some good ones. He might be one of them." Nathan grunted in agreement and handed the card back. "No. You keep it," said Bob. "You might need it before I do."

The following week he moved into his mother's apartment. Since their trouble with the Rider's she had left her job at the Cochrane RCMP detachment and compassionate friends had found one that buried her in the bowels of the Calgary Police Service. One of the first things Nathan did was ask her about Jerry Mitchell.

"I've never heard of him, dear," she said. "But if you like I can go downstairs to the department's media relations office and ask about him. Murray knows all the reporters and he'll know something about him."

'Sure, that would be great, Mom."

"What do you want to know about him?"

"Just what kind of person he is. Is he honest, trustworthy? That sort of thing."

"I'll find out for you tomorrow. Can your mother ask why you want to know about a reporter?"

An awkward pause followed, while Nathan thought about what to say to her. He eventually opted for the truth, but only half of it. "He's been snooping around trying to get in touch with me and asking questions. I'd like to find out what kind of person he is and what he wants to know before I call him back. You haven't heard from him, have you?"

"No." Emily Burdett shook her graying head. "After the trouble we had with the Riders, the boys did a good job of making me disappear. I doubt a reporter could find me." She looked intently at the hands in her lap.

"You're still scared the Riders might come back in some way, aren't you?" asked Nathan, as gently as he could.

She nodded ever so slightly. "I don't ever go back to Cochrane and only rarely call my old friends there."

Nathan reached out and took her hand. "I'm so sorry, Mom. It's my fault all that happened. If it could be undone I'd do it in a heartbeat."

"I know you would, dear." She patted Nathan's hand in a motherly fashion. "I'm moving on from there. Calgary has given me new friends and I'm using my maiden name with them, that's all. It's working."

Two weeks later Nathan finally phoned Jerry Mitchell, even though his mother's positive report had been delivered much earlier. He hadn't given a lot of thought about what to say, and when the reporter answered, Nathan quietly hung up. The reason he'd done that, he told himself, were his doubts that anyone, especially a skeptical reporter, would believe him.

He did know that what his mother had said about making new friends wasn't true. In the time he'd been there, his mother's phone had rung exactly five times and a total of one guest had come to the door. Two of the calls had been a telemarketer, two had been his sister and the other had been a 'friend' from work. The person at the door had been Bruce, the building manager, giving out notices about repair work to be done on the door to the building's underground parking. Two weeks, one phone call from a 'friend'. That was it. In a pig's eye, it's working.

Nathan found his second biggest frustration was finding effective ways to train with one foot immobilized. He did the best he could until the cast came off, which happened just before Christmas. A cast was a new experience, he'd never had one before, and the lack of mobility he had once it came off surprised him. The pain of physiotherapy surprised him even more.

Nathan found flexibility was something he had to buy back. The currency to purchase it was pain. And the person who extracted it from him was the physiotherapist. Every millimeter of joint movement was paid for in the coin of agony. However, he steeled his mind to what had to be done and learned that physical suffering was an acceptable price to pay for regaining the use of his foot.

When it was well enough that he could travel to the range, Nathan was anxious to try an idea that had popped into his head during the inactive periods of reading he had endured. A visit to a doctor friend gave him the prescription he needed, but only because he'd known this doctor since his days as an EMT.

Nathan had met Brad on a night they'd delivered the victim of another bear attack to the ER. A group of staff stood nearby discussing how this tragedy could have been prevented. The debate was alternating between bear bells or pepper spray when the new young doctor with the carefully trimmed beard spoke up. "Bells just help carnivores find you and pepper adds flavor. If you want to stop bear attacks, get real and use a .44 Magnum with 300 grain slugs." Some people took offense, most laughed. Nathan bought him a coffee. He learned Brad was a competitive shooter, too. A rifle shooter, primarily, but that was enough in common for them to develop a friendship.

Nathan doubted any other doctor would have authorized the potent substance in the little vial he'd carried home, and even so Brad had insisted that he be there when Nathan used it. They scheduled a mutually agreeable time at Gunsport Ranges and Brad brought the syringes.

"Where do you come up with these ideas?" he asked, as Nathan loaded magazines. "What sort of a warped brain do you have between those ears of yours?"

"Be careful now. I could take that as an insult."

"It *is* an insult. You are warped, pal. Can I make it any plainer?" Nathan tried to look offended but didn't succeed. "Do you want to do some control runs before we inject you?" asked Brad.

"Sure." Nathan produced a clipboard and timer and held them out for Brad. "We'll run through this scenario we've set up four times—two times left to right and twice right to left. That should give us a good baseline to train against."

"Yeah. If you're still alive by the time we're done."

"Relax, Brad. That's why you're here. You're the best ER doctor I know."

"And I'm the *only* ER doctor you know who would participate in something this crazy."

Nathan ignored him and shot through the stage four times. Then he reloaded, rolled up his left sleeve and presented the bare arm to Brad. "Fill 'er up, Doc."

Brad adjusted his glasses. "Okay. One half cc to start," he said, locating the vein. "This is a low dose. Stay aware of how you're feeling and we'll increase as required until you get a realistic reaction." He pressed the hypodermic's plunger and stepped back.

"Oh yeah!" breathed Nathan. "That's a rush—good drugs, man."

"Adrenaline is not a drug," corrected Brad. "It's a naturally occurring substance in the body, therefore it's not a drug."

"Whatever you say, man," slurred Nathan, in his best glassy-eyed, pot-smoking, bead-wearing, imitation of a stoned hippie. Then he straightened up, held his arms fully outstretched ahead of him and watched his fingertips. They were trembling slightly. "I don't think it's enough. I'll shoot with it but I don't think it's enough."

When he was done they compared times and scores. Brad made him wait thirty minutes before injecting him again. "Double dose this time," he said. "You're going on a trip, my friend."

This time the adrenaline drove through Nathan like a jolt of electricity. He felt the blood leave his extremities. His face went pallid. Breath came in short ragged pants; the shaking in his hands was almost uncontrollable. Brad looked on, a growing look of concern on his face. "We're there. Let's shoot," said Nathan. His voice sounded gravelly.

After four times through Nathan still hadn't dropped his gun. Brad was impressed and told him so.

"It's still with me but going fast. I'm on the edge of learning something so I'd like to shoot without scoring or timing 'til it's all gone. Okay?"

"Sure," replied Brad. "You're good to go now. If anything bad were going to happen to you it would've happened by now. Shoot as long as you want."

"Load magazines for me?" Without saying anything Brad held out his hands and Nathan dumped empty mags into them. He shot them up as fast as Brad could load, and fifteen minutes later when he was done the floor was littered in empty cartridge cases. Beads of sweat stood out on Nathan's forehead.

Brad noticed small curls of smoke rising from the joints and seams of Nathan's holstered .45. "I think you and your gun should cool off for a while," he pointed out.

Nathan looked at his pistol. "You're right, the lube is starting to burn off. Let's take a break. Can I get you something cold to drink?"

"No breaks," said Brad. "We're done. As in finished. You're through. Call it a day."

Nathan hobbled over to where the vial and hypo's lay on a table. "But there's still juice in this bottle," he said, holding it up to the light.

"And it's going to stay that way. You're system can't handle a dose like that again. We can come back next week."

A professional finality in Brad's voice told Nathan not to bother arguing. "Okay. Okay. I give up. But I sure could use something cold to drink. I'll buy, but it's a long ways for me to hobble to that Coke machine on a bum leg."

"You're darn right you're buying," scolded Brad. "And you're also right that you're staying here. Now sit down, relax, breathe deep and rest. Give me money and I'll go get us something wet. And nothing with caffeine for you."

The second can of fruit juice dropped out of the vending machine just as a wild burst of gunfire reached Brad's ears and in that same instant he knew he'd been conned. "Idiot!" he screamed, sprinting back to the range. The empty vial on the floor confirmed Brad's fears, but it was too late to do anything but dial 9-1-1. He pulled his cellphone out and checked signal strength—it looked pretty good for being in a concrete room—then he watched and waited. There was nothing else to be done. He wouldn't dial just yet.

Nathan wrote down a figure from the timer. Brad could see him desperately clutching at the pen, trying to control its movements. Then he shot again and wrote down another. Twice more and he walked over to the trashcan at the back corner of the range and vomited, hanging over the can, retching until the heaving stopped. Wiping his mouth with a sleeve he glanced at Brad and stepped back onto the line. Half an hour later he stopped shooting.

"Sorry about that," Nathan said as he brought the clipboard over to where Brad sat. "Say, you look a lot like my .45. There's smoke coming out of your crevices, too."

"You crazy idiot . . . you . . ."

Nathan cut him off by handing him the clipboard. Brad saw the pages quiver as he held it out in offering. "Work out these raw numbers would you. Just work on the times, the hits are all A's. I'm going to shoot some more. No point in wasting what's left in me."

Brad took the clipboard without replying, and when Nathan finished shooting offered him an orange juice. "That was stupid," he said quietly.

"I had to. I was on the verge of a new skill level. I'd crawled up to it and was peeking over. It was there to be seen but I couldn't drag my body the rest of the way. If I'd waited, even twenty-four hours, I wouldn't have made it. As it is I might still have to do this again to reinforce it."

"Not with me you're not."

"We'll see." Nathan drained half the bottle of juice. "What do the numbers say?"

"The numbers say four percent. You're last series was four percent faster than your control runs."

"Good."

"Good? That's not supposed to be possible, Nathan. Every top shooter I know is ecstatic if they can just manage to get their match day performance up to the same level as their practice scores, mainly because of the adrenaline that creeps into our system when we get nervous or excited. An adrenaline dump like you've simulated here should cut your scores by a third, not improve them. Adrenaline does make you stronger, but at the sacrifice of precision skills, which is what shooting is."

"I know. Most competitors try and stop an adrenaline dump from happening in the first place. And, no doubt, that's the right thing to do most of the time. It's just that sometimes circumstances are such that you can't stop it, and when it comes for me I want it to make me better."

"But this is reckless, Nathan. You don't have to train this hard."

"Yes I do."

"Why?"

Nathan emptied the juice bottle, set it on the table and squatted to the floor where he began picking up brass. "I don't know why, Brad. I just do, that's all."

CHAPTER SEVEN

Training and physiotherapy dominated Nathan's schedule for the next two weeks. Then Danny Forbes called him from Washington, DC and offered him his old job back.

"I guess I'm the first one to come back through the gate," teased Nathan.

"I should have known," conceded Danny. "You're the first one to do a lot of things. How much longer before your leg's ready?"

"Two more weeks should do it. I'm doing lots of range work in the meantime."

"Call me then. I'll have something for you to do."

Then, on an impulse, he called Jerry Mitchell. This time he talked to him. But he still didn't identify himself. Nathan asked him general questions about guarantees of anonymity and the paper's ability to investigate stories outside of their usual circulation area. Jerry's answers were positive and encouraging, but once again he hung up without leaving any information.

Two weeks later, to the day, Nathan called Danny and declared himself fit.

"Now that you're healed you might as well stay in Canada and work," he said.

Nathan perked up. "Sounds good, I think. What do they need me for up here?"

Danny hesitated before answering. "It's not really that they need you. It's just that . . . well . . . this is supposed to be an international project and we can't neglect any of the participants."

"In other words you're going to shuffle me off somewhere quiet where I can't get into trouble for a while."

129

Danny started to say something to the contrary but then gave up on it. "You called it. Kent's report wasn't exactly glowing, but I have to hand it to him, he was diplomatic. I would say he's leaving room for you to come back."

"And he can stuff that idea up his English nose." Nathan pictured Danny wincing.

"That's up to you, but like I said this is an international project and it's time to get you exposure in all the partner countries. It's partly political, I confess. But only to the extent that you're a shared resource and we can't hog you here in the US all the time. No urgent needs for you up North at the moment but it's still important you establish some credibility there for when you're needed."

The rustle of shuffling papers sounded over the telephone line. "This is what's up next, Nathan." A pause. "You're going to Ottawa. Ottawa is central to the Quebec-Ontario population base so it's a good place to drop you for the time being. We'll leave you there for a couple of weeks and you can work with the locals at whatever they happen to be doing. Training or operations, it doesn't really matter. This is just so they get to know you. Then we'll move you south to the Toronto area and maybe up to Montreal for a while too. In the process you'll make the Canadian contacts you need and hopefully get operational experience under your belt that will build your credibility in that jurisdiction. "Looks like you're going to be living out of a suitcase for a while. Sorry."

"What about Kim? Is she coming back too?"

"I haven't seen or heard from her since you went over to Kent's spook-shop and she went back to the Colonel. When I learned you were coming back I called him and he says she'll be available. I suggested he keep her within reach and doing something constructive until you have something happening. From DC she can be in Ottawa very quickly if you need her."

"Sure," said Nathan. "That'll do."

"I'll have Anne make the travel arrangements for you. She'll probably call you tomorrow."

"I'll send you a postcard from Parliament Hill, " said Nathan.

130

A week later, Jerry Mitchell checked his e-mail and found a message from his crime-reporting counterpart at the Ottawa Citizen. Jerry knew virtually all of his counterparts in the major Canadian dailies and had requested they let him know if any of their police contacts made mention of the arrival of a new 'assistant' with highly developed shooting skills. And here he was. Nathan Burdett arrived in Ottawa to work with the Ottawa Police Service two days ago. Jerry hadn't been in Ottawa for two years. This would be a fun trip.

On the open road between the international airport and the city of Ottawa, a stiff February wind sent a veil of snow drifting across the road. Not strong enough to lift it into a rolling blizzard, all the wind managed was a sliding shift along the ground, never lifting the powder more than a foot above the roadway. The softening effect it had on the pavement was smashed by the rental car, charging through the white film like a metal monster.

Kim glanced in her rear-view mirror to watch the swirling patterns left in the wake of the car's turbulence. In seconds the wind recovered its superiority and resumed the shifting veil pattern. "Look behind us. That's neat," she said.

"It's been awhile since you've seen snow, I take it," replied Nathan, closing his new cellphone and terminating the call. His satellite phone had gone back to Jenny, who wouldn't return his guns or clothes until the phone was on her desk.

"Not since we moved from Chicago to Israel. I guess that qualifies as *awhile*. It's been *awhile* since I saw you too."

"You were twelve, right? I mean when you left Chicago, not when you last saw me."

"Very good."

"You know, I really think I should be driving. You're not very experienced in winter driving."

Kim rolled her eyes. "Don't be silly. Besides, what am I doing wrong? This blowing snow isn't causing me any problems. My traction seems just fine and there's no visibility problem."

"Okay," conceded Nathan. "But both of those things can change in a second. Be careful."

131

"Worry wart," teased Kim. "What did your phone call tell you?"

"That was Barnes from their Domestic Abuse Unit. Nothing in addition to what I told you on the phone last night. At least nothing he's willing to give me over a cellphone. We'll get the rest when we get there."

"What's Barnes like?"

"I don't really know. I just met him briefly when he came up to the Firearms Training Unit yesterday looking for me. I understand they just started this Domestic Abuse Unit in Ottawa and he's in charge of it. Been around long enough to make Sergeant and he seems capable and enthusiastic in what he does."

Kim muttered something Nathan didn't catch.

"I've only been here a few days and was just getting to know the guys in the Firearms Unit when this thing started cooking and I called you."

"It still looks like it's going to happen?" asked Kim.

"No doubt." Nathan unfolded a map to check exits and streets. "It's supposed to be a simple arrest, but because the abused wife says her husband is armed to the teeth with all sorts of illegal firepower they're being real careful." Nathan tracked their route on the map and when he looked up again saw their sign coming up. "Turn off there," he said, pointing to an exit ramp on their left.

While Kim and Nathan drove in from the airport, Jenny brought Mr. Kent the morning mail and tea. Before she left, he asked her to have Leith come in to see him. Once he'd arrived, Kent wordlessly slid a phone record across the desk for his inspection.

"Ahhh, I see you're keeping tabs on Nathan's phone calls." Kent merely sipped his tea. Leith's finger pointed at two highlighted calls. "The Calgary Tribune? Sounds like a newspaper." Kent nodded in response. "What's he doing calling a newspaper?"

"The number is that of one Jerry Mitchell, senior crime reporter and now on special assignment at the Tribune. I phoned the helpful young lady at the switchboard and asked," he said.

"What special assignment?"

132

"That, she wouldn't say."

Leith slid the phone record back onto Kent's desk. It remained there untouched—the only paper out of place. "Do we need to do anything about this?" He already knew the answer or he wouldn't have been called into this office.

"Jerry Mitchell just caught a flight to Ottawa. As the call record shows, Burdett's in Ottawa, still working the domestic end of The B-Zone Project. Remember the last phone conversation I had with Nathan, the one in which I released him?"

Leith nodded. "You told me about it."

"There were sounds in the background that bothered me, so I ran the tape of that conversation past some technical friends." Leith nodded again, trying hard not to smile. "They picked up something interesting, the distinctive sounds of a tape machine being turned on. Mr. Burdett was recording our conversation." Leith couldn't help himself, he smiled broadly. "It appears, Leith, that we may have to terminate our involvement in this B-Zone project. I need you to go to Ottawa and make some inquiries. If it becomes necessary we may have to shut down the project and Mr. Burdett with it."

"What about Kim?"

Kent gave a dismissive wave of his hand. "People like Miss Corel are always available, Leith. But it's still too early to know what to do. These are disturbing developments, Leith, and I need you to determine if there are any serious breaches of security here." He sighed deeply and shook his head. "It's rare talents like Mr. Burdett that are hard to come by. *That* is the real shame. Remember, information is all I need so far. Do what you can and let me know when you're done. There's a good chap."

"My pleasure, sir. I've always enjoyed my times in Ottawa." Leith left the office whistling *Danny Boy*.

On an Ottawa stretch of the Queensway, Kim eased her car one lane to the left and took the exit, still slicing through the drifting snow. But the new route turned into the wind, and snow no longer sifted across the black pavement.

133

She made two more turns at Nathan's direction, skirting the bulk of the city and eventually entering an area of large country-sized lots and upscale houses. The trees were plentiful and even though they were bare and swaying in the cold wind it was difficult to see more than a couple of houses in any direction. The property owners had all used trees, shrubs and hedges to establish the kind of privacy large lots were capable of affording. Long driveways were the rule and houses were set far back from the street. Vehicle traffic was light and pedestrians non-existent.

Here, among the houses, snow no longer drifted and the only indication of wind was the rhythmic dance of naked branches. A pale blue Chevy Lumina, with one man in it, idled at the curb. Nathan waved to him and instructed Kim to pull into a driveway where an iron sign indicated the house number as *1092* and the occupants as *The Romanski Family*.

"Apparently Romanski is on the city's police commission, and with the target house only three doors down they convinced her she should do her civic duty and let them use the place as a command post," explained Nathan.

"Not so bad," suggested Kim. "From what I've seen, civilian police boards should get a little more first-hand experience in policing."

"So I've heard," nodded Nathan. "So I've heard."

Kim stopped the car beside several other police units. She was sure they were all parked on the family lawn—a foot of snow on the ground made it hard to tell—but no one seemed to mind, so she did the same. When she left the warmth of their vehicle the wind bit at her exposed cheeks and ears. The cold hurt her throat when she inhaled, and she was about to comment on it when Nathan walked around to her side of the vehicle.

"The house we want should be on the same side of the street, three doors down," he said, pointing to the west. "It's a white bungalow with gray trim and gray brick, a two car attached garage and an old-fashioned decorative lamp post out front that the house number hangs on." From where they stood no part of that house was visible. The trees and hedges around the Romanski house even made it difficult to see the street. The flickering shape of a car driving by was barely recognizable for what it was.

Kim noticed he wore no gloves and his jacket wasn't zipped up. Nathan looked east and then west, deep in thought. Kim turned up the collar of her wool coat against the wind and tried to fasten the top button, but with gloves on she couldn't do it. Nathan saw her frustration.

"Let me," he said, doing up the stubborn button. "When you have time, see if you can pick up a scarf. Nothing keeps you as warm as a good scarf."

"Not even a good man?" teased Kim.

"Nope. A Canadian man, even a good one, would be out ice fishing on a day like this."

"Yeah, right." Kim wasn't buying that one.

"You think I'm kidding?" he asked, raising his eyebrows.

"Ice fishing? Oh please! How gullible do you think I am? You're trying to tell me, you Canadians would be out fishing through ice on a day like this?" She thrust her gloved hands into her pockets and walked off towards the house.

Nathan followed, and was about to say something when two uniformed officers came out of the house, heading for their idling patrol car. Kim noticed they were dressed like Nathan—no hat, no gloves and open jackets. The two officers walked by Kim and Nathan giving them a perfunctory nod.

"Hello," said Kim, being polite.

Nathan, who was going to greet them the same way, noticed one of them wearing a lapel pin in the shape of fishing fly. "How's the fishing been?" he asked, instead.

They slowed. "Pretty good," answered the older of the two, sensing a fellow sportsman. "I caught an eight pound pike yesterday."

"What's working?" asked Nathan.

"For me, minnows on a tandem-hook quick-strike rig," came the reply.

"Thanks. I'll have to try that." Kim had stopped and turned around at the exchange. When the officers moved on, Nathan turned to her with a smirk. "The look on your face is better than catching an eight pound pike any day."

Kim snorted and with a disbelieving shake of her head took a more determined stride into the warm house.

Inside, the scene was familiar to both. The living room and attached dining room were becoming a small operations center and the Ottawa Police Tactical Unit was setting up in the large family room. The kitchen seemed to have been designated a common area with no official purpose other than a place to drink coffee.

Nathan, seeing someone he recognized, left Kim in the hallway. He spoke briefly to a man with a ruddy complexion and bushy mustache before bringing him over to meet Kim.

"Kim, this is Rick Lambert. He's the Tactical Unit leader here today."

They greeted each other and Lambert cut the small talk short. "If you two have any gear to bring in, do so. We still don't know exactly how we're going to do this. Once we have a formal plan I'll let you know. And don't worry, Nathan," he said moving away, "If there's a place for your talents we'll fit you in."

"Sounds like you've seen him shoot," commented Kim, causing Lambert to smile and stay a moment longer.

"Most of the guys on the Unit came up to the range two days ago while I was there working with Firearms Training," explained Nathan. "One thing led to another and before I knew it there was a shooting competition under way."

Kim groaned. Still speaking to Lambert, she pointed at Nathan. "He kick butt and take names, as usual?"

"Pretty much," agreed Lambert.

"How bad was it?" asked Kim.

"It was bad," he conceded. "We like to use bowling pins as reactive targets and so we took turns shooting them down against a timer. Nathan was far faster at it than any of us. But time is just numbers on digital display. We really didn't grasp how much faster until he made us set up two tables with five pins on each and put our best shooter against him. When he shot down all five of his and then all five of our man's before he even got his first shot off, then we understood."

"I know what you mean," said Kim.

"Anyway, it was nice to meet you, Kim." He addressed Nathan, "Give me ten or fifteen minutes to get some of my men moving and then I'll brief you on what we've got."

"They're no different than all the teams I've seen so far," volunteered Nathan, once Lambert was out of earshot. "Good guys, but not gun people." He looked pointedly at Kim.

"Yeah, I understand what you mean by that now," she said. "A year ago I wouldn't have. But now I do."

"I suppose it . . . ."

Nathan was interrupted by Barnes, standing in the doorway between the dining room and the kitchen. Instead of a uniform, he wore shirt and tie with a camel colored leather jacket he hadn't yet bothered to remove. The Domestic Abuse Unit Sergeant closed a cellphone and called out loudly, loud enough for everyone on the main floor of the house to hear him. "Attention people!" he paused. "Listen up." Another pause. Then, satisfied the room was quiet enough for everyone to hear him, continued, "I have just been informed the Chief is on his way here." The subdued groan from his audience seemed to be expected. Barnes carried on. "And that's not all." He paused again, this time apparently for effect. "The Mayor is coming with him." The next groan was not subdued and a number of curses were heard in the background. He carried on, ignoring the reaction. "So let's look sharp. The media won't be far behind. We want to look good here today. No screw-ups allowed. We're going to grab this gunny with good police work and grab some good press while we're at it. Let's do it!" he concluded loudly, sounding like a coach at a high school football game.

Kim looked at Nathan, a puzzled expression on her face. "Gunny?"

"Gunny," he nodded. "And it's news to me. I haven't heard that term for a while, but it usually means someone like me. A hunter, competitive shooter or a collector."

"I see. What's he done, gone psycho?"

137

"Sure. That might be it. Gone psycho." He walked off toward the Tactical Unit's preparation area. "Let's find out what we can about him."

They made it as far as the kitchen where a small sheaf of papers on the table caught Nathan's attention. He took one copy for himself and passed another to Kim.

"Bill Welter," she read aloud. "Offenses to be arrested for: Assault, Pointing a Firearm, Threats."

Nathan picked up the reading. "Also believed to be in possession of illegal full-automatic firearms."

"The rest is just vehicles owned by the subject, address and phone numbers," commented Kim. "This isn't very useful." Then ensuring only Nathan could hear her, "This is a planned arrest, Nathan, with time to organize and gather intelligence. It's not a developing situation and this," she gave the sheet of paper back to Nathan, "this drivel is the best information they can provide us?"

"I'm sure Lambert has more," suggested Nathan.

They killed time in the kitchen for another ten minutes until Lambert stuck his head in the doorway and motioned for the two to follow him. He led the way to a quiet corner of the living room and the three formed a tight knot against the wall as Lambert briefed them. "I see you have Barnes' little fact sheet," he said, pointing at the piece of paper still in Nathan's hand. "For what it's worth," he added. "It's not very complete but I think I can fill in the blanks for you.

"It seems this Welter character and his wife are having problems. He's been smacking her around for years and a few days ago he escalated to threatening her with a gun. She did the usual, ran off to a friend's house and the next day her friend convinced her to come in and see our shiny new Domestic Abuse Unit. That's where Barnes came into the case; when she told him her hubby owns lots and lots of guns, Barnes got authority for us to make the arrest."

"Sounds reasonable," commented Nathan.

"What's the plan to get him?" asked Kim.

"We've already had the house phone cut off and his cellphone disabled. Other than that, we're in a hold pattern until the Chief and Mayor get here. Once they're here, the uniforms seal off the streets and alleys. They also quietly evacuate the two neighboring houses and the one across the street. When that's done, some of my people move in and form a tight perimeter around the place and we send in an arrest team as soon as we can."

"Hard entry?" asked Nathan.

"Rock hard. Battering ram to the door, stun grenades, the works. With the guy owning as many guns as he does we can't take any chances."

"What kind of guns are we talking," questioned Nathan. Through the window overlooking the yard he saw a Limited Edition Jeep Cherokee pull up the driveway.

"Lots of rifles, shotguns and handguns. Barnes says the wife doesn't really know one from another. She claims some of them shoot really fast so he might have some full-auto stuff."

"If he's legal, his handguns should be registered," suggested Nathan. "What does your computer say he's got."

"I'll get the list for you," said Lambert. "There's about ten of them on it but it doesn't mean much to me. Wait here."

With Lambert gone, Nathan watched two men get out of the Cherokee and come in the front door. This would be the Chief and the Mayor. The Chief was in uniform, a gray-haired, overweight, older cop. He'd look like a chief even out of uniform, thought Nathan. The other man was half his age and dressed in an expensive overcoat. Exposed pant legs showed a gray pinstripe suit under the coat. The Chief had opened the door and was waving over Barnes who noticed them as soon as the cold blast from the opening door alerted him to their presence.

The Chief did the introductions. "Sergeant Barnes is the head of our new Domestic Abuse Unit, Mr. Mayor. He's the one who has put this investigation together."

"We've spoken on the phone," said the mayor, surprising the chief. "A pleasure to meet you in person, Sergeant." They shook hands. "Thank you again for all your hard work in getting your unit underway. You know how important it is to my administration to see that the women of this city are not victimized by abusive husbands. You're doing important work."

139

"Thank you, sir," enthused Barnes. "May I take your coat, Mr. Mayor?"

The mayor shrugged out of his overcoat with Barnes' assistance and the Sergeant hung it in the closet while the mayor continued, "Where can we have the press conference, Sergeant? My media coordinator will bring them over just as soon as you give the all clear. After all I don't want them, or myself for that matter, interfering with what you're doing."

"Nonsense, Mr. Mayor, you're never in the way of this police department," said the Chief, "and we'll accommodate the media in any way we can, as well."

"How about over here by the living room window," suggested Barnes, pointing to where Nathan and Kim stood watching. "As a matter of fact, why don't you come sit down and we'll get you a coffee."

The mayor crossed the floor, took the half step into the sunken living room and sat on the sofa. Barnes pointed at Kim. "You . . . Miss . . . would you get the Mayor a coffee from the kitchen please."

Kim didn't move. Her lack of movement was becoming awkward when the Chief spoke up. "Don't bother Miss, I'll get it. I need one for myself anyway." He scurried off in the direction of the kitchen as the mayor sat down. Kim and Nathan slowly moved off to the other side of the room.

"Your Chief tells me that this wife beater is also one of those gun nuts," said the mayor.

"He sure is," said Barnes. "That's why all the extra precautions. We can't be too careful considering the firepower this man has at his disposal."

"Well, I'm sure your men can give him some of his own back when it comes to firepower. Hopefully, of course, it won't come to that. Isn't it sad, though, that the potential for this kind of violence even exists in our city?" Barnes nodded. "Perhaps someday we'll be able to do more about it. But for now your new unit is our focus. My administration, Sergeant, is determined to create a city that's safe for everyone. There's no place for barbarians like this man here.

"Is there any chance," the mayor added, glancing at his watch, "that we can have this wrapped up in time so I can do my news conference before five? That way the stations could get it on the six o'clock news."

"Guaranteed," replied Barnes. "I'll personally make sure it's wrapped up by five."

Lambert returned with a printout of the handguns registered to Welter, and handed it to Nathan.

"Sergeant Lambert," Barnes called across the room, "No problem getting this wrapped up by five o'clock, eh? If we could do that it would fit nicely into the mayor's schedule."

Lambert looked at Barnes, checked his watch and began doing some mental calculations.

"No problem at all, Sergeant," said the Chief coming back with two coffee cups complete with saucers. Everyone else was using paper cups, Nathan noted, but the Chief had apparently rooted around the kitchen until he found the china. "Right Lambert? I would think you can have this done well before that. Say, by four o'clock," he added pointedly. He sat down beside the mayor and Barnes did too.

"Sure, by four o'clock. No problem," Lambert agreed, unenthusiastically.

Kim looked out the window and rolled her eyes.

Nathan's eyes rolled too but he had his head down reading the handgun list and didn't have to make any effort to look away.

Lambert turned his back on Barnes' entourage, quietly addressing Nathan. "What do you see there? Anything significant? Half of that stuff I have no idea what it is. The Smith & Wesson .357 and the .44 I know, but that's about it."

"There's seven handguns here," said Nathan, scanning the list. "The Walther GSP and Pardini PGP are Olympic grade bullseye match guns. With a price tag to match. The Caspian and Para-Ordnance are both 1911-style guns, similar to what I use. But the caliber on the Caspian tells me it's likely an Open Class match gun. Probably all tricked out with compensator and optic sights. He's got a CZ in .25 Auto too but that's not indicative of anything."

"What is that caliber on the Caspian," asked Lambert? "I've never heard of it before. It's nine something—that's not a nine millimeter is it?"

"It's 9X23." Nathan pointed to the designation on the sheet of paper. "Actually it *is* a nine millimeter. Same bore diameter as the nine-millimeter Luger you're thinking of, but the case is longer and stronger and it shoots a whole lot faster. It's an obscure caliber to be sure, but has features that some people like for IPSC competition."

Lambert's mind worked through this new information. "Fast enough to penetrate our soft body armor?"

Nathan considered his comment. "Sure. With the lightweight roundnose bullet that is the usual competition load and cranked up to a velocity that will make the compensator do its job, I suspect it would whistle right through your standard vests."

Barnes exploded out of his chair and took the three paces to where Nathan's group stood. "What! This nut case has a gun that will blow right through our vests?"

Nathan realized he'd badly underestimated Barnes' eavesdropping capabilities. When he thought back on it later it occurred to him that this was, no doubt, a highly refined skill of office politics. "Look," he said to Barnes, massaging his forehead before he spoke. "Sure, it will probably penetrate one of your standard patrol vests, but so will lots of other guns. Certainly any centerfire rifle he owns . . ."

Nathan was too logical and too late. Barnes turned on his heel and strode to the dining room table where the radio operator worked. He snatched the mike from her hand and in a voice loud enough to be heard in that entire wing of the house made his broadcast, "All units on tac four. Be advised that it's just been confirmed the suspect has access to firearms capable of penetrating our body armor. Take appropriate precautions and no chances." He repeated the message again, just in case, speculated Nathan, the chief and the mayor hadn't heard him the first time.

Nathan had enough. He brushed Lambert aside and homed in on Barnes. He'd made it two steps when Lambert appeared on his right side and gripped that elbow. Kim grabbed his left. His forward momentum and an extra-added push hustled him around Barnes, through the kitchen and into the crowded Tactical Unit ready room.

"Whatever you're planning on saying to him," Kim whispered as they passed through the kitchen, "it's not what's needed right now."

"I can't believe you two!" Nathan struggled to keep his voice down. He shook off their grasp and faced them. "Barnes and those two stuffed shirts are using this to promote their own agendas." He stabbed a finger in the direction of the living room. "They're distorting the truth and don't care about the consequences as long as it doesn't interfere with their careers or the six o'clock news."

"Leave it alone, Nathan," warned Kim. "In that room are two politicians and a Sergeant who wants to be one. They're just feeding off each other at the moment, that's all."

"They're harmless," chimed in Lambert. "It's how it always works. The street cops and the men on my team all know that. We're professionals and watch out for each other. We always build a safety factor into our planning to allow for the rotten information and orders that come from goofs like them. None of us will get hurt."

Nathan stood quietly. "You don't get it do you? You really don't get it. No, *you* won't get hurt. After all, you're smart professionals with good equipment and techniques. But what about your suspect? What about Welter? Is he going to get hurt? If he did everything his soon to be ex-wife claims, maybe he deserves to get hurt. But what if he didn't?" He pointed at Lambert. "What if she's using *you* to implement her personal vendetta?"

"Oh come on, Nathan, you're just speculating," countered Kim.

"No more than you are!"

Another Tactical Unit member appeared beside Lambert, interrupting them. "We got the word," he said. "The uniforms are blocking off the roads, time for us to go into position around the house."

Lambert acknowledged, "You two can stay here and argue," he said. "I have work to do." Before leaving he tapped Nathan's shoulder with an index finger. "You stay away from the three stooges back there. We have orders and we'll follow them. You're a cop, you should understand orders."

"Maybe that's why I see things a little differently," countered Nathan loudly. "I'm really not a cop. All I am is a sportsman who got sucked into this world and sometimes I'm not sure I want to be here." He turned and stormed out the side door of the house.

Kim found him standing in the front yard, watching a uniformed officer block the street with a car, yellow tape and his stoic presence. She noticed the men who previously wore no gloves or caps now added those items to their uniform. "You okay?" she asked Nathan.

Nathan detected something that sounded like genuine concern in her voice. He looked at her. "Sure. Personally, I'm okay. I just got a little hot, that's all. Coming out here cools a person off in a hurry." Nathan looked back to where the uniforms were working the street. "Professionally, I'm not okay, Kim. I don't like this." A couple of residents had seen the activity and come out of their homes to ask what was going on. Not long now before a crowd gathers, thought Nathan. Neighbors discussing and speculating amongst themselves about what was happening on their street.

"It's not perfect, Nathan. We both know that. Even Lambert knows that. I think we'd all do it differently if we could, but we're not in charge. We have to follow the command structure, even when we don't like the decisions."

"You sound like a Scotsman I know."

Kim's mouth tightened to a thin line. "What do you mean?" she asked.

Nathan didn't answer. He watched the people at the barricade for another minute. "Can I have the car keys please?" he held out his hand. Kim extracted the keys from her pocket and dropped them hesitatingly into his open palm.

"What are you going to do?" she asked.

Nathan laughed lightly. His laugh sounded forced to Kim. "Don't worry," he replied. "I'm just going to make a phone call or two, that's all." Then he strode rapidly to their parked car. Kim saw him start the engine, pull out a notebook and a cellphone and start dialing. She waited until it appeared he had connected with someone and then

144

walked in the direction of the car, doing her best to look casual, bored and a little cold. She reached for the door handle on the passenger side.

Nathan waited until Kim's hand touched the handle, then he triggered the electric door locks and smiled tauntingly as she slapped the window. Not content to leave it at that, she scooped up a handful of snow and threw it against the glass.

"Sorry Trent," Nathan said into his phone. "What did you say?"

"I said, I haven't heard from you for over a year. I've heard *about* you but not *from* you."

"Yeah, well, I've been kind of busy," replied Nathan.

"That's exactly what I've heard. There's a new rumor about you every week."

"Are they good or bad?"

"About half and half."

"Which ones do you believe?"

"Only the good ones. I know you. Remember?" Nathan didn't answer right away. "You still there?"

"I'm still here. Listen, I'm sorry I haven't been in touch. There's a lot of people I should stay in touch with, but things have changed, my life has changed . . ."

"You're friends haven't changed, Nathan." Again Nathan didn't reply. "I'm guessing you need something. Am I right?"

"Right as always."

"What do you need? Money, ammo, guns, men with guns?" Trent laughed. "Name it, I'll do what I can."

Nathan smiled. "Nothing that dramatic, Trent. All I need is information. Are you still Section Coordinator for IPSC Ontario?"

The voice on the other end of the line chuckled, "That's me. Still wearing the heavy mantle of leadership in the shooting sports."

"Do you know a Bill Welter?"

"Sure do. He was shooting with us until about two years ago when he had a bad accident. Got T-boned by a drunk driver downtown. Messed him up bad enough that he couldn't be competitive in IPSC any more. Then he took up bullseye shooting. I haven't seen him for about a year. Why?"

145

"This is where it gets awkward, Trent. I can't tell you. Will you trust me enough to answer my questions without asking any of your own?"

He heard no discernible pause. "No questions it is. Go ahead."

Nathan spent a hurried five minutes asking every question he could think of that might help him get a handle on Bill Welter. Trent gave him a verbal picture of a thirty-something, middle-class man with a passion for guns and the shooting sports. After asking about, job, family, character and personality Nathan had answers that filled the empty slots he'd created in his mind.

"Thanks, Trent," he said. "I kind of thought that might be the case. In a way I was hoping I was wrong." A puzzled silence followed. "I'd appreciate it if you didn't mention this conversation to anyone for the time being."

"Whatever you say."

When he stepped out of the warm car Kim was still standing near the front bumper. She was doing little bouncing movements on her toes to keep warm, her collar buttoned securely against the cold and her stare as icy as the temperature. "And just what is it you're doing?" she asked as Nathan pocketed the phone.

"Research," he mumbled turning away from her. Then he walked down the long drive to where it penetrated the massive hedge that separated the front yard from the street. He stopped at the sidewalk to look at the small crowd behind the yellow barricade tape. Kim caught up with him there. "What are you doing?" she asked again. A demanding note of urgency crept into her voice. Urgency mixed with foreboding.

"Get lost, Kim. Go back in the house." His voice sounded as biting as the wind. Nathan didn't look at her but strode purposefully towards the crowd.

She hurried after him, catching his elbow. But he jerked it violently out of her grasp and spun around, clutched her by the shoulders and pushed his face to within a foot of hers. "Back off!" he growled. His hot breath, visible in the cold air, cascaded across her face. "Back off and leave me alone."

146

On the exterior Kim remained silent but inwardly she uttered a mental gasp. The abrupt pounce, the iron grip on the shoulders and the anger in Nathan's face were things she had never seen directed at her. Nathan let go, but not before giving her a subtle push away from him. A final 'beat it'. He wheeled and walked the rest of the way to the yellow barricade tape. Kim saw him talk briefly to the uniformed officer sitting in the idling patrol car and then he walked over to where a small group of people stood huddled together on the other side of the tape. She shuffled in that direction as well, keeping her distance while trying again to look casual and disinterested, more for the benefit of the crowd than anyone else.

Nathan moved to where two twenty-something young women stood on the other side of the yellow tape. Kim saw the three of them cluster into a tight circle, talking animatedly, the words indistinguishable. Both girls were tall, fair skinned and prettier than they had any right to be. Their cheeks and noses showed a red glow brought on by the cold wind. Wisps of hair peeked out from under scarves they had wrapped over their heads and around their throats. The one with the blue scarf was a blonde. The one with the green scarf was a redhead like her. Even wrapped up against the cold it was a dead giveaway they were sisters. Something in the center of the group was the focus of conversation but Kim couldn't see what it was. She edged closer, still trying to look casual. "What's his name?" she heard Nathan ask.

"Max," replied the redhead.

Kim moved so she was almost at Nathan's side and saw a black furry head peeking out from the under the blonde's open coat. "He's a cockapoo," she volunteered, "a cross between a cocker spaniel and a poodle."

"Is he friendly?" asked Nathan, slowly extending his hand toward the black face.

"Just move slowly at first," she cautioned. "Then, once he gets to know you, he'll be your friend for life."

A nose as black as the face twitched at Nathan's fingertips. Within ten seconds the signal that the needed information had been collected came, as a long pink tongue darted out and licked Nathan's hand. He tussled the dog's ears and rubbed under his chin for a minute until the dog began to feel comfortable with him. "See. He likes you," said the redhead.

"Listen, ladies. I need a big favor," said Nathan. "I would really like to borrow Max for a little while. We have a situation going on here that he could help me with. I just need him for about ten or fifteen minutes. Do you suppose he would go for a walk with me?"

"Would he be doing real police work?" questioned one.

"You wouldn't let him get hurt, would you?" said the other.

Nathan chuckled reassuringly, "I assure you it's real police business and I guarantee you he'll be in no danger. He'll be beside me all the time. What do you say? Just for ten minutes."

The redhead nudged her blonde sister. "Go ahead," she said, "This will be the only chance Max will ever get to do police work. He's way too short for the K-9 Unit."

Everyone laughed as the squirming black dog was handed over to Nathan. Once he held him securely, the blonde pulled a retracting leash from her coat pocket and snapped it onto the collar. Nathan set him down and he immediately ran to the nearby police car and peed on the tire.

Both girls gasped, then broke into uncontrollable giggles.

"I think he had to go," said Nathan. After a few more words of reassurance to the owners he walked off, but not before throwing an icy stare at Kim. She watched to see where he went and in so doing faced into the wind. It bit into her exposed face making her cheeks tingle. The stare had been colder, thought Kim. She hiked up her collar as far as it would go and tried to shrink her neck, pulling her head down into the coat. A small tug on the back of her coat made her turn around.

The blonde pointed at the scarf wrapped around her own head. "You should get a scarf," she said, pointing at her own. "Nothing keeps the chill out better than one of these."

Her sister nodded. "Better than a man on a cold winter day," she said in agreement. "Especially an ice-fishing Ottawa man."

"Okay," Kim replied, throwing up her hands in frustration. She shrieked, "I give up! I'll get a scarf!" She didn't care if everyone in the small crowd heard her. "Would that make you all happy?" she yelled.

"If I got a stupid scarf, would everyone in this entire God-forsaken frozen country become deliriously happy if I got a scarf?"

The sisters shrank away from the apparently psychotic policewoman and Kim pivoted back into the wind. Seeing where Nathan and the dog were going, she stomped to the police car, flung open the door and plopped into the front passenger seat. Snatching the microphone from its cradle on the dash she addressed the surprised officer in the driver's seat as she pointed at the radio.

"Is this thing on tac four?"

He nodded. "The team just hit waypoint though. If you transmit it better be important."

Kim keyed the transmit button. "Lambert, it's Kim. Are you on the air?"

"Yes, go ahead." He sounded annoyed

"Nathan will be walking a dog down the street, past the target's house within a minute."

There was a long pause. Kim could imagine his mind working on that.

"Why?" he asked eventually.

"I have no idea."

"Tango 1—Sierra 2," said a voice over the radio. The codes told Kim it was one of Lambert's men, probably concealed in the winter vegetation somewhere in the neighborhood. "I can confirm that. I see him walking south on the opposite side of the street. So far it looks like he's going by. And he's got a black furry dog, about a foot high at the shoulder, running in front of him at the end of a leash."

"Everyone hold where you are until I get a handle on what's going on here," said Lambert. "Sierra 2, keep me posted on what he does."

"10-4."

Kim twisted in her seat to see Nathan still walking along the sidewalk. When he reached the area across from the suspect's house she could see him turn his head, studying intently what he saw on the other side of the street.

Half a minute later the voice of Sierra 2 came over the radio. "He walked right by, Tango 1. Looked at the house and walked right by."

"10-4," said Lambert. "I don't know what he was doing but when he gets to the barricade at the other end and is out of the way, let me know. Alpha Team, are you okay to maintain ready?"

Three distinct microphone clicks were his answer. Kim interpreted it to mean they were too close to the target to risk speaking.

"Standby for green."

Kim watched Nathan carry on south along the sidewalk. The black dog stood out starkly against the white snow, darting back and forth in a constant flurry of motion. She saw Nathan's right arm stretch out fully as the dog strained at his leash, relentlessly pulling Nathan. At least someone is enjoying this, she thought.

She continued watching until Nathan was almost to the barricade at the other end of the street. The dog was difficult to pick out and she was wishing for a pair of binoculars when she abruptly realized he could be seen clearly again, this time in profile. Nathan was crossing the street.

Sierra 2 confirmed it. "He's crossing the street Tango," said the unseen voice.

"Tell me what he does."

A pause.

"He's coming back Tango—north on the sidewalk—our side of the street."

"10-4. Condition is still Standby."

The dog became more visible to Kim as they drew closer to where she sat. The pair had walked about fifty yards when the dog's constant movement stopped. She saw him looking intently at a grove of mature spruce trees bordering the sidewalk. Kim watched Nathan catch up to where the dog stood frozen, studying the trees. Nathan faced straight ahead, pulled sharply at the leash and the dog carried on. She saw the black furry head look back twice before resuming its usual back and forth, leash-straining pattern.

The bodiless voice of Sierra 2 crackled over the radio. "They just walked by me Tango. I think the dog made me but Nathan didn't—still headed north—almost to the target house."

"Just walk on by," whispered Kim.

"Pardon me?" said the officer in the car with her.

"Walk on by," Kim repeated, watching the procession of two approach the drive leading to the suspect's house. "If he knows what's good for him, he'll walk on by."

Nathan changed direction ninety degrees at the driveway and strode up it toward the target house.

"Jerk!" yelled Kim, punching the dash so hard the glove compartment popped open.

"Tango 1—Sierra 2, he's walking up to the house. Still on the drive—headed for the house—walking up the ramp to the front door—he's at the door—still got the dog—he's reeled him in some though."

Nathan rang the doorbell and waited. Max sniffed around the door at his feet and eventually settled on the doormat. The little guy's feet must be getting cold, Nathan thought, I wouldn't want to walk barefoot on concrete in this weather. He was thinking of ringing the doorbell again when Max perked up, looking intently at the door. A moment later a noise within Nathan's hearing capabilities reached his ears. It sounded like the snick a deadbolt makes when thrown.

"Alpha Team—Tango 1, are you ready?"

Three clicks.

"Standby Alpha. Sierra 2, do you still have a clear shot at the front door?"

"10-4, clear and braced. I can count the fleas on the dog."

"I transfer green light authority to you. A shot from you or anyone else is, by default, a go for Alpha. Otherwise it's your call. I'm out."

"10-4."

The front door opened a crack and if Nathan hadn't been expecting it, he might have misinterpreted the shuffling movement

151

behind it. He took the slack out of Max's leash and as the door swung fully open looked down at the face that appeared. Nathan knew the man was in his thirties but his face looked older—add another ten years. He wondered what he'd look like in similar circumstances. "Bill Welter, I presume," said Nathan.

"Right the first time," replied the man. A puzzled look spread across his face, the sort of look that greets strangers at the door.

Nathan let Max have a little more leash, allowing him to move forward and sniff the new feet that appeared at his level. "I'm Nathan Burdett and this is Max. We've been out for a little walk in the neighborhood." Max stretched upwards, putting his front paws on the new knees, craning his head up, inviting to be petted.

"Max, I already know," said Bill. "He lives half a dozen houses down the street. But what can I do for you, Nathan Burdett?" Bill reached forward and tousled the dog's ears. He thought about asking what this guy was selling, but he'd never seen a door-to-door salesman, or even a missionary, with a dog.

"Subject has opened the front door," transmitted Sierra 2. "I have a clear shot if necessary. Everything looks friendly so far."

"Any idea what Burdett is doing?" asked Lambert.

"None whatever."

"10-4."

"Did you know subject's in a wheelchair?"

"What did you say?"

"Our subject, Welter. He's in a wheelchair. Did I fall asleep during that part of the briefing?"

"You sure it's him?" asked Lambert.

"It's him or we got the wrong photo too," replied Sierra 2.

Lambert swore. "Acknowledged." There was a lengthy pause. "No changes to the plan," he commanded. "No changes at all. You don't need legs to operate a gun."

"I think we have some friends in common," said Nathan. "Trent Heyden, specifically."

"I know Trent. Where do you know that old bullet-hole from?"

152

"Same as you. I'm a shooter."

The usual front door caution evaporated. Bill extended his hand. Nathan shook it. "Nice to meet you, Nathan. Would you like to come in? It's cold out there." Bill started rolling backwards.

"No!' said Nathan urgently. "Stay where you are. Keep the door open and don't back up."

Bill stopped moving. His eyes narrowed suspiciously.

Nathan took a deep breath and gave Max a little more leash. "There's an Ottawa Police Tactical Team surrounding your house, Bill. They're getting ready to do a hard entry. That means stun grenades, battering rams, everything that hurts. I suspect there's a sniper somewhere behind me who has his crosshairs on your forehead right now."

Bill's face went from suspicion to shock and back to suspicion. His hand slid to the edge of the open door and he started to roll slowly backwards again.

"Something's spooking our man," said Sierra 2. "Standby to go, Alpha . . ."

"Bill, you have to stay where they can see you!" The urgency in Nathan's voice escalated. Max picked up on the tension in the air and began to whine. Bill stopped but he didn't say anything. Nathan spoke rapidly, almost frantic. "Your wife is leaving you. She called the cops and reported you threatened her with a gun. I have no idea if that's true or not, but they're here to arrest you and because you're a gun owner you get the full treatment. You have to believe me, Bill. Give them half an excuse and they'll blow through your house like a black storm." Nathan stopped to take a breath.

Welter was starting to recover. "O-kay," he said, dragging out the word. "And just how is it you know all this? Are you a cop too?"

"I'm maybe half a cop, Bill." Nathan unzipped his coat and pulled it open just far enough for Bill to see the holstered pistol he wore on his right side. "I have a gun but no badge. It's too long a story to tell here but you have to trust me and come outside with me. Right now."

Bill didn't move.

"Government records show you own seven handguns, two Smiths, a Pardini, a Walther, a Caspian and a Para. You own a CZ .25 Auto too. There's a mistake on its registration though. It's listed as a revolver, not a semi-auto. Am I right?"

"Very good," said Bill. He removed his hand from the door and studied Nathan intently for what seemed a long time. "The wife left about a month ago. It's been nasty but I've sure never pointed a gun at her. She said that, eh?" He shook his head and looked down at his hands. "It's worse than I thought."

"Bill, we have to go outside. They'll be getting frantic by now. I'm not supposed to be doing this."

Welter looked up. "What do you mean, 'not supposed to be doing this'? And what does 'half a cop' mean anyway?"

Nathan glanced over his shoulder. "I don't have time to explain that, but you have to trust me, Bill. You have to come outside with me. Now!"

Bill seemed to think about that for a moment, then slapped his thighs. "Up Max." The bundle of black fur jumped and Bill grabbed him. "I don't suppose it would be a good idea to go get a coat then?" Nathan shook his head. "Okay. Let's go see who's outside."

Nathan tossed the retractable leash mechanism into Bill's lap as the man-dog combination wheeled by him, gently closed the door and followed. "Stay on the driveway, then go right on the sidewalk," he instructed Bill, half a step behind. When they'd made the turn, he stopped them just short of the cluster of spruce trees where Max had earlier indicated something unusual.

"I have Bill Welter for you," said Nathan loudly, addressing the trees.

In response, a figure dressed in black and white snow camouflage squirmed out from under the overhanging branches and struggled to his feet. Sierra 2 began to raise his scoped Remington 700, training telling him that the suspect had to be covered until searched. The rifle's butt was almost to his shoulder, when to the right of the suspect, movement from the barricade line caught his attention. He saw the media had arrived—photographers with million power telephoto lenses. A mental picture of tomorrow's front page flashed through his mind. He was on it, in full color. His .308 shouldered, covering a crippled man in a wheelchair, the little black dog in his lap, head cocked to one side, staring curiously down the muzzle. Sierra 2 lowered the rifle.

"Do you want me to hold your rifle for you while you search him?" asked Nathan.

"Uh . . . yeah, sure. No. Wait. The rest of the guys will be here right away."

Within seconds Nathan heard pounding feet behind him and deliberately didn't turn around. Two more similarly dressed men appeared on either side, flanking him and the wheelchair.

"Lenses!" growled Sierra 2, jerking his head in the direction of the barricade line. Four new heads swiveled to look. Nathan's too. He saw the photographers in the distance, and noted Kim walking toward their little group as well. She stopped a respectable distance away, waiting for the resolution.

Lambert's voice came from behind Nathan. "We'll take it from here," he instructed quietly.

Nathan turned and met his eyes. "Sure," he said, "I'll just take the dog back to his owners." He squatted beside the wheelchair. "Bill, everything will be okay now."

Bill's right hand left Max's head and extended in Nathan's direction. "Thanks, Nathan. I still don't understand completely what's happening but I know I owe you. Thanks."

Nathan took the offered hand and then guided Max down onto the street. He met Lambert's eyes again, but neither man said anything. Nathan left, following Max's lead to where Kim stood waiting.

"That's Bill Welter?" she queried as Max reached her. The black nose gave her ankles a quick sniff and then tried to carry on to his owners.

Nathan slowed his progress as he drew closer to Kim himself. His eyes met hers. "It is."

"How did you figure it out?" she asked.

"I didn't figure anything out, Kim. But, there were people here with an agenda. You saw that as clearly as I did. Only you chose to ignore what you suspected was wrong and follow orders. I just dug a little deeper that's all." The little dog looked back to see what the delay was and Nathan, seeing that, addressed him, "Let's go Max." He walked off without waiting for Kim to reply.

She was waiting for him when he'd returned the cockapoo. "Why the dog?"

"Because a stranger walking down the street or appearing at your door, is just that, a stranger. But a stranger with a dog is a person you know something about. He has a home, both for himself and the dog. He's also trustworthy, but only because people see dogs as trustworthy and by association the man is too. If you have a dog with you people tend to trust you more easily."

"That's quite profound," said Kim. "I'm impressed. And just how did you learn this?"

A sudden smile broke across Nathan's face. "When I was going to college, taking my EMT training, I used to borrow a friend's retriever. I'd sit outside in the sun with the dog and do my reading. I met more girls that way than you can probably believe."

Kim smiled broadly. "Very good." But her smile faded and she became serious again. "I think you should've kept Max. You'll need all the help you can get. Once we go back inside we'll find people upset with you again. This is getting predictable, Nathan. Why does it always happen?"

Nathan put his hands in his coat pocket and looked off toward the house that contained the temporary command post. He couldn't see into the windows but imagined some of the people left in there looking out at him, seething. "Sometimes people just get started down the wrong track. They need somebody to remind them that there's another, better route to the same destination," he said finally.

Kim watched as Bill Welter was loaded into the rear seat of a police car. Several officers attempted to help him but he waved them off. After maneuvering his wheelchair to the open car door he used his arms to lift himself up and heave his body into the back seat. He did allow the officers to fold up his chair.

The marked car drove out of the secure area past the photographers who rushed the sides of the vehicle to get their photos. Lambert walked over to where Kim and Nathan stood.

"Debriefing?" asked Nathan.

"Back at the station once we get our gear put away." He paused. "It might be best if you weren't there, Nathan."

"Sure, I can understand that."

Lambert walked away.

"Let's see," observed Kim, crossing her arms once Lambert was out of earshot. "You ignored the operational plan, you played the lone gunman and went off on your own without telling anyone what you were doing. You disobeyed orders, and then you captured the suspect all by yourself without a shred of violence and made them all look like a bunch of fools. Gee, I wonder why they don't want anything to do with you any more?"

Nathan found his car keys and started to walk toward their vehicle. "Are you going to tell Danny?"

"Absolutely." The word was firm but there was no conviction in the voice. She knew she would, but only because it was her job, a duty that must be carried out. The sight of Nathan pushing a wheelchair away from the house and the realization that he had risked his life and career to do the right thing had changed something inside of her. Personally, she'd never seen anyone do such a thing.

There were legends in her country. Legends of men and women who had done what was right even though everyone was against them. Stories of people who had trusted their beliefs and their faith more than their circumstances. They had prevailed and now they were heroes. The names went as far back as Abraham and Isaac. There were even one or two from the fighting that created the modern state of Israel, but there hadn't been a single one since. Now it seemed everyone did what was expedient, not what was right. She joined Nathan at the car thinking that if this had been a Mossad operation, he'd be dead by dawn tomorrow.

CHAPTER EIGHT

Three hours later Kim and Nathan drove along Ottawa's Elgin Street looking for a parking space. Kim's incessant fiddling with the radio dial finally paid off when she found the news conference she was searching for and they recognized the voice of the Chief.

". . . a wonderful example of the fine work our new Domestic Abuse Unit is capable of doing and, I might add, another demonstration of how this department is committed to using minimal force in effecting all of its arrests. Even in the case of a heavily armed and dangerous individual such as this. Members of our Tactical Unit placed themselves at considerable risk to ensure the subject was not harmed during the apprehension and that there was no risk to the public. I'm extremely proud of the way they conducted themselves. Now, are there any questions?"

By that point Nathan had found a parking spot and his turning off the ignition stopped the news conference. "Yeah, I have a question," he said. "How can he sleep at night?"

"Some people get by on very little sleep," answered Kim.

"And very little conscience."

Kim was quiet until they reached the middle of the next block. "Pancho Villa's?" she cried in amazement as Nathan led her down the brick steps to the basement restaurant. "Mexican food in Ottawa. That's great!"

"I thought it was fitting," smiled Nathan. "Sort of for old times sake. After all, it was in Arizona where we both acquired a taste for it."

"Is it good here?"

"So far I've only eaten here once, but I'm back. That should tell you something."

Nathan indicated a table at the far wall and the hostess led them to it. He sat with his back to the wall, watching the door. By now it was

158

habit and he felt uncomfortable and vulnerable with any other seating arrangement in a restaurant. As they talked he observed everyone coming into the small establishment but he also watched Kim. She had stopped to change her clothes, dressing in a white turtleneck and form-fitting green slacks. Kim looked as good as ever.

"You're still coloring your hair," said Nathan.

Kim smiled. "I like this shade of red."

"What color is it really?"

"It's dark."

"I'll bet it matches your eyes."

"It's been a long time, my friend," she said.

"Too long," agreed Nathan. "It's good to see you again. We used to eat together regularly."

"We did. Want me to order for you? I'll bet I can guess what you're *not* going to have—lasagna."

"Right," Nathan laughed. "I've decided my career as a naked lasagna server was a dead end."

"I'll never look at another pan of lasagna the same way again."

Nathan blushed, knowing that incident would never be forgotten. "Try the Pancho Special. You'll like it." Kim let him change the subject. "What have you been doing?" he asked after the waiter took their order.

"Now, Nathan, don't forget where I've been working. Spooks are secretive by nature but the rules still apply too. I can't tell you much. Mind you, like everyone else, we still gossip. I can always find out where the good-looking single guys are." She watched him furtively to see if he accepted that explanation. An awkward look at his menu told her he had. "I even know you hurt your ankle," she whispered conspiratorially.

Nathan looked up. "Very impressive." She asked how it was mending and he responded with his best macho brush-off. Kim had to repeat the question before he told her about the discomfort of the cast and the pain-filled physiotherapy sessions. She seemed genuinely relieved when he assured her it was almost as good as new. There were no questions about how it had been injured or how he'd occupied his time, and Nathan returned the favor. Instead, they talked about Danny,

159

other people from the ranch and what life had been like there. Politics crept briefly into their conversation when Nathan asked about her family.

Israel had been in the news lately, and violent clashes in the area seemed to be a daily occurrence. In response to his questions Kim admitted she hadn't been home since he'd last seen her. Nathan detected a longing in her voice for her family and homeland—certainly deep concern. The conversation took a more serious note when Kim asked about Nathan's work. "I don't need to know details," she said. "But I'm concerned how you're doing. Can you handle it okay? I know it can't be easy."

Nathan was about to give her the macho brush-off again, but it hadn't worked with the ankle and he suspected it wouldn't work here, either. So, he picked at his food and thought. When the silence became awkward he finally answered, "I had some real problems with the way Kent was operating. But you're right, I can't tell you about them, so don't ask."

Kim nodded. "I can imagine well enough."

Nathan looked up. "No, you can't," he fired back. Two people at the next table frowned at his outburst. He hadn't intended to raise his voice and sheepishly looked down at his food. "Sorry Kim, I didn't mean it to come out like that." It took a conscious effort to lower his voice. "You can't imagine what's going on."

"Want to try me?"

"No."

"So what can you tell me?"

"I'm going to turn what I know about Kent over to an investigative reporter. It's time he got put out of business."

Kim's fork dropped onto her plate with a clatter. She pushed the half-finished dish away. "Nathan . . ."

"Don't even start, Kim. I've made up my mind. Some things I haven't decided yet. But one I have. Kent was using me. He's a cold-blooded killer who thinks he's above the law and he's going down the best way I know."

"But you haven't even . . ." Nathan's look stopped her cold. If Nathan were an enemy she'd feel fear now. She'd seen the remains of that look on his face when the Riders attacked him through his friends the Coombs, and she'd walked into a room littered with bodies. His eyes, a combination of fire and ice, told her the decision had been made—no turning back. Time to act.

Nathan's revelation was like a blow, pushing Kim back in her chair. There had been no sign of this coming. In her world, the spotlight of publicity was a worst-case scenario. Nothing did more damage. Nothing. And Nathan was the one threatening to do it—idealistic, naive Nathan Burdett.

Kim twisted her napkin. What she really wanted to twist was Nathan's neck. No she didn't. Yes! She did. Well, at least give him a good hard slap. He needed it. For the time being the napkin kept her hands occupied. Her eyes avoided him. An amateurish mural of a Mexican village on the restaurant wall provided a safe place to look. Now what? Thoughts about the conflict it plunged her into raged through her mind. Turn in Nathan? She'd done it to others. Why not him? Because it was her job to protect her country, her agency and the foreigners they worked with, that's why. And all Nathan was trying to do was the right thing. No vendetta, no money to be made and no glory, just the *right thing*. The only thing he'd get out of this would be a bullet from Kent.

When she finally looked back her napkin was dead and her face pale, but she'd decided what to do. Truth and lies. That had always worked for her in the past. Truth and lies would do it again. It was just a matter of who you told what, and how convincing you were at it. "I care about what happens to you," she said. "Don't do this."

Nathan's shoulders tensed in frustration. "I know, Kim. And you're a good friend but sometimes it seems like we're in two different worlds. We see too many things differently."

Kim nodded. "Kent's a powerful man."

He shrugged. "So's free speech."

"He'll try to kill you if he finds out."

"I've thought of that. I'll be careful. It's really just a matter of a well-placed leak. I don't know enough to hurt him myself. If anybody's going to go after him they'll have to do a lot of digging on their own."

161

Kim leaned forward and grasped Nathan's hand across the table. "Nathan, you have to promise me you'll hold off on this for a while. I know people, too. Let me ask around, see what I can find out. Maybe there's another way. You can't do this."

"Watch me." He tried to pull his hand away but she wouldn't let go.

"Nathan . . . please?" No answer. Fire and ice. Her grip tightened. "Okay. Okay. So, you have to do it. But you don't have to do it right now. Why not wait a little? Maybe I can learn something that will help." She saw him softening. "Just wait, that's all I'm asking. Don't do anything until I get back to you. I'm your friend, I've earned that much, haven't I?"

That did it. His iron will bent. "All right, you win. I can wait a little. I won't talk to anyone until I've heard from you. But I won't wait long."

Kim's head slumped forward in relief her hair cascading around her face, but she didn't release Nathan's hand. When she lifted her head she let go. The color had returned to her face but there was something new—moistness around the eyes. She stood suddenly, surprising Nathan. "I'm going. Please, just stay here."

Nathan watched her go, puzzling at the emotion and the sudden departure. He pushed his half-eaten meal aside. The elderly couple at the next table looked relieved to see one of them leave.

Kim walked swiftly until a broad canal blocked her way. Lighted walkways snaked along either side. People skated up and down the canal's length, the night air filling with the sounds of laughter and the swish of steel on ice. She turned left, striding purposefully along the edge of the twisting waterway. But the determined walk was a sham; she had no destination in mind, nowhere to go.

She focused her attention on the skaters, slowly coming to the realization that there were only three kinds of people on the ice below her—families, friends or lovers. Certainly they were all people who lived normal lives and had normal problems. As far as she could tell, there wasn't a woman anywhere on that frozen water, with no real friends. Not one skater who hadn't seen her family in years and no one whose job it was to deceive others by winning their trust and then betraying them. A gust of cold wind blew into her face making her eyes water. She wiped at them with a sleeve and wished for a tissue.

Then her phone rang. For a moment she considered not answering, afraid it might be Nathan. However, there were a number of other people that it could be, so she dutifully answered the little hand unit.

"And how's my favorite red-headed lassie?" asked Leith.

"Not in the mood for idle conversation," she answered curtly.

"No idleness here, Kim. 'Idle hands are the devil's own tools' my mother always said. I do need to talk to you, though. Where are you?"

"In Ottawa."

Leith snorted in annoyance. "I am too. I mean where in Ottawa?"

"I've been walking along some canal but it looks like it's ending now. I just passed under a low wide bridge and I'm beside a sign that says *Ottawa Locks—Rideau Canal.*"

"I think I know where that is. Can you walk up to the roadway above you and I'll meet you on the bridge?"

Kim looked around behind her. "Yes, there are stairs going up and I can see people above me."

"Wait up there, I'll find you."

Fifteen minutes later he bounced his car up onto the broad cobblestone sidewalk and parked it in the middle of the walk. He tried some small talk but Kim threatened to walk away if he didn't get to the point.

"I just thought it's time for a formal report on how Burdett is doing."

"I've only been around him twelve hours. Kent can wait for the usual update."

"Now, now, Kim. Why so testy? Things go badly today?"

"No, they went just fine," she answered tersely.

Four teenagers arrived and took up residence on a nearby bench. A shared cigarette passed between them, pulsating intermittently as each took a drag. Leith guided Kim over to the edge of the ornate stone and concrete railing and looked down onto the frozen canal.

"Look, I'll get to the point. I've heard some nasty rumors about Nathan. I've heard he's been in contact with a newspaper reporter on a regular basis. A snoop named Jerry Mitchell." Kim started to say something but Leith held up his hands stopping her. "Before you say anything, understand this—I don't know what it's about. It could be perfectly innocent. You know as well as I do that it doesn't look good but I'm prepared to give him the benefit of the doubt here. And I haven't told that old buzzard Kent yet." He let it hang there, waiting for her reaction.

"I have no idea what you're talking about, Leith. And personally, I don't think Nathan would ever do anything like that." She thrust both hands into her coat pocket. "Now, is there anything else or can I finish my walk?"

"Nothing more, my red-headed lass." He motioned down the bridge with a flourish. "Walk away if you like."

She did.

Leith spent the next forty minutes phoning hotels until he found where Jerry Mitchell was registered. A short walk around Jerry's hotel, the Ramada, and an equally short drive to one of Ottawa's seedier bars yielded the rest of what was needed. His next call was to the reporter's room.

"I heard you came to town looking for information," said Leith, using the most conspiratorial voice he could manage.

"That's something a reporter is always after," answered Jerry noncommittally. "Do you have any?"

"I do. If you feel like going for a walk I'll meet you and we can talk."

"Sure. But talk about what?"

Leith considered for a moment how to answer and settled on the one common denominator. "Nathan Burdett," he said simply.

"Where and when?"

"In front of the courthouse right now. It's a ten minute walk from your hotel. Ask at the front desk and they'll give you directions." He hung up and waited.

Three minutes later, Leith, sitting quietly in the lobby of the Ramada Hotel, watched a man approach the front desk and ask her for directions to the courthouse. He left in a hurry and Leith casually followed him out the large rotating doors. Outside he approached two young men smoking at the curb. "That's him," Leith said, pointing at Jerry Mitchell's back

He was anxious and it was cold outside. Those two factors prompted Jerry Mitchell to take a shortcut between a large concrete sculpture and some obscure government building. So intent was he on getting to his destination on time that he was unaware of anyone behind him until a hand grabbed his shoulder, spinning him around.

"Hey, Skinny," rasped a voice in the darkness. "What's your hurry?"

"Yeah," said another as he turned around. "Hey, that's a nice leather coat. I'll bet that would fit me."

"Yeah, man, we're homeless and, like, we don't have anywhere to stay and we're wondering if maybe you could contribute a few hundred bucks or a handful of credit cards to help us out." They laughed.

Jerry panicked. He gave the closest one a quick shove and tried to run but only made it two steps. More hands grasped him and he collided with the ground. They picked him up as he flailed blindly at the voices. His attackers pinned his arms and slammed him against the sculpture's cold concrete. "Wait, I . . ." A fist smashed into his stomach cutting off the words. He gasped, straightened up, and received another gut wrenching blow for his trouble. Hands rifled through his pockets. He felt his jacket being yanked off. One of them was undoing his watchstrap when Jerry retched over the man's battered sneakers. That generated a curse and a flurry of kicks to his chest and head. As the ground came up to meet him once again he was dimly aware of footsteps fleeing into the darkness.

Jerry wondered if he was going to die. He felt like it. At least he'd tried to fight back. Not that it had done him any good. They could write that on his tombstone. If he'd only had his recently purchased CZ85 things would have ended differently. A close look at a .40 caliber muzzle would have scared them off. Or would it? Could he have shot these thieves if he had to? Jerry conceded to himself that five minutes ago he couldn't have shot anyone. But five minutes ago no one had ever done anything like this to him. Right now, if it happened again he could shoot.

Lying face down on the cold ground and hovering on the edge of consciousness, Jerry Mitchell learned time was irrelevant. Here only pain mattered. The waves of pain ebbed and flowed like the distant sound of traffic. Pain brought consciousness, or maybe it was the other way around. Not that it mattered, because when one left so did the other. He had no idea how long it was before he was able to turn himself over and lie there on his back. All that little piece of progress meant, he realized, was that he now had a permanent dose of both, pain and consciousness. Maybe he wasn't going to die after all.

As both increased he made out the looming sculpture above him. One of the surfaces was tilted at such an angle that it reflected the nearby street lamps. Jerry read the words inscribed in large letters on its polished surface . . . *all human beings are born free and equal in dignity and rights*. Perfect, he thought, struggling to his feet. Just absolutely perfect. Mugged and robbed right under some stupid colossus of a statue designed to make a statement about freedom, dignity and rights. Unbelievable! What a newspaper column this would make—that is, if he were writing columns. And that made him think about his contact. He contemplated struggling on to the courthouse but quickly decided he'd never make it. Besides, how long had he lain here and where was his contact now? The nearby sidewalk was the best he could hope for.

From there he flagged down a cab. The driver refused to take him to the hospital but was helpful enough to have his dispatcher call 9-1-1 and wait with him until a police officer showed up. Jerry thanked him, and while he waited in the warmth of the taxi asked the driver if he knew anything about the sculpture.

166

"I do, sir. There are many many tourists which come to this city and I must know much about these things for all of them."

"There are words carved into the top of it," Jerry motioned up into the darkness but the movement caused a spasm of pain. He gasped and took two slow breaths before continuing. "They're familiar, like I should know where they come from but I can't put my finger on it. Do you know?"

"Oh, yes, sir. I do indeed know that very well," he said, in his singsong voice. "Those words are the beginning of the Human Rights."

Jerry nodded. "Of course. That's it. The United Nations Universal Declaration of Human Rights."

"You are very much right, sir. Those are United Nations' words."

"You made it look like a random mugging?" asked Leith.

"Sure did, man," said the pimply faced one. "Just like you said, we hurt him enough to send him to the hospital. The sucker never knew what hit him."

"Good."

"Here's his room key and all his papers," said his friend. "You sure that's all you want?"

In the dim light of the alley, Leith looked at what was handed him. "This is all of it?"

The two looked at each other. "Well, yeah," said the first one. "You're letting us keep all the good stuff. What do we need with his papers? We wouldn't hold out on you." Crossing this short man with the broad shoulders and hard face hadn't even entered their dull brains. Such a move was too stupid even for them to seriously contemplate. Why he needed help in mugging the slightly built victim was beyond their understanding as well. All they understood was easy money and quick drugs and this was as easy as it got.

Leith slipped them each a one hundred dollar bill. "Good work, lads. Maybe we can do business again sometime."

The next day Leith stood in front of Kent's desk, briefing him on what he'd learned. "The notebook I got is about half full. There's

167

some stuff that seems unrelated to Burdett or us but a good half of what's there refers to Burdett. He's working that boy hard."

"Of course, that makes sense. If you have a new source of information you're going to check him out rather closely, aren't you?"

"Seems reasonable."

"Nothing in the hotel room?"

"A briefcase but not much of interest in that. Just an address book and a folder of photos."

"Oh?" Kent's interest perked up as Leith slid the large prints across the desk.

"They all look like long-range shots, some taken surreptitiously. The first one is of Burdett, that Forbes chap from the FBI and our Kim. Then we have myself and Burdett with a couple of local coppers on the library steps in Jasper and the last one is of Kim."

"That's how she looked in Jasper?" asked Kent, pointing at the photo.

"Aye. I'm sure it was taken there somewhere but I don't know where. And while we're on photos, there was a Nikon in the room as well. I developed the exposed film and got these." He handed Kent a packet of smaller sized photos. Kent thumbed through the twenty prints and shot a questioning look in Leith's direction. "All of them are of an Ottawa Tactical Unit operation mounted to arrest a dangerous character of some sort. The majority—the ones where Burdett and occasionally Kim show up—are from the arrest itself."

"Judging from the way he's zeroed in on our Miss Corel and Mr. Burdett, it's not hard to tell where his interest is."

"Not at all."

Kent tapped the last bundle of pictures. "I received a report on this earlier. It appears Mr. Burdett once again went off on some sort of tangent. My understanding is that he hasn't exactly endeared himself to another group of law enforcement officials."

"It doesn't change with him, does it? Oh, and here's Mitchell's address book as well. There might be something useful in there for you, but I can't pick it out."

"Thank you, Leith. You've done a splendid job as usual." Kent got up from his desk and paced the full length of the room, following the curve of the window. He stopped briefly at the far end to look out and think. Leith waited patiently by the desk, standing in a perfectly military *at ease* position. By the time Kent returned to sit at his desk, he had decided what to do.

"Leith, I want you to arrange the return of as many of the non-valuable items as possible to Mr. Mitchell. This was, after all, a simple robbery and the thieves would retain the valuable items. We will undertake that the others were discarded in a spot where some kind person found them, and seeing Mr. Mitchell's address in . . . say, this address book, he determined to do the chivalrous thing and return them to their rightful owner."

Leith nodded. "I'll have Jenny photocopy it for you first."

"Splendid. Now to the matter of Mr. Burdett." Kent neatly compiled the photos still spread across his desk before continuing. "Things are spinning out of control on this matter, Leith, and we've worked together long enough that I'm sure you know I find that unacceptable. In this business, maintaining control is an absolute necessity and the reason for this unacceptable state of affairs seems to be centered around Mr. Burdett. Therefore, Mr. Burdett must be removed." He sighed and shook his head. "Such a waste, Leith. Such a waste."

"When would you like me to do it?"

"There will be fewer questions asked if we first remove that cloak of protection Mr. Burdett enjoys by means of his association with law enforcement. I want you to wait until I have shut down the project. That will require speaking with a number of people, but fortunately he has provided us with ample reasons for doing so. It will be quickly and easily done. Then, once his protection is removed, he's all yours. Could you perhaps make it look like that nasty batch of criminals he had problems with about a year ago come back for him?"

"No problem there, sir." Leith reached across the desk, retrieving the address book. "This will be the first time you've had to sterilize one of your own projects, isn't it, sir."

"And it's a dreadful feeling," acknowledged Kent as Leith turned to leave. "On your way out would you ask Jenny to get the Director on the line for me? There's a good chap."

169

Jerry Mitchell was on sick leave and had every intention of staying that way. But then Frank phoned and told him some Good Samaritan in Ottawa had found a bunch of his stolen papers and sent them back to the Tribune. That was enough for Jerry to drag his bandaged ribs into his car and make the trip to the office. When he exited the elevator on his floor, a small crowd of people gathered near the photocopier diverted their attention from the machine to him. Sympathy and kind words were plentiful, as was the teasing.

Jerry tried dodging it by asking what made office machines so interesting.

"New equipment on each floor," said Frank. "All new shredders, high speed color printers, photocopiers—the works. All state of the art stuff."

"Did the delinquent advertisers finally pay their bills?" asked Jerry. Everyone laughed politely.

"Just time for a technology update around here," countered Frank. "Come on, hobble over to my office, you can have the crash course later."

Jerry was more interested in what remained of his file, so he left his co-workers with the new office machines and shuffled past the reporter's cubicles to Frank's office. Frank waited until he gingerly eased himself into one of the chairs before handing the courier package across the desk.

"I've seen week-old road kill that looks better than you do, Jerry."

"Thanks, Frank. I'm still pissing blood so that's about how I feel." Jerry opened the package and fanned through the contents. "Looks like most of it."

"Lucky for both of us," said Frank. "You have a lot of time invested in that file and we have a lot of money in it."

"I got beat up. I lost my watch, coat, camera, lap-top and wallet. I don't feel lucky."

Frank leaned back in his chair. "Getting this back could suggest you're wrong about the beating you took having something to do with Burdett."

170

"I don't know, Frank. The whole thing still stinks to me. It's all too coincidental. And you know how I feel about coincidences."

Frank nodded. "This is the covering letter that came with the package." He handed a single typewritten sheet across the desk. "The sender says he wants to remain anonymous. Ottawa postmark."

Jerry took the offered letter and scanned it quickly. "Anonymous eh? It smells, Frank."

"I know. It smells worse than you look. The question is what we're going to do about it. My first concern is your safety. Next time they might not let you off so light."

"Makes you wonder if I'm getting close to something, doesn't it?"

"Want to let it go, Jerry? Get up and walk away from it if you want. I won't make anyone follow a story that gets this nasty."

Jerry shook his head without looking up from the papers in his lap. "I'm in for the duration."

"That's what I figured." Frank sighed deeply. "Then how do we protect you?"

"I can look after myself," muttered Jerry.

Frank snorted. "Jerry, you're what, five feet eight inches and one hundred and forty pounds of scrawny pencil-pushing reporter. In a street fight, Barb could whip your butt."

"Gee, thanks for the confidence, Frank." Jerry began inserting papers back into the courier package. "But you're right. Well, what about carrying an equalizer then."

"A what?"

"You heard me, an equalizer. As in 'God made all men—but Colt made them equal'."

Frank leaned back in his chair, this time hooking his hands behind his head. "You don't even like guns, Jerry."

"I've been taking lessons, as part of my research on the Burdett story." He shrugged his shoulders. "I'm actually getting pretty good with a pistol. At least that's what Sue says."

Frank's eyebrows rose. "Sue?"

"My instructor."

"Your instructor is a *Sue*?"

171

"Sure. Why not? And she's way nicer than the grizzled, old, mostly-deaf drill sergeant."

"Than who?"

"Private joke, Frank. Never mind. But I'm serious about the gun. If you were to vouch for my need for protection I'd stand a chance at getting a permit to carry a pistol. Actually," Jerry sounded a little sheepish, "I've already bought one."

"*You* own a gun?" Frank came partway out of his chair.

"Hey. No big deal. I just got it. I've always been renting or borrowing guns for the courses I'm taking so I figured I might as well own one. That's all." Frank settled back in his chair. "How about it. Give me a reference letter for the permit to carry."

Frank thought about it for a minute. "It'd be a first around here."

"This story's a first."

Frank nodded silently and then seemed to think some more. "I'll do it. You start the paperwork and I'll write you a letter saying management at this paper supports your request for whatever permit it is you need. When will you need the letter?"

Jerry winced as he slowly extracted himself from the chair. "I'm not doing anything very fast these days, Frank. No big rush. I'll call you in a couple of days and tell you who to address it to."

"Watch yourself out there. It's a dangerous world."

Jerry stopped at the open door. "I know. And none of us are going to leave it alive."

Frank chuckled, gave him a knowing smile and waved him out.

CHAPTER NINE

Nathan looked out the window of the Airbus 320 and saw nothing but dull gray. They were still locked solidly into a cloudbank covering most of the eastern United States. The jet, fresh from takeoff, was still inclined upward so he waited for the moment they would break through the clouds. When it happened the crackling brightness stung his eyes, but he forced himself to look. Just breaking out of the clouds was the moment he liked best—looking out over their tops, being at their level, seeing all the peaks and valleys of the cotton candy formations and absorbing their three dimensional nature. But the aircraft's climb was relentless, and within minutes he was so high above the floor of clouds they looked like a white featureless field.

Nathan turned away from the window and considered that the last year and a half of his life may have been just like that moment of breaking through the clouds—the best part of the entire ride. And if that was true, it was now behind him.

The B-Zone Project was over. After Ottawa, they'd put him back at the Arizona ranch by himself and let him cool his heels there for a week. One week had dragged into two, two weeks into three. He trained and helped out with other duties wherever he could. On two of the weekends he'd found a couple of nearby matches to attend. They provided a pleasant diversion but he still held back and let others win. Neither Kim nor Danny ever showed their face. Rats deserting a sinking ship, speculated Nathan.

Eventually Danny called him back to DC, collected his guns and gave him a dozen forms to sign, informing him, while he wrote, that everyone involved had pulled their support. The ride had been good but it was over. Then he'd taken him out for dinner and bought him a seventy-five dollar steak. The steak had been excellent, conceded Nathan, but it wasn't worth seventy-five dollars. Danny said he'd called

Kim to let her know about the dinner but she never called back and didn't show for the meal. "She's back working for the Colonel and probably too busy," suggested Danny. They said their good-byes and Nathan boarded a plane for Calgary.

He moved in with his mother who made jokes about her twenty-seven year old son moving back home, but Nathan knew she was delighted to have him there. He told her he'd stay at least a month, then it would be time to find his own place. Friday morning of the second week in May Nathan was sifting through the paper, trying to get a handle on what was available, when the phone rang.

"Hello, friend," said Kim Corel.

Nathan dropped the paper to the floor. "Hi, yourself."

"I'm in Calgary and thought you might like to go for dinner. I think I owe you one."

"A good-bye dinner?"

"No. The last time we ate together it ended rather badly. I was hoping we could improve on that. And we do have some unfinished business."

"Oh yeah. That."

"Yes, that. It's your town, when and where?"

"Let's see . . . the downtown Earl's on Eighth Avenue, at six. Can you find that okay?"

"Sure. See you then."

Jerry ate his lunch while leafing through the same edition of the Tribune as Nathan. Red pen in hand; he circled another mistake. That was two in one issue. He stood up and, seeing Frank in his office, walked over and tossed pages two and seven on his desk. At least it didn't hurt to stand, sit down or walk anymore.

"What's this?"

"Mistakes, Frank. Look here," Jerry pointed at the first red circle. "This story we picked off the wire, calls the Vancouver policeman's gun his 'semi-automatic service revolver'. Give me a break, Frank. What moron wrote that? A revolver can't be semi-automatic."

174

Frank looked up at Jerry. "It can't?"

"No, it can't. And here." Jerry pointed at the red circle on page seven. "In this editorial piece on the new gun laws, you refer to magazines as 'clips'. They're not clips, Frank. Those long narrow boxes that hold cartridges and fit into guns are called magazines."

"They are?"

"Yes, they are."

"Then what are clips?"

"Clips are the little sheet metal strips that hold cartridges by the rim for loading into the magazines."

"Like small magazines?" suggested a confused looking Frank as he scratched his graying head.

"No. No. The full term is stripper clips. The difference between clips and magazines is that clips are designed to be discarded after use, magazines aren't. Even in the case of the M1 Garand, where the clip fits completely into the gun, it's still a disposable piece."

"If you say so."

"Look, Frank. If you like, I can proofread any stories we run that have firearms references in them. I don't know everything there is to know, but I'm learning and I've got enough time to help get things right."

"Jerry," said Frank, assuming a fatherly air and handing back pages two and seven. "Nobody cares. This is a newspaper, not a technical manual. Everybody knows what we mean. It's not a big deal."

"But . . . ."

Frank stopped him with an upraised hand. "Thanks for wanting to put your new-found knowledge to use, Jerry, but do me a favor and keep things in perspective. Okay?"

Jerry thought about arguing for a moment, but Frank wore his hard-nosed editor look and so he gave up on the idea. "Sure. Whatever you say." He was one step outside the door when Frank spoke again.

"The wife and I are barbecuing a salmon tonight. Want to come over?"

Jerry thought about that for a moment too. "I'd love to, Frank, but I can't. I have to load ammo."

"Load ammo?"

Jerry nodded his head. "I'm going to an IPSC match in Spruce Grove next weekend and I'm out of ammo. Well, not really *out*. I had some loaded, but when I chronographed it, I found it was too slow. It'll never make major. Either I load some new stuff or tweak what I've got. But I have to do something."

"Tweak?"

"Sue said I might be able to get it to make major if I tighten up the crimp a little, or maybe reduce the loaded length by ten or twenty thou'. It's worth a try." Jerry shrugged.

"Jerry?" said Frank, again in his fatherly voice.

"What?"

"I have no flipping idea what you're talking about."

"It's really quite simple," said Jerry, stepping back into the office. "If the crimp is . . . ." Frank stopped him with the look. Jerry retreated out the door. "Thanks for the invitation, Frank. And say hello to Betty for me."

"I'll do that, Jerry."

Nathan was ten minutes early and spent the time watching the door, waiting for her. When she came in he rose from the table and waved to get her attention. Kim brushed past the hostess without a word, pointing at Nathan in explanation.

"Hello, friend," she said, giving him a quick hug.

"I like to hear you say that."

"What?"

"Hello, friend. Nobody else greets me like that."

Kim looked surprised. "I say that often?"

"All the time. I hope it's still true—that we're friends."

"It is as far as I'm concerned."

"Even though you don't know you're saying it?" teased Nathan. Kim half rose from her chair and punched him on the shoulder. "Ouch."

"You deserved it."

"Where have you been? I left some messages for you."

"I've been overseas for a while."

"Get to go home?" asked Nathan.

176

"Unfortunately, no." Kim took a menu from the waiter. Nathan did the same. "What brings you to Calgary," he asked.

"I've finally got a few days off. I thought I'd come see you."

"Great. And if you still have a job to go back to, well, that's more than I've got."

"I heard. I'm sorry."

"No big deal." He was trying the macho brush-off again and he knew it. "They paid me the remainder of my contract in one lump sum. I'm okay."

"Sure you are."

They ordered drinks and meals, keeping up the easy banter of old friends while they ate. When the dishes were cleared away and coffee served, Kim changed the subject. It was time. "You haven't done anything about Kent yet, have you?"

"No."

Relief flashed across Kim's face. "Thank goodness. Very good. Did you change your mind?"

"No. Remember, you asked me to wait and I agreed?"

Now she looked bewildered. "And . . ."

"What do you mean? 'And . . .' You're my friend, I trust you, you asked me to wait. So I waited. There is no 'and . . .'"

Kim hung her head. "I'm sorry."

"The wait's probably been good. I've cooled off a little. So, what do I do? Have you checked with 'your people', can you give me any new insights, give me some good advice? I'll take whatever I can get. I have to tell you, though, I still feel the same way about Kent."

The hardness creeping back into his voice made her look up. "I don't have any new revelations for you, Nathan. All I have is a confirmation of what I told you before. If you try to hurt Kent and his operation he'll have you killed as dead as a stone. And, he has the resources to find you and do it no matter where you go. Not just his own personal resources, but also the security agencies of any country that's a member of the UN. They'll believe whatever he tells them. And trust me on this; he's good at manipulating people to do what he wants."

"So, I should give up my idea because it's dangerous?"

177

"Yes, too dangerous."

"Then give me an alternative."

"Forget Kent."

"Not an option."

"Nathan!" said Kim, slapping the table and cramming exasperation into every corner of her voice. "You can't right all the wrongs in this world. You do what you can and let the rest go."

"Sure, but this is one I can do something about." Nathan stiffened. "I'm not leaving it. Can you get that through your stubborn head? I'm not backing away."

"Stubborn? Well at least I'm not stupid. And that's what going after Kent would be."

Nathan leaned across the table and leveled an accusing finger at her, "You little red-headed . . . ." He caught himself and stopped in mid-sentence. This wasn't where he wanted to go. Nathan holstered the finger, shut his mouth and leaned back in his chair. Fixing his eyes on a spot across the room, he counted to ten.

Kim covered her face with her hands. "It's happening again isn't it?"

Nathan thought for a minute. "Yeah," he said quietly, making a conscious effort to relax. "We're having an argument." Then he added with a small smile, "You'd think we were married. Every time we go out to eat we have an argument."

Kim put her hands back on the table and took a deep breath. Truth and lies wasn't working. "What are we going to do about it?"

"Can we agree to disagree?" asked Nathan.

"Okay. Then I don't agree to attend your funeral."

Nathan reached out. "And I agree not to have one." He touched her hand. "See. Consensus. We agree on something. Now let's agree not to talk about Kent."

Kim smiled but an icy tension lingered as they tried to re-establish some common ground. They found it when they started talking about weekend plans.

"Want to hang around with me and my friends?" asked Nathan.

"You sure you want me?"

"I'm sure. Remember, though—no shoptalk. Okay?"

178

"I'd like that," came the reply. "What are you doing?"

"Tomorrow, I'm driving Mom out to Cochrane to visit one of her friends. You're welcome to come along and meet her. I'll even buy you an ice cream at Mackay's. Then I was going to drive up to the Homestead Range and watch some long-range rifle shooting at the competition there this weekend."

"Are you shooting?"

"No, just watching some friends."

"You're asking me to meet your mother, go for ice cream and watch shooting? I was thinking of something slightly more exciting, like whitewater rafting, skydiving, or maybe rock climbing."

Nathan shrugged. "I'm sorry. I think that's about all I can handle at the moment. If you want to hang out with me—it's mother, ice cream and shooting."

Kim laughed. "Sounds like an unbeatable combination."

"How about nine tomorrow morning?"

The waiter arrived with the bill and she snatched it out of his hand. "Perfect. I've got this. See you tomorrow."

"No shop talk."

"None." She touched him on the shoulder as she said it, gave the waiter cash and left Nathan to finish his coffee alone.

Later that evening after the sun disappeared behind the Rockies—as Calgary waited in that indecisive moment of spring twilight—Kim walked into an Irish pub on Macleod Trail and found Leith. He was sitting near the door, at a bar made of dark carved wood talking to a pretty barmaid dressed in green. When he saw Kim he took his ale and moved to a booth in a back corner. "What do you want?" she asked.

"Now, is that any way to treat an old co-worker?"

"I'm still waiting for what you want and why you called me?"

"Just keeping tabs on the pansy, that's all. I was in the area and Mr. Kent wants to make sure he doesn't do anything awkward."

"He's not a pansy." Kim fiddled with a cardboard coaster.

"I see. Well, let's just say 'weak-kneed' then shall we?" Leith saw a bright pink color flood her cheeks, it told him one of the things he needed to know. "Well, what's the lad up to this weekend?"

"Stick it in your ear. He doesn't work for you any more and neither do I."

Leith clucked his tongue and wagged his head. "My, my, but you're testy this evening." He paused briefly to make sure she was paying full attention to him. "Kimberly, you need to consider what Nathan might think if I were to point out to him what he doesn't know about you. For instance, that you helped set up that little party in the gunsmith's shop. The one with the Riders?" Leith stroked his chin, as if deep in thought. "And then there was the time . . . or do I need to go further?" Leith saw her hands clench and the muscular cords stand out on her bare forearms. He'd guessed right. Too bad. Burdett was nothing, but her loss would be a dirty shame.

"No," came the answer through gritted teeth.

"Good. So I'll repeat the question. What's the lad up to this weekend? Anything I should know about?"

"Just family stuff and watching a shooting competition."

Leith pulled a notebook and pen from his pocket. "Come along now, Kim. I need more details on our pansy than that. When and where, for starters?"

"What in the world for? Just leave him alone. He's finished in this sick business and . . . ."

Leith cut her off with a cold stare. "If I say I need it, lassie, then you'll bloody well give it to me. Understand?" He jabbed the pen in her direction to emphasize the last word.

Kim's nostrils flared and her cheeks flushed darker. She gave him the scant details she had in the briefest form possible.

"Anything else, lassie?"

Kim reached out and snatched the plastic ballpoint pen out of the Scotsman's hand, snapped it in two and stood up. "Yeah." She threw the pieces into his face. "Don't ever call me lassie again!" and she stomped out of the bar.

Leith watched her go, then one by one flicked the broken pieces of plastic off the table. When they were all gone he glanced back at the door to confirm she wasn't coming back. He picked up his unfinished ale and moved to another table near the door where one man already sat. "I think she likes me," Leith said.

His friend roared in laughter. "But did you get what we need?" he asked.

"Enough for a good try at it tomorrow. Are the guns and your two pals going to be here on time?"

"They drove across the border three hours ago. It'll be midnight by the time they get here. That'll be plenty early."

"Right. We're up at the crack of dawn to find this Homestead Range place. We'll play it by ear once we've done that." Leith raised his ale and saluted the other man's beer. "To a good day's work."

CHAPTER TEN

The day had dawned bright and sunny, but by the time Kim and Nathan drove west on Highway 1 at 10:00 a.m. the sky had changed. A high cloud cover had rolled in, and from horizon to horizon there was no blue to be seen.

Nathan watched the trees and bushes along the roadside trying to gauge wind direction and velocity. "This is good light for shooting," he commented, "but the wind seems to be switching a lot."

"Good light?" queried Kim. "Is there such a thing as bad light?"

"There certainly is. Ask a photographer if there's such a thing as good and bad light. All the competition today is with iron-sights and if you shoot that way, without the benefit of scopes, the nature of the light is even more important." He motioned with one hand out into the distance. "This light is flat and even. There's no glare and the lack of direct sun means there won't be as much mirage. The scores today should be good."

"How far do they shoot?" asked Kim.

"You'll see and you'll probably be surprised."

Kim accepted that and they listened quietly to the hum of the road noise until she changed the subject. "Your mother seems nice."

"Thank you. I think so."

"You certainly look after her." Nathan answered with a curt nod. Kim tried again. "Is that one of your duties, to look after your mother?"

"Only because she lets me drive her car until I get my own wheels again." Nathan patted the steering wheel. "Seriously though, I guess so. I've never thought of it as a duty, though. It's just what I do. It's who I am."

"Duty isn't a very popular word these days."

"About as popular as honor, integrity and responsibility."

"Is that who you are, too?"

Nathan shrugged. "Like everyone, I just try my best." He paused. "But the tough part is when they conflict. What do you do then, Kim? How do you handle it when the two conflict?" He waited for an answer but Kim remained silent. Eventually, he tried again. "What do you do when the two become mutually exclusive, Kim? What do you do when whatever your duty is, isn't the right thing to do?"

She answered, but it was a long time coming. "Go with duty."

"Why?"

"Duty is simple. Right and wrong are complicated."

"That's it?"

"Sure. Why not? It's simple and simple is good. Nobody needs complications."

"And that's what you like—simplicity?"

Kim didn't respond. She looked out at the passing scenery and tried to think of some way to change the subject.

They turned off Highway 1 and traveled south on #68. The clouds moved lower and a light mist sprinkled onto the windshield. "This road is one of the main routes into the Kananaskis," offered Nathan. "It's like Calgary's backyard, a controlled area in the foothills for everything from logging to hunting to camping and tree hugging. There's not much traffic today. Looks like the cool weather is keeping people indoors."

The road switched from pavement to gravel and back to broken pavement. An assortment of vehicles were parked in a broad pullout just beyond a Ranger station.

"Trailhead," explained Nathan. "If the weather holds we'll come back here and go for a walk later."

From a red Windstar van with darkened windows, four pairs of eyes watched them drive past the trailhead. One pair, aided by binoculars, confirmed the occupants. "That's them, lads."

"How are we going to do it?" asked the driver.

"That road up to the range is hilly and winding. They'll be driving slowly on the way out. The back roads in Northern Ireland are like that and I've seen how the Provisional IRA use it to their advantage. I'll show you lads one of the lessons I learned the hard way from them. We'll have to be patient though."

"Follow them?" asked the driver.

"No. Wait here. An hour, maybe two. Then we'll head up the road."

"The Homestead shooting facility is," explained Nathan, "made up of two separate ranges carved into the foothills of the Kananaskis Recreational Area. This branch road we're on ends at the ranges." They negotiated its winding turns, came out of a small valley, climbed a steep hill and passed a locked gate to their right. "Silhouette and Benchrest Ranges," said Nathan, slowing even more to let the vehicle bounce carefully over the evenly spaced steel pipes of a Texas gate set into the roadway. "Looks like nothing's going on there today. We're going on another half mile, where the access to the long range is."

"This is just short-range?" questioned Kim.

"Yeah, only five hundred meters."

Her eyebrows shot up. "*Only* five hundred meters?"

"That's all. But I will hand it to those guys," Nathan pointed a thumb back over his shoulder. "They do shoot it offhand."

"Offhand? You mean offhand, like in standing?"

Nathan nodded. "I mean standing. They shoot at steel targets from two hundred to five hundred meters away and they do it standing on their two hind legs with no support of any kind. Not even slings. You have to knock over the target to score. Just like the pistol shooting I do. It's great fun, and because you can see what's going on, it's one of the few shooting games that's also enjoyable to watch."

"But, we're going to watch long-range shooting?"

"Right."

"And I always thought five hundred meters was long-range."

Five minutes later, Nathan pulled into an access similar to the one they had just passed, drove through the open gate and parked beside a row of vehicles. Far from the flat, sterile military range she expected, Kim found this facility looked positively Swiss. Hillsides flaunting the lush green of spring rose to the west and she saw three buildings scattered around the parking lot. Their brown cedar siding and broad roof overhangs added to the Bavarian illusion. However, a quick look at the people milling about revealed no one in lederhosen or funny felt hats so she gave up on the image.

The terrain to the targets wasn't the pool table flat she expected, either. That part of the range was broken into a series of undulating ridges and valleys. A vehicle trail snaked around humps and shallow intervening swamps and led to a series of numbered targets in the hazy distance. Something moved beside one of the targets and she squinted slightly to discern a person walking.

"Okay," said Kim hearing Nathan walk up beside her. "How far is it?"

"Nine hundred meters," he boasted. "Or one thousand yards if that suits you better." Nathan raised an arm and pointed. "You see the raised grassy ridges between here and the targets? Not all the shooting is done at nine hundred. That's the furthest they go back, but they also shoot in hundred meter increments all the way up to three hundred. In this game they keep the targets in the same place and move the shooters. The target mechanisms are similar to the military ranges you might be familiar with. Competitors not shooting take turns working the pits under the target frames where they raise, lower and score targets from a position of safety."

"From here with iron-sights?" Kim couldn't get over it.

"Yeah, but with rifles not handguns," said someone behind her. She turned and saw Nathan shaking hands with two men. The youngest was close to Nathan's age, and the other she recognized quickly as Bob Coombs. When Nathan finished she said hello to Bob and was introduced to Brad. He wore what looked to be a hot, stiff and uncomfortable shooting jacket made with an assortment of leather, canvas, straps and padding.

"Nice to meet you, Kim," said Brad. "Someday we'll get Nathan competing with real guns," he added, casting a teasing look in his direction.

"Right," agreed Nathan. "And someday the Great Pumpkin will rise out the pumpkin patch and bring treats and goodies to all good little boys and girls." Everyone laughed. "Hey, I shoot rifles," added Nathan in his own defense. "But they're for hunting and for fun. You know me. The way I see things, it's handguns for serious competition."

"Oh . . . okay . . ." Brad said, slowly and reluctantly, as if conceding a point of honor. "We'll let you hang around with us anyway. But only if Kim comes, too."

"Sure," said Nathan. "We're a team. Wherever I go, she shows up." Kim smiled but his observation made her uncomfortable. Was he kidding or had he started to notice? "Come see my new rifle," suggested Brad.

"Love to," replied Nathan. The men followed Brad, but Nathan stopped and looked back when Kim didn't move. "Kim, are you coming?"

She was staring off toward the other end of the parking lot where another group of people had gathered. "No. You go ahead. I see someone I want to talk to."

Nathan followed her gaze and saw Frankie just leaving the gathering and walking across the graveled lot. "Great," he said. "She'd love to see you."

Kim ran to catch up with Frankie. She was rewarded for the effort when, in response to seeing her, a smile lit up the elderly face. "What a wonderful surprise to see you here, Kim. Come, I was just going to get a coffee."

"That sounds great. Are you shooting here today, Frankie?"

"Goodness no. I just come along with Bob. He doesn't shoot either but he always tries to come to these events and promote business a little. I wander around, talk to my friends and help out with scoring and paperwork."

"Well, since the guys are off doing their gun thing, do you think us babes can hang out together?"

Frankie chuckled. "Sounds like fun. And with no stores within thirty miles we can't even get into trouble."

"Who needs stores to get into trouble?" winked Kim.

Once they'd collected their coffee, Frankie directed Kim to a dazzling variety of lawn chairs scattered about a cold and empty firepit. She indicated a spot where they could sit and still watch most of what occurred on the grounds.

"You've known Nathan for a while now," said Frankie as they settled in. "Tell me, what do you think of him?"

Kim ducked the question. Carefully she repositioned the ball cap she wore, adjusting her ponytail where it protruded through the cap's rear opening. "He certainly seems to know a lot of people."

Frankie made a sweeping motion with her arm that encompassed the ranges and everyone on it. "In this world almost everyone knows him, and those that don't have heard of him."

"Why is that?"

"Because he's different, he's special."

"You mean his abilities?"

"Sure, that, but other ways too. Nathan has more talent with a pistol than anyone I've ever seen or heard of. Fortunately, he has the character to go along with it."

"Does everyone think that about him?"

"Everyone who knows him personally and certainly everyone who knows the stories." Frankie sipped from her Styrofoam cup. "That's one of our favorite pastimes you know."

"What is?"

"Telling Nathan Burdett stories." Kim's quizzical look prompted a knowing smile from Frankie. She pointed to the firepit, the nearby stack of dry wood, and to the empty lawn chairs around them. "Here, this evening after the guns are put away and once the boys break out their beer, everyone will sit around the fire, visit with each other and exchange lies about shots they've made and guns they've owned. But once the curious are gone and the new shooters have drifted on home, when just his old friends and the night wind are left—then we tell Nathan Burdett stories."

Kim was intrigued. "What kind of stories? Where do they come from?"

Frankie smiled. "You forget that Nathan grew up in this area. Most of us have known him since he was a youngster, and me, I've been watching him longer than anybody. It's also a small world, Kim. Somebody's cousin twice removed is a prison guard in New York state. Another shooter's sister's nephew is a cop in Portland. Everybody here knows Bob of course. And Jasper isn't very far away is it?"

187

Kim nodded in understanding. "Sounds like he's becoming a legend."

"How about you Kim, have you got any Nathan Burdett stories? I am the unofficial repository you know." Frankie waited for Kim to answer but after a minute of watching shooters on the firing line pack up gear there was no response from her. "It's just starting. You realize that don't you?"

Kim turned to look at her. "What is?"

"What he's here for. What he was born to do."

"I don't understand."

"Of course you don't. At first I didn't either. Remember, I told you he's special?" Kim nodded. "I don't know why, but I've known it since he first walked into Bob's shop. He was fourteen then and not much taller than a Winchester Model 12 is long. I knew there was something different about him and I encouraged Bob to take him under his wing and teach him. Bob did a good job, but with a student like Nathan it would be tough to go wrong."

"I've seen how fast he learns," agreed Kim.

"At first, Bob just saw that talent we've talked about. He missed the character. I noticed it right away, though, and over the years I watched and started to suspect that our Nathan has a destiny. Then Danny came for him. That's when I knew I was right."

Frankie continued. "I don't know, maybe you'll just write this off as an old lady's imaginings about a young man who's like the son she never had. But I believe there are things he has to do, things nobody else can do. It's why he's here, why you people took him away and why you gave him the next level of his training. You all think it's over now, that he's your creation and it didn't work out, so now everyone can get on to the next project. You're wrong. To him it was just another level in life. To him life is training and, of course, he trains hard. He has to."

Kim thought about that a moment. "So what's he training for?" she asked softly.

"I honestly don't know, Kim. But I can tell you this, it's not for competition and it's not to survive his next encounter with a criminal. He's training for something he can't even identify yet; something that's out there on the horizon—like a storm on the other side of these

188

mountains. In this valley you can't see the storms coming until they hit you, but if the wind is right you can smell them, even before you hear that telltale rumble in the distance. There's a darkness in the wind, Kim. He's smelled it and knows he has to be ready when it comes."

Kim felt a chill run through her and wished for a heavier jacket than the light windbreaker she wore. "I don't understand, Frankie."

Frankie shook her head. "Of course not. You can't. Neither of you can. When you're young, perspective is too short. Nathan understands he's extremely talented but he doesn't understand that he's special. But now you at least have some idea, Kim, because I've explained what little I know. It's all you need for now, it's all there is. Someday when I'm not there, you may have to remind him of it."

Kim was lost for words. She watched Nathan in the distance, talking intently with Brad. The subject of their conversation was the rifle being passed back and forth between them. She couldn't hear any of the words but suspected that even if she could, there would be no understanding—so obscure and technical would the conversation be. She watched Nathan and wondered about what she had heard until, Frankie gave a gentle touch on the arm, interrupting her thoughts. "Kim, do you know any Nathan Burdett stories? I can assure you we'll guard them, but it's important they be collected."

Again silence was her initial response but it was brief. "A few months ago I watched him defuse a potentially deadly situation with a gentle word and a little black dog." And she told about Ottawa. Frankie beamed at the outcome and Kim could see she'd made her day.

"Thank you, Kim."

"You're sure he needs someone to look after him?"

"We all need someone to look after us. Even you, dear." She reached over, took her hand and squeezed it gently, not letting go for a long time.

They'd been at the range three hours when Kim looked at her watch and tugged Nathan's sleeve. "I think we should consider leaving soon if you have to pick up your mother."

Nathan checked his own wristwatch and nodded in agreement as a bullet passed three feet over their heads—its sonic whip-like crack and a round hole in the paper target the only evidence of its passage. Nathan had taken Kim down into the target butts and now they'd have to wait until the current relay of shooters finished before leaving this concrete and earth shelter. A second and a half later the faint and distant boom of the shot that had launched the bullet came drifting over the targets. Nathan waited for the echoes to die away before answering. "This relay's almost done. We'll be out in plenty of time."

Twenty minutes later they said their good-byes, climbed into Nathan's mother's car and turned left onto the gravel road that would lead them home. Sharp turns, low hills and loose gravel kept Nathan's speed low. They'd driven half of the short distance to the Silhouette Range when, after a right turn that was also the crest of a hill, a van parked on the side of the road came into view. The hood was up and a frustrated-looking man leaned against the front fender, his arms crossed.

Nathan couldn't see into the vehicle because it pointed in the same direction they were traveling and it possessed the usual darkly tinted windows. He smiled at the driver's plight, speculating that inside was an irate wife who just had her weekend drive into the foothills ruined. Seeing their vehicle come around the corner, the man detached himself from the fender and crossed the road in anticipation of them stopping. Having been in similar circumstances, Nathan started braking and began lowering his window.

The glass was halfway down when Kim gasped. "Don't stop!" she yelled.

"What? Why not? He . . . ."

Kim cut him off by grabbing the steering wheel and stomping hard on the gas pedal. The car shot ahead. Not content to let the car follow its course down the middle of the road, Kim jerked the wheel to the left just enough to cause the walking man to turn into a diving one.

"Hey!" yelled Nathan in protest. But as their gravel-spewing Ford swept by the van, he caught sight of the left side sliding door being flung open. He glimpsed at least three more people inside. In the speeding blur, faces didn't register but the front half of several guns did—short black rifles with high front sights and flash suppressors—CAR-15's. That convinced him Kim had the right idea.

190

Kim relinquished her hijacking of the steering wheel the instant they passed the van. Nathan was fighting to regain control when the first bullets slammed into the car. Behind him he caught a mirrored glimpse of two men in kneeling positions in the middle of the road, firing rifles. Behind them another scrambled out of the ditch and slammed the hood. Then the rear window exploded in a blizzard of safety glass and lead. The first curve was less than fifty yards. Nathan accelerated, taking it on the inside. They made it around and out of sight. He doubted any of the shooters had fired more than half a dozen shots. They had a lead, but it was slim.

"Are you okay?" He stole a glance at Kim who had produced her SIG P229 from somewhere.

"I'm good. How about you?"

"Fine. What was that?"

"People who want to kill us. I recognized that creep on the road from a bar last night."

Nathan concentrated on his driving. Maintaining their lead was his best option. With just Kim's P229, he didn't want to stop and fight a vanload of thugs with semi-automatic carbines. He considered the Ranger station and dismissed it. They were too far and the rangers here were all unarmed. Stopping there might discourage whoever was after them, or if they were determined, it would add to the body count. As they neared the Texas gate Nathan slowed.

"Why are you slowing down?" asked Kim, facing backwards, her pistol up on the seat.

"If there's anyone on this range, I'll pull in. They'll have guns and that van might break off." Nathan leaned forward. "Gate's locked," he announced a moment later. "We're running for it."

Something was wrong with the car. It didn't feel right. It slewed badly but he straightened out, accelerating down the hill into a hard left where the road leveled out across a hundred-yard piece of boggy lowland.

Kim sensed the problem. "What's wrong?" She was still twisted in her seat, pistol up and ready.

"I think they got one of our tires. I'll run it down to the rim if I can keep up speed but we may have to hit the bush."

191

"Your call," she yelled.

Nathan started into the flattening left turn but felt it right away. Too fast! It was the right rear tire, either flat or getting there quick. With no traction the inertia of the left turn was forcing the rear end to slide out from under them.

"Hang on!" he yelled, "We're going in!" The rear of the car dropped over the edge of the raised roadway. But the front wheels held their traction and they slid sideways at an awkward upward angle, using up forward momentum until they stopped with a jolt. Not a bad stop, thought Nathan as he fought against gravity to open the door of the steeply slanted car. His exit was more fall than jump. He scrambled around the rear of the vehicle to Kim's side, to find her standing on the outfall end of a large steel culvert. She looked back up the road as a light breeze thinned the cloud of dust.

"Here they come!" she called, jumping down to where Nathan stood and handed him the pistol.

He pushed her into the tangle of the marsh ahead of him. "Go as hard as you can. When you hear me shoot, go down."

Kim took in the flat soggy terrain as she tried to run. Mostly, it was dense, waist-high brush and every fifty yards or so lived a scrawny spruce. Going down in this stuff would make you invisible all right, but in this flat bog there wasn't a solid piece of cover for a hundred yards. Brush clawed at her legs and the uneven ground was determined to trip her. Quickly though, she picked up a pattern to the ground. There were small channels where the water flowed, only six inches deep but a foot wide—enough to give her a more stable footing. She concentrated on picking the best route and not looking back. Nathan was behind her, she could hear him fighting the brush too. What's behind them is his responsibility, she thought. He has the gun. Then she heard him fire, the sound of it driving her down into six inches of cold water.

From her position in the shallow channel she looked back and was surprised to see visibility was good underneath the canopy of leaves created by the ground birch. Nathan was down behind her and crawling forward. He followed the narrow channel, crawled over her legs and stopped at her waist. "What happened?" asked Kim.

192

Nathan took a couple of deep breaths before answering, "I waited 'til they stopped the van, then I fired a round at the guy in the front passenger seat. A good shot but it was into the door. If the bullet made it through I got one. Mainly, I wanted to let them know we have a gun."

"You think now that their little ambush failed they might give up and go home?"

"Possibly. That *is* a public road and . . . ." A bullet ripped through the branches over their heads and Nathan vaulted forward, pressing Kim lower and pushing his face close to hers. Three more supersonic buzz saws cut apart the branches around them; one close enough to send bits of leaves raining down around them.

"Looks like they haven't gone home," whispered Kim dryly. "And Nathan . . .?"

"What?" he raised his head slightly, their faces so close he couldn't focus on her features. Her breath was warm on his cheek and the smell of perfume penetrated the musty odor of wet earth.

"You're on top of me for one of two reasons. Either you're protecting me or you have something else on your mind. I suspect it's protection and I don't need it." Nathan slid wordlessly back to his previous position. "Follow me," said Kim. " Let's see if we can slither like whatever animals use this swamp and put some more distance between us and those rifles."

They made progress, but five minutes later searching shots started raking the brush. Nathan picked up a difference in the reports and pulled at Kim's soggy ankle. "They've started to work around us. There's high ground on each side and they're taking it. Probably still one or more at the van as well."

"Want to pop up for a look? You might get a shot."

"Not with rifles on at least three sides of me."

"How far are we from the road?"

"Maybe seventy-five yards."

"That's all?" She readjusted the soaked cap on her head. They were immersed in cold water that was sucking the life out of them as surely as a bullet, just slower. She pointed that out to Nathan, then

193

added, "How about the shooters back at the range. We're not that far away. They should hear this. Won't they come to see what's going on?"

He shook his head. "No, it's just gunfire. They'll probably think it's people at the Silhouette Range. What we need is . . . ." Nathan's mid-sentence stop caused Kim to raise her head and look back at him. He tapped her twice on the thigh.

"What?"

"Have you got your phone?" Kim groaned and hung her head back down. Then she rolled over onto her back in the water, reached inside her jacket, and handed him a dripping phone.

"You're not calling the police I hope. They'll never get here in time."

"No," whispered Nathan. "And if they came in here it would just put good people in body bags." A sly mud-streaked smile crossed his face. "If these boys want to shoot rifles, I have friends who love to play that game."

Brad was surprised to hear his phone chirping its musical tone. When he'd geared up for the morning's shooting, he'd tossed it somewhere into the interior of his Nissan Pathfinder, thinking it was turned off—obviously not. He took a full forty-five seconds to successfully track the sound to its origin.

"Brad," said a distant whisper once he'd answered. "It's Nathan. I need help."

There was urgency in the voice that commanded attention. "Where are you? What's going on?"

"When we left the range Kim and I got ambushed by a bunch of goons in a red minivan. They've got us pinned down just . . . ." The distinctive sound of a bullet's supersonic crack carried over the cellphone. ". . . just down the hill from the Silhouette Range, in that first big flat." Brad heard the subdued thump of a rifle report with his non-telephone ear. No relays on this range were shooting.

"I can hear gunfire off that way."

"That's us getting shot at," whispered Nathan. "Right now *they're* doing all the shooting. It's several CAR-15's versus one 9 mm, Brad. And things are going to fall apart for us real soon."

Brad started to move. Two older men stood at the truck next to his Pathfinder. All the other shooters had moved up to the 600-meter range. He walked over and snagged their attention by waving and pointing at the cellphone to his ear. "What do you want us to do, Nathan?"

"Come bail us out. Give us some cover. Throw lead. Shoot these suckers!" Another bullet crack came over the phone. "Anything!"

"Hang on." The distant thump of a rifle shot again drifted in from that direction. It was a surreal experience—hearing a bullet crack over the phone, then seconds later listening to the shot itself echo in the distance. "Ken, John, grab your rifles and ammo and get in my truck!" They glanced at each other, and hearing the urgency in Brad's voice, hustled to do as they were told. Brad turned his attention back to the phone. "I've got two more riflemen. They're old-timers but it's all that's here. We're leaving now," he said, climbing into the driver's seat.

"Come as far as the Silhouette Range," said Nathan. "You'll see a red minivan on the road below you. That's them. At least four. Some are on foot following the high ground to try and get us in a crossfire. Kim and I are burrowed into the mud and brush somewhere in the middle of the flat."

"Hang on," yelled Brad. "Here we come." He snapped the phone shut and tossed it to Ken as he pushed the limits of physics in getting the SUV out the range gate and onto the road.

"What in the Sam Hill is going on here, Bradley?" questioned an irritated Ken as Brad's vicious left turn threatened to propel him out of the vehicle. "And who's an *old-timer*?" he added, grabbing for anything stationary.

"It's Burdett, somebody's trying to kill him again."

Ken clutched the dash and swore. John leaned forward, bracing himself with one big hand on each of the front seats. "We can't be letting that happen, Brad."

"I know. Get ready, we're going to deal ourselves in."

Ken used one free hand to control his rifle in the wildly pitching truck. "Didn't those bikers get enough the last time they came after him?"

195

From the back seat John spoke up as he pulled ammo out of a cartridge box and stuffed them in his pockets. "How about if we let them kill him. And then we shoot everybody who's left standing. Would that finally end it?"

"Kim's with him."

"Ohhhhh. I saw her," drawled Ken. "She's way better looking than Burdett."

"Yeah," agreed John, trying to recover a cartridge he'd dropped on the floor that was rolling from side to side. "I'll rescue *her*." He caught the errant round of ammunition and slipped it in the pocket of his shooting jacket. "We'll teach those dirtbags to mess with our womenfolk. Did I ever tell you about the time back in Korea when we caught . . ."

Brad cut him off, "John, reach behind you and get my rifle out of the back—and a blue ammo box. There's two, an empty one and a full one." John did as he was told and popped the lid on the plastic ammo box just as Brad turned a hard corner. Fifty shiny rounds of .223 with black moly-coated bullets spilled out onto the floor of the Pathfinder.

"They're both empty now," said John.

Brad groaned.

"Serves you right for calling him old," yelled Ken over the sound of the screaming engine and rattling gravel.

"Here's the gate!" called Brad a second before the speeding Pathfinder skimmed over the heavy steel pipes of the cattle gate. As soon as the vehicle was clear he locked the brakes and let it drift to a sideways position in the center of the road, its right side facing off into the valley.

John and Ken piled out the right side while the vehicle was still in the last remnants of its skid and jogged around to the driver's side for cover. John stuffed Brad's rifle into his outstretched hand. "Thanks for turning our side towards the killers," he added sarcastically. Both old shooters dropped flat to the ground at the front of the vehicle and pulled into their slings.

"How far to the van?" called Ken.

"Four hundred," answered a breathless John.

196

"In your dreams. It's five hundred if it's an inch."

"Well I'm going down fifteen minutes from eight hundred," John started twisting the elevation knob on his rear sight. "And three minutes of left wind."

"Hey, you guys, where's my ammo?" Brad had been frantically searching the floor of his truck for his spilled cartridges but found nothing.

"I'll see you on the wind but I'm only going down thirteen and a half minutes."

"See the guy up on the roof of the van?"

"Yeah, he just fired a shot."

"Let's take him first."

"Go ahead, I'll see if I can spot for you."

"John, you old cripple! Where is my ammo?!" Brad sounded frantic.

Ken's rifle roared but there was no apparent effect on the target. "Wait," said John. "I think he looked up. Hah! That means you're high. Spot this Ken."

John's prone position put his muzzle closer to the ground than Ken's and the blast kicked up a cloud of powdered road dust. The breeze cleared it quickly enough to see the shooter topple toward them and fall onto the road. "Told you. Four hundred," said John, just as the target picked himself up and limped around to the other side of the van.

"Four hundred, eh? You shot him in the leg, you old fart."

"Okay, so maybe we should split the difference. Make it four-fifty." Both men readjusted their rear sights.

"John! For the last time where is my ammo?!"

"It's on the road on the other side of the truck. The side facing the killers," he added with some satisfaction.

"What?"

"It's called inertia, Bradley. When you went into that fancy four-wheel drift that put our side toward the bad guys, Ken and I opened the door to get out while you were still moving. All that ammo on the floor left with us." He brought the rifle down from his adjustment. "Oh - oh. See the creep on this side of the bog? He just got in behind a big spruce. I think he's going to . . ." They heard a supersonic crack at the same time as the two rear windows of the Pathfinder blew out, one left and one right. ". . . shoot at us."

"Brilliant observation." Ken fired and the man broke cover, sprinting for the van.

"Apparently I can see better than you can shoot." John touched off a shot and the runner sped up. "Moving target," he said in explanation as another bullet cracked over their heads. "Where'd that one come from?"

"Other side of the bog. Just at the edge of the treeline." Ken fired and another bullet answered his. "It's really tough to see him in there," said Ken as he reloaded. "The runner's made it to the van. Why don't you hammer away at it and I'll take the guy on the other side?"

John's rifle boomed and the smack of lead on steel reached their ears a second and a half later. He cranked open the bolt, popping the empty out and while he was dropping in a fresh round the rifle beside him fired again. That started a rhythm—while one reloaded the other fired. Every ten seconds a new projectile was launched.

Brad peered over the hood of the Pathfinder, an empty rifle still in his hands.

"The van's starting to move," announced John.

"And my man's on the run," said Ken reloading. With no more incoming rounds, Brad seized the opportunity and darted to the far side of the SUV. Shiny cartridges littered the gravel and he paused long enough to grab a dusty handful. Brad made it back to the cover of the vehicle and the new runner was almost to the road when Ken fired again.

"You got him!" exclaimed a surprised John, watching the man go down hard at the edge of the road. The minivan braked and a figure leaped from the far side, running to the downed man. The rescuer boosted him up and hustled him into the van just as Brad went prone between Ken and John, slamming a cartridge into his rifle. He was sighting on the retreating van when two hands, one from each side, blocked his sights.

"You're too late, Bradley," said Ken. "It's over."

"Yeah," agreed John. "You missed everything."

Ken shook his head from side to side. "He never got to rescue anybody did he, John?"

"Nope. He's not getting any grateful kisses from Kim."

"It's just as well. His wife wouldn't understand anyway, would she?"

"No. But I'll bet we can get *Nathan* to kiss him."

Brad snapped, and the two elderly shooters took cover behind the Pathfinder, complaining bitterly about senior abuse. Brad threw every empty cartridge case and loaded round of ammunition he could find at them. When he finally ran out, they drove the still functional SUV to the bottom of the valley. Their collective shouts brought two soggy figures to their feet and stumbling out onto the road.

CHAPTER ELEVEN

Behind the friendly faces and kind smiles that came to their rescue, Nathan saw anger. Friends had been attacked—again. He saw it when they staggered back onto the road where laughing and back slapping couldn't conceal it. He saw it back at the clubhouse where generous and helpful people were plentiful as he and Kim were dried off, warmed up and loaned clothing. The assumption that Satan's Riders had returned to finish the job reigned supreme, and Nathan said nothing to counteract that. Personally, he wasn't convinced.

His mind replayed the brief glimpse in the rear-view mirror, just before the back window exploded; of two men in professional-looking kneeling positions in the middle of the road. When the plan fell apart, there was no stand up and blaze away like amateurs. Two shooters assumed identically solid positions and opened fire, while a third scrambled out of the ditch and slammed the hood. Someone else inside the vehicle, an unseen face, started the van for the chase. Everything was stamped with efficiency and professionalism—no simple thugs here.

And they'd both be professionally dead if Kim hadn't recognized the apparently stranded motorist at the side of the road. Nathan burned to ask her what her association was with him, but with one or another helpful hovering person constantly present it was a subject he dared not bring up.

Bob and Frankie Coombs gave Kim and Nathan a ride into Cochrane where the local Dodge dealership also served as host for the only car rental agency in town. Kim insisted on paying for the rental car, and once she came out of the office swinging a set of keys she gathered the four of them around Bob's truck.

"Bob would you pick up Nathan's mother and take her back into Calgary for us? We have some things to do." She gave Nathan a knowing look, hoping the other two would see it as well and not ask any questions.

"No problem," said Bob. "Consider it done."

"We can get her," said Nathan, looking at his watch. "We're not even late."

Bob looked at Kim, ignoring Nathan. "We'll pick up Emily and take her home. You and Nathan have bigger problems than getting her back to Calgary right now." Then he switched to Nathan. "Go deal with your big problems. Let your friends look after the little ones."

"Thanks," replied Nathan, sheepishly. "But don't tell her too much. She may not take this well. I'll have to figure something out before I get home."

"How about if we say you drove her car off the road and it's being repaired? And that you'll be home later this evening?" suggested Bob.

"Sure. It's even the truth. Just leave out the bullets and the rest is okay. Then she won't worry."

They said their good-byes and Kim and Nathan climbed into the rental. The thunk of Nathan's car door slamming signaled the beginning of privacy, and the question in his mind, clamoring to get out, did.

"Okay, how did you know?"

Kim started the car and put it in gear before answering. "Wait a couple of minutes. There's a few things I have to do first."

"No! I think you can tell me . . . ."

"I said wait!" The anger in her voice effectively stopped Nathan's questions and they continued in strained silence.

Kim drove across the railway tracks and parked at the west end of First Street, the start of the downtown business district. "Give me your wallet, Nathan."

"Why?"

"Because, right now, it would be the smart thing to do!"

He handed it over slowly, and she rummaged through the still damp contents of first his and then her own. The damp leather yielded nine credit cards to her searching fingers. Those and her cellphone were clutched in her right hand as she exited the car. "Wait here. I'll be right back," she said, tersely.

Nathan watched her walk east down the sidewalk. She stopped at the end of the block beside a litter container and looked up and down the street, as if searching for someone. Then, abruptly she lifted the hinged metal lid and her cellphone slid out of sight into the blackness. Watching her closely now, Nathan saw her cross the street, still walking east. As she hit the sidewalk on the other side, one of the credit cards fluttered to the concrete. Then he lost sight of her in the clutter of cars and pedestrians. When she reappeared she was on the opposite side of First, coming back west. She walked by on the other side without looking at him. Kim crossed the street at the end of the block and Nathan swiveled his head around in time to see what must have been the last card spiral downward and come to rest where the gray sidewalk met the cedar siding of Bentley's Books.

"What was that about?" asked Nathan once she had returned and was maneuvering out of the parking stall.

"That was Survival 101. For my own protection, my phone has a locating device built in. It works whether it's on or not. And credit card usage can, of course, be tracked."

"Of course."

"And if someone picks up the cards and tries to use them illegally they'll be tracking the wrong person."

"Of course." A pause, waiting for the explanation. She was stalling.

Kim drove out of town and turned south onto Highway 22.

"The creep leaning up against the van, I recognized him from last night. I saw him in an Irish pub in Calgary. He was sitting by himself near the door. I remember the smirk on his face when I stormed out—right after I told Leith off." She blurted the last part and waited.

Nathan exploded. "Leith? Leith's in Calgary? You *know* Leith?"

Kim drew in a deep breath and exhaled most of it before she replied. "We work together, Nathan. Leith and I both have the same assignment."

He looked at her in astonishment.

She replied to his unspoken question. "You. You're the assignment."

Nathan remained quiet. He crossed his arms and stared straight ahead. When he did speak his voice sounded confused. "I think you'd better explain," he said, through clenched teeth.

Kim's knuckles whitened on the steering wheel. "To steal a popular phrase, it's all about you, Nathan. It has been ever since your skill level jumped so far above everyone else's at the ranch. You were the 'golden boy', the one who could do things no one had ever seen or imagined. You have no idea how many strings were pulled and how many people were manipulated to test you, refine you and take you to where you are now. And, it's all for nothing. You can't be controlled and so you're being killed. And me too, it would appear."

"Who?" His voice still subdued.

"Leith. That whole crew was Leith's. I don't know if he was there himself but it was his job."

"I figured that much out myself. I mean who's been manipulated and who's doing it?"

Kim hesitated until Nathan shifted in his seat and stared at her. "I was brought into The B-Zone Project as the fitness instructor, but my other job was to represent the shared interests of the intelligence organizations involved. I was supposed to develop a friendship with whoever emerged victorious and issue a regular report for our people."

"Who did you report to?"

"Kent. With his UN link, his office is a focal point for a number of international undertakings."

"I see." Disappointment and disgust filled both words.

"No, you don't! You don't see anything. I've always worked for my government and still do. They just put me under Kent's authority for the duration of this project. Kent's had his hand in it from day one. And," she added as an afterthought, "Danny doesn't know anything about it. I'm sure he suspects Kent is pulling some strings from a distance but Danny's just what he claims to be."

"Who was manipulated?" Nathan wasn't letting it go.

"Please don't ask," begged Kim. "It's all in the past now. We need to figure out where we're going from here and . . ."

"Who." he demanded.

"You won't like it." Kim glanced over at Nathan but got only a cold stare back. "The Rider's were the first ones," she said finally. "Kent sent them after you as a test. You passed." She looked back at Nathan when the traffic allowed it. The same stare was still there. "I didn't show up at Bob's shop that night by coincidence," she admitted. "I was there to monitor you, help out if necessary and report. Leith was there too. He was up on the hill above the house."

Nathan muttered something, but above the road noise she couldn't make out what it was.

"Kent let a few months go by and then he reeled you in for himself. Anton and his cronies were another step in your development. Kent thought by the second time through you should have been getting used to killing. Maybe even enjoying it a little. At least relishing the adrenaline rush. It didn't work out that way though. Did it?"

"What about you, Kim? Do you like the killing?"

"No! I mean, I'm not a killer. Not like some people are. Some people like it," she admitted. Nathan didn't answer. "I was as surprised as them. The way you performed, it looked like you were enjoying yourself."

"Where were you?"

"At the treeline, between the freeway and the parking lot. Covering you with a rifle. That's how Leith knew where the fourth man had gone and where to send you to get him."

"And Jasper?"

"I was there too. But that was a weird operation." Kim's brow furrowed in thought. "It was handled differently. I got the feeling Kent didn't want you to go. That someone other than him was calling the shots on that one. And something went wrong with it—besides you disobeying orders, I mean." She scratched her head and pulled a piece of leaf out of her hair. "It was weird." And then in answer to the unspoken question, "I was in the background in case I was needed. As it turned out I didn't have to do anything."

"And what about Ottawa?"

"Just what it appeared to be. You were back in law enforcement so I was there with you."

"And you reported to Kent?"

"Yes."

"Thanks. That was the one that finally got me fired. Thanks a lot, *friend*."

"That's not right! That wasn't it!" she shot back.

Kim was driving too fast to make the exit ramp going back to Calgary and Nathan pointed at it as they went by. "You missed . . . ."

"We're not going back to Calgary."

"But . . . ."

"You don't get it do you?"

"Get what?"

"Later. First, you need to know it was your contact with the reporter that put Kent over the edge. That's why he's sterilizing you."

"You told him?" Nathan was incredulous.

"I didn't. You have to believe that. I never told him anything you said. But somehow Leith knew all about Jerry Mitchell. I don't know how."

"Your entire relationship with me has been a lie and now you want me to believe you on something? Good luck, lady."

"Look, I'm trying to come clean with you."

"From where I sit you're looking dirtier all the time."

Kim's cheeks reddened and she lapsed into silence. "Fine. I deserved that," she said finally.

Nathan fixed his eyes out the window, watching the passing scenery. He was afraid if he looked at her he'd explode in a fit of rage. This 'friend' had been manipulating his trust. She'd helped arrange circumstances so that the lives of those who were his real friends had been threatened. She'd helped lure him into circumstances where his life had been in danger and she'd taken part in trying to teach him how to kill—and like it. If she were a man he'd already have punched her.

"Why aren't we going back to Calgary?" he asked once he'd regained some composure.

"It's too risky. There are professionals after us now, Nathan; people with tremendous resources in manpower, money and technology. If Kent wants you bad enough, it'll be very tough to stay hidden. And we certainly can't go back to a place we belong."

205

"But I need to . . . ."

" . . . look after your mother?" Kim finished the sentence for him. "You need to stay alive, Nathan. Your friends will look after her."

"Then . . . ."

"No. You can't call her or anyone else. You can't make a long call, you can't make a short call, you can't send an e-mail and you can't mail a postcard. We have to disappear. Completely."

"Is that why we're headed south?"

"The border is south." Nathan nodded in response, but still refused to look at her. "What highway am I looking for?" she asked, trying to sound pleasant, hoping the worst of it was over.

"Number Two," he said without enthusiasm. "Once you've picked it up it's a straight run to the US border."

Kim made the turn fifteen minutes later and they drove another hour without a word being spoken, each of them alone with their thoughts. Initially the silence was welcome but eventually it deteriorated into a contest of who would speak first. Kim took the initiative, speaking softly. "I know you're angry and I don't blame you, but don't go off half-cocked." She hoped the old firearm cliché would be something Nathan could relate to.

"I'm not," countered Nathan quietly. "I'm going to hold my fire," he paused briefly, "until I can see the whites of the eyes."

Kim opened her mouth to reply, but then snapped it shut as she thought better of it. "Fine," she replied in resignation. She glanced to her right and examined his face in the fading light of day. Anger was plastered all over him, she expected that. What she was looking for was its direction. Was he still struggling to come to terms with what she had done or was Kent the focus of his feelings now? The flimsiest tendrils of friendship still seemed to exist between them. He was allowing those to remain. He was still talking to her, letting her take charge and he hadn't punched her lights out yet. Those were the good signs. There were too many bad ones to think about. The connections were damaged, but maybe it wasn't terminal. In an effort to stop the growing chill, she forced a smile and changed the subject. "Let's stop talking in clichés, shall we? We're both being hunted now and we need to work together."

206

Nathan ignored her comment but he did talk to her. That made her hopeful. "Ever stop to think how many clichés and trite little sayings we've picked up from firearms? Things like 'don't go off half-cocked'."

A high degree of certainty crept into Kim's voice as she replied, "I can definitely say that's something I haven't given much consideration to."

"Think about it," he said pointing off to the west towards a low rise of hills. "About five years ago Bob and I got snowed in at a hunting camp up there in the Porcupine Hills and we had to sit in our tent for a day and a half waiting for the blizzard to blow out. One of the things we did to pass the time was see how many firearm clichés we could come up with. It's amazing how the vocabulary has penetrated into everyone's language and most people don't even realize it."

"Okay," said Kim, still faking her smile. Nathan's voice sounded preoccupied. This wasn't where his head was. This was a fresh coat of paint over a collapsing building. She kept painting. "How many can you remember?"

"No," replied Nathan. "You first."

"Oh, all right. Let me think." Her brow furrowed as she drummed her fingers on the steering wheel until an idea worked its way to the surface. "Son of a gun!" she exclaimed, trying to sound excited.

"Not bad," he said flatly. "Try again." He still didn't look at her.

"Not a chance," countered Kim. "Not until you tell me what it means. Come on. You're the expert. Where did it come from?"

"That one goes way back. If I remember right it's a phrase that originates from the time of sailing ships. The cannon on the decks of military ships had gunners to service and fire them and they basically lived beside their guns. Occasionally women were allowed to live right there with them. Children happened, and in the social order of the day they became illegitimate bastards and the phrase 'son of a gun' was coined to refer to them. Weird how the meaning has changed. Try again."

"No, it's your turn now."

"Sure. Lock, stock and barrel," he offered easily.

"And I think I even know what that means," said Kim. Then she added, "How about, 'going great guns'."

Nathan nodded. "A shot in the dark."

Kim laughed but she noticed Nathan didn't join in. Still, the tension retreated just a little. Under better circumstances she would be having fun with this. But who was doing the manipulating now, she wondered. Nathan's perception of her betrayal hadn't changed, she was sure of that. This talk was just a pleasant little veneer to pass the time and avoid the issue. She didn't want a fight and it appeared Nathan didn't either. By unspoken mutual agreement they were both burying things, at least for the moment. It would come back, she knew it would.

"He's shooting blanks."

"She's a flash in the pan."

Kim paused. "All right, help me out again. I know what it means but where did it come from?"

"Black powder and flintlock muskets. Sometimes the flint would ignite the powder in a flintlock's pan but for various reasons the main charge wouldn't light, so all you got was a flash and a bang with no actual shot fired."

"I'll buy that. But 'she'?"

"Why not? If *he* can shoot blanks, *she* can be a flash in the pan."

Kim was quiet for a moment. "I guess that way no bullets fly and neither one gets hurt."

"Sure," said Nathan, pulling the lever that tilted his seat back. He closed his eyes while dropping the seat to a reclining position, a signal the conversation was over. "That way neither one gets hurt."

Nathan slept the rest of the hour and half drive to Lethbridge. Either that or he pretended to sleep, Kim wasn't sure which. She was just glad his eyes were closed when the tears came. She had to wipe at them for a full minute before they stopped.

When she braked to a halt in the parking lot of the first mall she saw, he opened his eyes and sat up.

"There's things we need," she explained. "Clothes especially." She pointed at the Sears sign visible through the car window to

208

Nathan's right. "Unless you're planning to wear those borrowed coveralls forever. Get a basic wardrobe, a shaving kit and a suitcase to put them in."

"And what do we use for money?"

"I'm sure there's a bank machine in there I can use."

"*Those* withdrawals should be easy to track?"

"Only if the people doing the tracking know about the account. Nobody knows about mine but me. I can keep us supplied with clean money but we have to pay cash for everything."

"Sounds like you were ready for this," said Nathan as Kim locked the car.

"Just prepared," she replied. "In this business it's important to be prepared."

"Survival 101 again?"

"I can keep us alive and functioning and I can get us across the border. That's part of what I do. Then it's up to you to end it. That's what you do."

Nathan reached out and opened one of the entrance doors to the mall for her. "We'll have to talk about that."

"It's a long drive south, Nathan. We'll take turns driving and sleeping. And we're not stopping for anything but gas until Vegas. This is your last chance for a good meal 'til then."

"Why Vegas?"

"We need a big city in which to dump this car and get lost in. Vegas is as good as it gets."

With new clothes, a hot meal and a full tank of gas they again followed the highway south. At the border Kim assured the guard they were both Canadian citizens and were going on a short holiday to Great Falls, Montana. When questioned about the rental car, she explained how her own useless bucket of bolts had blown a head gasket two days ago and now she had to go through the hassle and expense of renting. Her convincing smile and a good story were enough to get them waved through.

"You're suggesting we kill Kent, aren't you?" asked Nathan somewhere in the empty plains north of Great Falls.

209

"We have two options, Nathan. Hide forever or eliminate the hunter. Kill or be killed. I have no intention of hiding forever."

"Where do your people fit into this? Have they sold you out or are they going to support you?"

"Generally our government is very protective of its people. I suspect that's how they'll act towards me. You, however, are nothing to them."

"Then, you haven't contacted them yet?"

"No."

"Why?"

"To protect you."

"I'm supposed to believe that?"

"You can believe it or I'll drop you at the next gas station. Without me you'll be dead in a week, probably within four days. Your choice. You either trust me now or you don't."

Nathan looked out into the passing darkness. "I'll agree to follow your lead for the time being, but don't ask for trust. That's too much. I'll watch my own back."

"I can work with that."

"And how will it work if Kent is gone? Won't someone step in to fill his shoes?"

"No. Kent's not exactly what he claims to be. His operation is not an official part of the UN or Interpol, even though he takes great pains to portray that. He's a well-connected, well-financed freelancer who contracts his services. Most governments love using him for dirty work because it gives them distance and deniability."

"Most . . . ?"

"We don't. When it comes to enemies of our country, Israel has an official policy that allows for their termination. A legal procedure has to be followed, and the fact it exists isn't secret. We call it extrajudicial execution."

"Is that what I was supposed to become, an extrajudicial executioner?"

"Only if you wanted to."

"I don't want to."

"I know that—now."

"I don't know what's scarier, that you do it or that you have a legal-sounding name for it."

The next day, shortly after sunset, Kim and Nathan drove into Las Vegas. Their route in search of someplace to eat took them down the strip to the front of the Paris hotel and casino. "The S.H.I. convention is on," said Nathan, pointing at the marquee sign in front of the complex.

"S.H.I.? What or who is an S.H.I.?"

"Safari Hunters International," explained Nathan. "The world's largest international hunting organization. They have an annual convention here in Vegas. I know a couple of people back home who are members but other than that, I've never done anything more than read about them. From what I hear they're a great outfit–high standards, lots of conservation work, good people."

"Sort of like you?" asked Kim, stopping at a red light.

"Sort of." Nathan rolled down his window to get fresh air but the noise of the strip came with it. He had to speak louder as a result. "The difference is, these guys are hunters first and shooters second. People like me are shooters first and hunters second. It's just a matter of where you put your emphasis."

"What's Kent?"

"From what I've seen he's definitely a hunter first." Kim gave him an expectant look. "What?"

"Tell me more about this S.H.I."

"Well, they have a reputation for being upper crust. I'm sure there are lots of ordinary working stiffs as members but there's a real group of high rollers in the club as well. Keeping up with them would be completely out of my league."

"What about Kent's league?" asked Kim.

Nathan considered that. "Sure," he nodded in thoughtful agreement. "There were several S.H.I. books in his library. One was a big game record book. Kent seems like a serious enough hunter that he probably has some animals recorded in it."

"Do you think he might be here?"

211

"He told me he doesn't hunt much anymore. 'Forced retirement' he called it, so I doubt it."

"But there might be people here who know him?"

"Sure. If I'm guessing right and he's got trophies recorded in either the *Boone and Crockett* or *Rowland Ward's* record books, some people here will know him." Nathan thought about the possibilities. "Hmmm. It wouldn't take me too long to find out, either," he added.

"One of the first things they teach you in spook school is that knowledge is power. Why don't you hang around here for a day or two and see what you can learn about him? I'll go on to New York and scout around there. Once we've pooled our research we should have enough to figure a way to stop him from coming after us."

Kim didn't wait for Nathan to agree. When the traffic started moving again she made a couple of quick turns and stopped at the Aladdin. "Let's get you a room here." She pointed back the way they had come. "You're just down the street from the Paris, so it should be accessible without being too close. I'll set you up with enough money to do what you need here and buy a ticket to New York when you're ready."

"And you?"

"We'll eat here. Then I'm going straight to the airport. I'll bury this car so deep in one of the Park and Ride lots they won't find it for a month."

The next morning Nathan didn't get up until nine. He ran five miles on a treadmill and worked weights in the Aladdin's health club for an hour. Then, he wandered over to the Paris. After paying the non-member's door fee to get into the merchant's displays, he bought copies of *Boone and Crockett* and *Rowland Ward's* big game record books. A leisurely brunch in a quiet corner, thumbing through the books, yielded a total of four listed hunters with the last name Kent. Nathan realized for the first time that he had never learned Kent's given name. Which was the right Kent? Was that even his real name?

Considering what he did know about Kent, the place to start looking was with people the man's age. He needed an old-timer with stories to tell. Nathan smiled to himself. That shouldn't be too tall an order at a hunter's convention.

Frankie walked out onto the raised deck attached to the rear of the Coombs' house and breathed in the smells of a new spring. She shaded her eyes against the late afternoon sun and looked down to where Bob sat at his shooting bench, test firing the .17 Ackley Hornet. Earlier that day, when he'd come in from the shop for lunch, he'd mentioned that it would be ready to test today. She waited until he fired three more rounds, and when he got up to retrieve his target she walked down the deck's steps and over to the bench.

"Looks good," she said, when he returned with the perforated paper.

"Yeah. And this was fire-forming brass. This one's a shooter." He took out his pocketknife and proceeded to cut the paper target, intent on saving the cluster of bullet holes as a record of the gun's ability.

"I've been thinking," said Frankie, while Bob worked. "That we should have a little talk with that young man from the paper."

Bob kept on puttering. "I suppose we could. He is getting to be a bit of a pest. If I call him up and get firm with him, maybe threaten to call his boss, we can probably get him to stop coming around."

"No, that's not what I mean. I don't think we should run him off. I think we should tell him everything."

Bob looked up and straightened. "And just why in the world would we want to do that?"

"I just got off the phone with Susan, Bob. You remember Susan?" Bob nodded. "Well, I guess she's getting to know him and from what she tells me and from what I've heard from others, I think he'd understand."

Bob sat down and rested his elbows on the bench. Absentmindedly, he rolled an empty cartridge case between his fingers as he spoke. "Frankie, there's no chance at all that he's ready. He'll never believe it. You're kidding yourself."

Frankie reached out and plucked the cartridge case from his fingers. "When this case went into that rifle's chamber, Bob, it looked totally different than it does now. But when you fired it, the heat and pressure of firing made it change shape. It's not the same cartridge any more, is it? Now it can do things it never could before. I think that's happened to our newspaperman."

Bob held out an open cartridge box and Frankie dropped the case into it. "I'm just a gunsmith, Frankie. You're the peoplesmith. I know better than to argue with you about something like this. You do whatever you think best."

Frankie kissed him lightly on the forehead and walked back to the house.

One hour from the time he started looking seriously, and five merchant booths later, Nathan found a likely suspect—an old-timer with stories to tell. He'd dropped Kent's name with likely people at a Rocky Mountain Elk Foundation display and then at the Arctic Safari booth. No bites. Federal Ammunition and the big Winchester array were also zeroes. His luck changed when he tried Weber & Markin, a builder of custom guns. The tall man standing among an assortment of exquisite rifles and shotguns hesitated before answering. When he did speak it was with a German accent. "Ya. I haf heard of him. Robert knows him." He pointed with one of the brochures in his hand at a man autographing books forty feet down the aisle.

"Thanks," said Nathan, moving on as quickly as possible.

The title of the book was *Sixty Years a Hunter* and the name on the cover, Robert Novick. Judging from the crowd at the signing table it was a good book. Nathan avoided him and bought a copy from a young girl at the other end of the publisher's booth. "I'm in a hurry to meet someone right now. I'll have to catch Mr. Novick later for an autograph. Is he going to be here long?"

She looked at her watch. "He'll be with us another hour and then he's scheduled to take a long break and come back at four this afternoon."

Again Nathan moved on as quickly as possible, applying Leith's lesson about not chatting anyone up. 'People remember you if you chat them up'.

An hour later Nathan watched as Robert Novick excused himself from his fans and walked out of the hall. Nathan followed him to the taxi stand outside the Paris. A quick conversation with the next cabby in line and Nathan tailed the old man a short distance down the strip to another casino complex, the New Frontier. He remained a discreet distance behind Novick as he made his way into a quiet lounge. This watering hole was only marginally different than all the others Nathan had seen. Perhaps a little older and not quite as upscale, but flickering slot machines, a smoky atmosphere and some background music were the constants. This lounge had a western theme. Country music drifted over the sound system, and rather than sports on the large screen TV's there were old western movies.

Nathan found a stool affording him a view of the lounge's interior, then ordered a drink and nursed it. The movie soundtracks were muted, the random country songs on the sound system providing all the background noise. Once in a bizarre moment of coincidence, when John Wayne was having woman problems and a twangy voice sang a cheating song, the music matched the movie.

Nathan noticed no shortage of badge-wearing S.H.I. conventioneers, even here. He thought about that a minute before figuring it out. This was the closest western bar to the Paris. No doubt there were some people at the convention who could only take so much champagne and crepes. Those people were here. They congregated in groups of twos, threes or more, eating rare steaks washed down with beer and whiskey. Loners like himself were the exception. This, after all, was a time for socializing, renewing acquaintances and telling stories.

Novick wasn't alone either. At a booth near the center of the lounge, he joined a woman. Silver haired and as old as him, she carried her age with dignity and poise. The years had been kinder to her. They ate slowly, talked comfortably in short interludes; their conversation punctuated by lengthy periods of silence. At ease with each other during the quiet moments, Nathan suspected they had been together a long time.

Because of her, he feared this effort was going to be for nothing. But when she gathered her sweater and shopping bag from the bench beside her and the old man didn't move, Nathan realized he may have lucked out. As he watched, she patted him on the hand and took her leave. When the waitress came and cleared away the dishes the old man pointed to his empty glass. She returned quickly, brought him another drink and Nathan made his move.

He slipped off his stool and started down the aisle that would take him past the old man's table. Book in hand, he made as if to walk by, but when the old eyes lifted and met Nathan's he stopped. "Say. You're Robert Novick, aren't you?"

The old man straightened his slumped shoulders and leaned back to look at who had intruded into his thoughts. "That's right."

"I picked up your book today. But you weren't around to autograph it. Could I trouble you to do that?"

"Sure thing. Have a seat." He indicated the opposite bench, which the woman had vacated. "No trouble." His hand reached for a pen.

Nathan did as he was told. "This is really great, bumping into you like this. I was supposed to meet a fellow here but it looks like he's a no-show. He was going to put me onto some good African outfitters but I guess I'll just have to work the trade show floor tomorrow to get those." The African outfitter ploy was Nathan's impromptu response to the bolo tie the old man wore. His black braided leather tie had silver tips on the string ends and a slide composed of the head of a cape buffalo set atop the continent of Africa. The material appeared to be aged silver and well worn. "What are you drinking?" asked Nathan. "Can I buy you a fresh one?"

"No. No need for that. I just got this one. I'm good. So you're going to Africa?" The old man scrawled a signature into the book.

"That's the plan, if I can line up a good outfitter. The name's Nathan, by the way." He extended his hand across the table.

The old man responded in kind. "Robert," he said. "Not Bob, or Rob, just Robert."

Nathan laughed politely. "Nice to meet you Robert. Have you been to Africa?"

"I have indeed, Nathan, many times. And there are lots of good outfitters in that part of the world. The majority are honest, hard-working professional hunters that have the client's and the game's best interest at heart. The list of good ones is a whole lot longer than the list of bad ones so you won't have any trouble."

"That's good to know."

"What's more important from your perspective, Nathan, is having a good handle on what it is you want to hunt, and what your budget is."

Nathan nodded wisely, trying to look intent on picking up everything the old man was saying. It wasn't a difficult act. The idea of an African safari was a dream. As far as he could see there was no hope of it ever happening. But now he played the role of a smart young entrepreneur with a lot of money and a passion for hunting. Robert talked freely and Nathan asked the kind of probing insightful questions that would garner the man's respect. He gave it a full hour to build rapport. They talked through outfitters, the availability of game and destination areas until political circumstances provided the opening he was looking for.

"My dad told me," said Nathan, "that he has a friend who can open some African doors for me. He says this guy is well connected and can help get permits and licenses without having to endure the long waiting period and the bureaucratic hassles I hear plague those countries."

"I think it's obvious that knowing the right people can help you get things done faster in Africa, but that's where your outfitter comes in. A good one will have those connections. He'll make sure everything is done on time. He knows how Africa works and he'll have it done. In my experience if you try and interfere from this end it'll just cause problems."

"My father says, and he's not a hunter by any means, he just knows this guy from business, that this fellow can even get me into places where other people can't hunt. Now I don't know," said Nathan shrugging, "I'm new at this. Are there places in Africa where you need special permission or connections to get in to hunt?"

The old man bristled visibly. "Sure there are places like that. And there's a name for people who get into those places—poachers.

There's a name for people who let them into those places too—corrupt officials. And there's a name for how they get in, it's graft and bribery."

"Whoa." Nathan held up his hands. "I want no part of something like that. I hunt by the rules or I don't hunt at all. That makes it simple. I'll tell my dad to forget his connections and I'll work through channels and through some of these names you've given me."

He saw the old man relax. Okay, he thought, now take the bait. I've laid it out there, you can smell it and your curiosity is up, all you have to do is take it. Nathan held his breath and waited.

"So, who is this fella with all the connections? Sounds like someone we should watch out for; turn him in if we get the chance."

Got him, thought Nathan. His heart beat faster as he tried to slide the information out as naturally as possible, making an effort to sound helpful, ignorant and slightly disinterested all at the same time. "The last name's Kent, but I don't know a first name. He's a Brit., I know that, probably between sixty and sixty-five. I've seen him once, distinguished looking, if you know what I mean. He works for the government but I'm not sure in what field. Probably a consultant or something, he was vague when I asked him about it."

Nathan studied the man across the table from him, looking for a reaction. There was no dramatic response, but there was recognition; a small nod of the head, a stroke of the chin and a long gaze into an almost empty whiskey glass. Half a minute passed and the only response was his vacant stare into the amber liquid. Nathan probed a little further. "Do you know him? Ever heard of him?"

The question brought his gaze up. "I know him. Haven't seen him for a lot of years but I know him."

Nathan didn't reply, he waited quietly with an expectant look on his face. The old man cooperated. "Even hunted with him once."

"A good hunter?"

The old man lowered his eyes to the whiskey glass and kept them there. "You could say that, Nathan. He researched and studied the game he hunted until no one knew it better. His intellect was massive and he used it to his advantage. He knew everything written about the species right down to the Latin name."

218

Nathan didn't have to fake interest anymore. He put his arms on the table and leaned forward to catch every word the old man spoke.

"Same thing with his technical knowledge about firearms. He knew every ballistic formula, everything worth knowing about every rifle ever made, and he had the money to afford them all. His bush skills were good too. Certainly not in the same league as a tracker or professional hunter but considering the amount of time he spent in the bush he did very well. But, no doubt, he approached that the same way he did everything else; methodically researching, analyzing, disciplining himself and again using his intellect to collect the information and then process it."

"That's the impression I got from him," said Nathan. "A feeling that he's a very intelligent man."

Robert took a sip of whiskey. "And he was, as you say, distinguished looking. That was thirty years ago, and handsome would have been more appropriate then. On the surface he appeared to be the ultimate sportsman. At least that's what we all thought. Eventually we learned he was missing something."

"What was that?" asked Nathan.

"Ethics."

"Ouch."

"Ouch is right. He hurt us bad."

"What happened?"

Robert shifted his attention from the glass to Nathan's face and then to a waitress walking by. "Another round," the old man told her. He looked at Nathan. "The same for you?" Nathan nodded. The old man tossed back what little was left in his glass and handed it to the waitress. When she left he refocused on Nathan. "It's a long story," he said heavily. "Not necessarily a pretty one. But every so often it needs to be told, especially to the younger generation. Those of us in the club who lived through it, we learned some lessons; lessons that need to be passed on. And since it's not something we're proud of, you'll never see it in writing or in the official history—that means it's unofficial history, like what the Indians do. The elders pass on the old stories so that the young people can learn from them, and not make the same mistakes."

Nathan nodded his understanding.

"There's only two ways to learn, Nathan. You learn from your own mistakes or you learn from somebody else's. It's a lot less painful to learn from someone else's."

Nathan sat in silence, thinking of a similar lecture, delivered by Bob. The words were different but the message was the same. Just like then, it was best, now, to let the teacher tell it his way.

"As you can imagine from what I've told you already, Kent, like us, was a passionate hunter. He was born into money. His family is part of that upper ruling class that seems to run things in Britain, and so he had the time and the resources to devote to his passion. He got in at the ground floor when the club was started and because of his charm and natural leadership abilities it didn't take long before he worked himself into an executive position. He was the consummate great white hunter, Nathan, traveling the world in search of adventure, trophies and hunting opportunities. He was well known in our circles. He gave generously to the club activities and conservation projects. Everyone liked him. As I recall he did a workshop at our first convention called 'Finding the Right Outfitter'."

Nathan smiled at the irony. The old man didn't return it.

"Don't bother trying to find it in the archives," he said. "We destroyed all the copies. He did write some articles in the club's magazine as well. If you can find some old copies of those, they're still there. I remember him telling me he was working on a book too. It was going to chronicle his hunting adventures. I think he pictured himself as some sort of O'Rourke or Capstick."

"I imagine he put a few heads in the record books," interjected Nathan.

The old man nodded. "The scuttlebutt was that he intended to have an entry for every single species. And not just *Boone and Crockett* but *Rowland Ward's* as well."

Nathan let out a low whistle.

"He was well on his way too. Had a number one eland and probably three others in the top ten, and a bunch of lower numbers."

"Sounds like a guy who had the world by the tail. No need to work for a living. Go hunting anywhere and whenever you want. I think I'm envious."

"And don't forget, Nathan, that he had the respect and admiration of a lot of people. That, was very important to him. He wanted to make his mark in the sportsman's world. His ancestors had done it through exploration, colonization and building the British Empire. Well, that's not there anymore and this is the age of leisure, so his intention was to become known as one of the greatest hunters who ever lived, one of the greatest sportsmen in the world. He wanted his name to be used in the same breath as Jack O'Connor, Elmer Keith and Capstick."

"Well, it obviously didn't happen. What went wrong?"

"The lion is born to hunt, Nathan, that's what God created him to do. That's his place. Every so often however, something changes in a lion, and while he still hunts, the reason he hunts changes."

"Man-eaters?" volunteered Nathan.

The old head shook from side to side. "Not necessarily. Lions kill for food, either to feed themselves, their young or to share it with their pride. But that's the reason they hunt, and it's a moral-ethical reason. Now, I know lions don't think in abstract terms like morals or ethics, but for the ones that go bad it seems they lose those reasons and then they deteriorate. It can be a man-eater. Though, you know, most man-eaters kill their prey for food, the same reason they'll kill a zebra or an antelope, it's just that the two-legged prey gets easier to catch once they're old and weak.

"But there's the odd lion that'll kill because he enjoys it. They kill for the sake of killing and with no other apparent motivation than that. I saw the results once in a cattle herd. Again, easy prey, fenced in, confined. The lion came in at night, of course, and in the morning all the farmer had left were twenty-seven dead cattle. I've never seen it, but there are stories in Africa about lions who have turned bad and hunted people."

"The Ghost and The Darkness?" volunteered Nathan.

"Yes, The Ghost and The Darkness. They were unique in that they were a pair of lions who killed for the joy of it. It's bad enough when one goes bad, but when two join together, well, you no doubt saw the movie or read the book." The old man shrugged. "As far as I can tell that's what happened to Kent. Somewhere along the way he lost the hunter's ethic."

"Any idea what caused it?"

"Personally? No. I suspect it may have something to do with the aristocratic British tradition he was raised in. We are the lords and you are subjects. The lords can do no wrong, they are the ruling intellectual elite. Combine that with the sort of intelligence he possesses and you have a man who says I am superior to you in every way and the rules don't apply to me. Rules, either man's or God's, are for the subjects not the masters, and therefore I'll do what I want, when I want." An edge of bitterness entered his voice.

"What happened?" asked Nathan, keenly aware that everything he had heard up to now was just background.

"We started to hear rumors about him. At first they were dismissed as personality conflicts, individual jealousies or just campfire stories. We should have known better. When you're downwind from something rotten it's going to stink. Anyway, we finally got some first-hand information.

"Kent went after bighorn sheep up in British Columbia. He and his guide hunted hard for a week, looking for a big one. They finally found him just as a snow squall was running through the valley they were in. The stalk was a tough one, and so was the shot, but Kent pulled off both. Problem was, when he got up to it, it was smaller than what he was looking for. A good legal ram, mind you, but not nearly what he or the guide had estimated on the hoof. Hey, it happens to all of us. But rather than tag it and come back next year to try again, he handed his rifle to the guide and with a good heave pushed it over the edge of a two hundred foot cliff. Then he turned to the guide and announced it was time to carry on with the hunt."

Nathan's stomach churned. A poacher. Somehow it fit.

"When the guide refused, Kent offered him money. The guide walked off the mountain, untethered his horse and rode off. By the time Kent came off the mountain, his guide had pulled base camp and that was gone, too. Kent was livid, but there wasn't much he could do. It

222

was a two day ride back to civilization but fortunately for him the guide never reported it to the authorities."

Nathan exploded. He couldn't help himself. "So he got away with it . . . ."

The old man stopped his outburst with a single upraised hand. "After that incident he didn't book with his usual outfitters any more. Well, occasionally he would, but by and large he used guides that were unknown, or if we asked him, he wouldn't say. The rumors didn't stop, though. We kept hearing those.

"Now, the sheep story made it to our club executive who were as concerned as the rest of us. The last thing they wanted was someone inside the club not hunting by the rules, not respecting the game and not working by our code of ethics. I wasn't aware of it, but they apparently hatched a plan to set Kent up.

"One of them approached him as a conspirator and volunteered information about a man who claimed to have a line on a world record rhino. The only problem being, the rhino was in a national park. But the man had a way in and out and was selling the opportunity to hunt the rhino to the highest bidder.

"They did a real number on him, Nathan. They set up a phony meeting in a motel room, they taped the encounter, and they even got him paying a five thousand dollar advance to the poacher. That was three months before our annual convention. They didn't spring anything on him at the time. They waited until the convention. Their intention never was to prosecute him; it was solely to cause him as much embarrassment and shame as possible.

"Kent was in the running for a board of directors' position that year and when his turn came to make his election speech they called him up to the podium and announced to the gathering there were a few things they needed to be aware of. The president started by announcing that Kent had just made a five thousand dollar donation to The Black Rhino Habitat Fund. There was, of course, a large round of applause for him and lots of cheering. Kent was rather perplexed. I was there; I saw it. Then the president announced the donation had been made unwittingly. He detailed briefly what they had done and then played the audiotape from the motel room.

"Kent turned purple. The rest of us in the room were almost insane with rage at the thought someone we trusted had betrayed us like that. The president was barely able to maintain order, but when he got things quieted down he directed someone at the back of the room to open a door. With that done he addressed Kent. Told him to get down on his hands and knees and crawl out of the room like the lowlife he was, never to set foot in our club again and that he wasn't welcome anywhere in the world that sportsmen gather. Kent of course didn't crawl. He put his chin up, raised his aristocratic British nose and walked to the door."

"I'll bet he didn't get there unscathed," mused Nathan.

The old man smiled, the first time he'd done that all evening. "I take full credit for being the first," he said. "I was seated up front, right on the aisle. It was a morning session so I had a cup of coffee in my hand. When Kent walked by I threw it at him. He didn't even flinch, completely ignored it and kept on walking. He was a scalded mess by the time he made the door. But you know, he never let anything show, eyes straight ahead, marching just like a soldier."

"That's unbelievable," said Nathan. "How come I've never heard this before?"

"Remember, I said the intent was never to charge him. Part of the reason for that was we didn't want to make this a public deal. We wanted to clean our own dirty laundry, at least that's what the executive felt at the time. In hindsight I'm not sure that was right, but that's what they did."

Robert paused and sipped whiskey. "Kent was a traitor, in every sense of the word. Countries aren't proud of their traitors and neither are organizations. As a result, this became something you won't find recorded in the club's history. It never appeared in the minutes of that meeting, but it's what we pass on to the next generation. The story becomes a way of teaching them our values and what we believe. It's a way of making sure this never happens again. Because if it does, Nathan, we'll stand the next guy up there too. We'll strip him of his pride and his reputation and his dignity. We'll humiliate him publicly if we have to, but we will not compromise our ethics or integrity. We're determined to maintain the tradition of the hunt and keep it sacred for all those who follow after us."

"Did Kent retaliate?" asked Nathan.

"Not as far as I know. We also made sure every other hunting and sportsman's organization he belonged to struck him from their roles. He was declared *persona non grata* everywhere that hunters and sportsmen gather. Eventually he just dropped from sight. Those of us who knew him, hear about him every so often. People like you show up, mention they've run into him or his name comes up in conversation. Indications are his burn scars healed and his ego is bigger than ever. He's the sort of slippery eel that will no doubt have ingratiated himself into some power structure somewhere and be doing their bidding. He has the money and the connections to remain well looked after. Except for his memories of that day, I doubt any part of him is suffering."

Nathan sat in silence for a time trying to work through what he'd learned, then the old man interrupted his thoughts.

"Find out what you needed to know?"

"Uh . . . yeah . . . sure. I've got the list of outfitters . . . I'll start making contacts tomorrow."

"You can cut the bull, son. You don't need outfitters any more than I need a new wife. You came in here hunting me right from the git go. Takes a hunter to know one. You sat on that stool over there, caught wind of me, watched and stalked me and then came over here and took your shot." Nathan felt his face changing color as the old man stopped to take a breath. "Do you really know Kent?"

"I do," said Nathan. "And I know him a lot better now."

The old man nodded. "What's your business with him?"

Nathan watched the waitress serve two customers seated in front of slot machines on the opposite side of the room as he considered how to answer that. "It's probably best you don't know."

"I see. Are you going to be seeing him?"

"I expect I will."

"Can you give him a message?"

"Talking to him may not be an option."

"It's come to that has it?"

"It has."

Both men sat quietly for a time and then Nathan abruptly drained the contents of his glass. "I'd better be going," he announced.

"If you get the chance," said the old man, as Nathan stood to leave, "tell him you were talking to me."

"You sure you want me to do that?"

"Don't worry, son." A smile spread across the face. Just tell him you were talking to his old sheep guide, Robert. And tell him I still feel the same way. He's made his pact with the devil and he'll go to hell for it."

"If I get the chance I'll tell him," said Nathan. "If not, I may have to send him there."

The next morning, as Nathan continued to snoop around the S.H.I. convention, Jerry Mitchell drove northwest out of Calgary to Cochrane. Fifteen minutes beyond the small town he turned off a main county road and parked in front of Bob Coombs' gunsmith shop. Frankie stepped outside into the morning sunshine and greeted Jerry as he slammed his car door.

"Hi, Jerry. Thanks for coming."

"My pleasure, Mrs. Coombs." Jerry took the offered handshake. "From what I've heard, no one knows more about Nathan Burdett than you and your husband. And if you'd like to talk about him," he shrugged, "well, I'm a reporter and I'd love to listen. I have to tell you, I was very excited when you called and asked me to come out."

"Wonderful, Jerry." Frankie put a hand on his arm and ushered him towards the house. "You're right, of course. I've known Nathan a long time and nobody knows him better. There are so many things about him you need to know, Jerry. And there are other things too, things you may find hard to understand. I need you to keep an open mind. Can you do that, Jerry?" Her face broke out into the most disarming smile he had ever seen.

"Of course I can, Mrs. Coombs." This was it, he thought. Pay dirt! The break he needed. Jerry's heart beat faster. He had no idea what had made these people change their minds but he was certainly glad they had.

As they approached the door Frankie's smile abruptly faded and her voice became serious. "There are, however, some conditions to our little talk." She stopped and looked at him intently.

Jerry's momentary elation sank. Here it comes, the old 'everything I say is strictly off the record' line. He took a deep breath and carried on, trying to sound cheerful and positive nonetheless. "And what would that be, Mrs. Coombs?"

"We have to sit in the kitchen, Jerry. I always entertain my guests in the kitchen. And you have to have some of my cinnamon buns. I just baked a batch this morning and they're warm and fresh." The smile returned and a wink came with it.

Jerry laughed. He'd just been had. "Cinnamon buns, eh? With raisins or without?"

Frankie's serious air returned. "The only correct way to make cinnamon buns, Jerry, is with *lots* of raisins."

"I love raisins," said Jerry.

"In that case, step into my kitchen," said Frankie. "You're not going to believe some of the stories I have to tell you."

CHAPTER TWELVE

"That one?" asked Nathan, pointing at an office tower reflecting a gold colored hue wherever the sun struck its windowed sides. He leaned forward in the car to try and see the top.

"About thirty floors," volunteered Kim in response to his searching gaze.

"It's plenty close enough," Nathan acknowledged, slowing and eventually stopping the car in response to the traffic light that turned red a half-dozen cars ahead.

"It's not too close?" asked Kim.

"Not if you're down here waiting for me."

"Trust me," she said. Nathan thought about that. Trust didn't come easily yet. Eventually maybe, but not yet. "Go, get whatever you need," said Kim. "I'll get us in." She opened the car door and stepped out onto the pavement. "Is seven o'clock tomorrow evening okay for you?" Nathan nodded. "Great. Over there at seven," she said, pointing at a doorway with a green awning that projected over the nearby sidewalk. "Be ready." An impatient honk sounded behind her and she closed the car door.

Nathan drove as rapidly as New York traffic and his knowledge of the city allowed. He estimated the trip to Shooter's Haven Indoor Range would take half an hour. What had happened last night occupied his mind during the trip to the range.

Kim had picked him up at the airport and they'd skirted Jamaica Bay on the Belt Parkway driving to the hotel where she had spent the previous two nights. They had traded information during the drive and when they were done Nathan unfolded a newspaper and held it so Kim could see the front page. "Look at this," he said. "It's a Calgary Tribune I picked up at a newsstand in the Vegas airport."

Kim glanced at the paper as she drove, taking in the headline. "Three bodies? That's all?"

"Apparently. All found in a burned out red minivan. Each one shot in the head."

"Sterilized."

"Very."

The hotel she drove to was in Flatlands, at least an hour drive south of downtown. She explained it was her intention to work Kent at his downtown office, therefore a home base well away from that location made sense.

After getting Nathan checked in they went for a walk, scouting for someplace to eat. The restaurant they found was a short distance from the hotel and sufficiently crowded that the topic of Kent was avoided until they made the walk back.

"Stone cold simple," Kim said reassuringly. "I can get you into position somewhere between three and five hundred yards from him. With a good rifle that should be easy. Right?"

"I don't think assassination is easy at twenty yards, Kim."

She hesitated. Nathan imagined she was mentally kicking herself. Served her right. "I know it won't be easy for you," she said. But you do agree it's the only way?"

"It's the only way I've been able to think of—so far."

"Just remember, it's really self-defense. If he . . . ."

"Save your breath, Kim." Nathan cut her off. It was rude but he really didn't care. They walked on in silence, passing an open liquor store and a closed and shuttered electronics dealer.

"Can you get the equipment on your own, or will you need my help?" asked Kim.

Nathan took a moment to think about what he'd need to carry out Kim's plan; in response, a sudden idea, popped into his head. The result was a broad smile. "I don't think I'll have a problem. I know where to go."

The unexpected smile seemed to make Kim relax. "Good. That's great. We'll drive in tomorrow and tour by the place. If it's okay, then you can leave me downtown and I'll finish what I need to get us in. You can have the car to get your gear. I'll get around by taxi."

Nathan stopped and zipped up his jacket to ward off the damp breeze. Thrusting his hands into his pockets, he announced, "I'm going for a long walk. What time do we need to leave in the morning?"

"Would you like company?"

"No, I wouldn't. I need to think about what we're doing. What time tomorrow?"

Kim put a hand on his arm. "It's the only way. You understand that don't you?"

"I do. What time, Kim?"

"Breakfast at nine. We'll miss rush hour that way. I'll knock on your door."

At that point he'd made some type of affirmative comment and walked away. They'd been good friends once, thought Nathan. Now they were barely acquaintances. If everything worked out Kent wouldn't be a problem within forty-eight hours and they'd go their separate ways. Each of them back to the life they had before all of this started. Just as well, they were too different anyway.

A sprawling mall occupied a large part of real estate half a mile down the street, and with no better destination in mind he walked in that direction. The mall was on the opposite side of the street, and Nathan crossed four lanes of busy traffic to get there. He did it in two short sprints. The first one got him onto the broad concrete median. The second gained him the mall's parking lot.

Once inside, Nathan walked every corridor in the place. The only stores he found were the usual clothing and gift shops. The only people he saw were senior citizens and teenagers prowling the corridors with him while bored husbands waited outside the stores for their wives. When he was sufficiently bored himself he sat down with a coffee in the food court. The coffee was bitter enough to qualify as originating from the bottom of the pot, but that was to be expected at closing time when all the food vendors were shutting down. Pedestrian traffic in the hallways was dissipating as surely as a morning fog and the mall grew progressively quieter. Nathan stayed put. An idea had drifted across his mind and he was afraid that if he moved it would vanish like the crowds around him. He played with it until a security guard started giving him a look as cold as the coffee.

Reluctantly he drifted out the nearest exit and then walked entirely around the outside of the building. Three hours after walking the perimeter a second time he finally returned to the hotel. It had taken another two hours to fall asleep.

The next morning, promptly at nine, Kim had knocked on his door and they started the day.

When Nathan arrived at Shooter's Haven Range, Phil still occupied his space behind the counter. "Remember me?" Nathan asked, in his friendliest manner.

"Sure do. Haven't seen you around for quite a while. It's Nathan, isn't it?"

"Yeah—been out of the country." Phil's dark eyes narrowed a little but it was a knowing look. "I lost a bunch of equipment. Is the company tab still good here?"

A smile accompanied Phil's answer. "Nobody's told me any different. You're still on the list." Nathan gave a curt nod. Just as he suspected, no one had bothered to let this man know that Nathan was out of the loop. "What do you need?"

"Let's start with a scoped rifle, two good pistols and ammo for everything."

Phil nodded enthusiastically. Nathan smiled back. He was probably going to make this guy's day. The gun-shop employees Nathan knew liked dealing with government agencies and with knowledgeable people. Most of the time those two were mutually exclusive. When one of those rare exceptions showed up he quickly became a treasure. No hassles about price and the bill was paid at the end of every month. Just like clockwork.

"Rifle first?" asked Phil.

"No. Rifle ammo first. What have you got in Federal's Tactical line? I need a bullet that holds together. And no .223, I need .30 caliber minimum."

Phil stroked his chin. "That stuff is hard to get. Let me go check what I have in the back." He emerged a moment later with three silver and blue boxes. "Sixty rounds of .308. That's all I've got."

231

"That's plenty. Now what have you got in a heavy-barrel bolt action that will shoot it well?"

Phil turned around and scanned the rifles on the rack behind him. He walked towards the end of the row and Nathan followed on his side of the counter. "Here's what you want," he announced, pulling a black rifle down from the rack. "Accuracy International AWP. This one even has their folding stock. You may not need it all the time, but it's a nice option to have."

Nathan took the offered rifle and worked the action and safety and removed the magazine. "It comes with the bipod?"

"Yup. Standard equipment."

Nathan pulled out the bolt and set it on the counter. Then he folded the stock into its collapsed position. "I see what you mean," he said. "That could be handy. Have you got a short padded case?" Phil nodded. "What about scopes?"

Phil reached under the glass-topped counter and laid out several. He drew Nathan's attention to the last one. "It's a Leupold Mark 4 with mil-dot reticle, and the usual target knobs and side adjustable parallax. I brought it in from Premier Reticles for a customer who backed out on the deal. They bumped it up to 24X. If the relatively high power isn't too much for you, it's one sweet piece of glass."

Nathan picked it up and checked the details Phil had described. "I like it," he announced with enthusiasm. "Find some solid rings and we'll mount it." Phil produced rings and while Nathan removed the packaging, he once again disappeared into the back, returning with his scope mounting tools. "Please don't take offense," said Nathan as he extended the bipod and set the rifle on the counter, "but I would rather do this myself. If you don't mind? You're probably good at scope mounting but I don't know you well enough to be sure of that."

"No explanations required," said Phil. "I don't get many guys like you in here."

When he had the scope mounted and bore-sighted, and the rifle cased, Nathan added the cleaning essentials. "I need a laser range finder too."

"Is a Bushnell okay or do you want to go all the way to a Leica?"

"How much more is the Leica?"

"About five times more, but they're top notch binoculars at the same time."

"Nothing's too good for government use, is it?"

With that out of the way, Nathan moved to the pistol display and looked at the offerings under the glass. "Ideally I'd like a full-race .45, with a C-More sight, compensator, you know—the works. And an iron-sighted compact as well."

"The compact's not a problem," said Phil, locking back the slide on a Springfield Armory pistol and handing it to Nathan. "But you know how long it's been since I've seen a full-race .45? Everybody shoots .38 Super in competition now."

"I know. I've always had them built specifically for me. It's just that I prefer something harder hitting than a Super."

"Can't help you on the big .45, Nathan. I've got a couple of Supers . . ." He paused, as if something just came to mind. "Hey, how about a race gun in .357 SIG? Now there's a hitter."

Nathan gave a tentative nod. "Let's take a look at it." And then as Phil disappeared into the back called after him. "And let me take a look at what you carry in hollow-points for that caliber."

A muffled "Got it," came from the back room.

By the time Phil returned, Nathan had checked out the Springfield Armory Compact and declared it ready to test fire. Phil handed him a tightly crafted STI race gun. "A friend of mine that used to work for STI built this one," he explained. "I can recommend his work. All the bells and whistles. And ballistically the .357 SIG is the semi-auto equivalent of the .357 Magnum revolver. That's as good a hitter as you're likely to find."

Nathan nodded, silently putting the pistol through a detailed check. "Ammo?"

Phil slid a cartridge box across the counter. "Federal 125 grain Hydra-Shok. It's rated at 1350 feet per second at the muzzle. I've got two cases of it."

"All right," said Nathan. "Let me test the handguns and if they check out okay, I'll take them. Any ammo I shoot I'll pay for regardless."

233

"Deal."

With holsters and mag holders, a Surefire light, more cleaning supplies, a new pair of electronic ear muffs and an hour on the range working through the handguns Nathan was starting to feel prepared. "Where's the nearest outdoor range I can use to sight in the .308?" he asked.

Phil handed him a brochure complete with directions and a map. "This is the one we recommend, Brookwood. It's on Route 25, about an hour and a half drive."

"That's fine," replied Nathan as he completed the signatures on the forms Phil passed him. "And can you do me a small favor? If you see Leith, don't tell him I was in. He doesn't know I'm back and I'd really like to surprise him."

"No problem," agreed Phil. "He'll be surprised will he?"

"And not just him," nodded Nathan. "Others too."

The next evening at seven, Nathan drove up to the green awning. There was no place to stop so he drove around the block three times before Kim appeared on the sidewalk. He paused long enough in traffic for her to jump into the car. She pulled a wine-colored nylon windbreaker from a shopping bag, unfolding it so he could see *NK Satellite Services* embroidered on the left breast. The jacket she wore was identical.

"What's this?"

"Our ticket up."

"NK?"

"Nathan and Kim, of course. I know it's not very original, but on short notice it was easier for the monogram shop at the mall to do initials than some fancy logo."

"And what is it we do exactly?"

"*We* do the best satellite dish repair in New York city. As a matter of fact we're so customer service oriented we even work after hours to get our clients' connections restored for the next business day."

"Service is our business," added Nathan, catching on.

234

"Now you're getting the company spirit." Nathan kept driving, looping the car around a four block circle. He kept it up for a half-hour while they talked about the job, outlining plans and covering possibilities. When the topic was exhausted, Nathan parked the car around the corner and out of sight of the main floor of the building. Before she got out, Kim asked, "Are you ready?".

"Everything's in the trunk. The rifle Kent bought me works great."

"That's not what I asked." She shifted in her seat to look directly into Nathan's eyes.

"Yeah. I'm ready. Go get us in."

Kim tried to convince herself of that as she stood outside a heavy glass door and pushed an intercom buzzer. She gave the security guard on the on the other side a little wave as the door's magnetic latch popped free. Kim approached the guard and identified herself as Kelly from NK Satellite Services. "Got a call to service to bad dish on the roof," she said.

When the security guard hesitated she produced a phony work order that ten minutes of work on a library computer had generated. The name was the same as that of one of the companies listed on the building's directory in the marble covered foyer. She had no idea what the company did, or even if they used a satellite feed, but she suspected the security guard didn't either.

"Okay," the female guard, agreed. The nametag on her shirt said *Lois*. "But the other guard on shift, Perry, will have to go up on the roof with you and stay there while you make your repairs."

"Not a problem." Piece of cake, Kim thought to herself. They were in. A rent-a-cop security guard with little training would be easily handled. "I'll go get my technician and his tools from the van."

"I'll radio Perry," said Lois. "Wait for him by the elevators, please."

Kim was doing a masterful job of distracting Perry, observed Nathan, as they waited for the elevator. The security guard hadn't given him and his three foot long Pelican tool case any more than a passing glance. Kim was working a delicate balance, being noticeable and still looking like she performed a service function. But, Nathan acknowledged, she was pulling it off. Her tight black jeans and an equally tight yellow sweater with a plunging neckline were definitely distracting Perry. Nathan conceded it was easy to get distracted around Kim. Her athletic build grabbed your attention first, and then deep brown eyes held it. Too bad the inside wasn't as pretty as the outside. Unlike Kim, Nathan kept his jacket zipped up. He had things they *didn't* want Perry to notice.

Once they exited the elevators, Perry directed them to a clipboard hanging on the wall and insisted they fill out 'relinquishments of claim'. While they wrote he hooked his thumbs behind the gun belt that supported both a 9 mm Beretta and his massive stomach, explaining in detail how company policy required this of anyone who ventured onto the roof. The way he watched Kim's yellow sweater, Nathan was surprised he remembered what floor they were on, let alone building policy.

Perry led them to a single flight of stairs leading to the roof access. He motioned Kim to go first and made a point of walking up behind her, leaving Nathan to manhandle his tool case up the narrow stairway alone. Exiting the single door of the service access hut deposited them on the flat roof. Perry directed them to the right where Nathan saw two satellite dishes mounted among half a dozen conventional aerials. The usual three foot high safety ledge ran around the entire circumference of the roof, and other than the aerials and dishes only the massive anchor points for the window washer lifts protruded over the dark edge. Most of the city's lights were concentrated in the thirty floors below, making it noticeably darker up here than at street level. Nathan pulled a flashlight out of an inside jacket pocket and made a show of inspecting the nameplate on both dishes until he selected one. "This one's ours," he announced, picking the one closest to the edge of the thirty-floor drop.

"Need my help?" asked Kim.

"No. When I need you to check the calibration I'll call. Go enjoy the view. Once I have the problem identified it won't take very long."

Kim took her cue and walked away, engaging Perry in conversation as she left. Nathan looked busy until she'd led the guard to a point where the small service hut providing stairway access to the roof blocked them from his view. From the large case he'd carried up, Nathan withdrew the smaller rifle container and another padded case filled with his other gear. He laid it all against the edge of the low perimeter wall, next to a window washer anchor. The ledge was a comforting security blanket, shielding him from the mind-numbing drop on the other side of that short dark wall. Now he needed time and nerve; a little time and lots of nerve.

Nathan shuffled around the edge of the service hut to check on Kim and Perry. He saw them at the other end of the roof, bathed in the artificial glow of a city making the daily transition from office work to nightlife. Kim was still talking and looking at the view, occasionally pointing to where the World Trade Towers used to stand. Perry still watched Kim. Nathan slipped back to his work and five minutes later walked to where the two stood, the crunch of roof gravel underfoot announcing his arrival.

"Kelly, I can't find my field-strength meter. You know, I think we left it on the roof at that last job over on West Thirty-Fourth."

Kim groaned. "I was sure you picked it up. I thought I saw it in the van." She pretended to think for a moment. "Why don't you go down and see if it's there. Leave your tools here and give me a call on my cell once you've checked the van." She turned to Perry. "He can get down on his own right? If he has to come back up we'll have to go down and get him?"

Perry nodded. "You can get down from here all you want. But you ain't getting back up without me." He tapped his chest to emphasize the point, and his importance. Nathan left them, disappearing around the side of the hut as Kim asked Perry, "And what happened then—when you suspected he was a terrorist?"

Ten minutes later Kim's phone rang and after a brief conversation she announced to Perry that the instrument wasn't in the van and they'd have to call it a night—without getting the job done. As they walked to the other side of the access hut Perry volunteered to help Kim with the tool case. She quickly declined, afraid he'd notice the light weight and become suspicious. Kim wished she hadn't when Perry resumed his thumbs in the belt pose and patrolled around the satellite dish Nathan had been pretending to work on. Kim held her breath and considered calling him back to help with the case. She was about to call out, when he wandered back in her direction. "I really need to get going," she said.

"Sure," grunted Perry. He held the door open as she wrestled the awkward case into the stairwell and started down to the next floor where the elevators began.

When Kim reached the street she made the short walk back to the car. It took all the self-discipline she possessed to resist looking up.

Nathan thought he heard the doorway to the roof slam shut, but it was impossible to be sure. The traffic on the street below was noisier up here than he'd expected and the sounds of roaring buses and squealing brakes ricocheted around these canyons of steel and glass making individual sounds difficult to isolate. That would work to his advantage later, but now it meant he'd have to stay longer in this position. Physically that was okay—so far.

Mentally, he wasn't as sure. Fear had found him. That was expected—he could handle Fear. He'd done it before. But here, at the taut end of a swaying rope, where three hundred gut-wrenching feet of free fall separated him from certain death; Fear had brought his big brother—Panic had slithered along. It surprised him to discover Panic was still alive. Fifteen minutes ago he would have made an intellectual argument to the effect that his training and experience had killed it. Now he knew that wasn't true. It had been there all along, hiding in some dark recess, an animal devouring rational thought and willpower; carrying with it the disease of blind, gasping, paralyzing terror. It had crawled up out of the hole where it hid and now stalked him.

Nathan gave his head a violent shake and imagined his eyeballs rattling. He concentrated on looking up, and inhaled the cool night air in steady even breaths. He tried convincing himself he was sucking in logic, willpower and knowledge, and exhaling terror, confusion and the unknown. Slowly, the moment and the slide into darkness eased enough for him to function. Panic pulled back, circling just out of sight beyond the ring of light. Waiting. Waiting for the light to fade enough for one quick, sudden rush. Nathan forced himself to tense his muscles in preparation for regaining the roof. The light grew brighter as he started to move. He resolved not to underestimate the tenacity of the creature again.

The black rope he dangled on had loops tied every eighteen inches and he used them now as hand and foot holds to move up six feet to where it was secured to a window washer anchor. Nathan's head cleared the ledge first, but only enough so his eyes could scan the rooftop. Nothing moved. He held the position for another minute to make sure. Still nothing, so he hoisted his trembling body up over the ledge and onto the security of the flat gravel surface. With his back to the ledge and his shoulder against the cold metal of the anchor he watched and rested. Nathan let his cheek touch the heavy post and felt the steel draw heat out of his face. He continued to watch and listen but more importantly he rested his muscles and his mind. In five minutes every trace of the mental brute he'd glimpsed was gone. Once again Panic had retreated to its lair. Only a bad memory remained, and he could easily have convinced himself that, because of his training and experience, Panic was a beast he'd never see again. .

Heaving an audible sigh he got up and performed a quick crouching patrol along the perimeter of the roof, pausing only long enough to insert a security wedge at the access door. Surprise visitors would not be welcome while he worked. Arriving back at his start point, he pulled up the rope that had been his lifeline. The padded nylon rifle case came over the ledge first. He unhooked the carabiner that held it to a rope loop and pulled up the last eight feet, bringing the second equipment bag onto the roof at his feet. When it was unhooked, he carried all the equipment to the northwest corner of the building and extracted the rifle. It was a simple matter to unfold the stock and lock it into place, extending the rifle to its full length. Ammunition was next and the loaded magazine snapped into its recess with an authoritative click. Once he'd removed the scope caps, he retrieved the Leica range finding binoculars and put his eyes to work.

Nathan recognized the building easily and he knew the floor number. That allowed him to focus in on the Starbucks at street level and lift the binoculars, counting audibly as lighted windows flickered past his optically enhanced vision. When he reached thirty he went back down one to compensate for the thirteenth floor that didn't exist, and slid his vision laterally to the corner office. Bullseye. The lights were on. And somebody was home. He could see movement but couldn't recognize who it was. That was expected—the seven-power magnification of the binoculars was too low to identify anyone at this distance, so he didn't bother trying. Instead he steadied his elbows on the ledge, settled the binocular's red crosshair on the distant window and depressed the raised button on top of the right hand lens assembly. In a fraction of a second an invisible laser made the trip to the lit window, bounced off the glass and came back to the rangefinder's microchip. An internal display recorded the distance—three hundred and forty one yards. Easy shot, Nathan thought. Dead easy.

Before lowering the binoculars, he established a mental picture of where the window was located in relation to the patchwork of black and white that made up the illuminated and darkened offices of the distant building. Then he reached for the rifle.

Three subdued bursts of light from his flashlight were necessary to prepare the scope. With the first he consulted the trajectory chart he'd worked out at the range and taped to the side of the stock. The second flash illuminated the markings on the housing of the scope's vertical adjustment turret as he dialed in the right setting. With the third flare of light, Nathan set the scope's parallax adjustment to a point midway between the three hundred and four hundred yard settings. The rifle was ready.

Nathan didn't use the bipod, but let the AWP's forend rest on the padded case now draped over the ledge. Finding the corner window in the scope's field of view was easy. He felt his heart rate jump a notch as he recognized Kent sitting behind the desk. Kent sat facing the wall and his computer monitor, hands moving across the keyboard before him. Nathan imagined he heard the clicking of the keys—so distinct was the telescopic view in the clear night air. What was he working on? Another plan to kill him? Was that his exclusive focus now or was it business as usual? Was Nathan Burdett just a minor nuisance that needed to be swatted? As he asked himself those questions, the tiny black dot at the junction of the Leupold's fine crosshairs hovered over Kent's right ear.

A sudden tremor in the crosshairs made them dance across the balding head. Nathan stopped. It wasn't the rifle's fault. He looked away, blinked several times and rechecked the breeze, still nothing of consequence. He took three deep breaths, expelling everything as he exhaled. Then he snuggled in behind the rifle again and drew in another deep lungful, this time releasing only a third. The crosshairs returned to the ear—solid and steady.

Nathan's right index finger absorbed half of the trigger's pull weight. The crosshairs remained steady so he kept applying pressure in a smooth even increase. His finger felt the sear release, a picture flashed through his mind of the firing pin's powerful spring driving it forward, and in the same instant he heard it slam home. Through the twenty-four power Leupold, Nathan's right eye saw the consequences of the firing pin's mechanical journey as the crosshair twitched right, moving as far as Kent's temple.

Nathan shook his head in disgust at the rifle's movement in response to the firing pin's fall. He rechecked the buttstock's position on his shoulder and his own grip on the rifle but found nothing wrong. Finally, reaching under the rifle's forend he explored the padding between it and the ledge. He shifted a flap of fabric from one of the integral side pouches that had partially bunched up under the forend. When he was satisfied that the AWP rested on a smooth, even platform he cocked the rifle and repeated the same drill. This time, when the firing pin fell on an empty chamber—with the same deadly efficient mechanical click—the crosshairs didn't move. Satisfied with the rifle's stability, Nathan jacked a round into the chamber and reacquired his sight picture.

At street level, Kim sat behind the wheel of the car, her arm out the window, fiddling impatiently with the rear-view mirror. She was keeping her window down, straining her ears for a distant echoing boom that would mean Nathan had done it. Hopefully it was possible to hear the shot down here. *If* he made it. Was it too much to hope for that

241

he would actually put those crosshairs on Kent's balding head and pull the trigger? She allowed herself the luxury of thinking he might really do it. He'd said he would. Or had he? In her mind she replayed their conversations about Kent.

"He'll never stop coming after you," she'd told Nathan, on the way in from the airport.

"I know," he replied. "I've learned that much about him."

"But it's a one-man show. He runs that little operation of his alone, and he's the only one threatened by you. If he's gone so is your problem."

Silence and his distant blue-eyed look were her only reply.

"Essentially it's self-defense," she continued. "If you don't kill him, he'll kill you. You don't have a problem with that do you?" No reply. "I know how you could do it."

That broke the stare and he'd turned to look at her. "How?"

"He's in that office of his until all hours of the night. One side of it's all glass windows. You're good with a rifle. If you're good enough . . . ?" She shrugged, leaving the question hanging, waiting for his response, baiting him.

"Sounds easy."

"It would be. And it's self-defense." She knew she had to keep pushing that button. "He'll do it to you if he gets the chance. And you can bet he's working on a way to make that chance happen."

"What makes you think he's careless enough to continue hanging out in the breeze like that, when he must know I could airmail him a bullet any time I wanted to end this whole thing?"

Kim knew the answer cold, but she hesitated, trying to think of something else to say—a coloration of the truth, a little white lie— anything to encourage him to do what she knew he must. If he didn't they had no chance of surviving. But his blue eyes remained fixed on her and they melted the lie she was formulating. "He believes he understands you well enough to know you won't shoot him in cold blood."

A knowing smile crossed Nathan's face, then he answered. "He always researches his quarry and learns everything there is to know about them." Kim returned a puzzled look. "Just something I learned about him in Vegas."

"Well, it's absolutely right. But the flip side is, if you don't act in the way he anticipates, you—we—have the advantage."

The eyes turned away and once again fixed onto something in the distance. Minutes dragged by without a reply. She could see he was thinking. Eventually he'd spoken, but without looking back at her. "Let's take a look at it."

That was all he'd said. Further attempts to draw him out had been met with silence. But he'd kept working in the right direction. Sometimes, though, it had felt like she was pulling him along, that he wasn't moving on his own. Still, he kept moving.

At one point she'd contemplated doing it herself. Her rifle skills were marginal, but she might be able to pull it off. And what if she did? Kent would be gone, the problem solved. Or would it? If she assassinated Kent, would Nathan be gone too? She was unsure enough of that possibility that she didn't want to risk it. Kim had disciplined herself to being positive about the outcome, focusing on a future without Kent; acting confident that Nathan would punch Kent's one-way ticket to hell and free them both from a future of dodging death.

Two patrol cops appeared around the corner, the sight of them jolting her back to the present. They turned and walked toward her. Like a two-headed creature their heads pivoted, eyes searching, analyzing everything in sight. They gave her and the car a careful inspection as they approached. Kim tapped her fingers on the steering wheel and faked an impatient glance at her watch. It was enough to keep them moving in their suspicious measured stride. She watched them in her rear-view mirror until they turned a corner and disappeared from sight. Other pedestrian traffic was light and nobody seemed to notice her sitting in a darkened car at the curb. She waited. Listening.

With the rifle's chamber now loaded and the safety off, Nathan checked the wind. He found nothing more than the mild breeze that had been weaving its way through the skyscrapers all evening. The shot would go almost directly into that current of air and no allowance for lateral drift was needed. He thought about going to the other side of the

243

building and looking down, to see if he could spot Kim's car. Would she be there—waiting for him? Yes, he believed she would, but then he realized that wanting to go look meant he wasn't sure. With a determined effort Nathan put it out of his mind and focused on what he saw through the telescopic sight.

Kent still worked on his computer, hands alternating between mouse and keyboard, blissfully ignorant of the crosshairs superimposed on his skull. Nathan scanned to the left. From his slightly elevated position he saw the top of the desk. An open file and the usual telephone and desk accessories were neatly arrayed on the walnut surface. Beside the phone, the stone polar bear still loomed over the Inuit hunter and his feeble white spear, the ever-faithful dogs still badgered the giant beast in defense of their master. Beyond that scene and into the rest of the room Nathan saw no one else. Neatness and solitude were present in equal amounts. As he continued watching, Nathan reached inside his jacket and fumbled briefly in a shirt pocket.

Through the scope he saw Kent abruptly stop typing, turn toward the desk and pick up the telephone's receiver. Nathan saw Kent's lips mouth a word and simultaneously, "Hello" sounded in the cellphone near his left ear.

"You're looking for me." A statement not a question.

A brief moment of silence and a straightening in the chair preceded the reply. "Well, well, Mr. Burdett. This is a surprise."

"You have no idea."

"And to what do I owe the honor of this phone call?"

"I thought it was time we talked."

"I think that's a splendid idea. But I am . . . ahhh, in the washroom at the moment. Allow me to put you on hold, will you, I'll just get to my desk and . . . ."

Nathan's icy tone cut him off as Kent's left hand reached for the telephone. "Put me on hold and it could be the last thing you ever do." Kent's hand paused in mid-air, a look of temporary indecision on the face. "No tracing." Kent's hand settled on the desktop, fingers tapping the surface.

"You're far too suspicious, Mr. Burdett. I have no intention of tracing this call."

"And all you want to do is talk, right? This has just been a misunderstanding and we can straighten everything out if I only come in and see you, or maybe meet you somewhere. How about a dark alley somewhere, just me and you?"

Kent said nothing in response. During that moment of silence Nathan saw him cradle the phone under his ear and hold it in place with a hunched shoulder. Turning toward the computer, Kent reached for the mouse with his right hand, his left hovered over the keyboard.

"Stay off the computer too," commanded Nathan.

For the second time that evening Kent's hands froze in place. This time his head turned slowly towards the window. Behind his wire-rimmed glasses a pair of pale blue eyes were visibly wider.

"Off the computer, I said." Kent's left hand dropped down to his lap, the right drifted back to the receiver. "Now touch your nose." Nathan saw the slightest hesitation and then Kent's left hand rose to his ear. "I said your nose, moron, not your ear." The hand moved to the nose. "Good boy," mocked Nathan. "Now, has that aristocratic British brain started to figure out what's going on here yet?"

"Where are you?" he asked softly.

"You look good in crosshairs," said Nathan. "Most people don't, but they suit you."

"I see." Nathan saw Kent turn his chair to face the window and settle back into it. "And what is it you want? I presume there's something or you would have shot me by now."

"Robert, your old sheep guide, says hello."

Even at three hundred and forty-one yards Nathan saw his face change color. "And how is Robert?" Nathan heard an audible chill in his voice.

"Robert says you've made your pact with the devil and as far as he's concerned you can go to hell."

"He always was overly emotional."

"Like me?" Kent didn't bite. "People usually get emotional when you betray their trust," said Nathan.

"Is that what you're planning to do, Mr. Burdett, betray me?"

"The way I see it, getting rid of you would make the world a better place for everyone."

"And my opinion is that getting rid of you would make the world a much better place for me."

"Then it seems we have an irreconcilable difference of opinion. I guess I'll just have to kill you first."

"I suppose so, Mr. Burdett."

"Do you realize you'll hear the shot before the bullet gets to you, Kent? Think about it. The phone will transmit the noise faster electrically than it can travel in air, and a lot faster than the bullet."

Kent considered that for an instant. "Why, you're right. Now isn't that a bloody wonder. Now what made you think of that little quirk?"

"A friend pointed it out to me shortly after Leith and his band tried to ambush me."

Silence dragged across the connection for what seemed like a full minute, the traffic noises from the street and the wail of a distant siren the only noise. Nathan adjusted the crosshairs slightly to the left as he felt the breeze shift direction and become two inches worth of crosswind.

Kent broke the silence. "Is there a problem with shooting me, Mr. Burdett?" No response. "You didn't really expect me to beg for my life, did you? Or perhaps promise to leave you alone in exchange for not killing me this evening?"

"No, I don't think I expected that."

"What's this all about then?" No answer. "Come now, Mr. Burdett." Kent's voice grew stronger and more confident by the second. "Either shoot me or go home, Mr. Burdett."

It was time. "You're a hunter. So am I. Some of the game we hunt is more dangerous than others, I just thought you might want to give the most dangerous game a try—personally."

A smile slashed across Kent's face. "Most intriguing, Mr. Burdett. And could I nail your head to my wall afterward?"

"If you get it, you can do anything you want. But first it's just you and me, hunting each other in a concrete jungle."

Kent nodded his head thoughtfully and slowly pivoted his chair back to the desk where he lifted a pencil from the ivory penholder beside the telephone. "Where and when, Mr. Burdett?"

Nathan gave him an address. "And come alone."

"Of course, just the two of us." Kent looked down at the desk. "I'm just curious about something," he said.

"Go ahead."

"How can you be sure I'll show up at all?"

"And how can you be sure I won't kill you right now?"

"Because I know you well enough that . . . ahhh, I see, so you think you know me also, do you?"

"Better than you know."

"And just what is it you know, Mr. Burdett."

"I know the Inuit hunter wins."

Nathan saw a puzzled look cross Kent's crosshair-bisected face as he glanced back out the window and then turned to the large sculpture on the table beside the telephone. "Whatever do you mean, Mr. Burdett?"

"I've been thinking about that sculpture and the conversation we had. There are two reasons the Inuit hunter will win."

Kent gave a small laugh. "Do enlighten me, please?"

"Training," said Nathan. "He's been training all his life for this. It's not something he knew was coming, not exactly anyway. But he felt that bear's teeth every time the East Wind cut through his parka, and he sensed this day would come just as surely as an Arctic winter. No, he didn't train specifically for this, but every time he walked twenty miles across frozen tundra he was training. The time he fell through a patch of soft ice and got soaked at forty below, he survived because of the skills his father taught him and a determination that keeps a man going when he should be dead. Two years ago and a hundred miles from home one of his sled dogs went mad and tore his leg open. He killed it with his bare hands and then he sewed up his own leg with a bone needle and caribou sinew. And you know what, Kent? He didn't go home. He finished the hunt. His family was counting on him to bring home meat. That man lives in a place where life *is* training and he trains hard, Kent. It's train or die—he'll survive because of that."

"You have quite an imagination, Mr. Burdett."

"It's not imagination. The story's there. The artist carved it into the stone, all you have to do is see what he put there." Nathan's finger tightened on the trigger. The switch in the breeze was holding but its speed had increased. He added another two inches of windage. That made four.

Kent leaned forward slightly, apparently searching the statue for the story Nathan saw there. "You said 'two reasons'. What's the other?"

"The hand of God."

Kent snorted in derision but Nathan didn't hear him, the muzzle blast of the rifle drowned it out. Three hundred and forty-one yards away, over a telephone's earpiece, Kent heard the shot and in that instant knew a bullet was coming. The one hundred and sixty-five grain projectile required half a second of flight time to the glass window. Enough time for Kent's brain to communicate fear and imminent death to every part of his body. When the bullet blew through the window his bowels and bladder were beginning to void. Performing as designed, the Federal bullet smashed through the heavy window, exiting intact and spraying the inside of the room with razor-sharp crystal shards.

Lead and copper spinning at one hundred and ninety-two thousand revolutions per minute and traveling at two thousand feet per second slammed into the chest of the stone polar bear. The upper half of the bear and all of the bullet disintegrated in an explosive mist of copper, lead and stone dust. Blowing out in all directions it shredded everything in its path. Paper, cloth and skin frayed under the withering erosion of the high-velocity cloud. Kent's glasses protected his eyes and the expensive suit his body, but in the ballistic snowstorm his exposed skin eroded into a bloody version of bullet-induced road rash.

When the rifle came down out of recoil the bullet had already hit and Nathan had time only to see Kent topple over backwards in his chair. The top half of the bear was missing and the window had a ragged hole adorned by a spiderweb of radial cracks. He watched long enough to see Kent claw upright onto his hands and knees and to glimpse a bloody mess of a face. Nathan snapped the bolt open and the empty case flicked out and over the ledge into three hundred feet of open space, pirouetting downwards in a lazy flattening arc.

248

By the time it bounced onto a deserted sidewalk and rolled into a New York gutter, Nathan was at the access door to the roof. He kicked out the security wedge and ripped open the door, hitting the stairs two at a time. The bolt handle of the rifle slung across his shoulder dug into his kidney with every jarring step as he sprinted for the central stairwell. He rejected the elevators—too chancy. A late working secretary could stop him cold with an innocent push of a button. The stairs would be deserted and they were all downhill. Still, it was going to be a long thirty floors.

He did five floors before realizing every single landing was a sharp turn to the left. Over sixty high-speed left turns. The plan was to blow past the security guard at the desk and be out the door so fast she wouldn't have time to react. Nathan realized now that by the time he hit bottom he'd be so dizzy it would be all he could do to stand up.

The booming echo of the shot made Kim sit bolt upright in the car. "Yes!" she exclaimed, starting the car and unlocking the doors. She ratcheted her vigilance up to maximum and focused her attention on the front of the building, waiting for Nathan to burst out of the glass doors. He did it! He fired the shot. Since a miss wasn't within the realm of possibility, it meant Kent's brains were splattered on his office wall and they were free. Now they just had to get out of here. She took a moment to look around.

Two pedestrians across the street stopped and looked up. They'd heard something but she guessed they didn't know what. This city was spooked. Losing over six thousand citizens in one terrorist attack would do that to you. Kim checked the street ahead and then her rear-view mirror for police cars. Nothing. She heard no approaching sirens. Her eyes swiveled back to the building's doors. Her hand tapping impatiently on the steering wheel. Nobody. Anxiously, she checked her watch. How long had it been since the shot? She hadn't bothered to take note of the time and now she cursed her sloppiness. Five minutes? Ten minutes? Impossible—closer to five. How long would it take him to get down? What if he tripped and broke a leg?

The Ground Floor sign on the stairwell's exit door was barely decipherable to Nathan's spinning brain when he hit the door's release bar and burst out of the stairwell. A wild swing to the left and he ricocheted off a marble wall on buckling knees, fighting to maintain equilibrium. The dark blue uniform that appeared in front of him looked like it was at the bottom of a swirling pool of water.

To Perry, the man who had just materialized out of the stairwell was one of the stranger sights he'd seen in this city. Soaked with sweat, matted hair clung to his scalp and from the way he staggered it was obvious he was stoned on something. But, that was all secondary to the black rifle slung across his back. Perry needed no other encouragement to claw his Beretta 9 mm out of its holster.

"Freeze!" he shouted, using both hands to level the pistol at the swaying wild man who stumbled to a halt four feet in front of him.

Nathan groaned and gulped as much air as he could into his aching lungs. He tried to keep the room from moving and his legs solid. Slowly the swirling room steadied. "It's me, Perry," he gasped, trying to unbalance the guard. "The satellite dish—the repair guy—I got it fixed."

"What?" Perry adjusted his grip on the gun. "But you left . . ."

Nathan moved a step closer. "I had to come back . . ." A gasp for air. "I forgot this on the roof." He patted the barrel of the rifle that protruded over his shoulder.

"But . . . ."

Nathan took another step. The room was stabilizing. "Didn't Kelly tell you?"

Perry took one hand off the Beretta and looked over his shoulder at the desk. "Hey Lois, did that broad from the satellite company . . ." He felt a touch on his pistol and whirled back to Nathan, pulling the 9 mm closer to himself in an instinctive protective reaction.

The wild-eyed man in front of him was still there, swaying slightly, and he had a black piece of metal in his hand that hadn't been there before. It wasn't a gun. Maybe a short club or a folding knife. "Freeze right there!" repeated Perry. "I'll shoot you. I mean it."

Nathan saw Lois frantically dialing the phone. He wasn't sure if it was in response to what he'd just done or if was simply because there was a man in the lobby with a big black rifle. Phoning was good. Nathan doubted she could phone the police and shoot at the same time.

"I'm sure you would, Perry," said Nathan, turning to leave. "But I don't have time for this, I have to go."

Perry didn't hesitate. He'd grown up on the mean streets of this city and no one walked away when he drew his 9 mm and told them to stop. He jabbed the Beretta at Nathan's disappearing back and pulled the trigger. At six feet there was no way he could miss.

The metallic click the pistol's hammer made as it fell was the loudest, scariest sound Perry had ever heard in his forty-two years of New York life. A misfire? He'd never ever had a misfire!

His mind raced to remember what he'd been taught to do in case of one. A mental picture dashed unbidden through his mind. In it the intruder, in response to the ominous click, pivoted smoothly, shouldered his rifle and with a single scorching blast vaporized Perry's head. Tap and rack—that was it! That was the drill he'd been taught— tap-and-rack. He slammed the bottom of his pistol's magazine with his left hand to ensure it was firmly seated. Then he reached for the slide to rack it back and chamber a new round. Missed the slide! He tried again and missed again. Perry slowed down, trying desperately to focus in spite of the wild fear building within him. The man with the rifle was running now. Didn't he care that an armed guard had just tried to shoot him? In the subdued light of the night lobby Perry slowed enough to look closely at his gun. What he saw grasped tightly in a trembling death grip scared him more than that deafening click he'd heard a moment ago.

The top half of his pistol was gone—missing. Perry clutched a complete Beretta frame in his right hand. He could see the magazine resting inside the grip and the shiny top cartridge nestled there waiting its turn to be fired. But it wouldn't be fired. It couldn't be fired. The barrel and slide were both gone. He looked up in time to see Nathan hit the exit door's release bar and run to a waiting car.

CHAPTER THIRTEEN

"Present for you, Kim," said Nathan, throwing the top half of the Beretta into her lap and tossing the rifle and binoculars in the back seat as she put the car into gear and moved into traffic.

"What? Where did this . . .?"

"Perry got the drop on me when I came out of the stairwell," said Nathan. "But if you're within arms length, never point a Beretta 92 at somebody with fast hands," he added, as if that explained everything.

"But how . . .?"

"They disassemble from the front, Kim. Beretta 92's disassemble *very* quickly, from the front."

"You took the top half of his gun away from him?" An incredulous smile spread across her face. "What did he say to that?"

"He actually tried to shoot me with what was left in his hand, so I think he's still trying to figure out what happened. The poor guy means well but Perry doesn't catch on too quick."

A traffic light changed to yellow and Kim accelerated, pushing the signal's limits to make it through the intersection before the light turned red. She needed to drive a delicate balance, trying to gain as much distance as possible without attracting attention from law enforcement. She checked her rear-view mirror and breathed a sigh of relief. Then jerked a thumb at the back seat where the rifle lay. "I thought you were going to leave that thing on the roof?"

"You're going to need it," said Nathan quietly.

Kim's fingers tightened on the steering wheel until her knuckles turned white. Her voice went as quiet as his. "I heard a shot. Why would I need a rifle?"

Nathan heard the brittleness and hesitated before answering. "Because Kent is coming after us and I'm sure he'll bring a platoon of goons with him. I need you to watch my back."

252

Kim balled her right hand into a fist and pounded on the steering wheel in cadence to the words she spit out. "I knew it." *Pound.* "I knew it." *Pound.* "You couldn't do it." *Pound.* "You jerk." *Pound.* "It was too simple." *Pound.* "You're an idiot." *Pound.* "You couldn't do it." *Pound. Pound. Pound.* She took a deep breath. "Why not?"

Nathan waited for her fist to hit the steering wheel again but it didn't come. "Rules of the kill," he said eventually. "It would've been murder."

Kim flexed and stretched her fingers, exhaling slowly. "I thought we agreed it was self-defense?"

"You had yourself convinced, not me."

Kim's hand balled into a fist again, her voice tightening to match. "Rules of the kill?"

"Rules," echoed Nathan. "You remember those don't you? We use them to define the limits. In this case they're *my* rules and they define *my* limits."

"Sure. I remember."

They drove the next two blocks in silence.

"Where are we going?" asked Kim.

"Head back towards the hotel. I'll direct you once we get close."

Kim nodded. "How can you be sure Kent will be there? He'll probably just send cannon fodder."

"I challenged him personally and I peeled a lot of skin off his face. That'll be enough."

"You peeled skin off his face? With a bullet? Care to explain?"

Fifteen minutes later Nathan had briefed Kim on what happened on the roof. That still left forty-five minutes of driving in silence until they reached the south end of Flatbush Avenue. He directed her through two more turns until they parked at the mall across from their hotel.

"That's what you were doing two nights ago. Scouting this place."

"There's one guard on duty during the night. As far as I can tell he patrols the corridors and public areas. The stores, of course, are locked up. With the water fountains, food courts and weird architecture that place has, it's a real maze in there. Sort of like an urban jungle. The guard wanders in and out of the north doors to light a smoke every hour so they can't be alarmed."

"Is he armed?"

"Yeah. He looks like Perry's baby brother." Nathan grinned.

"And how were you planning on getting him out of the way?"

Nathan shrugged. "Distract and surprise him somehow and then tie him up unharmed 'til it's over."

"And me?"

"The roof," Nathan said. "With that." He indicated the rifle.

"And what if somebody hears shots and a whole precinct of blue uniforms show up?"

"Not likely. Kent wants to hunt me down undisturbed. A few well connected phone calls from him will no doubt inform the locals there's some special spook operation going on, and no matter what, to stay away until they get the all clear."

Kim abruptly jumped out of the car and leaned back in through the open door. "I'll take care of the guard," she instructed. "You go find a way for me to get on the roof."

"But . . . ."

Kim paused briefly before slamming the door. "Some things I'm better at than you, Nathan. Distracting men is one of them. Now pop the trunk. I need a tool pouch. I see a satellite dish on that roof that needs service." She tapped the *NK* logo on the breast of her jacket. "And service is our business."

"You didn't hurt him, did you?" asked Nathan, when Kim appeared at the back of the mall fifteen minutes later.

"He's tied up in their little security office. The most damaged thing about him is his ego. I suspect that by the time he gets around to telling the cops about who dropped him I'll be some three hundred pound gorilla with tattoos and a ring through his nose."

Nathan laughed. "The poor guy didn't stand much of a chance. Not with you still wearing the yellow sweater." Kim threw the tool pouch at him.

He caught it and dropped it in the open trunk. "*I'd* never admit to being flattened by a good-looking redhead." Reaching into an equipment bag he pulled out ammunition. "From yesterday's sighting in, testing and the one shot tonight, this is all I have left." He passed her twenty-six rounds of .308 and then the rifle. He hung the binoculars around his own neck. "Time for you to take the high ground. There are four big domed skylights in the roof. Depending on where you are, you'll be able to see some of what's going on. Generally though, I'll handle the inside and you can cover the outside. Okay?"

"If you say so. But just remember, once I'm up there my rules aren't the same as yours."

"I realize that. You know, it doesn't have to stay that way. You could start to see things the way I do."

"I was thinking it would work the other way."

"I know you were. But it won't."

"No kidding."

Nathan pointed to a dumpster pushed against the back wall and clambered onto it. He took the rifle from Kim and waited for her to join him. Then he boosted her up onto the flat roof. "How does it look up there?" he called.

"Not nearly as high as the last roof we were on. You sure you want me up here?"

"I am."

Kim had to lay flat on the roof to reach for the rifle and binoculars he readied below her. She looked down at him, barely visible in the darkness. "You know, I could just finish them all off when they show up."

"I doubt it. There'll be too many and they'll come from all directions at once. Besides, you're not good enough."

"And you are?"

"I'm better than I've ever been." He looped the binocular's neck strap over the rifle butt and pushed it up at her.

"That doesn't answer my question."

"I know."

"Why are you doing this?" Kim grabbed the strap and hauled up the heavy glasses.

For a moment he didn't answer, thankful there wasn't enough light for her to read his face. "It's who I am."

"So you've told me. And it's very profound," she added sarcastically. "But what made you that way?"

"I don't know, Kim. I don't think there's any one thing that makes us what we are. We're the result of everything that's happened to us over however many years we've been breathing. The result of our circumstances and of the decisions we've made—good or bad. But more than that, too. We're not all born as a blank slate. We're individuals and I believe we all start out different."

"Well you sure ended up different." Kim's right arm reached downwards. "Okay. Pass me the rifle."

Nathan didn't move. "What's so different about wanting to do what's right?"

"Nobody I know carries it as far as you do."

"It's like training, Kim."

"Huh?"

"Training. It's like training. First you work on the small easy skills. They become the building blocks that take you to the complex ones. Life is like that. We get to practice on the little stuff in life, doing what's right or doing what's wrong—it's our choice. Then, when the big ones come along we get to use the skills we've learned and the strength we've built up to tackle those."

"Life is training. That's it?"

Nathan lifted the rifle to her outstretched hand. "But you have to train the right way, Kim. Come on, you're the fitness expert. Physically speaking, if you train properly you get faster and stronger. Then, when a conflict comes, an opponent has a tougher time beating you. That's like a law of nature. What if the same law holds for the way we behave? If we behave properly we become stronger for it."

"And tougher to beat?"

"Sure. Why not?"

"Then doing what's wrong makes you weaker?"

"I've done it."

"Going after the Riders when you should've left it alone?"

"Uh-huh."

256

"And now you're going to do this. And it'll either kill you or make you stronger."

"I can't do it any other way." He waited for her to answer but there was no reply. "Be careful up there." Still no response. She had already melted into the darkness.

Nathan jumped down, walked back to the car and pulled out another equipment bag. The iron-sighted .45 and concealment holster behind his hip were both stashed away in favor of the competition belt and holster rig he wrapped around his waist. No point in concealing anything now, he thought. And in his hands the bigger gun with the dot sight was, at indoor distances, as accurate as a rifle. Loading the magazines gave him a chance to look around.

One other car occupied the parking lot. A fine wet mist covering its exterior indicated it had been there all night. Beyond it, on the distant street, traffic was sparse. Kent's people would drive in on that main entrance but then hold back, scout the place from a distance. That's what he'd do. But they still had to get in the building.

Earlier, he'd counted five entrances to the mall. If there were enough men, they'd hit all five at once. That would be best. Did Kent even have that many men? The thought of it forced him to remember the odds. Who was he to think he could take that many gunmen? This was insane! A philosophical discussion with Kim was easy. Stepping up to the line and doing it wasn't.

His opposition didn't even have to be good. Just one lucky shot, one stray bullet, one ricochet off a concrete wall was all it would take to kill him. And yet something pulled him on. That was what he hadn't told Kim. It was there, swirling somewhere between the fringes of what he knew and what he believed—an undercurrent dragging him along to an unknown destination. The unmistakable feeling there was something more at stake here than what rippled across the surface of his life. That belief had towed him this far. And now as his mouth went dry and his hands wanted to tremble, Nathan uttered a silent prayer that he was right and jammed the last cartridge into the last magazine.

With all the mags loaded, the one remaining cartridge box still contained twenty rounds of ammo. He dumped those loose into his right hand pants pocket where a Lightfoot folding knife was habitually clipped.

Into the belt pouches arrayed across the front left of his torso he had inserted five of the magazines as he'd loaded them. Ten rounds of .357 SIG hollow-point in each gave him a total load of fifty on his belt. He snapped the sixth magazine into the compensated and ported STI and turned on the C-More holographic sight, adjusting the intensity of the red dot that glowed in the center of the single lens to a brightness optimum for the conditions. A quick cycling of the slide stripped the top round off the magazine and into the chamber. Ejecting the magazine, topping it off with a single round, then reinserting it, left him loaded to capacity. Nathan snapped on the safety, locked the gun into its holster and donned his electronic earmuffs. He closed the trunk softly and scanned the roofline for Kim. She was there, somewhere, maybe with her binoculars focused on him. Perhaps wondering if she'd ever see him alive again. He walked through the front doors hoping she would.

CHAPTER FOURTEEN

Nathan was struck by the idea that the empty mall looked like an urban version of a frontier ghost town. Empty shops with darkened windows lined the corridors. In front of each of them stood vacant benches the way hitching rails lined western streets. The wooden water barrels had been transformed into concrete and steel trash containers. Even a faint breeze moaned through the hallways, but it didn't blow from the distant mountains, or smell of sage and pine. No, this breeze came from the heating system and it smelled of oiled machinery.

No tumbleweeds. Not a single round thistle had drifted in off the desert to be bounced around between man-made structures until its friend, the wind, freed it once more to run through the open plains. And no dust anywhere. Everything was pure, neat and sterile. Everything you could see, anyway.

The struggle's the same, thought Nathan. Some things never change—men fighting to the death. And fighting for what? Why *was* he doing this? Sometimes it was easier to understand the other side than himself. Power, greed and hate were more understandable. They were all the motivations necessary to kill and were still around in warehouse-sized quantities. The men who used them as justification needed to be stopped, and people like him had been trying since the beginning of time. Now it seemed to be his turn his time. Was *that* the reason? Was it just his time?

Nathan turned left down a smaller corridor and gave himself a mental slap. He needed to focus on the environment. In the dim lighting, with the stores sealed up and no people milling in the hallways, the terrain was entirely different. To survive he needed to learn this structure before they came. He needed to take advantage of being here first and study the building, and he needed to learn to use it to his advantage. Walking rapidly he scanned left and right, working in a pattern that covered each corridor twice and took him back to where he'd started. Within thirty minutes he traversed the entire complex.

The main corridors were linked like a large 'H'. Four big chain stores were anchors located at the ends of the top and bottom legs. In between was the usual assortment of clothing, gift and specialty stores with a food court in the core. Four street level entrances opened into smaller hallways that fed the main corridor, each feeder hall was near one of the anchors.

Nathan chose the northeast entrance as the place to wait. These doors were no more likely to be an entry point than any other, but twenty yards from the entrance an alcove in a dark corner gave him a spot to hide. The alcove led into two clothing stores associated in some way. Two fake pillars in front of the stores narrowed the entrances at midpoint and gave him something to hide behind. He tapped the pillars—decorative. Doubtful they'd stop a bullet. The pillars and the lack of lighting provided concealment but no cover. Still, it held a significant advantage.

He walked into the hallway and studied the alcove. The lighting out here was subdued, but the difference was enough that anyone crouched back there was difficult to see. Glass surrounded most of the position, but the cluttered window displays made it impossible to see through and pick out shapes, especially stationary ones. Nathan slipped back into the darkness, snapped the .357 SIG out of its holster, sat on the tiled floor and waited. Forcing his mind to work through *what if* scenarios kept Fear and Panic at bay.

His watch told him he had been there an hour and a half when the sound of shattering glass drifted down the hall. It was distant—not from the entrance closest to him. Seconds later another crash reached his ears. This one was further away and fainter, but the amplification of the electronic muffs made it sound musical. He waited, listening. Ten minutes passed. He was about to abandon his position and move in the direction of the sound when the flicker of a flashlight beam caught his attention. It came from the doors nearest him. Muted voices sounded from the same area as the light. The sound of a glass explosion came a moment later, followed by a rhythmic crunching noise—the interaction of glass fragments, floor tile and boots.

At least three groups, thought Nathan, easing into a crouch. Not very coordinated in their entry. Were they amateurs? Professionals whose timing got screwed up? The darkened window across from him reflected moving shapes coming his way. With each step the crunching sounds grew fainter as the scattered glass dissipated. Through the glass behind him, peeking between the legs of a mannequin, Nathan saw them coming. Three men walking slowly, one on each side of the hallway and one in the middle, searching for him, probing.

The one on the far side carried the flashlight, using it erratically enough that they might miss him. If they spotted him in this dark hole they wouldn't be the first. Fear had discovered him with the first crunching steps. So far Panic hadn't come along. Fear he could handle.

The STI pointed up, hiding the sight's faint red glow from three pairs of hunting eyes. The closest man paused at the alcove's entrance. Nathan glimpsed a sawed-off shotgun. After the briefest pause he moved on. Nathan counted slowly to five then slipped out of his burrow. He checked left towards the shattered doors and saw no threat in the direction he was about to turn his back to. Nathan poked his pistol around the corner to his right, at the broad back of the shotgun-wielding gunman twenty feet away.

"Freeze."

The gunman exploded into a blur of motion as he twisted, crouched and brought up his shotgun all in one whirl of movement. Nathan wasn't ready. He had expected him to pause mid-stride or at the very least to hesitate while processing this unexpected development. The twelve gauge roared but the blindly-fired shot sprayed high.

Nathan recovered, slipping into the mental slow-motion state of tachypsychia as the killer slammed back the pump gun's slide, and sent a smoking hull twirling out of the ejection port. The hull was still performing its aerial dance when Nathan fired three times. Three new orifices, two in the chest and one between the eyes prevented the shotgun's slide from being driven forward for a second try. Nathan tracked to the center man.

The middle one was already turned and bringing a handgun to bear. Sideways! Nathan fired twice. He let the recoil from the second shot lift his dot up onto the man's nose, then fired again. Three empty cases arched out of the .357, less than two inches of air between each spinning piece of nickeled brass. The man sagged to his knees as Nathan shifted to the last and furthest gunman.

The one he'd just shot held his pistol sideways! He'd seen it in movies but it was hard to believe anyone actually tried shooting like that. It told Nathan something about who these people were.

The third gunman's pistol was up. They fired their handguns at the same instant—thirty feet apart, two men, the same age, one a career criminal who fired his 9 mm only when he was killing his latest victim; the other a determined competitor with a lifetime count of one and a half million rounds downrange. One pistol a scratched and scarred Ruger P85 bought in a dark bar for two hundred dollars; the other a hand built machine worth the price of small car. One man clutched his pistol one-handed, desperately trying to hit a target further away than anything he had ever shot in his life; the other in a tight two-handed isosceles stance who trained every day to hit faster, further and harder than the day before. Brain matter splattered across an elegantly decorated shop window.

Nathan stepped back out of sight as he pulled a fresh magazine from his belt and performed a tactical reload. Fear was gone. Panic didn't exist—never had. Rage left no room for either. Kent had gone to the streets and hired punks. Then he'd sent them in here to face Nathan Burdett. 'Cannon fodder', that's the phrase Kim had used. That's all these people were. Kent might as well have lined them up against a wall and shot them, their death was that certain. Only he was dumping the job of killing them on Nathan.

Voices and the sound of running feet came from around the corner, in the direction of the first entries. Nathan sprinted along the wall in that direction. "Wait," he yelled when he neared the last store. The voices stopped. "Don't come any further!"

Shouted curses and the sound of shuffling came closer.

"Your three friends are dead!"

Silence. But at least the movement stopped.

"Listen to me," shouted Nathan, his mind racing, looking for words to frighten these people into saving their own lives. "I killed them all and you'll die too if you come around the corner."

Excited whispering drifted to him from the main corridor, the words indistinguishable.

"You're out of your league," prompted Nathan. "The man who hired you knows that. He's using you." He paused. No response. "Leave now. Turn around and go back the way you came. Forget this place. It's not your fight! This is between me and him but he doesn't have the guts to face me alone!"

"Yo—man."

At last a response. "What?"

"You gonna die slow, man."

"No! Listen, I'm sorry about your friends. I didn't have any choice. You have to leave. I don't want to kill the rest of you too."

Laughter echoed down the corridor and Nathan hung his head.

"My man. You know how many be ready for you?"

"It doesn't matter!" shouted Nathan, desperation creeping into his voice. "Don't you people understand? I'll kill you all. You don't stand a chance."

More laughter.

"We be comin' for you now."

An idea flickered across Nathan's mind. "Wait!"

The same voice. "Too late, man."

One last chance. "You ever do one-on-one?"

Silence.

"Come on. You boys must have grown up doing one-on-one."

Silence.

"How about some three-on-one?"

"Say what?"

"Three-on-one, punk. I'm calling you out for three-on-one."

More laughter. "I don't be seein' no hoop nets 'round here. What you thinkin', man?"

"Not hoops, idiot. Guns. Ever watch a western? Three of your best against me. In the middle of the hall. Right here. If you kill me, you kill me. If I win, you all leave."

"Thought you didn't want to kill none o' us." Laughter.

"I don't. But with three I can work around that. Three of you get ready in the hallway. The rest pull back to the food court. I don't suppose any of you have real holsters, so stuff your guns in your pants. I'll come around the corner when you're ready."

"You kiddin' me? You be stupid!"

"I'm serious. Three-on-one. Here and now. I'll bet you've never done that before. Make you a big man if you can pull it off," he taunted.

"You seen too many westerns, man. You madness, but you *on.*" Excited voices and shuffling preceded the shattering of a distant window succumbing to a fatal blow. Nathan started. "Just doin' a little shoppin' for a video cam," said the familiar voice. "Keyboard's gonna be standin' to one side to catch it all on video—don't be shootin' *him* now." The owner of the voice laughed. "If I don't got pictures, nobody but nobody is gonna believe anybody as stupid as you."

"Fine. As long as we do it." Nathan waited. They were going for it. Three of them would end up crippled for life, but that beat dead. And from his perspective it sure beat having to kill them. The others were supposed to leave if he won. Whatever their intention right now, he doubted any of them would stick around once their buddies, and probably their leader, lay writhing on the floor.

Five minutes later he still hadn't heard from the voice. Nathan was about to call out when the muffled blast of a .308 shattered the stillness behind him. He spun around in time to see a body crumple to the sidewalk in front of the broken entrance door. Kim, doing her job. She was staying with him.

Nathan turned back to the corner. "You shouldn't have done that! Now he's dead too."

Five more minutes dragged by before he heard the voice again.

"We be ready. Wassup now?"

"No more tricks?"

"No, man. I'm all out."

"Okay, I'm coming." Nathan crept to the end of the solid wall. A glass display window replaced it the rest of the way to the corner. He tried finding a spot that allowed him to look through into the other corridor. No luck. Moving ahead slowly he found the right combination of glass and open space that allowed a confined peek through the corner shop. Three young men stood in the center of the far hallway fidgeting nervously, pistols stuffed into their waistbands. The center man had two. Perfect. Nathan checked his chamber and magazine. Ready. The STI clicked into its holster and then he checked his primary reload. Ready.

When he stepped into the open hall the fidgeting stopped. They watched him walk to the center of the corridor and face them—fifteen yards away.

"Cool, man," said the middle one. He was the voice. "Major cool, man."

"We don't have to do this," said Nathan. Sixty yards behind these three he saw two more gathered at the railing defining the edge of the raised food court. "You can still leave. Nobody has to get hurt."

"Oh—oh." Two-Gun nudged the man on his right. "I do believe he be changin' his mind." Then addressing Nathan, "S'up, bro? Don't like the odds now dat it's all hangin' out?"

Nathan smiled as broadly as he could. The smile was forced but they didn't know that. A psychological edge could be gained here and he was going to play it as long and as hard as they would let him keep talking. "I told you before. This is the big leagues. You and your friends," he gestured towards them with his left hand "you're not ready to play here. You can't even comprehend what's standing in front of you. The dead ones behind me, they'd tell you if they could. They'd say 'Go home. Run for your lives. Run and never look back. Hide and pray the blue-eyed one doesn't come after you'."

The *dead ones* reference generated nervous glances from the short one on the right. Nathan turned up the rhetoric. "Walk away and I'll let you live. None of you need to die." There was a lottery kiosk behind the Shorty and he looked ready to duck behind it and hide.

Two-Gun must have seen or sensed his partner's discomfort. He turned, calling over his shoulder, "Keyboard, you gettin' all this. I ain't never heard so much brass. I want this, Keyboard. Don't mess up on me bro'. This goin' to be my favorite snuff piece." Keyboard kept his face glued to the video camera's eyepiece. "Where you from, man? You talk funny, like a tourist or somethin'. Whasat over your ears? And what kinda gun you got there? That's mine when we snuff ya."

"That's what I'm trying to tell you. I live in a world you don't even know exists. There, guns like this are normal. And we can do things with them you can't imagine. I know it's hard to believe, but the three of you can't beat me. Trying, will get you killed."

Two-Gun rolled out his best sneer. "Ohhh—now we really be scared. So, what are you, Mista Fancy-Gun, a cop?"

"No. I'm not a cop. I'm . . . ." Nathan stopped. He was about to say 'half a cop'—his normal line. But an image from a hostage-taking in a foul prison flashed through his mind. A brusque Situation Commander harried by the same question had answered it in one word, universally understood. Besides, this was for Shorty. Nathan let his voice go hard and deep, leaving the reply to echo down the empty corridor, all the way to the food court. "I'm a gunfighter."

Two-Gun blinked. Twice. Shorty licked his lips and started wiping palms on his trousers. Perfect. His nerve was almost gone. Shorty just qualified to be shot last. With any luck he'd break and run before the dot got to him. Two-Gun was first, the one on the left was next and then Shorty if need be. Perfect.

Two-Gun snapped his fingers, three times.

From inside the lottery kiosk behind Shorty, Nathan heard a whisper and then shuffling. A head popped up. Then two more. Three men rose silently out of hiding. Hands hanging loosely at their sides, pistols stuffed into waistbands they made the short walk to where Shorty stood and fanned out to his right. Shorty appeared to take comfort in their presence. Nathan wasn't comforted at all.

"So, what you think of them odds, Mista Gunfighter?" sneered Two-Gun.

Nathan couldn't let them see it, but a fourth man had shown up with these three ringers. It was his old friend Fear and this time Panic wasn't far behind. "Six-on-one isn't what we agreed on. You shouldn't have done that, friend."

Two-Gun folded his arms and looked up and down the line of killers beside him. "Maybe I flunked school and I don't count too good. Maybe, I like six-on-one better."

Nathan tried to bring the smile back, but now he couldn't even fake it. He settled for a cold stare. "I lied to you. I wasn't going to kill you. I was going to cripple you and let you live. I can do that with three but I can't do it with six. With six I have to kill you all. This doesn't have to happen. Go home *now!*"

Two-Gun didn't budge. Neither did anyone else. Five of them were stone cold solid. How much was true confidence and how much was bravado, Nathan couldn't be sure. Not one of them believed him, so Nathan guessed they weren't far from finding out. Only Shorty still showed uncertainty.

Nathan took two steps toward them. All bluster. What he really wanted to do was run.

Two-Gun reached in his pocket and pulled out a silver dollar. He flipped it two feet into the air with his thumb and caught it quickly when it came back down. "When the silver hits the floor, Mista Gunfighter. That's when you die. When the silver hits the tile—listen for it." A full arm heave sent the coin spinning upwards into the highest reaches of the domed ceiling. There was no turning back.

Nathan had enough time to point a finger at the third man from the left. Maybe he could save one. "You ready to die, short man?" Then his eyes tracked to the right end of the line, and he heard the ring of silver on stone.

Someone on the line in front of him yelled, but his mind shut it out. What was said and who was saying it was pushed back into the realm of the irrelevant. Only three things mattered now, and in the fraction of a second that it took his pistol to travel from holster to arms length his mind focused on them to the exclusion of everything else. Target, dot and trigger were now his world. Individually those three elements were separate, but his mind pulled them together the way a cosmic black hole sucks in matter. And when all three collided, the flash they created would tear apart the silence of the corridor and everything in its path. Even his thoughts were left behind as his body moved faster than verbally based thought processes allowed. Only visual images flickered through his mind, analyzing, interpreting, pushing him to the limits of his ability.

267

Starting to move, hand clawing for gun . . . target-dot-trigger—flash
Almost touching the gun . . . target-dot-trigger—flash
Hand onto the gun . . . target-dot-trigger—flash
Skip one
Both guns out . . . target-dot-trigger—flash
Gun up . . . target-dot-trigger—flash
Back to Shorty . . . gun out . . . target-dot-trig . . . break and run.

Nathan's mind tripped out of overdrive as the sounds that resulted from his five shots merged into a symphony of death. The physics of gunpowder and lead relinquished its authority to gravity as five empty cartridge cases tap-tap-tapped onto the tile floor to his right. Lifeless bodies fell, generating a spiritless *thud*, followed by the louder *crack* of perforated skulls following their individual torsos down in response to the law of gravity. Four pistols fell with them, following the same law, onto a hard floor. Two-Gun's clunked down first, then that of the last man to die. Shorty's came next but with a sliding sound, as he tossed it and ran, sprinting with the speed only a person who came face to face with death possesses. He dashed past Keyboard and the camera's crash to the floor was gravity's last victory; the sound underscored by the pounding feet of four men fleeing.

Their mamas had lied to them. The Grim Reaper didn't wear a black hood and carry a scythe. Not anymore he didn't. Not in New York city. Here Death was fearless, had blue eyes, carried the strangest looking pistol they'd ever seen—and he wasn't human. They knew that because they saw him do something no human was capable of—God or Devil, they didn't know which. They didn't care. They'd seen him and lived. Each one of them intended to keep it that way.

Nathan slid four steps back, crouched behind a concrete planter and executed another tactical reload. Rage came storming back. Five more deaths to hold Kent accountable for. Five more lives consigned by Kent to the trash bin of hell. Five more reasons to make sure Kent didn't leave here until his own life had been weighed in the balance.

Nathan waited until the two bodies on the right stopped twitching. The first two shots had gone high, and high brain shots typically caused an electrical storm that generated spasmodic muscle contractions. Each body spasm drove Nathan's anger up another notch.

Kent was here already, he was sure of it. The cannon fodder had served its purpose and kept him busy while Kent slipped in for the kill. Using other people was Kent's specialty, that's what he did, that's how he operated. Well his time had arrived. Time to hunt him down, find him and destroy him. Nathan rose from his concealed crouch and froze mid-step as a spark of logic flared in the darkness of his wrath.

That's what Kent was counting on—anger clouding reason—rage replacing tactics. Nathan took a deep breath and returned to his position. Kent was out there waiting for him to do something stupid like stalk the corridors looking for him. Kent wouldn't step out to fight. He'd shoot him in the back and then spit on his body. The only assurance Nathan had was that the territory up to the food court was clear, everything beyond that was a potential killing ground for Kent.

Nathan slipped down the corridor to the railing where the spectators had recently stood. He took cover behind the raised floor of the food court, peering carefully over the edge, searching his memory banks about what lay ahead and planned his next move.

A spring sales promotion was about to start and the mall was being readied. The far half of the food court was already hung with banners, balloons and ribbons, while the half nearest Nathan had decorations stacked in strategic spots along the floor. Also left behind were two ladders, suggesting the workers would be back this morning, before the mall opened. On the other side of the food court the ladder was still up, ready for the morning's work; on Nathan's side it was down, laying along the floor. Between the two ladders was a high broad beam, the intended location for the decorations. The architecture was such that if he used the ladders and the beam he could cross the open killing ground before him without being seen. His objective was a raised stage with red skirting—probably set up for a coming fashion show—and the clear area beyond it.

With his pistol holstered, Nathan stayed low and slid on his left side along the smooth floor. Crossing the stairs and ramp leading to the upper level, he reached the wall. Grabbing the wooden ladder he pulled it back into his safe zone, setting it up against the wall as quietly as possible. A last look confirmed everything was clear so he scrambled up, not stopping until he reached the beam. A quick scan confirmed he was safe to go and in a crouching shuffle crossed the food court hidden from any waiting ambushers. A similar pause at the other end and he started down.

Nathan was at the ladder's midpoint when a voice spoke from behind him.

"Don't move, Nathan." A pause. "Don't even twitch."

Here, suspended in mid-air, there was no choice. He did as he was told. There was no mistaking the Scottish accent giving the businesslike commands. At least Leith hadn't shot him outright. That was a good sign. But where had he come from? Where he was positioned now didn't take any imagination. The short ex-commando would be back there in the deep shadows with good cover. And he'd have a rifle or an SMG. Nathan was only alive because Leith wanted it that way.

"What brings you here, Leith? I thought this was a private affair." Nathan was careful not to move. He stayed in a half-step position, most of his weight on his left leg and hanging by the arms.

"Mr. Kent tells me that when he hunts he often employs trackers or beaters. I guess you could call me one of those."

"Like the eight others I just killed?"

"Eight, you say? That'll be why a herd of them went by here like the Devil himself was biting their arses. Very impressive, Nathan."

"Not very sporting of the old guy though, is it?" countered Nathan. He kept his voice calm but his mind raced, trying to figure out what to do next. Leith solved the problem for him.

"Nathan, take your left hand off the ladder and reach around to your pistol. Punch the magazine release button and let the mag fall to the ground. Make any attempt to get your fingers around that gun butt and I won't have any qualms about killing you immediately. You're too good with that short-barreled piece, lad. I can't risk you touching it at all. You push the magazine release with one left finger only and eject the mag. Nothing more."

Nathan didn't respond. He calculated his options but didn't like the way the numbers came up. Eventually he performed the requested task and heard the mag hit the polished floor beneath him. The thud was followed by the skittering sound of several cartridges as they popped out from the impact and spring pressure sent them sliding across the tiles.

"Very good. You can climb down now. Slowly."

That's odd, thought Nathan. He's letting my pistol stay in the holster with only one round in it? He really is worried about me getting a hand on it. He slowly eased his body down the ladder and when his right foot touched the floor, Leith cautioned, "Keep your hands up, Nathan. I don't want them anywhere near your gun."

Nathan turned slowly and saw he was right about Leith's location. A good twenty yards from the ladder, hidden behind a concrete planter was a corner of Leith's face peering over the top. Most of it was obscured by the muzzle end view of an AR-15.

"Where were you?"

A short laugh came from the shadows. "Under the stage, lad. It's empty under the stage. "Now reach down with your left hand and dump all the remaining mags out of their pouches and drop them on the floor in front of you."

Leith still had him cold. There wasn't much he could do in the hands of a professional like this. Nathan pulled one of the remaining mags and dropped it loudly to the floor. Loose rounds popped out again and slid across the marble. He was reaching for a second one when he heard the faint sound of footsteps coming from beyond the food court to his left. "Come on," urged Leith. "The other ones too."

Nathan obliged him, moving slowly so as not to startle Leith, but also giving himself more time to think.

Leith was disarming him, slowly and methodically in a totally professional manner. Prepping him for Mr. Kent's arrival and presumably his amusement. He knew Nathan's abilities and wasn't going to let him get anywhere near his pistol. The way in which he was doing it kept him safe, Leith had all the advantages—distance, cover, a rifle and lighting.

Nathan dropped the rest of the mags on the floor, then raised his left hand up to shoulder level again. "That's all of them." Now we'll find out what he wants me to do with the gun, he thought. One last chance.

"The half empty ones in your pockets too, lad."

271

With a mental curse Nathan did as he was told.

Kent appeared on Nathan's left weaving in and out of the food court tables, moving in their direction. He carried a bolt-action rifle at port arms. Nathan was mildly surprised to recognize it as a Steyr Scout.

"Splendid," said Leith, relief coloring his voice. "See Nathan, you *can* follow instructions. It just requires the right kind of motivation." Nathan watched incredulously as Leith stood and walked in his direction, the rifle now held at the waist—his readiness status down a full level. He caught a glimpse of Leith's Hi-Power as his black jacket swung open and he knew then what Leith was thinking. The consummate military man with excellent skills but only a thorough knowledge of his personal weapons was still laboring under a false assumption. The assumption that all pistols, like his beloved Hi-Power, had a deactivating safety that rendered the gun useless when no magazine sat within the grip. A wrong assumption.

He had a chance.

As he faced Leith, Nathan was aware of Kent slipping up on his left side and stopping ten yards away. Kent would see the magazines and ammo littering the floor at Nathan's feet and take his cue from Leith, trusting the professional to have rendered Nathan harmless.

"Well, Mr. Burdett, it appears I have won this little hunt."

Nathan turned his head, looking over his left shoulder as he spoke. "You're face doesn't look so good, Kent." He concentrated on keeping his torso between Kent and the holstered gun, trying to hide from him the still present pistol. Kent had proven he wasn't as naive about 1911's as Leith.

Kent gave a half-hearted shrug. "You may have done me a favor. I might need a new face before this is all over. Just think of where I can go and what I can do if that were done." Nathan did think about it. "What's his condition Leith? He's a very dangerous fellow, as I'm sure you know."

"He's toothless Mr. Kent. Don't worry. The mighty Nathan Burdett is toothless." Then Leith flicked the AR-15's safety on and laid the gun gently on the planter. He pulled his Hi-Power from its holster and set it there too. As he started to walk forward he spoke. "Keep him covered, sir," Then to Nathan. "Turn around and we'll get that pesky gun off your belt—and keep your hands up too."

Kent yelled, "Stop! Where's his gun? Haven't you disarmed him?"

Leith took two more steps forward before stopping. He chuckled slightly. "His gun's still in the holster, but I made him drop the mag. Relax. He's toothless. Turn around, Nathan, and show Mr. Kent."

Nathan turned slightly towards Kent; just enough so that the edge of the holstered STI became visible.

Kent gasped, "You idiot!" he screamed, starting to throw the Steyr to his shoulder. In that instant he saw a puzzling expression flash across Nathan's face. There and gone, too quick to categorize—a flash of a smile or just a grimace? He couldn't tell. Whatever it was, left him feeling cold, and then just as quickly that changed too. A hot blast of fire hit him as though the Grim Reaper were grabbing him by the throat and laughing in his face, his breath tinged with sulfur and brimstone. Or was it only burnt gunpowder he smelled?

After all, the young man standing in front of him had just fired his pistol. He knew that because an empty cartridge case spun out of it in a twirling silver arc. He hadn't seen how the gun got into his hand but he knew where it came from. All he recalled was that slight grimace. It was gone now, if had ever been there. Now the face just grew dim. And then it vanished too. Vanished into a stifling blackness. A deep swirling blackness thicker than the darkest African night he had ever experienced. He felt himself falling. That was predictable; he knew he'd just been shot. But he had expected to stop falling once he hit the floor, instead his fall didn't end. Further and further into the blackness he sank, until he heard screaming. He wasn't sure what it meant until a fiery blast of flaming sulfur hit him and then he screamed too.

The nickeled cartridge case continued its spin through the air as Nathan pulled his gun down, crouched to pick up a magazine from the floor and pivoted to face Leith. There are reloads and then there are mandatory reloads, he thought, snatching a mag from the floor. The

273

round on top was slightly askew. He pushed it into place with his left index finger as he brought it up to the gun.

Leith had been over halfway to Nathan when Kent's yell stopped him. At the shot, he hadn't gone back for the rifle or the Hi-Power. Instead he chose to charge, his hand clawing under his coat and pulling out a black blade by the time he completed his second step.

Nathan's eyes were fixed on Leith. Eyes that didn't need to look at the gun to reload any more than people need to look at their hands to applaud. Leith was four strides away. Nathan saw the blade come out as his magazine found its way into the pistol's mag well—three strides—slammed the mag home—two strides—racked the slide—one stride.

Leith saw he was too late, one stride, one heartbeat, one fraction of a second too late. Nathan would shoot and kill him but he'd have to do it just right to stop from being killed himself. He had the momentum. He'd be on top of Nathan no matter what. If Nathan didn't make the perfect shot he could still kill him.

Then he too saw an empty case spin out of the gun and felt a scorching blast to his face that short circuited movements and brought on a choking darkness. He plunged into a liquid pool of darkness with a nightmarish feeling of never-ending horror. Like the cartridge case, he spun and fell, but never reached the floor. Just as the thought occurred to him that the falling may be forever, he heard screams. They were getting closer. It took a second before he recognized them as Kent's. But Kent was already dead. How could Kent be screaming? Then he smelled the sulfur.

Nathan left the bodies where they fell. He retrieved his magazines and scooped up the loaded ammo littering the floor, but didn't bother searching for the fired cartridge cases. It broke all the sterilization rules Leith had taught him but he didn't really care. On the way back out he noticed the camera Keyboard had dropped. He found the eject button and pocketed the tape, then walked out the front doors looking for Kim.

"Looks like Mr. Kent didn't make it, ma'am," said the driver when he saw Nathan walk out of the mall. He tried to keep his voice flat and professional to mask his astonishment. This kid, whoever he was, had obviously just killed Kent, Leith and a handful of others. Most of them had been amateurs but not Leith. Kent was a cagey old man and Leith—Leith was one of the best. Together they must have been a formidable team and yet this punk she'd described as a target shooter and a hunter had just eliminated them. He was one lucky punk. Had to be luck, because nobody was that good. If she only let him carry a gun in the car he could finish it from here. One good rifle shot was all it would take. "What do we do now?"

"He's no concern of ours," she said. "Nathan Burdett doesn't even know we exist. We're going home. Our work continues. It was rather vengeful of Mr. Kent to invite us to be present for Mr. Burdett's demise, don't you think?"

"And, as it turns out, presumptuous."

"Poor, Mr. Kent."

The driver nodded silently and pressed the button that raised his window. He maneuvered the blue Mercedes out of the parking lot and onto the quiet street.

Not seeing Kim as he exited the mall, Nathan whistled. She stepped from the shadows in response. "Anything going on out here?" he asked.

"There's a Mercedes limo parked at the end of the lot but that's all. Maybe Kent's driver waiting to take him home for a pint of bitters? There it is." She pointed with her left hand, the right still held the rifle, its butt nestled into her hip. "You can see it leaving now."

"Mercedes? Let me see." Nathan held out his hand for the binoculars. He focused them in time to see the driver, a large black man, raise the window. Nathan continued to watch as the long car made a tight left turn and wheeled out of the lot. Blacked out windows eliminated any chance of seeing who, if anyone, was in the rear seat.

This was the same driver and no doubt the same dark blue limousine that had been in front of Kent's office building six months ago. Only he hadn't seen the plate then. Nathan shifted his binoculars to the limo's rear license plate.

Now, he read it clearly and as he did the impact of it took his breath away. Deciphering the meaning of the reflective lettering had only taken a second. Filtering it through his mind had taken another moment and the links it now made were unmistakable. The inference was that of evil, and it traveled the world in a blue coach with Lies and Corruption as its footmen. Nathan slowly lowered the binoculars.

Kim didn't notice the change that came over him. "Come on," she said, nudging his arm. "Whoever it is, he's leaving. Let's go. It's over."

Nathan handed back the binoculars but his eyes remained fixed on the receding taillights. "No, Kim. It's not over."

"What do you mean?"

"I don't know if you'd understand."

His voice carried a frightening tone that grabbed her attention as effectively as reaching out and pulling her upright by the lapels. She walked in front of Nathan, looked at his impassive face, and then at the rapidly disappearing car.

"Listen, I don't understand you at the best of times. Of course you could try something *really* novel—like explaining it to me."

"I can try but you may not believe me. I'm not sure *I'm* ready to believe it. And I don't think I'm ready to face it."

She gazed at where the limo had vanished into the remnants of the two o'clock morning traffic but saw nothing that meant anything to her.

Nathan's eyes broke loose from their fixation and shifted to Kim. "The license plate. It's a vanity plate. It says: *G-R-8-R   G-D.*"

She answered him with a puzzled look.

He reached for the rifle and started her moving toward their car. "I'll explain it while you drive." Then quietly in a voice she barely heard, "I'm not ready," he said. "It's too soon." A desperate shake of the head. "I'm not ready."

He slung the rifle over his shoulder as they walked, pulled empty magazines and loose ammo out of his pockets and began reloading.

EPILOGUE

"And what are you smiling about, Jerry?" asked Barb as she slid a single sheet of paper into the photocopier at the reporter's workstation.

Jerry looked up from the shredder's digital command screen. "These things are getting way too smart," he said, unable to wipe a spreading grin from his face.

Barb came around to where he stood and read the lines on the shredder's screen. Bewilderment showed on her face. "I don't get it," she said finally.

"It's a shooter's term," explained Jerry. "I loaded the shredder's feed hopper and the machine chewed up all the paper I gave it. Now, it's telling me that if I want to do any more I have to refill the hopper." He pointed to the last two words on the command screen.

"*Mandatory Reload*," read Barb. She looked at him in exasperation. "So?"

"So? That was the Burdett file. I just shredded most of it." Jerry lost it and burst out laughing.

"Jerry!" screamed Barb. "You just shredded the story of a lifetime!"

Jerry stopped laughing quickly. "No, Barbara. Yesterday, I learned where the real story is, and it's not what I thought. This was all unnecessary background fluff." He waved a hand in an airy gesture. "The real story is just starting. I don't know when or exactly what form it'll take. But it'll be soon and Burdett's in the middle of it. Count on it." Jerry punched the *OFF* button, gathered up the few papers that remained in his file and walked away. It was coming. He knew it now. The only thing that puzzled him was why he hadn't seen it before this.

277

ABOUT THE AUTHOR

Al Voth, like many of his generation, grew up on a family farm and began a lifelong interest in firearms by hunting small game with a single shot .22 caliber rifle. After graduating from university with a degree in sociology, he began a career in law enforcement and has never left that field. This included work as a patrol officer and nine years of service on an Emergency Response Team. Along the way he has won numerous awards in rifle and handgun competition, usually building and modifying his own match guns in the process. He currently works at a forensic laboratory as a firearm and toolmark examiner and still shoots competitively and hunts as much as time permits. This is his second novel.